DESOLATION ROAD

by

Ian McDonald

Voted BEST NOVEL OF 1988 BY A NEW AUTHOR

by *Locus* readers

"This is the kind of novel I long to find yet seldom do—extraordinary and more than that!"
—Philip José Farmer

"*Desolation Road* is wild, original, exuberant, profound, moving, magical, hilarious, fantastic, fabulous. . . . It is also good science fiction."
—Don C. Thompson, *Denver Post*

"Most exciting and promising debut since Ray Bradbury's. . . . Here's a first novel brimming with colorful writing, poetic imagination, and outrageous events recounted in a persuasively matter-of-fact manner. . . . Hugely readable."
—Shaun Usher, *Daily Mail*

". . . destined to be a classic . . . perhaps a work of true genius. *Desolation Road* will drift along timelessly, undoubtedly outliving its creator—though may he live long and prosper—and occupying its own special place by the dust-blown literary highways traveled by countless generations of future readers."
—Peter Crowther

"A spectacular first novel. A lively wit leavens the dense complexity of this epic tale. From the Greatest Snooker Player the Universe Has Ever Known to a mysteriously transported Glenn Miller (father of the Martian swing craze) and the technoevangelist Inspiration Cadillac, the characters are madly memorable, the most extraordinary mix of human and not-quite human since Cordwainer Smith's tales of Norstrilia."
—Faren Miller, *Locus*

ARES EXPRESS

ARES EXPRESS

Ian McDonald

an imprint of **Prometheus Books**
Amherst, NY

Published 2010 by Pyr®, an imprint of Prometheus Books

Inquiries should be addressed to
Pyr
59 John Glenn Drive
Amherst, New York 14228–2119
VOICE: 716–691–0133
FAX: 716–691–0137
WWW.PYRSF.COM

14 13 12 11 10   5 4 3 2 1

Library of Congress Cataloging-in-Publication Data

McDonald, Ian, 1960–
    Ares Express / by Ian McDonald.
        p. cm.
    Originally published: London : Earthlight, an imprint of Simon & Schuster UK Ltd.,
a Viacom Company, 2001.
    ISBN 978–1–61614–197–4 (pbk.)
    1. Mars (Planet)—Fiction. I. Title.

PR6063.C38A89 2010
823'.914—dc22

                                                                2009050115

Printed in the United States

*H*ere comes Sweetness Octave Glorious Honey-Bun Asiim Engineer 12th. She is eight, and this is the manner of her coming.

First, you see the sand. It is red and of a particular grain type produced only by wind action. It smells electric; there is much iron in it. It draws lightning out of the occasional clouds; once or twice in a long year, rain. Where the lightning strikes, veins of slag-iron strike deep into the sand. This is rust-sand, strewn profligately about this contourless landscape. Red sand, rust-sand, red dust, a desert of iron studded with ugly stones. The wind never ceases out here on the plains of the high high north. It has teased the sand into steep-sided ridges, long meandering sifs, crescent moon barchans. This is a sinuous, sensual landscape, curves and seductions from the slip-sliding dunefaces to the curve of the close horizon.

A solitary hard erection confronts the soft northern desert of iron. Five metres high, a slim steel shaft, scabbed by the excoriating winds, scarred by summer lightning. It is a natural victim for summer lightning. On top of the shaft, three lights, red topmost, amber in the middle, on the bottom, green. Signal lights. In the middle of a rust-desert.

Now you see the rail. Two perfectly parallel lines of Bethlehem Ares steel, rolled in the mills of New Merionedd, married together by pourstone sleepers, tied down by figure-of-eight tie-bolts: pinned, plated and bolted. Straight and absolute as a geometrical proposition. Get down. Hunker down—not too low, under this sun your cheek will stick to the hot rail and rip. Just enough to sight along them, gun-barrels aimed at the place where horizon and heat-dazzle meet and melt. Straight and absolute. You can go over the edge of the world and they'll run straight and absolute for seven hundred kilometres. In the cabs of the big transcontinentals there are red buttons that the engineers must touch every twenty seconds or the brakes will automatically apply. It's easy to fall asleep over the speed levers out here. It's a hypnotic land. It draws your soul out through your staring eyes along the twin steel rails, to whatever dwells in the silver shimmer at the edge of the world. Occasional track-side tangles of sand-polished metal prove the dangers that lie in the long straight track.

But we drive ahead of ourselves here. We must stay a while at the signal light, and ask questions. Why signal what? What is there in this dust and rust of any significance? Two things. The first is the passing loop. This patch of desert is the only place within two hundred kilometres where trains may pass and gain access to the single mainline. Here crews exchange ancient brass tokens—part key, part shield—to unlock the line. Conversations too, news and gossip, sometimes family members, or body fluids, if they are the big slow ore-haulers whose timetables allow a little society. The second thing is that, if you look up the line, you will see it part company with itself. This is Borealis Junction: one line drives forcefully on into the snow country of the north pole, where the cold can glue an Engineer's hand to the throttles as this heat will seal flesh to steel. Up and over the top of the world, and down into the old lands of Deuteronomy and Dioscu: green places replete with grazers and herd-beasts, where every village roof-tree is high and holy with prayer kites. The other line drifts to port until it curves out of sight among the thunderous chasms of Fosse mountains, spanned by treacherous trestle bridges and pour-stone viaducts, that disgorge nerve-wracked Engineers out on to the bleak mesa-lands of Isidy. For half a quartersphere the lines are drawn together by mutual magnetism until they meet once again at Schia-parelli Junction to run westward along the vast synclinorium of Great Oxus and the thousand towns of Grand Valley, where the Worldroof sparkles on the horizon like a reef of morning-lit cloud.

So this signal light is more than an arbitrary stop-go in the wilderness. It is the prefect of line safety, it is guardian of the line tokens, it is the gateway to new landscapes. And, no less than any of these, it is Sweetness Octave Glorious Honey-Bun Asiim Engineer 12th's Uncle.

It is time she made her entrance.

You become aware that the rail burning the sole of your desert boot is trembling. Bend down—don't touch! Yes. Rail humming. Train coming.

You squint under the shade of your hand down the long straight line. What is real and what is potential is still undecided in that haze. But the rails are singing now: a deep, tight, harmonious keening. A sharp dry clack. You have to look around at the nothingness several times before you can see the small but significant change. The points have switched on to the passing loop.

Peer again: shapes moving in the haze, flowing so you cannot be certain it is one thing or many. Silver in silver. Then the shadows flow, silver out of silver: a winged woman, wing-arms folded back, breasts out-thrust, hair streaming in the wind. In your amazement you almost do not notice that the track is roaring. Red dust bounces up from between the sleepers. Now you realise your mistake. This is no angel. Its shadow flows out behind it into a shield of darkness: you are looking at the boiler-cap and figurehead of a great train. A very great train indeed: the faceless land has been playing tricks with your perspective. You had thought the winged woman pixie sized, maybe a medium-grade Amshastria, but close and manageable. No. This silver angel-woman is enormous, the curved prow of the boiler gargantuan. The train is kilometres away. But it is very very big. Airship big. City-block big. Ocean-liner big, if this world had oceans fit for liners. The buffer plates, held out like a prize-fighter's weaving fists, are three metres across. The cow-catcher, baroquely ornamented with figures from the Ekaterina Angelography, could sweep entire phyla from its path. The eight bogies are each the height of a decent house: the spokes of the drive wheels are the crucified arms of windmills. The drive shafts, the thickness of a thick man's body, pump with the regular, tireless ease of a Belladonna sweat-house laddie. The headlamp is a monstrous cyclops eye, furious with heat, all revealing. It is hooded now, but with the magic hour, it sends its sheer white shaft kilometres ahead of it, a vanguard of the divine. The steam that blasts from the sharply raked stack is so hot that it travels a third the length of the fusion boiler before it condenses into visibility. This train leaves a pure white contrail downtrack for ten kilometres.

Another glance at that smoke-stack. Down at the base, where it flares into the main caisson, is that a *handrail*? Are those *staircases*, is that a *balcony*? Those gleams of highlight, could they be *windows*? There, just above the halo of the Bethlehem Ares Railroads angel, is that an arc of glass, like the bridge of a ship? And balancing precariously on the swept-back piston housings, spilling steps and ladders over the buffer cylinders, what else can those be but low *buildings*? A swathe of bungalows clings to the skirts of Bethlehem Ares Railroads Class 22 Heavy Fusion Hauler *Catherine of Tharsis*. And there, on that perilous railed-in viewpoint underneath the smoke-stack, is that a *figure*?

Nearer now. Yes, a sun-brown lank of a female dressed in the uniform orange track vest of her clan over a flirty floral-print frock. A tousle of black curls tosses around her face, combed back from great cheekbones by the speed of passage.

And *now* you notice how close the train is to you. Too much time spent staring at the girl on the high balcony. It's on top of you. You should—you must—run. But you cannot. The whole world is quaking to the pound of the engines, and you are transfixed in its track like a hopper in headlights. A steel avalanche rears over you. Crushing death pants in your face. The black and silver angel looms over you like judgement, and turns away. *Catherine of Tharsis* swings on to the passing loop, tucking her three kilometre tail neatly behind her. Brakes shriek, steel and grit bite and grind. It takes a lot of space for the big transpolars to stop. This is by no means the largest. There are tripleheaders hauling ten kilometres out of Iron Mountain. The magic thousand trucks. Those mothers are visible from orbit, like steel rivers.

The caboose clears the points. It's a frantic congeries of railroad utility and Cathrinist whimsy. *No Step Here*, with hand-painted round-eyed icons of the Seven Sanctas. Grit boxes and prayer flags, now windless and limp. The Bassareeni are a gaudy people. Socially below the salt, but the Engineers have always got on well with them, outside the Forma. There was a mingling of genes some generations back. The Stuards have never forgiven, never forgotten, but the Stuards are a notoriously anal Domiety.

A trickle, a creep, a hiss of steam. Thirty-three thousand tons of Bethlehem Ares steel balances on two ten-centimetre ribbons of metal under the hot, high sun.

Clunk. The points have switched over again, back to the mainline. The signal light has gone from caution to green. New train coming. But that is not part of your story. Your story is ended here. Your part as observer of these events is complete. Your eyes have shown us what only the desert things and

God the Panarchic see, at this forsaken junction in the high polar desert. You are dissolved back into a greater story that begins here, the story of Sweetness Octave Glorious Honey-Bun Asiim Engineer 12th.

*N*aon Sextus Solstice-Rising Engineer 11th always experienced a little death when he took his hands off the drive lever. Post coital. He coyly shrugged the thought away—exaggeration—but that first time when his own father Bedzo 10th had taken his hand and laid it on the drive bar, when he lifted it off again, had there not been a tiny damp spot on the fly of his pants?

Twenty years rodding and railing had made him acute to every whisper and vibration of his machine. The fusion fires ebbing in the magnetic pinch-torus was a languid decay, a sorrowful limpening. Flaccid. He was never truly himself while the fusion engines slumbered. He grew distracted and irritable. All his family had learned this decades ago and were wise.

He called up a track report from North West Regional Track at Suvebray. The mottled quartersphere resolved in the projector focus, the mainlines a web of throbbing vessels like the arteries of a womb. The fast Northern Lights Express was still twenty minutes down despite its Engineers rattling every valve up into the ochre on the long Axidy incline. Derailment at Perdition Junction, down to a single track. Damn locals, jammed with commuters and roof-riding goondahs, stopping at every hole in the hedge. Woolamagong! Serendip! Acacia Heights! Atomic Avenue! Naon Sextus was not a man who bore delays with grace. Every lost second felt pared from the exposed end of his life, like hard salt cheese. As a child he had read and memorised timetables. For fun. He snatched the monocular from its peg, peered impatiently down the branchline but even the vantage of the bridge of *Catherine of Tharsis* could not penetrate the haze.

"Tcha!"

Casting around for an object on which to flog his annoyance, he noticed through the grille of the catwalk overhead a pair of yellow desert-boot soles. He turned his lenses on them.

"Mother of plenty, has that child no shame?"

A woman's voice answered from behind him: Child'a'grace, Mrs. Asiim Engineer 11th, floury to the elbows, folding samosas in the domestic galley.

"What, dearest?"

Firmness was as much a part of Naon Sextus's character as good time-keeping. Many a time the unexpected voice of his wife had almost tricked him into speaking but he had never lapsed, not once, in four years. He tightened his lips, gave the nasty cough that was the sign for his wife to look at him. Naon Sextus turned from the control board, enough to glimpse Child'a'grace, but not so much that she might think he was looking at her.

No underwear! his fingers said, shaking with indignation.

"It's a fine day," Child'a'grace commented, deftly sealing a pastry triangle and flipping it into hot fat.

The shame! Naon Engineer signed.

"Who's to see?"

Every staring soul on the thirteen twenty-seven Northern Lights Express! For something was emerging from the liquid light dazzle. *Due in three and a half minutes!* As a coda, his thumbs added, *What will they think?*

"They will think," said Child'a'grace breezily, here fishing samosa from the fry-bath with a chicken-wire scoop, "That there is a fine young woman of nearly-nine with the body of an Avata and the impatience of a rat whom you and I both know, husband, should long since have been married." She drained the golden oil back into the pan. "And if by some chance, the passing winds should blow that skirt up—which they might, for if I remember, it is quite short and floaty—and they see that she wears not underpants, then the more fortune to them and I hope their sleeps are tormented by wants for many a night."

Before leaving her family at an unnamed water stop under the volcanoes, Child'a'grace had been Susquavanna, a catering people who for two long centuries had hawked hot savouries up and down the platforms of the northwest quartersphere. Pastry was in their genes, like steam in the blood of the Engineers, but she resolutely refused to observe the proprieties of caste, namely the eternal distinction between *track* and *platform*. This was deeply grievous to Naon Sextus, a son of his father and his line before him. Truly, the dowry had cleared up the matter of the remortgage, but he frequently wished that

Grandmother Taal had matched him with someone a little less *platform*. But after eleven years, the food was still exciting. The sex can go, the conversation will go, the respect may be trodden into a familiar track of predictability, but by the Mother of Mercies, cooking endures.

But the girl had no underwear, and one under-dignified marriage was enough. Women with no knickers ended married to Bassareenis and dropping their sprogs in the caboose. His fingers prepared to riposte this to Child'a'grace but the shapes were blown away by the sudden slam of the express train's passing.

3

*T*here was a moment that Sweetness Asiim Engineer treasured above all other distinct moments. She had travelled long enough around the globe to admit it as almost sexual, but it was entirely her own. It began with a brief flutter, an intake of breath, a stirring of hair and clothes: the pressure shift. At this point you obtained best effect by closing the eyes and listening to the swelling thunder of wheels. Hold the dread: fight the instinct to look at the source of that unholy noise. Then, the second pressure point: *there*. Sweetness opened her eyes. The fast train reared like a cliff before her. The world was nothing but steel and steam and blasting, shattering sound. Sweetness unleashed the deep, dark fear: *You're on the wrong track, the points have failed, sixty thousand tons of train are about to meet head on at three hundred and fifty kilometres per hour, and you're right between them!*

It would be quick, and glorious.

The mountain aimed itself at her heart and, at the last instant, turned away.

The pressure wave punched her hard, blinded her with steam and dust. Then the slipstream yanked at her: *You, come.* Sweetness needed no invitation. She leaped after the blur of chrome and black. Along clattering catwalks. Down iron staircases. Across vertiginous gantries, over platforms, hurdling the sprawling legs of brother Sleevel, lolling idle with his best mate Rother'am watching the afternoon pelota on a handheld.

"Sle."

"What? Uh. Just my sister."

Sweetness raced the faces behind the tinted window glass but the faces were always going to win. The wind that dragged her was failing. It dropped her in a little iron-framed oriole high on the side of the starboard tender coupling. She leaned out over the brass railing, raised her hand in salute to the glass observation car, the rattle in the express's tail. On the open rear balcony was a fine city lady in a sheer lace dress. Wake turbulence tugged her parasol from her fingers. It soared up and away, a bamboo and waxed-paper flying saucer. The city lady looked up, vexed, and in that moment her eyes met those of the black-haired girl in the orange track vest in the wrought-iron carbuncle on the flank of the big hauler.

Lady and train were a thin black snake winding across the red desert. Carried high on the winds, the parasol floated into invisibility. The haze swallowed all. Gone again.

"You're a fool to yourself," the voice said after a decent interlude. The thunder of wheels had masked his approach, but Sweetness had deduced Romereaux's presence from his smell. All the Deep-Fusion people had a distinctive musk, like electricity and cool evenings after hot days, or concrete after rain. Sweetness imagined it was what atoms smelled like.

"You think."

He was leaning against the turret door in the easy-pleasey way men can when it's not important for them to be looked at. Romereaux's people shared hair colour and quality with the Engineers—and body fluids, certain generations ago—but he was slight and pale, with a narrow shadow of attempted goatee. The sun did not get to the Deep-Effs in the heart of the big train.

"Two hundred years of Engineer tradition says I know what I'm talking about."

He was a year and a half Sweetness's senior and, bad genes or not, next corroboree he would marry a Traction daughter off the Class 88 *Four Ways*. She would miss him.

"There's a first time for everything."

He saw the way she looked down the long straight track and wanted to lie, to promise unpromisable things, but he had never been able to lie to Sweetness in all their years growing up together on *Catherine of Tharsis*.

"Sle will be Engineer 12th. You know that."

She did, she knew it like she knew the sun would rise tomorrow, but she still growled, "All Sle's interested in is pelota and grab ass. And he's not even any good at them."

Romereaux smiled palely. She went on.

"There are other branches of the Domiety have women drivers. The Slipher Engineers. The Great Western folk. Down in New Merionedd every other Engineer is a woman. And couldn't you just pretend, eh? Couldn't you just for once tell me, yeah, sure, Sweetness, you'll drive, you'll be up there with your hand on the drive lever? Would that be so hard, for once?"

"Sweetness . . ."

"I know."

He said, "Have you been to see your uncle yet?"

"Mother'a . . . I near forgot. How long've we got?"

"About five minutes."

"I'll go now, then. You coming?"

"If you don't mind."

Trainpeople, Sweetness thought as she waited for Ricardo Traction to crank down the access ladder. We can go any place we like in the whole wide world but only as long as we stay on the rails.

"Regards to your uncle!" *Tante* Miriamme Traction called from the tiny window of her laundry room as Sweetness hopped down on to the red sand. Stay on the rails. Bad luck will come in the night and climb up through your nose and through your ears if you wander off the safe track. Superstitions, litanies, observations. Casual coincidences that have become baked over years into causes and effects. Believed truths. Like daughters don't drive. But she still glanced over her shoulder when she could no longer feel the psychic closeness of *Catherine of Tharsis* on the back of her neck. The big train stood like a black monolith fused out of rust sand.

Romereaux paid his respects first. A quick press of the palm to the sand-scoured shaft of the signal light. Everyone—crew, that was, *passengers* never counted—on *Catherine of Tharsis* was related in some way, even the boisterous Bassareenis, but Romereaux's connection with Uncle Neon was tenuous and he had never really believed that a soul could exist in a railroad signal. That might have been why he had never felt anything but Bethlehem Ares galvanised steel, Sweetness thought. He bowed and stood back.

Sweetness clapped her hands twice. The sound was small and flat in the huge and flat desert. She uncapped the flask she had collected from *Madre* Marya Stuard and poured a libation of cold tea. It frothed and stained the red sand like urine. Sweetness closed her eyes and boldly pressed her hand against the shaft. As ever, it began with sound-shadow, steel-slither, the hum-thrum of wind and wheels on rails, a memory of a life in rapid motion, twin ribbons of metal singing like the tines of a tuning fork. Her hearing opened like wings, was down at the bottom listening to the strum of the silicon and the songs the stones sing, then up through the wind-tumbled grains, listening to them building into harmonies of sand, a slow sea breaking grain by grain. Outward still, until she could hear everything contained within the girdling horizon. The rhythms and pulses of her own body joined with the chord of sand song. For a divine moment the great northern desert was a single quantum wave function, modelled in sand like a Shandastria scrying-garden. Sweetness stood at the locus of maximum probability.

She opened her eyes. As ever, she was somewhere else. In this place there were no rails and no train and where the desert met the far mountains the red bled up into the sky. Blood-red sky, a pink zenith. No clouds in that sky, neither hope nor memory of rain. The rocks around her feet were salted with frost. The sand on which she stood seethed with static electricity. In all the world there were only two things, her and the upright of the signal light, rooted obstinately in the alien earth.

Sweetness had always understood three things about this place. First, that neither of them should really be here at all. Second, that it should be as instantly lethal to her as if the soil were acid. Third, that this was their private place, her uncle and her, and that she could never tell anyone about it. Not even her family. It had been bad enough with Little Pretty One. They had talked Flying Therapist. This . . .

"Uncle."

When he spoke, he sounded less like the practical, piratical man she remembered, and more like she imagined God the Panarchic. In a voice that seemed to come from a great distance, he asked, "What year is it?"

"Same as last time."

"When was last time?"

"Duoseptember. The autumn equinox. The Cadmium Valley contract?"

"Oh, yes." Like a sandstorm subsiding. "What year is that, exactly?" She told him. He said, "I lose the track, here."

As she knew that these conversations with her uncle took place outside normal space, Sweetness also understood that they occupied a special time, neither past nor present nor future, but other, real-time inverted. Dream time.

"So," Uncle Neon said. "Sle . . ."

"Still thinks he's going to be a big pelota star. 'Cept he's got two right feet and a fat gut and his head is fried from too much television and wanking."

"He hasn't married that Cussite girl with the fifteen gold ear-rings, yet?"

"Not yet."

"Has he . . ."

"Met her yet? Not that, either."

"Ah. I see." He did too, much and wide, but unfocused, like a distorting lens. Sweetness frequently tripped over Uncle Neon's nostalgias for futures that might never happen. And sometimes the branching future he picked in this mother of marshalling yards was the mainline ahead.

"They want you wed," he said.

"Tell me."

"To a Stuard. A *Ninth Avata* Stuard, on the Llangonedd run."

"Mother'a'grace . . ."

"Don't worry yourself."

"Don't worry myself? You've just told me I'm going to blow my wild years brewing samovars of mint tea for Cathar pilgrims."

Uncle Neon had an appropriately scary laugh. It felt like sand scouring the inside of your skull. Sweetness winced.

"Sweetness, your wild years are far from blown," he said, and sang an old nursery rhyme about a sailor who sailed across the sky and brought back his love a silver fig and a diamond rattle. He did not sing well, even in death, but Sweetness was patient with relatives. When he had finished she left a polite pause before asking, "Is that it?"

"That what?"

"I'm going to marry a Stuard and my wild years are far from over?"

In the pause that followed, Sweetness imagined the three-bulbed signal light cocked to one side, quizzically.

"Yes. That's it. Don't worry, though. Trust me. Now, tell me, how is she?"

By "she," Sweetness understood *Catherine of Tharsis* and that she would see no more of her future. She huffed through her nose in exasperation at the unruly oracle.

"The aft containment field still isn't seating right."

"Is it making a sound like this?" *This* being a twittering, hissing whistle.

"More like this." Sweetness added a tweeting click, on a rising cadence.

Uncle Neon clicked his tongue.

"You want to get that seen to. What are those Deep-Fusion folk about? I don't know, since I died, she's gone to pieces. No one has any respect for good machinery any more. *He* certainly doesn't. His head's completely up his arse, and I don't just mean trains. Look at that poor sow he married—your sainted mother, I mean." Uncle Neon's telepathic apology felt like two crossed fingers circling Sweetness's frontal lobe in blessing. She loved the feeling. It made her purr. "He's still not talking to her."

"Not a whisper. He signs."

Another neural tut.

"It should be you. I've always said that. You'd get that field generator set right *toute suite*."

"I wouldn't have let it get into that state in the first place," Sweetness said proudly. Too many dead-end tracks toppling into glossy green craters were the monuments to sloppy tokamak maintenance. The Tracksters laid fresh rail around them but the blast craters stayed hot for lifetimes, glowing sickly in the high plains night. Thinking of them, Sweetness flared, "But I'm going to marry a poncing Stuard on the God-shuttle and make tea and almond slices, amn't I?"

"You are?"

"You said you saw it."

"I see a lot more than I say. That I can say."

Says who? Sweetness wanted to say but the words were sucked off her lips by the sudden dust wind whipping up around her, a dust she knew was not dust, or rust, but moments. Granulated time. She was being drawn back. The journey home was always quicker and more precipitous than the way out: a swooping giddiness, a rustling blackness, a sense of wings wide enough to wrap the world, and then *there*; the big big desert and the hot hot sun.

Romereaux was squatting on his heels by the rail, scooping up palmfuls of dust and trickling them through his fingers. Idling time away.

"How do you do that?" he said.

"Do what?" The other place took a moment to blink away, like grit in the eye.

"Whatever it is you do. Wherever it is you go."

"Go?" Suspicious: what had he seen? "I don't go anywhere. I mean, you're there, but you're not there."

"But where are you?"

"What's this about?"

Romereaux shrugged, opened his hand, looked at the earth and small stones clutched there.

"I'm just interested in what you do, where you go."

"Well don't be."

"You're very defensive."

"I've got to have something for myself." On a train where five families live on top of each other in a tapestry of territories and societies. "Some place for me."

"So you do go somewhere."

"What's this to you?"

"Nothing. They've whistled."

That brought her up.

"What? How many times?"

"Twice."

"Mother'a . . ."

Three whistles and the train left. With or without you. Fare or family. We've got a railroad to run, don't you know? Timetables to keep. As Sweetness sprinted for *Catherine of Tharsis*, steam plumed up from the calliope mounted where the main boiler joined the tender. The impudent notes of "Liberty Lillian's Rag" swaggered across the desert as *Madre* Mercedes Deep-Fusion's asbestos-gloved fingers hopped across the seething keys. All aboard that's coming aboard! All a-ground that's staying behind. Skirt hitched around her thighs, Sweetness pounded down the track. Romereaux passed her effortlessly. Behind them, Uncle Neon closed his amber eye and opened his green eye. *Catherine of Tharsis* cleared her cylinders with a shout of steam. Cranks flailed, wheels spun. Like a crustal plate shifting, the behemoth began to move.

Sweetness saw Romereaux snatch at the bottom rung of the companionway as it retracted. Then it was past her head and moving in utterly the opposite direction. Sweetness spun on her heel and raced after the receding ladder. House-high wheels churned beside her head. Romereaux crouched on the lowest step, hand outstretched. Mother'a'grace, it was going to be close.

"Romereaux!"

The reaching hand was pulling away. With the dregs of her strength, Sweetness leaped. Romereaux's hand was an iron manacle around her wrist. Sweetness slammed into the relief valve on the luff housing. Winded, she swung from Romereaux's grip. Drive shafts hammered beside her ear.

"I can't . . ." Romereaux's face read; youthful strength overstretched by sharp reality. Sweetness swung, tried to kick herself toward the diamond tread of the rung. Nailtips grazed steel. The sleeper-ends beneath her were a blur of concrete. Fall now, and it would be worse than miss the train. She kicked again, reached.

"Ahhh!"

Fingers locked around metal rung. Romereaux pulled her up until both hands had a firm grip. He gathered a fistful of track jacket and floral-print summer frock and hauled Sweetness on to the companionway. Metal scraped bare shin, she paddled with her feet. Boot treads found stair treads.

Home.

"Close one," *Tante* Miriamme called, sheets a-folding as Romereaux and Sweetness scurried past her window. "And Sweetness, in the desert? A true lady never forgets her underwear."

Two hundred kilometres up, the orbital mirror caught sunlight from beneath the edge of the world and winked it into Naon Engineer's eye. Momentarily blinded, he dropped the thread of his argument to the floor of the Confab Chamber.

"Erm . . ."

"The marriage portion," svelte, dangerous Marya Stuard hinted.

Blithe and holy, the five-kilometre disk of silverskin wheeled down the orbital marches after the setting sun.

"Oh yes. Of course. What had I suggested?"

"Five thousand dollars in the chest."

"Ah, yes."

A glance at Grandfather Bedzo, drooling in the Remote Steering Cubby under the copper curls of the cyberhat. Tanking up should be straightforward enough a process to entrust to the decrepit old Engineer, but Naon 11th did not like the way the old man's wall eye was rolling.

"Plus . . ."

"What?"

"Two percent on the next five years."

A beat of fist on the live wood conference table. Grandfather Bedzo started in his decades-deep senescence. He remembered the hard edge of his wife's hand.

"Never!" Grandmother Taal declared. She was a little, pickled kernel of a woman, packed with meat and life and potential. At forty-two she still shunted the weightiest of bargains when the locodores in their red flannel tailcoats came loping in their sedan chairs into the sidings to call the day's contracts. Her eyes were sharp little black flies. "One percent, over three years."

Naon Engineer 11th glanced again at his sire. He was banging his foot against a riveted bulkhead in time to the swash of water through the reservoir pipes. Naon prayed the Lords of the Iron Way that Bedzo would resist an incontinence attack. It would make the marriage bargaining so very much harder.

"One and three quarter percent and four years."

Engineer and Stuard matriarchs locked eyes over the bargaining table. On this oval of wood, reputedly an Original Branch from the Tree of World's Beginning, the Articles of Operation had been signed twelve generations and a billion kilometres back by Engineer and Stuard the First.

"Were he of your lineage, *Tante* Marya, I might concur," Grandmother Taal said. "But this . . ."

"Narob," piped Salam Serene Stuard, youngest of the Domiety, first time at the big table and blessedly ignorant of the social games the formidable old ladies loved to play. His great-aunt glared at him.

". . . is a lad of *prospects*." Meaning, *and your granddaughter is just a daughter. A womb, a ladder to history.* "He is *Chef du Chemin*. He has his own galley."

"In stainless steel," Youngest Salam said, with some envy. He had only just been promoted to Linen and Tray Service. Grandmother Taal scooped up his unwise attempt to recover *coup* like a hot *nimki* from a station tray-hawker.

"On the *Ninth Avata*!" she said.

"Yes!" Naon exclaimed, feeling as if he had missed a couple of turns in the game. "One and a quarter percent, and three and a half years!"

"Naon!" Mother-to-son voice. "You are without doubt the finest throttleman in this quartersphere, but that is exactly the reason men drive and women bargain. Now . . ." She turned to her adversary. "She is Engineer born in the bone. She has steam in her soul and oil in her heart and iron in her thighs and fusion fire in her eyes, she has left a million used-up kilometres behind her, she is true granddaughter of this grandmother and know this, she will carve up your *Chef du Chemin* Narob with his own fine knives, in his own stainless steel galley and serve him with a little salt and chilli to his clients and that is why she will go to *Ninth Avata* for nothing less than one and half percent for three years and twenty-four months. Stick. Stop . . ."

But before Grandmother Taal could call *stay* and seal the deal, Marya

Stuard worked her thumbs behind the gold-embroidered lapels of her tunic and called out, "Yes, Engineer, *but what is she doing now?*"

It was an evil blow that ricocheted across the table from open mouth to raised eyebrow, deflected off Naon Engineer's dismayed brow, through the porthole, two hundred kilometres up into the evening sky to bounce off the reflecting dish of the big vana, as it slid over the terminator into night, back down to earth two and half kilometres north to the Inatra Fillage Number Six Water Storage Cistern in which Sweetness Engineer joyfully swam. She felt it as a prickle of gooseflesh on her bare back as she stroked toward the concrete lip where Psalli sat, toes teasing the water. Sweetness glanced up; the knuckled rim of the escarpment had risen above the sun. That would explain the sudden shiver. Magic hour. The triskelions of the wind-pumps were lazy silhouettes on the deep blue.

"You going to be much longer?" Psalli called as Sweetness tumble-turned into another length. She was a solid, sullen-faced creature, a true Traction. At eight-and-not-a-day more she was Sweetness's closest female contemporary, thus friend, though Sweetness wondered would she have been had their lives been less mobile. She could be a whining cow.

"You go on back if you're cold," Sweetness said, elbows hooked over the further ledge of the tank.

"Nah," Psalli grunted.

"Don't let me stop you, now."

The girl shrugged her meaty shoulders. Sweetness kicked off from the far end of the cistern. Two strokes brought her sliding in front of Psalli.

"Why not?"

Psalli glanced beyond the stepped terraces of water tanks to the truck gardens.

"They won't bother you," Sweetness said.

"They keep looking and waving."

"So? Okay. Then we'll give them something to look and wave at." A heave brought Sweetness out of the water in a cascade of fat drops. Balanced like a gymnast on the narrow lip, she drew herself up to her full one point seven five bare-ass metres. Honey-skin dewed with billion-year-old fossil water. She scraped her hair behind her ears, put her fingers in her mouth and whistled. It pierced the indigo cool of Inatra like a stiletto. All the dark doll figures that had been clinging to the tall foliage at the edge of the irrigation canals turned as one.

"Hey! Boys! See this?" Sweetness wiggled her hips. "Well, you can never, ever have this." She turned a slow cartwheel on the edge of the pool. The watching boys of Inatra were each and every one struck through the eyes so that ever after they could not love right because tattooed on their retinas was a vision of unattainable youth and loss with arcs of old, cold water flicking from its heels. Sweetness bounced upright. "Just thought you should know, right?" The figures slunk away into the greenery.

Hands on hips, she surveyed her conquest. Inatra was a spring-line town, a place of wells and shafts and pumps, of water shivering silkily down mossy runnels from cistern to cistern, of gurgling irrigation canals and sagely nodding *yawnagers*, of aloof water-towers and lithe brown children who pranced in the rainbow spray from the leaking fill-hoses. Here the gradual tilt of the great Tanagyre plain cracked like a broken paschal biscuit into the kilometre uplift of the Praesoline Escarpment. Here the big fusion locos paused for a long drink of water before the toil up the ramps and switchovers of the Inatra Ascent. Here, while the trains drank, train people played in water.

"Sweetness Octave Glorious Honey-Bun Asiim Engineer, you have no shame," Psalli said.

"Great, isn't it?"

By now her piercing, two-finger whistle had penetrated *Catherine of Tharsis*'s Domiety Chamber and, though weak, it still had enough strength to climb into Marya Stuard's ear. She smiled. Everyone around the table had as good a guess as her as to its source. She laid her hand palm upright on the polished wood.

"Three thousand, one point seven percent and three years thirty months. Stick stop stay."

She held Grandmother Taal's look. The old Engineer woman shrugged.

"Tinguoise."

"Major's Gate."

"Ethan Soul."

The formula was complete. No one living or undead knew its source, neither could they unsay anything it sealed.

"I'll contact the *Ninth Avata* people and have the contract drawn up."

Marya Stuard rose from the table with her delegation. As she swept out, Child'a'grace muttered, "Too cheap."

Her husband roared.

"Tell that woman . . ." he commanded Grandmother Taal but she had departed in a rustle of many-layered skirts, so he signed, *She is only a daughter!* His fingers added, *Half a daughter*.

Child'a'grace rose in a blossom of sudden fury.

"Never . . ."

Sorry sorry my mistake, Naon Engineer signed. He had committed a cardinal sin. He knew that he had handled the negotiations badly. His hands might be on the throttles but he was afraid of Marya Stuard. Afeared, and indebted: no one in any of *Catherine of Tharsis*'s Domieties was let forget that she had single-handedly faced down the notorious Starke gang as they fleeced a carriage of Lewite Pelerines. Her defiance had cost her a needle in the hip that troubled her when it was political for it to do so, but her example had woken the demons in the milk-mannered pilgrims. As one they had risen, seized the dacoits and ejected them at the next mail drop. Marya Stuard herself had been so incensed at the needle in her side that she had laid out old, dreaded Selwyn Starke with a silver salver flung frisbee-style.

"Some day, and, please God, soon, that woman's account will be overdrawn," Naon Engineer mumbled as he went to clean Grandfather Bedzo's tubes and change his bags.

*I*t was full dark now over Inatra. Under the first glimmerings of the moonring, that tumble of orbital engineering that sustained the world's fragile habitability, Sweetness walked home alone along the tracks. Psalli had made the most of the space caused by Sweetness's display and slipped off to her cabin before the rude boys drummed up a scrap of courage between them. She walked between the sleeper-ends and the shanties. Sweetmeat and patty vendors roused themselves from their scavenged human-dung smudgefires, then settled back into repose at the sight of an Engineer orange track vest. Androgynously thin boygirls, ungendered by hunger, shook fistfuls of copper charm bangles at her. *Good luck, good luck girlie, a prayer on every strand.* Sweetness shook her head. The wire was filched from switchgear relays. Aside from the occasional electrocuted bangle-wallah, a prayer on every strand often meant a derailed front end.

Catherine of Tharsis rose from the night, as monolithic as the scarp she was preparing to climb. Riding lights twinkled, windows beckoned. But a whisper turned Sweetness aside at the last booth before home.

"Sees all hears all knows all. Past present future. Uncurtain the windows of time, lady."

The voice was a reptilian whisper, but strangely attractive for that; a reptile with a gorgeous jewelled skin, an ornate crest, a coiling blue tongue. An unsuspected seduceability in Sweetness responded. She heard herself say, "Oh, all right then. How much is it?"

"Very little," lizard-tongue replied. The booth was a sagging leopard-spotted yurt. As she ducked inside, the door flaps brushed Sweetness's nape. They felt like *skin*.

"It's kind of little in here."

Littler than the exterior hinted. She could hardly make out the lizard-lips man across the octagonal table. He seemed small and hairless, his skin oddly dark even among a dark-skinned people. She could have sworn it was *green* in the dull glow from everywhere and nowhere.

"Shouldn't you be asking me to cross your palm with centavos?" Sweetness asked. The yurt smelled ripely of green and growing, mould and leaf, pistils and fresh-spaded soil.

"If you like," the fortune-teller said. While she fiddled in her hip bag for silver, he placed a device like an overweight egg-timer on the table. Its upper hemisphere was filled with small white beans. Their progress to the lower hemisphere was prevented by a *cheval de frise* of spills inserted through a mesh.

"This do?"

The fortune-teller scooped the trickle of centavos up to his mouth and swallowed them.

"Should you . . . ?"

The huckster leaned toward her. He was green and the source of the smell of verdure. He flared his nostrils.

"You've been swimming."

"My hair's wet, o great detective."

"You smell of water. Here." Quick as a striking rat-snake, he whipped a spine out of the hour-glass. It had a blue tip. Burned on with a hot needle were the words "Fulfillingness First Finale" and "One for free." The little green man studied the motto. "Worse places to start." He laid the spill on the table. "Now, you play. Remove any stick you like, and the aim of the game is not to win, because you can't win a game like this, but to delay the fall of the beans as long as possible. Then we shall begin our reading."

"No problem." Sweetness reached for a stick.

"One rule. Whatever you touch, you must draw."

"I get ya." She confidently drew the stick at which she had aimed her finger. The first five moves were simple, even mindless; then, as the beans rattled and sagged, it became a true game, with demands of thought and foresight. She sucked her lower lip in concentration and hovered between two spills that crossed deep in the heart of the bean heap.

"So, how does this work anyway?"

"You pull the sticks. Gravity supplies the rest."

"I mean, how does it tell the future?"

"How should I know?" the green man said. "All I know is it does."

Her fingers seesawed, decided, decided again, locked firmly around the spill that stuck out at thirty degrees. She could feel the beans grind over the wood as she withdrew the stick. A lurch. A solitary bean hit the bottom of the future-machine. She found she had been holding her breath, and released it in a relieved sigh.

"Some beans will always fall," the green man said, taking the stick. "Hm. Queen's Canton."

"Is that good or bad?"

"It is, that's all." He laid it next to the others in an orderly row.

"I've got an uncle can see the future," Sweetness said matter-of-factly. She squatted low, hands on the table, eyes level with the web of spills.

"Indeed?" said the green man.

"Though he'd tell you it's not so much seeing the future, it's more like having a wider now."

"An interesting perspective."

"That's what he says. But then, he is a signal light."

"That would give . . . novel . . . insights."

"He was working on the pylon when he got hit by lightning." Sweetness drew a stick like a Belladonna rapieree drawing a swordstick. "There!"

"Bravo," said the green man.

Three sticks later there was a click and a sag and all the beans hit the bottom of the jar like goondah-flung pebbles on a widow's window.

"Oh," said Sweetness. The green man was now crouching, studying the pattern of the remaining sticks. He turned the future-ometer over in his hands. Sweetness noticed that he was frowning. She thought of ploughing.

"Bone Sandals in parallel with Boy of Two Dusts, crossing Innocent Excesses obliquely. But Boy of Two Dusts overruns Scent of Lavender, then exits hole eight eight, upper right quadrant; the Deserted Quarter."

"Meaning?"

The green man raised a finger to his lips. He held the hour-glass up to the light that came from everywhere.

"See? Golden Thumb-ring is quite, quite horizontal, and in an isolated quadrant; notice that the only stick that approaches it is Eternal Assistance. Your family wants you wed."

His eyes—which Sweetness noticed had yellow irises—challenged her to be amazed.

"That's not hard. A trackgirl, my age? You're going to have to do better than that."

"I don't see a marriage, though."

"That's more like it. You mean, ever?"

The green man held the future-ometer out to Sweetness.

"Not within the frame of the story."

"What story would that be?"

"The one you're in. The one we're all in. This." The green man's hands cupped the wasp-waisted glass torso. "Stories are made up of lives but not all of life is a story. Only parts have the narrative construction, the dramatic energy, the confluence of incident, desire and coincidence that are the elements of *story*. Within here"—he again caressed the glass—"is the story of your life. Here and here"—he touched either green-tipped end of a scrying-stick—"are where you fade out of the once-upon-a-time and into the happy-ever-after. The rods, of course, go on forever." His fingers described extensions in the air. An instant of other-sight: Sweetness saw them stretching out beyond his reach, through him, through her, through the soft walls of the yurt and the softer walls of night and time. "You think that everything that has happened to you in your life thus far has been chance? To be so blessed! Everything you have been leads to this place, this story-jar, this confluence of forces. Of course, you can look at it the other way." His chartreuse hands turned the oracle one hundred and eighty degrees. A different phalanx of quills menaced Sweetness. "If the universal laws are as reversible as the sages insist, then it is also true that the what-you-will-become influences your decision of what-you-are-now."

"And these beans, are they like God's shit, going to fall on me if I do this or don't do that?"

The green man pursed his lips.

"If you consider that, to me, shit is an excellent fertiliser, and to these people, how they warm their lives, maybe. Then again, you could consider them the weight of undecided events that must be shed for the bones of your story to emerge."

Sweetness cocked her head and folded her arms and looked a challenge from under her fringe of dark curls.

"Do I get to drive a train or not?"

"You do a lot of driving."

"Driver, or driven?"

The green man rotated a spill between thumb and forefinger.

"Grey Lady's Visit, crossing Trumpet of Alves, acute. Both, my dear. Words of advice. Hold on tight to fast-moving objects. Don't trust too much to appearances; then again, first impressions are lasting impressions. When climbing, look at the hands, not the feet. Be aware that the marvellous is always around you. Don't discount family. Don't drop litter. Always expect unexpected assistance. Take a toothbrush and at least one change of underwear. Small change is bulky and too easily rolled out of pockets. Keep notes in your sock. Angels exist, if you know how to use them. Read a little every day. The desert teaches drought, the city bathing. Your body odour is usually worse than you think. Some day, soon, you will cost the world a moon. Your grandmother loves you very much. Easy on the throttle until the cylinders expand. The world is very much more than it seems. When you see green, trust it, for it's all one with me and I will be there in some form or another. Never pay good money to trackside hucksters."

The green man pulled the remaining sticks and set them beside the others on the octagonal table. The future was spoken.

"That's it?" Sweetness asked, in case it wasn't.

"Yes, that's it," the green man said with the same considering look, as if Sweetness's every syllable was loaded with wise ore.

"Keep your eyes open and bring a change of underwear? Anyone could tell you that. What happens to me, where do I go, what do I do, who do I meet?"

"You want me to give the story away?" the green man said.

"This is balls," Sweetness Asiim Engineer declared. "I want my money back."

"Have beans instead," the green man said and threw a fistful of legumes at Sweetness's face. The beans flew apart into dust. Sweetness reeled back from the blinding beige fog that, as it settled, became common Inatra road dust. The soft skin yurt and its resident were, of course, both gone.

"Hey!"

In the dust at her feet Sweetness saw three gleams of silver. Her coins. A hissing: she looked up: wisps of steam were leaking from *Catherine of Tharsis*'s shaft couplings. The Ascent beckoned. A flicker in her peripheral vision distracted her; a wink of light, minute as a five centavo piece, floated over the top of the escarpment. Quick as silver it slithered between the wind-pumps, leaped over the zigzags of the Ascent, glimmered across the tank terraces. Every moment it grew in size: over the trucks, gardens, the water-towers and hose gantries, aimed true and proper at Sweetness. Fear and wonder transfixed her. The spotlight from heaven dashed across the sidings, over the cardboard roofs of the poor, swept over Sweetness. And stopped. She was embedded in light. The air about her seemed to sing. Dust rose from the ground. The night smelled electric. Sweetness held out her hand. The three centavos in her palm shone like burning platinum. But she was not afraid. She shaded her eyes with her hand and squinted up the beam to the orbital mirror at its source. The light squeezed tears from her eyes.

"Thanks, but I got to go now!"

She stepped out of the enchanted circle. The spotlight followed her.

Sweetness giggled nervously.

Be aware that the marvellous is always around you.

She stowed the three centavos in her hip-bag and walked home shrouded in light.

6

*S*hortly after four a.m. *Catherine of Tharsis* completed its climb up the Inatra Ascent and dragged the last of its hundred ore-cars over the escarpment lip on to the down-grade into Leidenland. At twenty to five Sweetness Asiim Engineer 12th was woken in her narrow bed-box back of the aux-com by a burning tingle along her left flank, hip to floating rib. By the time she was fully awake, Little Pretty One was crouching in the mirror on the cabinette door. As ever, she was dressed in the clothes Sweetness had been wearing the previous day.

"They've done the dirt," she said without preamble, as was her way.

"What time is it?" Sweetness asked.

"'Bout three hours from Juniper. Look, if you're not interested . . ."

"You'll tell me anyway."

Eight and a half years teaches you the moods and toyings of your imaginary friend. But not as much as being joined flesh to flesh, bone to bone, organ to organ, hip to floating rib.

Twins were a blessing among trackpeople: two firm rails on which to run a common life. So when the mountainously pregnant Child'a'grace had felt something stir in her waters and Naon Engineer (then speaking words of love to her) had rushed full-throttle up to the floating Midwife at Dehydration, and the midwife had run her foetoscope over Child'a'grace's belly and pronounced definitely, "twins," there had been rejoicing. Even if they were girls. So no one had really listened when the midwife added, "They seem close. Very close."

How close became apparent five months later, in the Obstetrarium of the Flying (as opposed to Floating) Midwife's dirigible, docked like an egg in a cup in an old impact crater just south of the high, lonely Alt Colorado line.

"A girl!" No surprise. "And another girl!" So quickly? Naon Engineer had peered at the tangle of limbs and blood and tubes. Suddenly it all made visual sense, and he let out a cry of pure superstitious dread.

Siamese twins.

"Seen worse," said the Flying Midwife, a great, ugly-lovely woman called Moon'o'May as she ran her scanner over the squawling, raisin-faced humans. "See?" Naon Engineer could make nothing of the false-colour images of bones and organs and pulsing things. "Shared kidney—could be a problem with that, later. Same with the ovary. But no neural interconnection. The spinal columns are clear, and the hips are anatomically ideal."

"So you can separate them," Naon Engineer said, even as his wife was sweating and smiling and trying to make sense out of the unexpected complexity that had unfolded from her uterus.

"It should be straightforward."

"Then do it."

"I'll come back in a year, when they've grown stronger and the organs have settled."

"No, do it now."

Afterward Naon Engineer would always justify it by arguing that you could not have twin-trunked creatures obstructing *Catherine of Tharsis*'s narrow corridors and gangways. If there were a pressure leak, or, please God, a plasma breach, the creature would not only endanger itself but the lives of every other family member. Child'a'grace, still vertiginous from the birthing drugs, had understood that he feared others might suspect bad genes in the Engineer Domiety. Too close to the tokamaks. Uh huh. And there's a shallow grave, just off the McAuleyburg branch. Oh yes. Well, of course there's nothing left now, the condors get everything. But just you look at the collar bones, and count the vertebrae.

"So," the Flying Midwife said as she printed out the consent forms and laid the little red squawling thing on the white table under the white lights, "who gets the kidney and who gets the ovary?"

"She gets the kidney." Naon Engineer pointed. "And she gets the ovary."

"Okie dokie," the Flying Midwife said, and called up the surgeon she worked with in Belladonna. He was on a marriage-repair weekend on the canals of New Merionedd, so the locum slipped his hand into the waldoglove and put on the cyberhat. In his windowless office on the fifth underdeep of

Belladonna he waggled his fingers. In an Alt Colorado impact crater, scalpel-blades danced over the infants. The robot arms wove, the fingers flashed and at the end of it the one with the kidney lived and the one with the ovary died and in truth there was a shallow grave, by the side of the branchline, unmarked but much spattered by the soft, bloody faeces of condors.

Child'a'grace, half-joyful, half-despairing, hung a mobile of mirrored birds over the survivor's cot and that night, Little Pretty One came into them and watched over her sibling, though the eyes of Sweetness Octave Glorious Honey-Bun Asiim Engineer 12th had yet to learn to focus.

That was the story as told by Little Pretty One.

"I just hope you like the smell of hot fat," the twin ghost said in her bedroom mirror.

Sweetness surged out of her bunk with as great a surge as her tiny couchette would allow.

"Grandmother Taal . . ."

"She's got powers but she's not omnipotent. She got as good a deal as she could . . ."

The night, the dust, the gentle rock of the rails beneath her, the warm presence of constant velocity, the background bass hum of the tokamaks, the cool of the ancient waters of Inatra, the reek of dungfires, the verdant perfume of the green man's booth; all drowned out by the rattle of pans and plates and the blatting of orders down the gosport. Sold. To a Stuard.

"*Ninth Avata?*"

"Who told you?"

"My uncle."

Little Pretty One pouted, put out. She disliked having an oracular rival in the family.

"Did your uncle tell you his name?"

"Tell me."

"Narob Chi-Ora of the Southern Circle Stuards."

"Is he?"

"Cute enough. Black hair. Nice ass. Nice eyes too. He'd be kind. He's got ambitions. Catering director for the entire North West Quartersphere. He could get it too."

After eight years, Sweetness knew that Little Pretty One's *coulds* usually meant *will*. Somewhere in the Panarch's ninety-seven nested heavens, she suspected her ex-Siamese twin had met *others*.

"When?" Heavy question.

"Next corroboree." Heavier answer. Twice a long year, on the spring and autumn equinoxes, the Trainpeople gathered on the great sidings of Woolongong flats, ten trains to a track, five hundred tracks. Five thousand noble locomotives, tenders and cabooses decked with bunting and flower garlands and hard-won iron rosettes for speed and endurance and bravery and heavy hauling. Here the Domiety heads boogied and the daughters were traded away. Economies of money and honour were exchanged out on the shimmering flats and, often as not, were that same day lost over card and snooker tables. Commodius vicus of recirculation of the commodifiable. Sweetness had seen the young women in their mothers' dresses, bags in hands, nuptial kerchiefs on their heads. Seen, pitied, resolved never to join.

"Oh God!"

The big ore-load was bound for the foundries of Steel River. Three days deadhead from there up to Shelby to pick up a forest fermenter—raw trees at Shelby, fifteen kinds of liquiplastic and hydrocarbon fuel by the time it decoupled at Wisdom. There, an immediate shunt on to a pilgrim charter to the Murmuring Mountain at Chernowa, then a fast run to Belladonna for a month heading up the pride of Bethlehem Ares Railroads itself, the Ares Express. And after that the sun would stand vertical over the equator and divide the world into equal day and night and she would get to live in a strange man's galley and her black curls would smell forever after of hot fat. So little time, so few kilometres.

"You can't let this happen!"

In the mirror, Little Pretty One spread her hands in the way ghosts do when they tell the living, *I'm a ghost, remember*.

Sweetness did remember. Something else.

"The green man!"

For the first time Sweetness saw Little Pretty One taken aback.

"The what?"

"The green man. He said . . ."

"You met a green man? Where? I didn't see that. This changes every-thing."

He said, I don't see a marriage yet, was what Sweetness would have said but for the smart rap on the cabin door, followed by the swift, fierce itch that was Little Pretty One exiting the mirror and entering the long scar up her side.

Brother Sle opened the porthole and bellowed.

"Uncle Billy!"

The formula was ancient, irrevocable and universally respected. Not even the Domiety historians agreed who Uncle Billy had been, if he had been any more than legendary, but he had saved generations of Engineers from peril, crime, police, debt, rivals, badmaashes, wanderlust and misjudged relation-ships. He had warned of threats gross and subtle, shysters, dunners, weigh-bridgemen, bindlestiffs and freeloaders.

"Whereaway?" Sweetness called.

"Railrat," Sle answered.

A roofrider. A freeloader. A faredodger. Pausing only to scratch her haunted wound, Sweetness threw on shorts, shoes, shirt. Sle was waiting in the corridor with the flashlight and djubba-stick.

"You be careful with that," he scolded as Sweetness reacquainted herself with the short, chubby railfolk's weapon.

"What, like this, brother?" She aimed the blunt club-head at Sle. He danced back; the compressed gas charge could shoot out the djubba-stick with force enough to dislodge the most tenacious roof rider.

"Don't waste the gas," he said sourly. Sweetness gave his retreating back a thumb of disgrace as he exited the port sidewalk. She popped the overhead iris hatch with a gasp of steam and shinned up on to the roofwalk. Up on the roof had always been the place Sweetness had gone to think and feel and be alone, a savoury delicacy on crowded, bustling *Catherine of Tharsis*. Here, on the brilliant nights when the moonring was a diamond prizefighter's belt, Child'a'grace had always known she could find her daughter out of all of a big train's hundreds of hiding places. Sweetness unclasped her hair and shook it out in *Catherine of Tharsis*'s eternal slipstream. With the innate grace of the trainborn, she poised herself against the slow rock of the engine. She breathed in the night air. Steam wreathed around her. Several times since sprouting hair she could sit on, she had come up to take her clothes off and let the white vapour and the night caress her. At first she had felt perverse and sinful. Midnight nudist *and* aspirant engine drier. Then one night, buttoning up her blouse, she had spied Nugent Traction not merely take his gear off, but enjoy a slow, nocturnal wank, launching his effort in an elegant arc over the side of the water tender.

Tonight, an Uncle Billy. Sweetness instinctively checked her tunnel-warning beacon, though there was no tunnel within two hundred kays, hitched the djubba-stick to her belt and set off down the gently swaying roofwalk toward the tender.

A sound.

She froze on the top rung of the tender companionway. Her inquisitive torch beam swung hither and yon. Romereaux's grin greeted her from the lee of the main water inflow.

"Don't do that man, I could've djubba-ed you."

"Sorry, did I spook you?"

"Nah. Course not."

She saw Romereaux's face change and knew what he was going to say. She did not want to hear it. He did anyway.

"About . . ."

Sweetness flared.

"How come everyone hears about this before me?"

"I'm sorry . . ."

Well, Engineers can't marry Deep-Fusion people anyway, so you're scuppered there, she thought of saying but he really did not deserve words like that so she said, coolly, "Where've you checked?"

"Starboard side's clear. Suleiman is still down port. Chagdi's coming up from the caboose."

"I'll do the tops of the trucks."

"Okay." A pause. "Sweet . . ."

"Don't talk. Okay?"

It was good and physical to leap over the dark chasms between the ore-cars and flash her torch down among the clanking couplings.

"Come out come out."

She sent her beam dancing over the angled planes of the truck roof. Behind this one, three hundred more. More distant than she had imagined, another sway of light, Chagdi working his way up.

Father Naon had tried to impress the family horror of railrats on Sweetness but she had seen the indignity of old tramps impaled on signal stanchions and sad goondahs, shaken from the bogies, guillotined in half by the wheels, and the dreadful look in the eyes of the bums as they spat red dust from their mouths and banged red dust from their coats and then saw five hundred kilometres of it on every side of them. Freeloading was stealing but every time she was sent up on the roof Sweetness regretted that she must be part of the punishment. Were tales of the terrible fates of roofriders not told among the indigent orders that breed and were buried under the great termini? Or was whatever they were escaping worth any risk?

Escape.

A noise. Not family this time. The torch beam dodged left. Movement down on the sloping flank of ore-car eleven. Behind the vent stack. Sweetness hurdled the gaps between trucks, light fixed on the hexagonal mound of the vents. Steel mesh clanged beneath her feet. Yes. Yes. There. *Fingers*. She crouched by the handrail, sent her light this way, that. Her right hand unhooked the djubba-stick. Fingers, pale knuckled around the metal vent. Thin fingers, dust ingrained in the knuckles, black jam under the nails.

Sweetness considered the fingers for a long time. Then she laid the djubba-stick on the roofwalk and said, softly, "Hey. You're taking a wild risk, you know."

The fingers were silent.

"You get all kinds of stuff gassing up off the ore. A kind of relative of mine fell in once when they were unloading. Came out like a teacher's handbag. True. If that thing valves, it'll blow you clear off the car."

The fingers twitched.

"You know, I wouldn't pick that place at all. Hanging down the side? You want to get gravity working for you, not against you, see? I'd go right up the front, down on the cow-catcher. It's right in front of everyone but it's kind of like a blind spot, you can't see it from the bridge. True. Really. But, well, you're here, so what you need to do, when you fall off, is make sure you land right between the tracks. That way the train goes right over your head. Mind you, you have to get down kind of fast, you don't want to get anything tangled up in the grit pipes. You could be dragged for like kilometres."

The fingers twitched in her torch beam.

"So, how long've you been down there?"

Nothing. Then, a whisper almost lost in the wheel rumble, "Since Little Rapids."

"Mother'a . . . Your fingers must be coming off."

"Yes," came the small reply that was full of knotted nerves and locked sinews and muscles numb to everything but dumb survival. Sweetness came to a decision.

"I'm going to send something down to you. Grab ahold of it."

"No," came the answer.

"You what? I'm trying to help you."

"Don't trust."

Sweetness was sincerely perplexed at the rejection of her offer of rebellion.

"Why so?"

"Trick. Try to knock me off."

"Listen, if you've been hanging on there since Little Rapids, you don't need me to knock you off. Sooner rather than later, my friend."

The train lurched over points. Fingers groaned. Fingers slipped a fraction. Sweetness ducked under the handrail, anchored her feet over the lip of the roofwalk and stretched down over the sloping truck side. One-handed, she aimed the djubba-stick as close as she dared to the fingers.

"This is going to come fast, so don't shy away or anything stupid like that."

A second lurch threw her aim. The club-head shot within a whisker of the pale soft hand. The fingers almost flinched. Almost.

"Grab hold!" Sweetness shouted. "It'll hold you."

"Yeah," came the voice as the fingers felt for the telescopic shaft of the stick. "But can you?"

"I can hold any damn thing," Sweetness said, affronted. One hand, then the other grasped the stick. The sudden tug almost tore her loose.

"Hang on," she gritted, to herself. She fumbled for the retract key. And *twist*. The djubba-stick kicked like Nugent Traction's organ as first the hands, then the arms, then between them, a hunger-sunken face beneath the mat of black hair were hauled up over the edge of the car.

He's kind of young, Sweetness Asiim Engineer thought between the rip in her shoulders and the tear in her calves. *What, just gone eight?*

They were almost face to face, lip to lip. Sweetness felt the last of her strength go.

"Grab the rail!" she hissed. He seized it just as the djubba-stick fell from her fingers and clattered down the side of the ore-car into the dark. Sweetness rolled on to her back. The railrat knelt over her, head cocked to one side like an inquisitive songbird.

"Why are you doing this? You could have knocked me clean off."

"Have," Sweetness panted. "Plenty. So"—a swallow—"what ya called?"

He was desperately thin. The fall would have snapped his little chicken bones. He had big brown suspicious eyes that mistrusted everything in the universe from under his urchin fringe. He was desperately cute. Worth saving just to look at.

"You saved me, you tell first."

Sweetness sat up.

"My name," she said, "is Sweetness Octave Glorious Honey-Bun Asiim Engineer. The twelfth."

"You trainies have big names."

"So, how big's yours?"

"Pharaoh," the boy said.

"Pharaoh something? Something Pharaoh?"

"Pharaoh nothing."

"Just Pharaoh."

"It's enough, where I come from."

"And where would that be, little-name?"

"Meridian."

"That's . . ."

"I know how far Meridian is."

Half a planet.

"How?"

"I won the meat lotto."

"What is this?"

A crossing bell clanged away into the past.

"Everyone puts up a steak. Then the Boss of the Roof draws the feathers."

"Whoa whoa whoa. Everyone? Who is this?"

"The people. All of them. The underfolk."

"Ah." The deep dregs; the faces you glimpsed looking up at you from between the sleepers in Meridian Main; the hands that reached out from under the platform when you dropped a centavo and it rolled over the lip. Small loss to you, to the fingers down there in the access tunnels and bogieways, food and glam and power. "You lived there like for always?"

"This life, the one before it, probably the one after it too."

"Don't get cute, railrat."

"We got names for you people, underneath. Anyway, you dropped your punch-stick over the side, remember?"

"Yeah, well I can still pick you up and throw you off." They knelt, challenging each other under the circling moonring. "So, how old are you?"

"I'm near ten."

"Had you for younger."

"How much younger?"

"Younger. So, what steak?"

Kid Pharaoh finger-combed back his lank hair. No left ear, instead, a puckered grin of deaf scar.

"An old woman bought it. She had cancer of the lobe."

"Don't get a lot of that, cancer of the lobe."

"Sometimes, when the wind's right, I can hear what she's hearing, in here." He tapped the earless curve of his skull. "That's how I know who got it, after."

"What did you win for that?"

"The ticket out. Anywhere. And the golden purse. A thousand dollars."

A tangential thought demanded Sweetness voice it before it faded.

"So, how many times did you go in for the, ah?"

"Meat lotto? Second time lucky."

"The first time?"

"A big toe. Don't balance too good."

"Who got the toe?"

"Don't know. Not much sense in a toe."

"I suppose there're one's've been up for it a lot of times?"

"Well, there's a kind of natural limit . . ."

"I suppose so." Up ahead in the night, Naon Engineer whistled. Three short blasts, one long. Coming up on Juniper. Sweetness felt the great train shudder beneath her, brakes gently gripping.

"So, what happened? I mean, if you had a thousand dollars . . ."

"Got stiffed."

"Where?"

"Suniyapa. Three big girls. Must've heard that they give out the Golden Purse with the lotto. They were looking for poor kids riding rich. They had suits. Looked like regular coh-mute-ers. Big damn blakey-toe boots, but."

"Sorry."

"What for? You were going to knock me off your train, so? Any road, they throw me off at High Plains and then I hitch a ride on some shit dead-header across Chryse because Mr. Engineer he's expecting to ride the whole rig with me hanging off his lizard and when I don't he dumps me out. Walked three days to Little Rapids."

"I'm an Engineer," Sweetness said quietly.

"Yeah, and like I said, you were going to knock me clean off. Anyway, I wait there and one two three trains go by, and then you come along and you're the biggest by a way and I reckon, bigger the train, better to hide, and then one of youse spies me and I have to hide down over the edge, so."

Sweetness gave him her full regard a moment. She rocked back on her heels.

"So, where's this all going to end?"

"Grand Valley, I'd hoped." No hesitation. "I'm not comfortable 'cept there's a roof on the sky."

The brakes were squealing now, biting down hard on raw steel. Within their familiarity, Sweetness was able to make out another sound, a Bassareeni voice, calling over the car tops.

"Quick," Sweetness ordered. "There." She pushed Pharaoh toward the gap, mimed with her hands for him to crawl face flat and hushed.

"Down there?" he whispered, peering down the ladder into grinding darkness.

"Down there," Sweetness hissed. "And be quiet about it." Railrat Pharaoh slid over the top rung. His upturned face caught the moonslight.

"Hello? Who dat dere?" Chagdi Bassareeni called from too damn close.

"Listen up," Sweetness hissed down into the dark abyss. "We're pulling up for Juniper. Don't wait for the train to stop, there's always someone looking out when we pull up. Wait until we're dead slow, *dead* dead slow, then do what I told you back there, drop down between the carriages on to the track. There's plenty of room if you lie flat, on your back, not your face. Wait until you can't see the taillights any more, then you're safe. Juniper's a *merde*-hole, but the Xipotle Slow Stopper's through in a couple a days and they've no dignity. You can ride the roof for two centavos. When it gets to Xipotle, it splits; front half goes on to become the Grand Trunk Rapido. Take you right to Grand Valley."

She glanced over her shoulder. Fat-thighed Chagdi was standing at the far end of the truck, sending his torch beam swinging around like a jive-dancer.

"Got to go. Luck."

"Thank you. I owe you."

"You do, but I don't mean to collect, so I'll write it off."

"Sweetness Octave, why did you do this?"

Heavy feet on steel roof.

"I don't know, I haven't time."

"I want to know."

"Okay, okay. I don't like seeing people getting trapped in things they can't get out of. Especially by other people."

"That'll do."

"That's all you're getting."

The face was swallowed by the grating black. *This is the last time I will ever see you, Pharaoh*, Sweetness thought. *Quick and desperate and unprepared.* But all partings should be sudden. Sweetness stood up. Chagdi's beam dazzled her.

"Watch it with that thing."

"It is you."

Light-blinded, then night-blinded. Phosphenes flocked like bats across Sweetness's retinas.

"You find anything?"

A soft, gritty thud, then the brakes reached a crescendo. Can't see a smile in the dark.

"Hey, what happened to your djubba-stick?"

"Bastard caught hold of it. Took it with him."

"You djubba him?"

"Right off." A whistle and a downward curve of the hand.

"And is he?"

"Couldn't see. Don't think so."

Plump Chagdi's face resolved out of the dazzle. He looked piqued. He had a reputation for capturing and tormenting caboose vermin and probably resented that his had not been the thumb on the djubba-stick trigger.

"Pity you lost the stick, but."

"Yeah." Sweetness sized up the dark gulf she must leap to get back home. "Pity."

*F*orty-two long years on the iron road buys a woman a measure of dignity. When Grandmother Taal made one of her increasingly rare progresses down *Catherine of Tharsis*, she stopped, and the train moved for her.

"Honoured Grandmother," *Tante* Miriamme cooed from her cubby by the crew companionway. Grandmother Taal grunted acknowledgement and shuffled down another painful step. God smite these shoes.

"Fine morning, *Amma* Taal," called Finvar Traction, penduluming across the feed pipes and plasma buffers in his abseil harness. No one believed that all this swinging and dangling was necessary to his routine repairs but he clearly enjoyed it and he was one of the sights of the railroad.

"Umph." Too damn hot in layered skirts and tight-laced bodice on a day like this. Electric blue sky. The hottest colour.

"Regards to thee and thine!" hailed cheery Silva Deep-Fusion, eternally white to the elbows in flour.

Grandmother Taal nodded and grabbed for the handrail as the train jolted over points. Son and heir he might be, but Naon was no part of the Engineer his father had been, in his day. But neither was he cyberhatted into the autonomic systems, the drooling autopilot on the long, boring straights. Grandmother Taal waited for the last creak of brake and huff of steam before stepping down to the ground. A tip of the finger to Prevell Watchman Junior in his shunting turret.

"Grandmo'r!" he yelled in warning. She was already pulling on her track vest. Not so old, nor yet so incontinent, as to forget the laws of the universe. *Catherine of Tharsis* dragged her long load past Grandmother Taal. She fished in her waist purse for her needle case. Her thick thumb opened the leather wallet, felt out the smooth shaft of the delicate obsidian needles, anticipating power and pain. Had they no respect for a woman in her forties, that they make her stand under hot sun and stitch coloured silk through the pallid skin of her forearms? But her magic had never been respected. It was too useful, despite its limitations. Her clients found creative ways of bringing their woes into its peculiar bailiwick. Had there been someone she could have thanked and cursed, she would have, copiously, but her power was not a gift. It had just happened, the day of her womaning. The best she could work it out was that the power had gone out of her into the brown smear in her pants, then from there to every other brown thing in the world.

The ore-trucks clunked past. The tail of the beast appeared around the slow bend. Henden Stuard was waiting at the foot of the galley stairs, hat of office outheld in salutation. He whispered into the gosport. Three hundred cars forward, Naon Engineer applied the brakes. The companionway came to a halt with such precision that Grandmother Taal need only step up.

"What is your need?" she asked.

"He is constipated," suave Henden said.

Junior Stuard kitchen hands and vegetable peelers bowed out of Grandmother Taal's way as she moved through the galley car to the Pursery. There Brellen Stuard greeted her gravely.

"He is constipated."

Shafto Stuard sat enthroned among golden cushions in the observation box. Light stained by painted glass dappled his strained features.

"It is eight days now," Brellen whispered.

"You have tried dried fruit?" Grandmother Taal said.

"And marmalade," Shafto said, uncomfortably.

A slight lurch told Grandmother Taal *Catherine of Tharsis* was under way again. She watched the track unfold from under the bay of the observation box and wondered how it might flavour a family's soul, to be always looking at where you have come from and never where you are going.

"I suggested a hemp bandage, soaked in oil of paraffin," Brellen said. "But he could not swallow more than a finger of it."

"Nor I," said Grandmother Taal.

"Please help me," Shafto pleaded.

Grandmother Taal contemplated a moment. It was good for the mystique.

"It is doable."

"Is there anything you require?" Brellen asked, head bowed. Mint tea would have been good but Grandmother Taal remembered that once Brellen's Aunt Mae had offered her tea in a smeared glass. Her opinion of the Stuards as a Domiety had never recovered.

"Nothing, thank you." She took out her needle case. "Children are advised not to watch." She squinted in the stained-glass light to thread the right silk through the proper needle. The track outside, she noted, was now a blur of sleepers. She felt more secure in her power with fast steel beneath her. Immobility troubled Grandmother Taal. She uncapped her fountain pen and bared her forearm.

"Try to be concise, but poignant. It should express all your feeling."

Shafto Stuard looked the old woman in the eyes, then took the pen and wrote STRAIN in bad lettering on the veined pale skin.

"Very well." Grandmother Taal picked up the purple thread and commenced the humming. It had no significance and little tune—a medley of toe-tappers off that All-Swing Radio the young ones listened to—but it kept her voice busy while she embroidered the word *strain* on to her forearm.

It still hurt.

She tried something more closely related to the pain, reading the memories of past magics in the white scarifications of her arms. Those arcs and loops, buried under successive woundings like the surface of a cratered moon, had been that time she moved the big earth-making machine off the line when it had upped and died inconveniently. Easier done, alive and dead. At least the teams slopping brown paint over its orange and blue mottled hide had been spared the moaning and hectoring about fine points of contractural detail endemic among earth-makers. That time the magic had been strong enough, and the paint sufficient to hold it, to flip the cussed thing half a kilometre into an old impact crater. Odd, that the power was not a scalar thing. It had been so much more difficult and painful to change Levant Traction's brown eyes blue for one night of passion with a track surveyor for Lombarghini. Her wrist bore the memory of his few, sweaty hours; the white scar of the word *pretty*.

She glanced down. On the "A." Blood welled from the stitches, soaked the silk, stiffened. Bad to put in, worse to take out. Brellen looked politely revolted.

"How are we?" Grandmother Taal asked her client.

"I can feel something," Shafto said with a curious light in his eyes. "Moving."

"Deep within?" Brellen asked. Shafto nodded. Grandmother Taal kept stitching.

"Oh," cried Shafto.

"Ah," murmured Grandmother Taal. Almost there. The downward slash of the "N," then the blissful ascent to the finish. Done.

"Ohh," moaned Shafto Stuard. Brellen mopped his brow with a paper coaster.

"Ah," said Grandmother Taal, letting the needle fall and swing on the end of its silk. Blood paraded in thick drips down the thread.

"Oooh," Shafto said, eyes opening in wonder. "Oohhh."

"Ah," said Grandmother Taal, feeling behind her for a chair.

Eeeeee, said an entirely new voice. *Eeee. Eeee. Eeeeeeee.* For an instant, puzzlement on every face. Then realisation: *Catherine of Tharsis* herself was crying out, the top-C shriek Grandmother Taal had last heard the night Marya Stuard had driven off the Starke gang.

The emergency whistle.

All hands rushed for their duty stations, never to reach them. A tremendous wrench threw everyone from their places. Shafto was flung hard against the stained-glass bay and went down in a heap. Brellen floundered among golden cushions. Grandmother Taal found herself toppling eyes-first toward her neatly arranged needles. She grabbed at a cupboard handle and twisted herself aside. Cutlery and crockery sprung from racks, a full samovar of tea flung itself from the spirit-burner to spill boiling liquid across the floor. Chairs tumbled, tables capsized, antimacassars flew. Grandmother Taal was rolled toward the spreading stain of scalding tea. Somewhere she was conscious there was a sharp pain in her hip. She would bother with that later; if any of them survived this thing. She kicked her legs and swung herself away from the deadly tea on the hinged door.

What was happening? A wreck? A derailment? Yet more dacoits? God forfend, a head-on, a containment breach? No, not that, the failsafes would blow the tail of the train free and send the locomotive shrieking on ahead to its final thermonuclear immolation.

And it ended. Like that. With as little warning or manners as it had begun. Everyone lay where they had fallen, stunned motionless. The silence was eerily oppressive. Not even the familiar creaks and clicks and hisses of track life. *Catherine of Tharsis* stood on the mainline, inexplicably halted.

8

*T*he dead stop jerked the bone slug out of Sweetness's ear. Before it had even hit the decking, she was out of the cabinette door on to the sidewalk. The little gristly device muttered surds and improper fractions to whoever had ear to attend. Education abandoned, Sweetness swung around the stanchion on to the port observation deck. What she saw stopped her as surely in her tracks as it had stopped *Catherine of Tharsis* in hers.

They have a saying for it in the *patois* of Old Belladonna, whispered from the perfumed balconies, tier upon tier upon tier lining the great cavern walls, growled in the dripping, fetid runways under the deepest of underdeeps: *gobemouche*. Mouth catching flies. Flygobbed. Sweetness stared at the precise circle of alien landscape dropped foursquare across the Trans Oxiana mainline.

What she saw first was *colour*. Oranges, yellows, deep blues blobbed like a drip-painting on to the burned beige of the highlands. Once a Flying Optometrist had tested her for colour-blindness with patterned discs that reminded her of this; dots, swirls, crazily eddied colour. Try and make out a pattern. This was what she saw next; *shape*. More difficult by far than an Optometrist's numbers and letters; these shapes were completely other, so entangled she did not at first know what she was looking for. Then she caught edges, curves, lines. *Those* tall, ribbed things were three-sided derricks, *those* low, curved things that caught the light as they flapped in the wind, some kind of kite-aerofoil. *Here* there seemed to be knots of thorny vine-pipe, *there*, that bright blur might be some kind of rotor. *This* was a whip-tipped aerial-thing, tall as a house, that was a translucent bladder that swelled and ebbed, swelled and ebbed like the throat pouches of painfully unpleasant frogs.

Shape gave *substance*. The little rigs that supported the whizzing rotors looked as if they were made from purple bone; the sheets of the kites had the gloss of pure nylon, the guys that tethered them grew gas bladders like seawrack. The orange-green ground cover had the nap of a handwoven carpet, the cups of the big flowerheads looked like nothing more than satellite dishes spun from styrene foam. Plastic, a polymer jungle, a Bakelite rain forest.

From *substance* to *purpose*. What was this? Did it have a name? A nature? Laws, ethics? Business? Predictabilities: was this all there was of it, would it expand, would more of it appear, like chicken pox? Would it disappear as abruptly as it, apparently, had arrived? Was it friendly to people and their trains? Did big terrible things hunt in its heart? Was God to be found there, navel-deep in a pool of crystalline water? How had it come here? Dropped out of the sky? Just growed? Miraculously verbed into being by the angels of the Panarch? Domestic magic? Had some herder kid been mucking with the Stones of Saying, despite all the Prebendaries' sermons to the stern contrary?

What was it, where had it come from, how had it got here, how were they going to get rid of it?

All of which, clamorous in Sweetness Octave's head expressed itself in one soft, awestruck, "Wow."

Others had joined her on the balcony. Miriamme Traction had forsaken her scullery. Marya Stuard stood agape. Naon Sextus had even relinquished the drive rods to stand and stare. A whirr, Grandfather Bedzo had unhooked himself from the cyberhat and was haltingly negotiating the ramps and sharp corners in his power-chair. Onlookers moved aside to give him a place at the rail. His bleary eyes rolled over the circle of otherness that lay square across the track. His words spoke for everyone.

"What the sweet suffering frig is that?"

The young were organised into scouting teams while the Domiety elders gathered in confab. Things were hideously amiss for North West Regional Track not to have issued a warning. Somehow—impossibly—it had slipped in under every single one of the thousands of watching eyes up in the moonring.

"Bugger *hows*," Uncle Tahram Septus Engineer boomed over the great table. "Give me *whens*." He was contracts clerk, but spoke for everyone's fear of missed connections, rescheduled haulage deals, cancelled contracts and Wisdom's bankers in their ground-scraping beige coats and little round purple data-specs. Customary inter-Domiety bickering was forgotten. Clan heads drew up schemes and hurried to their various stations to expedite it.

Equipped for the alien with track vests, notebooks, walkie-talkies and djubba-sticks, Sweetness and Romereaux eyed the intruder with mistrust.

"I don't know," Sweetness said. She stood between the rails, a few steps from where they disappeared into the other. "What if it smells bad, or something?"

Romereaux leaned forward, took a generous sniff.

"Smells okay to me. Sort of like when we haul a forest-fermenter."

"It might be poisonous."

"I don't think so."

Sweetness took a hesitant step toward the borderline. The rails were not smothered in other-growth. They stopped. Terminated, clean as a laser cut. Likewise, where the plastic factory-jungle abutted the everyday world the plant-machines were sliced though with surgical precision. A parasol-like leaf was sectioned along a chord, a windmill gantry was exposed down one side. Stems and vines were neatly truncated, oozing ichor the colour of long-dead batteries.

"I mean," Sweetness said, "if we go in there and . . ."

"One way to find out." Romereaux unholstered his djubba-stick. He positioned himself *en-garde* to the line of division, shuffled an uncomfortable moment or two, aimed the weapon. "Right then." He pressed the trigger. The club-head shot out, clacked off a gantry upright well beyond the line of division. The shaft remained whole, unparted. He retracted the device.

"So."

"So."

But Sweetness still tippy-toed across the boundary, like an old seabather testing the water. Then something darted at her, feathery and diaphanous and whirring, and darted away as she swiped at it. She glimpsed helicopter rotors, a fragile crystalline body, great blinking eyes framed, incongruously, with long eyelashes. It was no larger than her hand. The autogyro-bug blinked at her, emitted a soft purr and released a stream of phosphorescent spores from its belly. The spores settled on Sweetness's skin like thistledown. They sparkled in the sun. She heard faint far tintinnabulations, smelled summer and palm wine and spent fireworks, felt delicious weals of cold stitch across her flesh.

"Oh," she said. And, "Ah."

The thing blinked again, dipped on its rotors and spun away. Without understanding the impulse, Sweetness followed. The will-o'-the-wisp led her into wonder. In groves of derrick trees five, six times her height she ducked under swooping sails. Gentle breezes scented with syrup and electricity fanned her face. Through copses of translucent orange bottle-plants, wide bellied, tight lipped, corked with plugs of matted fibre. Within, coiling things somersaulted in thick liquid. Luminous midges swarmed in her face, shifting patterns of light and density. As she moved inward, Sweetness heard the potplants uncork like deeply resonant belches. Looking back, she saw them ejaculate hundreds of long silver streamers. On, and in, over a carpet of glistening blue pebbles that, when she stepped on them, grew legs and fled from her. She padded through a parting sea of iridescent beetles. She stopped to pick one up, yelped, dropped it. The thing had hit her with an electric shock. It lay on its back, thrashing its cilia legs until one by one they locked and froze.

Onward; parting webs of thick, pulsating vines to be sure she was on the track of the fluttering lure. Bulbs and nodules burst between her fingers, staining them with coloured juices that smelled of stale beer, cinnamon, fresh buttery plastic, window polish, Grandmother Taal's herb *tisanes*. One smelled so powerfully of ginger sorbet she remembered from a trip to Devenney on the Syrtic Sea she almost sucked her long fingers. Almost.

Onward: through curtains of transparent lace; along narrow twisting alleys confined between towering crimson tube walls, like the neatly coiled intestines of an eviscerated giant; crawling under umbrella-canopies of ground-kissing mushrooms; through flocks of creatures like tiny silver flies suspended from gossamer balloons that wheeled and darted with surprising agility from the touch of her shadow.

At some point Sweetness remembered that Romereaux was not with her, had never been with her. At another point, she realised she had been walking much much longer than she should have been able to. At yet another, she saw that the edge of the world was a good deal closer than she had expected.

Another still, and she discovered she had no idea where she was. Further yet, she realised she did not care.

Pushing through swags of knitted moss, she failed to see the glitter of water and almost fell headlong into the pool. Sweetness grabbed fistfuls of moss, they tore like widow's curtains. She fell to her hands and knees in shallow, metallic-smelling water. Water. She remembered who what where she was. She looked around. The flying tantaliser was gone, of course. She looked up at the sky. It was a shade or two darker than the norm. Verging indigo. She thought of that other strange sky, in the place where Uncle Neon dwelled alone in his steel pole. Was this like that, another other? Was what had fallen on to the Trans Oxiana mainline a circular door, an infinite number of ways in, so that when you were on the other side, you found that it was bigger on the inside than the outside? The twenty-seven heavens of the Panarch were stacked like that, each inside the one below it, each larger than the level that contained it. She had walked a long way; the sun—if that was the sun she knew—was close to the edge of the world.

A panicky thought. Some doors open only one way. Once through this door, could she get back? Could she even get back to where she could get back *from*?

Something moved in the water. A face, pale, framed by writhing black snakes. St. Catherine preserve us, the Lamia of the Pool. The snakes were black curls. The face was her own. But it was not a reflection. Little Pretty One lay under the shallow water, rising slowly through the rippled surface. A hand thrust out of the water. Sweetness seized it, pulled her psychic twin out of the pond. Little Pretty One was dressed in the work shorts, tie-waist T and big boots Sweetness had worn the day she refused to djubba Kid Pharaoh off the side of the ore-car. Little Pretty One gobbed and hawked out a mouthful of water.

"What were you doing in there?" Sweetness asked.

"Drowning, tit-breath," Little Pretty One spat. "Sweet Mother of sewage . . ."

"No, I mean, how did you get here?"

"You're asking particularly inane questions today," Little Pretty One said, wringing out the hems of her shorts. She and Sweetness stood facing each other ankle-deep in the strange water. "Same way I always get anywhere."

"Where are we?"

Little Pretty One squatted, dripping, on a gnarled fist of translucent, spark-speckled polymer. Sweetness found a perch on a swag of liana.

"Now, what would have been a much better question is 'when' are we rather than 'where'?"

"Well, when then?" For a psychic twin, Little Pretty One was damn irritating.

"That's tricky." Little Pretty One stretched her fingers out and examined them. "God! Bloody prunes!" She held up wrinkled pads for Sweetness's perusal. "I mean, if you think of time as a railway line, you have a problem. There isn't anywhere but forward or back. Think of it more like a shunting yard . . ."

"But one with many thousands of tracks . . . Done this one before."

"Where? When? You didn't tell me."

"My uncle."

"Oh. Him. And where is your uncle, exactly?" Little Pretty One looked theatrically around her. "So, did he tell you it's a probability thing?"

"He didn't tell me anything. I thought it up myself. When I was there." Conversations concerning invisible relatives tended to the surreal of the metaphysical, Sweetness had found.

"Well, my little mathematician, if you can imagine that the tracks closest to the mainline are more likely than the ones on the outside. Like a train to get on to a track has to roll three dice. So, to get on to the outside tracks you need a three, or an eighteen; it's going to be much easier to get on to the ones where you need a twelve. Except, the odds are way way longer than that. Like rolling a hundred Eagle-Eye-Jacques in a row. Maybe less likely, but the thing is, it can happen, and you'd be on that track way way out there. It can happen first time, even. Space-like time. Time-like space, but that's something else."

Railway children grew up natural relativists, where time and distance were freely interchangeable as they moved at speed across whole landscapes.

"So, where does this when come from?" Sweetness asked. A cellophane rustle. Little Pretty One looked up. Her eyes opened. In a trice she dived back inside Sweetness. She left a damp stain on Sweetness's shirt and track jeans.

Pink plastic fronds parted. Fingers pushed through. A face followed. Romereaux's. Sweetness saw him, frond-freckled. Romereaux saw her, water-dappled. And it went *crack* between them, the thing that had been here every moment in every breath and word and look between them, that they had never dared talk about, that the ways of the Domieties and the customs of the trainfolk and the Forma had denied, but here, in a place outside the Forma, outside the world of laws and formas, they could play. *Crack* like Uncle Neon in the middle of routine signal maintenance, flashed into somewhere else. *Like that* Sweetness found her fingers untying the draw strings of his pants. Loosening the elasticated waistband from the crinkled skin. *Like that* she found her track vest floating in the water, found fingers working up and under her T, found Romereaux's attempted goatee prickling her chin. Then *tongue*. Then *tongue* back and the pants dropped around his ankle like a vanquished battle flag and the discovery that he, too, flouted Domiety prescriptions on underwear.

"Ooh, you filthy bugger," Sweetness giggled as it kicked hard in her hand like a pet lizard and he just smiled.

"In there." He nodded at the pool.

"In the water?"

"The water."

"So, you've always wanted to . . ."

"In water. Ah hah."

"You are a filthy bugger."

She unbuttoned her shirt. It fell in surrender like Romereaux's many-pocketed pants. Sweetness took a step backward. Cool alien water sucked at her heels.

"Hello?"

She turned to stone. Romereaux was paralysed. The windmills wound and the whirligigs whirled and fritillaries frilled while they stood, two statues, too stunned even to pull their clothes on.

"Hello? There's someone there, isn't there?"

The little pet house lizard had gone down, limp and sad.

"There is someone there. I'm sure of it. Hello?"

The trance was broken.

"Cock piss bugger bum balls!" Sweetness scooped up her shirt and fled into the pink frond forest while Romereaux struggled, one legged like a stoned stork, to pull on his sodden pants. They were both sliding into their track vests as the figures emerged from the finger-forest on the further shore of the pool.

"Hi there!" Romereaux waved with one hand. The other scraped back his tousled hair.

"Hi yourselves!" called the leader of the other party, a cheery-faced, chubby man in his early tens. With him was a spookily thin girl who squatted on pinched thighs and looked resentful, and a dumb-looking seven-year-old boy whose face said *I'm hugely confused here.* Track vests and djubba-sticks marked them as track. "Where are you from?"

"*Catherine of Tharsis,*" Romereaux shouted.

"Back there," Sweetness added.

"Ah!" cheery-face called. "*Bishop of Alves!*"

Sweetness knew the train, a good, tough little Class 14 freight hauler. Well-maintained and proud, but definitely second class.

"Where's yours?" Sweetness asked.

"Back there." The Bishoper pointed back through the finger-forest. "You walked long?"

"Seems like it. Couldn't say."

The Bishoper nodded.

"We must've been walking for a couple of hours. This place seems to get bigger the further in you go."

"I think this is the middle, though," Sweetness said.

"Thank God," the chubby man called. "My name is Esquival Nonette D'Habitude Dharati Engineer 5th. Do you mind if we come round?"

"We'll meet you halfway," Romereaux said. But neither party took a single step, for with a rushing like the wings of all the angels in the Ekaterina Angelography beating at once, the sun was eclipsed.

Everyone looked up. An edge of something huge and dark, and curved almost as gently as the world, moved over the trainfolk. Projections, protuberances, masts, aerials, unobvious sticking-out bits: then they were in deep shadow. Not darkness: the belly of the great machine was starred with lights. A clutch of those lights unfolded, swept fingers of light across the canopy of the plastic jungle before capturing each of the trainfolk explorers in a personal spotlight.

Sweetness shaded her eyes with her fingers and peered up into the beam. As she had half expected, a voice spoke out of it. As she had also expected, it was big and booming.

"Caution humans," it said, not in the air, but inside Sweetness's skull. "This is ROTECH Real-systems Repair Monitor eleven thirty-eight. You are in peril. There has been a reality dysfunction in this sector. You are advised to leave forthwith. Further slippages may result in your being marooned when the breach is repaired. Please follow the moving lights. They will guide you to the exits."

Sweetness did not listen beyond the fifth word from the sky. Danger, reality breaches, so? ROTECH was here, stooped down from heaven to touch the earth. The people who made the world had come.

*T*here was a steaming that night, hosted by the Stuards of *Bishop of Alves*. Spits were set up, great joints of grazebeast slung on spears and hoisted on to brackets. Women and juniors repaired to a safe distance to prepare salads and flat bread and barrel-up beer while the Deep-Fusion men, in silver heat-refraction suits, orchestrated the superheated steam blasts from the overheat valves, dextrously turning the dripping beeves.

All were invited and by now *all* was many. Stacked behind *Catherine of Tharsis* were *Count Tassaday*, *Three Great Shepherds*, *Doughty Endeavour* hauling a dangerously overreacting pulp processor and *Lords of the Iron Way* with forty carriages of express service passengers now as steaming hot as the cooking roasts. *Passengers*, of course, could not possibly be invited to a track jamboree. Down the track from *Bishop of Alves* were the famous *Indomitable*, then a nameless, low-caste ballast unit from Suvebray—its Domities huddled apart at the steaming and, as Psalli noted, all bearing the sunken chin, bug eyes and bulging, translucent forehead that advertised *incest*. Most available and despicable of track crimes. Behind the *Ballasteros* stood the venerable *Mountain of Great Peace* and a recently refitted *JahSpeed!*, her pipework and tubes the envy of every Deep-Eff. Bringing up the rear was *Freight 128*, an ill-omened workhorse, stained with rumours of radiation leaks, bad fortune and piracy on the mainline which only persisted the harder her grim Engineers denied them.

Over all hung the ROTECH machine. Tulsa Engineer, inheritor of Tahram's contractual mantle and smitten with an inappropriate love of all things airborne, had checked it up in his *Big Book of Aircraft and Angel Recognition* but it fitted no known format. By day it had been an oppressive presence, like the legendary flying city of Hooverville, torn from its bedrock and sentenced to roam the jet streams as punishment for cheating an angel of the Panarch in a frame of snooker. An obscuration. A total eclipse. A crushing satellite, a steel cloud. By night it was a deeper darkness on the black Oxus sky, a hiatus in the moonring where the belly-lights made up new, geometrically regular constellations. It would have been almost forgettable, but for its activities at the heart of the plastic jungle. This was a tug of war by light; vivid cerises, lilacs and turquoises from on high strove with flashes of vermilion, white and poisonous green from where the surveyors had mapped the mirror pool to be. Occasionally there would be a particularly dazzling exchange and the ground would tremble. It cast a fine, party illumination over the entertainments.

Beef-stuffed chapatti in one hand, mug of small beer in the other, Sweetness was not having a fine time. Small beer, small fun. Romereaux cast a ROTECH-machine-sized shadow over her pleasure. She queued up for her food, he was there, mug in hand by the beer fermentory, not noticing her. On to the musicians' awning to watch the fingers fly over the keys and strings and the women entice the men to dance; tapping her foot, but Romereaux was talking with Domiety brothers from the other trains with a set to his shoulders that insisted, *No dance, never dance.* To the beer pavilion for her mug fresh from the teat, and now all his attention was given to shoving a fat chapatti, dripping grease and garlic sauce, sideways into his mouth while the lads laughed and cheered, *Go on go on go on you boy!* Eventually she turned her back on him but he did not notice that either.

The ground shook, the strongest tremor yet. Venerable matriarchs shrieked and tottered, flagons of petty beer slopped. Great trains swayed on their bearings, a spit of meat capsized in a hurricane of steam. Silver-suited Deep-Fusioners dashed through the billows to right it. Under cover of confusion Sweetness ducked between *Bishop of Alves*'s drive wheels and crouched in the oily dark, avoiding everyone. A twitch in her side told her that the oil pool between her feet was now inhabited.

"Nice party," Little Pretty One said. Sweetness offered her the remains of her chapatti. Little Pretty One devoured it decorously with her fine white teeth. "This ain't bad, this. Any idea how long it is since I last ate anything?"

"Take it all," Sweetness said. "There's beer too. You dried out?"

"Some." Little Pretty One took the pot, sniffed it. "Thanks." She drained it in one.

"Tell me this, and tell me no more, why do they do it?"

"Who do what?"

"Men. One moment, they're all over you, next . . ."

"Oh, that. Whole different world."

"What, us and men?"

"Well, that too. Holiday romance."

"Change of scenery . . ."

"Change of climate . . ."

"Everything commonplace becomes special . . ."

"Then you come home . . ."

"And they never write or phone."

"Bummers."

"That's the way they are. The thing about males, my corporeal friend, is that what they really really want isn't sex, or power, or money, it's a quiet life. Everything easy. One-night stands included."

"It wasn't even a one-night stand."

"Tell me." Little Pretty One burped. It seemed to take her by surprise. "But it's not going to be a problem."

"I live on the same train as him, I see him every day, hell, five times a day, every day."

"Not a problem. Train's a-coming."

"Trains is always coming. And going," Sweetness said.

"This one's special."

"So? How?"

"This one's a Great Southern. *Ninth Avata*."

In a life without many surprises, Sweetness thought of sudden shock as *numb thing*, a sensation right behind her nose between freezing and wet mud turning to cracked clay under summer sun. Numb, dumb, paralysed, incapable of action. Shot through the will.

"*Ninth Avata*. Good catering facilities," Little Pretty One continued. "Stainless steel galley, and everything. This wasn't timetabled. You were supposed to have zapped past each other three hundred kays south of here. But now, they're thinking, well . . . Look." Little Pretty One squatted beside Sweetness, pointed out between the spokes. There they were, all the traitors, Marya Stuard in her best epaulettes and braid, Naon Engineer flanked by Sleevel and Rother'am, Child'a'grace looking little and happy, even Grandmother Taal by the beer fermentory, talking animatedly with a group of similar-faced women in many skirts and petticoats.

"They're talking pins and ribbon," Little Pretty One said. "Dowries and percentages. They're saying, why wait for corroboree? We're here, you're here, they're coming and we've got the money here, now, in our hands . . ."

"No!" Sweetness moaned. Revellers turned, startled by the noise from beneath the train. Another grumble from the divine battle distracted them. "Some invisible friend you are. This is the worst day of my life. What am I going to do?"

"There's another train back there. Just pulled up."

"So? Can't move for trains."

"That one's still a-coming, but this one's here."

"What are you talking about? Why don't you just do something useful for once rather than hand out stupid proverbs like they're wise or something?"

"Okay," Little Pretty One said. "Okay. You want me to do something. Watch this. You won't see this again in a hurry."

On cue, the earth shook again. Not a shiver, nor a side-of-beef-toppling quiver, but a sustained quake that made Sweetness glance up, suddenly alarmed by the thousands of tons of metal over her head. Out at the party, people reached for anchorholds, failing those, each other. Sweetness remembered some School of the Air bone-slug piece about how, unlike Motherworld, this world was cold-hearted and had not stirred since the fires that built Olympus a billion years ago. She was about to protest the geophysical impossibility until Little Pretty One nudged her and said, "Look."

The light play between heaven and earth had become a battle. Rapiers of lilac and blue from above clashed with sabres of slashing scarlet stabbing upward and were parried. Blades and guillotines of light struck and shattered; ball lightnings arced fizzing through the air; pyrotechnics met and mutually annihilated in cascades of sparks. It would have been pure fiesta but for the vibration. Sweetness could feel the earth groan in her teeth. *Bishop of*

Alves's every bolt and rivet rattled. Rust flakes snowed down on her hair. Dust was sprung from the grass and spun away into scampering devils. Sweetness put out a hand to steady herself and yipped. Her second electric shock that day. The steelwork hummed with static.

"I couldn't really recommend staying here," Little Pretty One said. In illustration, a fat blue spark dropped from axle housing to wheel. Little Pretty One and Sweetness skipped out from her hole like a rabbit. *Bishop of Alves* came alive with lightning.

Party was over. The *son et lumière* had been entertaining, but everyone was afraid now. Here were forces beyond their reckoning. Engineers' hair stood out from their heads; their clothes ballooned away from their bodies. The battle in the jungle was now a blinding cylinder of light, earthy crimsons and heavenly lilacs swirled together like a cosmic fool pudding. Trainfolk watched, eyes shaded by hands. Sweetness and Little Pretty One stood *gobe-mouche*. For the lilac was winning. The crimson was turned back on itself, confused and confounded and pressed down until it formed a boiling line of scarlet interrupted by the silhouettes of the fantastic jungle plants. End game. The whirling cylinder of light stretched to a column, to a single sun-bright beam. The earth spasmed. People staggered. Spits tipped, a beer fermentory split, spilling its heady cargo around spectators' feet. The party was ruined. No one noticed. Again, the earth shook, throwing up cataracts of dirt which were sucked into the vortex of light. Electricity cracked continuously between the apex of the hurricane and the insulating plastic forest. Derricks fell in showers of sparks, windmills detonated, crazy sails spinning as they blazed, severed creeper-pipes thrashed like beheaded snakes, spraying jets of vapour. It was most spectacular. A third time the earth heaved, hard enough to imagine the end of the world. Sweetness and Little Pretty One clutched each other. There was a cry, long and wailing and terrible, a voice, but none any present had ever dreamed of. The cry was in their heads and it went on and on and on and on and the earth danced like a poison-maddened mongoose and everyone decided they really wanted it ended now before things went wrong that could not be put right again, even by divine energies, and just as they were certain, absolutely certain that it never would and it was all over for everyone, it did.

The earth erupted in a stupendous gout of soil and plastic chaff like a hard-pulled tooth. The unseen battler flew clear. The trainpeople saw a soft-edged cube, blue and orange tiger-striped, hang in the shaft of light. The bulk of the hovering ROTECH device played tricks with its dimensions; the newcomer was the size of a Class 15 freight hauler. A fall of red dust and coloured confetti spattered the onlookers. Sweetness's hair was a party of rust flakes, plastic spangles and red ochre. The quaking settled and ceased. The cube started to spin, faster, faster until it was a blur. And it seemed to be shrinking, as if the intense violet exerted an irresistible pressure inward.

It all ended suddenly and spectacularly. With an echoing boom of inrushing air, the cube imploded into a black dot and vanished. The beam of killing light exploded outward, engulfing the spectators in momentary blindness. In the same instant they heard a rushing mighty wind and a voice spoke in every head: *This unit was defective. It has been scrapped.*

An orph, Sweetness breathed to herself in the eye-blinking, carpet-patterned after-dazzle. Every child knew the hagiography of the machines that built the world before their fourth birthdays: most of the orphs had returned to heaven after the manforming, but some had refused the summons of St. Catherine and remained, buried deep in the ground, pumping out humus and microbacteria and going ever so slowly insane.

This unit was defective. It has been scrapped.

As she repeated the doom, her vision returned. Heaven-machine, orph, plastic other-world place, tracks, Oxus plains, all were gone. The twin queues of trains faced each other across two kilometres of bare earth.

"Wow," Sweetness said. "That was a blast."

What did I tell you? Little Pretty One skull-whispered as she slipped back inside her host.

Unsure of exactly what they had witnessed, the people stood staring at the stripped earth. All, but one. The unmistakable prickle of alien eyes on back of neck alerted Sweetness. She turned to see who was impudent enough to seek her out with eyes, and give him a gobful of her best disdain if it was Romereaux. The victim was a short skinny Waymender boy, easy to recognise by his flat, inbred nose. One eye was a milky film, the other stared shame-lessly at her hip.

Sweetness put her hands on her hips and leaned back, as she had seen the heroine do in *Feisty Grrrl* comic.

"Like it, then?"

The kid frowned.

"What's that hanging off your hip?"

10

*H*is name was Serpio and Sweetness saw in the dawn with him, tailbones chilled and alert against the cold iron of a number five driving wheel. With the dawn the tracksters went out. Hours of talk had left Sweetness post-conversational, ravenous and slightly high; a nudge in the ribs poked her back into reality.

"Look. See?"

It was a sight too splendid to be kept only for the unpopulated dawn hours. The big Waymender train was a caterpillar of windowless service cars, yellow and green, bearing the red globe-and-rails clan colophon. At the touch of sun the cars opened like yawns. Ramps crept forward, tested the temperature of the ground, settled. In the shadows, motors trembled, big machinery woke. With a gleeful shout, the survey buggies leaped into the high plain tallgrass. Their riders were keen-faced, clench-teethed teens. They wore goggles and mouth-scarves. They arrowed out across the pampas drawing tails of rising dust. Ranging lasers flickered mensurations, theodolite mirrors heliographed responses. Next, unfolding like thermophilic insects, the levellers stepped from their cocoons. Clawed feet shook the morning dew from the grass blades. Piggy-backed jockeys pulled levers. Long orang-arms, shovel-handed, scooped and shifted soil. Wheel-heeled graders ponderously descended their ramps, stomped the soil into submission. Surveyors darted around the heavy shanks of the big earth-movers. Watching them, Sweetness wished more than any wish that at that moment she was a badmaash Waymender and not an exalted Asiim Engineer. She wanted scuffed work boots and cut-off T-shirts and heavy gauntlets. She wanted dusty goggles and headscarves that waved their tassels in the dawn wind. She wanted to twist handles and pull levers and have machinery—any machinery—do her bidding. She wanted not to have Narob Stuard approaching over the close horizon in his wedding shirt and hat and vest with the dollar bills pinned all over it.

Almost, she blurted all the things in her heart to Serpio but they stalled on her tongue like a back-country air-fair barnstormer. The grand finale to the show was gearing itself together out of the back three carriages. Roof sections tilted and lifted, bogies swung out and back, gear trains and conveyor racks unfolded. The foremost carriage mounted the centre one like a Swavyn Ecstasy priest his catamite. The rear car completed the unlikely steel troilism by ducking underneath the central car and, by a complex series of extrusions, unfolding itself into tractor treads and bucketwheel booms. So much metal was performing so many unnatural acts that Sweetness's head reeled with the dynamism of it all, but Serpio's pride in his people's work was warm beside her. It meant much to him, and thus to her.

She had learned early—after the wee-est ones had been sent to bed and before the trysters started trysting—that they were fellow oddballs. Outcasts. Bizarres, berefts.

"Like, all the time?"

"When it's open."

He didn't mind her looking into his cataract. It was of a plasticy translucence. You could tap it. It made a kind of fingernailly click, and no pain. He didn't mind her doing that either.

"Ghosts?"

"And angels. Anything sort of spiritual."

"That thing." Sweetness's chin had jerked in the direction of the extracted orph. "Could you see that? What did it look like?"

"It's kind of hard to describe what it sees, it's like things extend out beyond themselves, into other kinds of worlds."

"Like, tentacles?" Imagining things from two-year-old dreams, which are the big ones that scare you all your life, the dreams of loss and horror and the death of your parents by things with cable wrists and hooks for hands. And red light-bulb eyes. Imagining tendrils coiling out through puckered holes in the universe into mystery.

"No, it's like I see you and you're high and wide and deep . . ." She smiled inside at the warm glow of his eyes measuring her physicality. "But there's other kinds of like, dimensions, beside those. You go out a long long way. That orph, when I looked at it, it had wings. I mean, they opened like wings, and I think there was some other kind of dimension it lived in some of the time where it could fly with them. They held it up in the air, if you know what I mean."

She didn't but the way his lower lip drooped when he was earnest pleased her so much she nodded and asked, slowly, "And when you look at me?"

"Which of you?"

His vision was both exciting and shaming; a striptease of the spirit. He looked at her and saw through his milky film a thing that had been private to Sweetness so long she had almost come to disbelieve in its objective existence. Baring, prying and enviable; Serpio needed no mirror. He looked at the world and his cataract reflected its flipside. But to see it everywhere, for everything you looked at to be populated with angels and ghosts. Too much. Too bright. You would go blind if you had to look at that too long. She could see it in Serpio. There was Trickster beneath that spiky thatch of gelled black hair. She liked it. She wanted to lick it. But she did not trust it. Only a fool or a track-side mark trusts his centavos to Trickster. She did not trust that it was Sweet-ness Octave Glorious Honey-Bun Asiim Engineer 12th he liked, and not a Little Pretty One she could not see as he saw. She might have brighter eyes. She might have nicer hair. She might have better tits. Maybe he was turned on by whatever junction it was that joined them, meat to spirit.

Maybe it was both of them, together.

Bad thought. She'd only just met him, and he was nice—even if he'd had his Astral House changed by deed poll because of an uncertainty over which side of the Diurnal Line his carriage had been on when his mother heaved and squeezed him into the world. Uncertain house, strange boy, Grandmother Taal had warned.

Later: after the trysters had departed on their missions and before the drinkers achieved horizontal, she asked him, "Were you born with it?"

"No, I got it," he answered and there was a worm of bitter in it. "There was this old hooker in Plazaville. They said she was a shapechanger—if you wanted to do it with a dog, or a big cat, or like a grazebeast, she'd turn into it for a pile of money. She worked out of this sprayed concrete dome home on the edge of the Rimbauds." All railway children had heard of Plazaville's Rimbauds, that iridescent, uncertain industrial district where used tokamak hotcores were stored. At the centre, the energy levels reached such intensity that reality broke down into a blur of many-coloured alternatives, the stories told, but you could never reach there. The power that flowed through the streets would turn you astray, and all the time the radiation was gently basting you. "All the kids used to rip the shit out of her, call her things, do the burning bag trick, throw ball bearings on the roof so they'd run down, you know? It was this real cheap house: there was this one tiny window, like a slit, and we were daring each other to go up and take a jeek in, maybe see her doing someone, or turning into something. So I pulled the card and even though I was scared, in case she was something out of the Rimbauds, I got a crate and went up and stood on it and jeeked in. It was a real tiny window, I could only get one eye."

"And? Was she an animal or a machine or what?"

"I jeeked in, and there was a fat guy with a hood on hanging from this crossbar by his hands and feet and the hooker, she had her back to me, but she had this thing in her hand that looked like a claw, you know?" Serpio spasmed fingers into a Hand of Glory. "Well, you see something like that, you just have to keep looking, especially when the hooker, she started raking the fat guy's ass with this claw thing and leaving all these red scrapes. And he was thrashing around up there but there was nowhere he could go and in like no time, his ass just all red, and there was blood dripping from it on the floor. And I'm still up there on the crate, staring. Then, it was like when you know someone's looking at you but you can't see them, like a warm feeling that there're eyes on you? The hooker, she suddenly stands up straight, and I should've got out then, I should've jumped off and run like a champion, but I couldn't you know? It's like I knew something awful was going to happen, but I had to stand there and see what it was."

"And was it? Something awful?" This, asked in the semi-wheedling tell-me voice of childhood ghost stories. And the answer, in that same intimate, mutual-conspiracy-of-let's-be-scared voice: "She turned round and she looked right at me and all I can remember is her face. Where her face should have been, was silver. All silver. Not a mask. Like molten metal. I could feel the heat off it. I could feel it on my eye, I could feel it sucking all the moisture out of it, I could feel it shrivel up and go dry and hard and blind. That's what I thought, it was blind, then when the eye-patch came off, I realised that I was still seeing the silver I'd seen in her face, but the silver was the like the colour of the light in another world where all the things from all the legends live."

The linger after the end of the tale of the cataract seemed to request a response but Sweetness did not know how to best fill it. So she said nothing but edged a little closer to strange Serpio.

"So," he said. "What about you?"

The question felt like a warm, intrusive probing between Sweetness's thighs. She gave a little gasp at the violation of her selfhood, then yielded herself to it. Things she had not even told Uncle Neon she told Serpio Waymender. The drawing out of them felt like she imagined sex to feel, mutual and releasing, yet very very private. All night Serpio teased her out with questions until, with the first dip of the horizon beneath the sun, the story ended and Sweetness Asiim Engineer found herself tired and yawning and gritty-eyed and needing a wash but strangely exhilarated on the cold trackside.

"You hungry?" she had asked, thinking scraps and shavings among the party detritus; then Serpio had poked her in the third rib and said with voice forty-sixty longing and pride, *Look, see?*

Now the carriages had almost completed their evolutions: panels fixed and locked, joints and couplings met and mated. The machine outheld boom arms above wide metal skirts, above both rose a command torso of pumping engines and grinding conveyor trains. In a high glass cupola, the oldest and most experienced Waymenders steered the juggernaut over the grass past the procession of stalled trains. It made a tremendous noise. Dawn-grazing plainsbeasts skittered from its path, Surveyors rode them down on their terrain bikes, scooping up dust-hares and striped piglings. The machine inscribed sixteen parallel wheel tracks deep in the earth. It found the sheared track ends and settled over them like a venerable dowager of many skirts taking a piss. The booms dipped to the ground. Bucketwheel fingers threw up red dust. Conveyors spun their wheels.

"What are they doing?" Sweetness asked.

"Come and look."

Serpio took her hand. Sweetness found she did not mind that. His was soft, with rather long nails. A nonworking hand. No handlebar or lever for it, the eye that guided it was as blinded by seeing too much as by too little. She felt sorry for that hand, as they sneaked around the side of the big machine, dodging flying clods, and so she squeezed it.

To make talk, she asked, "What do you think happened to the orph? I never saw one before, I thought they were all gone long ago."

"Don't know," Serpio said. "Don't care. Well shut of it. Well shut of them all. Poxy things were always going wrong; they weren't very well made."

This was mild blasphemy to an Asiim Engineer. The prickle of reflex impiety surprised Sweetness. She had thought herself young and free-thinking. She asked, carefully, "Is this because of your . . . you know?"

"Eye?"

"Aye."

"You mean, because my angel-sight means I can't work on the track?"

"Aye."

"Maybe. Maybe." He sounded as if the insight had genuinely tripped him up, like a diamond in a midden. "But I think it's mainly because I don't think they should be here. We don't need them. So, they say they built the world, and they keep it running, and so we call them angels and say prayers but they're machines and even if one machine makes another machine makes another machine, at the bottom of it all, there's a person, not a machine. A human who designed the machine, and programmed it, and gave it a mission and a name and a purpose. They're the ones built the world. They're the ones we should be remembering, not bits of metal and plastic. Those orphs, they're stupid. Big cow-machines. Cows got more sense'n an orph. I tell you, when you've seen as many as I have go ga-ga."

"What do you mean?"

"I got a job, see? I don't do nothing, no one does nothing on *Iron Lion*. I got a job. I guide the train. I stand up there on the fo'c's'le and I look down the track and I see angels boiling off the horizon like dust-devils. Angels? Balls. Tired, bad, mad machines."

"St. Catherine . . ."

"Woman. Like you." Serpio looked at Sweetness askance from the eaves of his thatch of glossy black hair. "Nah. Not like you. St. Catherine, she was tired, mad, bad too. But she was a woman."

"Who tells you all this?" An itch of irritation in the voice. She'd only known this boy one party and a night and he was niggling her already.

"Harx," Serpio said and no more. While Sweetness was still deliberating if the monosyllable was a cough, a name or a Waymender curse, Serpio ducked down to peer through the dust-bunnies billowing up from the big machine's hem. "Down here."

Sweetness hunkered down on her hams beside the dark-haired boy. Through the soil and shredded grass, she glimpsed alchemy. The big machine ate soil and shat steel. Two gleaming parallel lines of steel, new forged, shimmering with heat-haze, married together by smoking obsidian sleepers.

"It's making it straight out of the ground," Sweetness said, amazed. Serpio nodded the nod of workaday magic, but Sweetness knew her delight had pleased him. Squatting side by side, they watched the steel rails creep across the gap of raw earth. *Centimetre by centimetre*, Sweetness thought. *Measuring the time until the rails are joined. Shortening the gap between me and Narob and his stainless steel kitchen. A joining, and a joining. Grain by grain. Centimetre by centimetre.*

Too dismal a thought by far for a crisp cold clear Deuteronomy morning. Serpio read the sudden gloom in her muscles.

"I'm hungry now. Come on. Let's eat. They'll be barbieing up by now."

Under the ribs of a lone umbrella tree the Surveyors had dug firepits and slung spits. The flee-kills were being gutted, skinned, skewered. Cracks and flares of burning fat sent spirals of aromatic black smoke through the leaves of the shade tree. There were three barbecue pits under the tree. At one the Waymender bike girls were gathered, roasting bustards. They greeted Serpio with a toss of the chin, Sweetness with a suspicious glance over their goggles. Sweetness admired and envied their bike gear, the amount of dusty muscle it showed, the casual toughness with which they wore it.

"Anything going?"

The girl with the biggest muscles spoke. "Might be. Who's that you're with?"

"Sweetness Octave Glorious Honey-Bun Asiim Engineer 12th."

The leader tried the name out on her tongue, twice.

"So. Nice hair. You with Squint?"

"I've been talking to him."

"Well, I suppose someone needs to. There's rail-rabbit if you want some."

They took the charred haunch wrapped in old survey charts to the trunk. It tasted to Sweetness like hamadryad thigh. A bike wireless burbled New School Deuteronomy flute-and-tabla and Sweetness thought, *In this place, at this moment, I am perfectly happy.* It could not last. The ending was exactly as Sweetness had seen in too many incarriage Range-rider movies. The cool touch of shadow, the boots foursquare on the earth, the silhouette blocking out the sun. Three of them, in classic vee-formation. Each could have taken Serpio like a haunch of rabbit in two hands and bitten him in half. And they wanted to. The bike girls' gruffness had fronted a sororal affection. These Waymender boys hated him.

"You don't eat that, Squint."

A heavy-soled boot kicked the meat from Serpio's grip. As he reached for it, a lieutenant pushed him over on his side down into the dust and twisted his spine until he was looking up at his chief tormentor.

"Breakfast, boy."

The leader carried meat: a roasted pigling penis, smoking hot. Serpio struggled and spat but the two lieutenants had him held firm.

"This is what you eat, Squint."

They pried his mouth open with sharp fingers pressed hard into the angle of the jaw. Serpio kicked and thrashed against the big boy's attempt to shove the pig's penis into his mouth.

"Hold him still."

They did and it went in. Serpio choked and spat.

"Eat it up now."

The lieutenants moved his jaw, mocking mastication.

I know why you are doing this, Sweetness thought. You see him with someone, doing a thing your rules for him do not allow, you see him doing a thing for himself and not asking it from you, and you hate that. She wanted to speak out. She wanted to kick them hard in the balls, go for their eyes. She wanted to stop them doing the thing to Serpio that was for her benefit. But she was off-territory, out-clan. Amongst aliens.

"Salp, let him be."

The leader twisted his mouth in a moue of disappointment but the girls had spoken. They were not impressed. It was over. The boys left without a word. Serpio flung the foul pig-thing away from him, spat and spat and spat again. Sweetness went to him but she was afraid to touch him. She did not know the decorum of the Waymender Domiety. To offer a hand in comfort might be a worse insult than that done to him by the bike boys.

"I'm sorry," she said, feeling how lame the words were on her lips.

"Sorry?" Serpio struggled to his feet. "What are you sorry about? What have you done?"

"Sorry," she said again, no better than before.

Serpio flung soil, kicked grass, dry-spat after his persecutors.

"Bastards! Bastards! You think you're something, Salpinge, well, you're nothing! You are nothing!"

He settled into a damaged, trembling sulk. His world-eye glowed dark.

"It's over. They're gone." Sweetness knelt, carefully putting herself between Serpio and his bullies.

"Harx," Serpio whispered, so quiet and venomous Sweetness almost mistook it for a natural phenomenon.

"What?"

"He'll show you," Serpio muttered. "He'll show everyone. You'll all see!"

"What is, who is, Harx?" Sweetness asked but he did not hear and she knew the words were not for her. She saw a reflection in Serpio's angel-eye where the sun was not; a glint of silver.

Serpio stood up. He balled his fists and roared at his tormentors, a howl of energy that drew years of shame and rage and alienation like a vacuum in the soul. Sweetness was not sure she liked boys who howled. Serpio gasped into a hunch of humiliation, but the howl roared on, changing shape and tone, becoming something other, a note, a whistle, a train whistle, coming up the track. She knew that song. She knew the song of every train on the Southern Grand Trunk. An ear within had been listening for it since Little Pretty One told her in the night the name and nature of her intended. The song of the Class 44 single-tokamak fusion hauler *Ninth Avata*.

11

*F*unny, she was to think kilometres later, how simply these things are decided. In all this piece of the Great Oxus there was one upswelling —a shallow, egg-shaped mound a spit or two long and less high, a flaw in the world-making like a bull's-eye in cheap glass—and Sweetness and Serpio were hiding behind it. They lay side by side, belly-flat on the grass, passing a stolen pair of Surveyor's glasses between them.

"What are they doing now?" Sweetness demanded. She was a poor passive listener. She was eye that looked, not ear that heard. Thus, from childhood she had had a fear of going blind, perhaps in whimsical divine punishment.

"They're processing," Serpio said.

Too much. She snatched the binoculars from his grasp, almost throttling Serpio with the thong. The hillock lay a kay and a half west of the mainline—so the ranging equipment on the glasses told her. Good little glasses, light, clever: they focused automatically. She turned them on the twin ant-trains mutually approaching against a backdrop of colossal engineering. Asiim Engineers to the right, Stuards to the left. They leaped into resolution: first Naon Engineer, sweating but superb in the robe, hat and gloves of his mystery. A pace behind him: Child'a'grace, heartbreakingly elegant in her Susquavanna marriage gown, unfaded, unshrunken and unpatched. Like her. So precise were the survey-glasses that Sweetness could even make out her smirk of small pride at her husband's splendour— knowing full he would never see it. Then came brother Sle, sulky still, with the casket that held the bank draft for three thousand dollars; Rother'am, sulkier still. Behind him came a Hire-priest—a spotty adolescent in rented regalia. Sweetness watched his lips move as he rehearsed the sentences and responses. His inexperience would have been inaudible over the sound of the *Catherine of Tharsis* Inter-Domiety band immediately following. Sweetness could hear them parping and cracking notes all the way from her grassy knoll. Non-wedding party, non-musicians straggled after, minor Domiety members and important Septs, the curious, those who liked a bit of a cry, those who wanted any distraction from the mundane nomadism of life on the line. The sides of the waiting trains were hung with religious banners, good-luck ribbons and the faces of those who loved a good wedding. Sweetness swung the glasses widdershins.

Narob Stuard strode well ahead of his people. It showed nuptial eagerness. He held his chin up, and kept his eyes steely-slitted. The wind rustled the banknotes stapled to his waistcoat and tousled the tassels of his wedding shirt. Every few paces he touched his hand to his wedding hat to steady it against the rising high-plains wind. It seemed to irritate him. He is good-looking, Sweetness thought. *But then many men look good walking into the wind, and that's no reason to marry them.*

They hadn't missed her yet. The affiance. On the first meeting between the partners, the bride-soon-to-be was supposed to feign a demure reluctance. But soon they would wonder what was taking her so long with her clips, or her veil, or her garland, and the unmarried girls would be sent to look. They would be sent to look, and a kilometre and a half away on a grassy knoll she realised she had not thought what to do when they did not find her. It was a big thing to realise. It lay in her stomach like morning hunger, or the sway when a train hits a set of points you aren't expecting, or magic hour moments when the edge of the world is just over the sun and the sandstone fingers of the Big Vermilion country are still glowing with the heat of it—you can feel it on your face—and the sky is so blue it aches.

Sweetness Octave Glorious Honey-Bun Asiim Engineer 12th, the feeling said, at this moment, you are free to do one of two things. You can get up from this bank and go to your cabin and put on your clips and your veil and your garland and go out there to meet your husband-to-be. You can get up from this bank and go to that terrain bike over there and take that bike and this boy and go wherever you want in the world. That's it. That's your two choices. Sorry there ain't no more. That's your lot.

Sweetness put down the glasses, but it wasn't readjustment to new perspectives that made the world swim around her. It was those two and two-only choices, and the certainty that in this moment, she had to decide. The world went white. Certainty blinded her.

Sweetness suddenly found words inside her. She did not want to have to think too much about them, because that might have killed them, so she opened her mouth and let them come out. They tasted like something she was spitting up, strong and biley, something she had to get out of her.

"Hey Serpio."

"What?" He had been reaching for the glasses, but Sweetness rolled on to her back and looked at the sky.

"You hate it."

"What?"

"Here. This. You hate it. I hate it. So let's go."

"You mean?"

"Let's go. Now. Why not?" Thinking: *Hurry up, get on with it, say yes, don't keep asking stupid questions because each one eats a bit of that blinding white certainty and I don't want to have to go back there, I don't want to be married and have a stainless steel kitchen and no, I don't know what's going to be out there with you, but I do know that it's none of that back there. And this is a very very very long moment indeed.*

She saw his lips open. It was like a replay on the pelota, but with a tiny rope of saliva between tooth and top lip that caught the sun.

"Okay," he said. "Okay."

And so they ran away.

But it wasn't that quick, or clean. You don't just run away. People who do that on the Deuteronomy trampas end up raven-picked and wind-polished. Even an Engineer girl knew this.

Timetabling made the raid easier. Engineers and Stuards were hither and thither, up-track and down, but North East Quartersphere regional control had stuff backed up all the way to Grand Valley and a railroad to run, God damn it, so all the running around was against a backdrop of track-mending gear folding itself neatly into its manifolds and tokamaks firing up in impressive gouts of steam and crews swinging themselves perilously on to companionways as cranks turned and wheels ground. Marshals with red flags and whistles backed trains up to the sidings and engaged in impressive feats of impromptu shunting as intercities nudged past slow freighters and priority diplomatic transports slipped in ahead of big chemical processors. In the confusion of steam and costumes, Sweetness could slip up the Number Twelve access ladder, over the top of the water tender, wriggle down the relief pipe that no one over the age of ten could ever make it down, along the midway and through the open porthole of her cabin unseen.

Kilometres later, she would also be amazed about how simple the choice of items was. Two hundred and twenty-seven dollars rolled up in a waterproof can. A jingle of change, though it was heavy and rolled too easily out of pockets. A torch. An all-weather lighter. A pen and a little paper. A fistful of tampons. A leather-bound copy of *The Evyn Psalmody* that Grandmother Taal had marked up in red highlighter. A Bakelite cat—quite small, but dense—that she knew would never forgive her if she left it behind. Some glue, and a small screwdriver. Shampoo. Water purifying tablets. BootsT-shirtslongpantsshortpantsposh frock(in case) gloves*good*socks. A long-fingered comb. A gold filling, to sell. Sachet mint tea, sachet ersatz coffee (appropriated from Stuard country). Tin mug. Spoonknifefork, folding. A whistle, in case she really couldn't trust Serpio. A decent blade, partially ditto. A little solar wireless. Something unimproving to read. Remembering the advice of the green man of Inatra, a toothbrush and at least one change of underwear. Her charm, to watch over her. An emergency spell, a sixth birthday special from Psalli, purchased with many frissons and some guilt from Mammy Wulu the Budget Witch of Belladonna Main.

It all looked very small in the bottom of her black everything-proof bag, precious little eggs in a dark nest. But it had been easy. Just reach out and take it. The thought had been put in long before. Some quarantined fold of her mind had been planning this for years.

Something else. Oh yes. Her smelly sleepsack. And food. It might be a while before she got something to eat.

Voices and distant whistlings from beneath her porthole told her *Catherine of Tharsis*'s people were still abroad, trying to search the other trains for the runaway fiancée before they pulled out. She listened a second at the hatch of her cabin, then darted swiftly down the dark wood-lined corridor to the Domiety refectory. As ever, Sle and Rother'am had left all the stuff with no meat or that was in some way healthy. It all went into four greaseproof paper bags, and, with six bottles of oxygenated water, into the bag.

Those ten items suddenly made it heavy enough to root her to the spot.

The bright certainty was fading. One moment more of this greasy, scored wall panelling, that ingrained sweat of hot fat and onions, those smeary framed photographs of Great Trains passing over Photogenic Terrain, that phlegmy rattle of the neon wireless on the window-sill, those cheery plastic condiment bottles in the shapes of smiling vegetables with their crusted necklaces of dried drips, and she would be trapped forever. Pickled like a festal egg.

"Sweet?"

Too slow. You lost it.

Cock piss bugger bum balls. It had to be Romereaux, standing in the doorway with his mouth open in a way that told her without words he had worked it all out in one glimpse.

"Don't." She held up a warning finger.

"Sweet, where are you . . ."

"Don't say another word."

She backed away from him.

"Don't try and stop me, don't try and talk me out of it. I'm not marrying Stainless Steel Kitchen. I've got a life waiting for me."

"Sweet, I just wanted . . ."

"Shut."

"Wanted to say . . ."

"Up. Shut up."

"To say, good luck."

It was so wrong a thing for him to say that she was halfway to the door before the double-take hit. She turned.

"What?"

"Good luck."

"You're supposed to try to stop me. You're supposed to have arguments about how hurt everyone will be, and the honour of the family, and the disgrace I'll bring on everyone and they'll all have to go round with their hair uncut for three years. When that doesn't work, you're supposed to ask me if I know what I'm doing and do I know where I'm going and that it's a big wild world out there and I'll get very hurt very fast, and I'll come crawling back like *that*. And when I say I've got it all sorted, you're supposed to go all soft and say you'll miss me and that you've always really loved me, and that you had this brilliant plan to buy out the contract and we'd have our own train and go off in a cloud of steam into the sunset and we'll found our own Domiety and one day they'll name a station after us and that'll stop me for ten, maybe twenty seconds—if you've played it right—and I'll say something like, well, I always loved you too, like for years, since you were *this* size and I was *that* size and all those years, we never knew it, and now it's too late because I've got to go, I've got a life waiting for me, and I turn around and walk right out of here and that's it."

"Um, no."

"What do you mean no?"

"Like, no."

"I mean, you did love me, and you could never tell anyone about it, right?"

He sighed from his cheeks.

"Well, that time, by the pool?"

"What about it?"

"Well, I wanted to . . ."

"So did I."

"But I didn't really . . . love you."

"Oh."

"I wanted you. But that was just . . . wanting."

"I see."

"Sorry."

"Well, I suppose I'll go then."

"Yes. Go on. Go on then. Get out of here. Get wherever you're going, and don't come back. There's too much of you for this place, always going somewhere but ending up nowhere. You're too good for Stainless Steel Kitchen. You should have maharajahs and riverboat gamblers and Belladonna assassins and interplanetary ambassadors. You should have canal barges and silk-lined airships and gold-plated Praesidium Sailships and big low cars with bars in the back seat. There's stuff out there that's worthy of you, and if you don't go you'll never find it. So get out of here."

She turned in the corridor. She told herself it was because she wanted to ask a final favour, but they both knew it was for a final meeting of eyes.

"Romi."

"Go on. What is it?"

"Can you cover for me?"

"I think I can do that."

She told herself she must not look back again, but she did it anyway because she knew she was perverse. Romereaux was gone.

Having exhausted all other possibilities, the searchers were returning home for the fingertip scrutiny of crannies and hidey-holes. Sweetness slipped past the denim-clad arses of Sle and Rother'am cooeeing up an airco duct, but *Tante* Marya patrolling the undercarriage stopped her dead. One glimpse at her face promised a punishment worse than marriage to the Stainless Steel Kitchen. She was head of the Domiety. She had made the match. The shame would be excoriating.

Sweetness ducked down under the porthole as she heard feet clang on the metal steps. She pressed herself hard against the sun-warmed wood. Marya Stuard's face deformed itself against the glass as she tried to squint out every possible line of sight. Clang clang clang. Away again. But she was out there, between herself and the things Sweetness deserved.

The ripe fanfare of the calliope almost tricked a yelp of surprise from Sweetness. Bite it off, bite it off. Again, the steam organ tootled a riff.

"There she goes, there! Look!"

Romereaux.

"Look, there, going east! Somebody stop her, she'll be away!"

Feet clattered in the corridor. The opposite door slammed open, the same feet rattled down steps.

"Where where where?"

Again, the calliope parped the alarum. Sweetness dared a peek. *Tante* Marya was ducking under the carriage—a heinous sin, which every child was warned off on pain of gravest censure. She flung open the door, was down the steps and running. Now one look back. And there was Romereaux, a tiny silhouette standing on the saddle of the big steam calliope, asbestos-gloved hand pointing in exactly the wrong direction.

Serpio took the terrain bike easily.

"What kept you?"

"Things." Sweetness slung herself up behind him. The engine trembled between her legs. She pressed her belly and thighs against his work gear.

"Is she comfortable?" he asked.

"Who comfortable?"

"Her. Your friend. She doesn't look comfortable. Half her's dragging on the ground."

Sweetness rolled her eyes and mimed heaving some mass on her right side.

"Can we just go now?"

"Certainly."

He twisted the handle and they went. Like that. Sweetness whooped and Serpio gunned the little alcohol engine and it was fast and dusty and sexy and in a direction she had never travelled before, which was perpendicular, and in all the speed and excitement she quite forgot to worry about the effect of Serpio's angel-eye on his driving.

*T*he rain was gruelling now. Sweetness loathed getting her hair wet, but stuck her head out from under the shelter of the seat. She thought she had heard it again.

"It's nothing." Serpio coaxed a small fire of grass stalks and wood splinters. It sent a wan spiral of smoke up to haunt the ribs and buttresses of the underside of the chair seat.

"It's not nothing if it's thunder." She scanned the sky that had slowly curdled from the west until now it was a moiling blanket of grey on grey.

"You don't get thunder from that kind of cloud." Serpio was trying to rig a trivet of stones over the now-glowing fire.

"Well, I hope you're sure, because in case you hadn't noticed, we're sitting right under a twenty-metre wooden chair, and not only is it wood, and the tallest thing in fifty kays, it's also right on top of what passes for the major hill in this neighbourhood."

"I'm sure."

"How do you know?"

"I seen plenty of weather."

"So've I."

I've got an uncle fused into the regional signalling grid by plenty of weather, and a relative hit by lightning gives everyone a nose for thunder, she wanted to say but Serpio's forehead was furrowed and his tongue peeking pinkly from the corner of his mouth as he stacked his stones. "I'm soaked," Sweetness said instead. "Let me near that." Wet hair momentarily blinded her. Her foot brushed the tripod of stones. It promptly collapsed. Serpio swiftly plucked the rocks from the fire before they crushed out its last breath. Then with the Zen patience of card-house builders, he set about rebalancing his rocks. Sweetness squatted on her heels and showed her hands to the three flickers of heat and thought about how quickly it had all gone like the weather.

For the first handful of hours the novelty of travel at right angles had thrilled her. Off the track. Beyond the lines. Turn those handlebars and you can go in any direction you like. The track doesn't take you. You take the track. Maps among the trainfolk are grids, networks, interconnections of coloured lines with black circles. All this two-dimensionality was *wooeeeee!* stuff. This flat, almost treeless rangeland was full throttle terrain. Glancing behind her—comb black curls out of her eyes—Sweetness exulted at the plume of dust rising up behind her. One part of her soul warned her she was advertising her egress for a hundred kilometres around. Another did not give one fig. Outliers of a great herd of grazebeasts cantered, roll-eyed with fear, from the speeding bikers. Encouraged, Serpio aimed his machine at the heart of the dark wall of the main herd. It parted before him. The terrain bike drove a dust-coloured wedge through the mass of bovine bodies, splitting it in two like an amoeba.

"Woo-hoo!" he hollered.

Sweetness thumped Serpio on the back. When he stopped the bike, she took the little wireless and wedged it between the handlebars. Thereafter, Hamilton Bohannon and his Rhythm Aces and Cool Cat Jazzy Jee rode with them over the outwash hills of Lesser Oxus into West Deuteronomy. Like hormone-troubled adolescence, the smooth face of the land was breaking into bumps and ridges. Straggles of wire tried to entrap the trampas. Dusty meanders in the grass became tracks, became double-rutted roads. By unspoken agreement, they stayed clear of these, and the fields that had appeared in between the long, low ridges, the farms and the stockyards and the pens. Occasional gangs of stockmen in dusters and cartwheel hats nodded to them. Their long-legged destriers minced nervously, offended by engine whine. Fence-crews working on the wire from the backs of huge eight-wheel yutes raised a hand in passing greeting. A taciturn folk, the Deuteronomians, given to their land and their past and the arcane formulae of their society.

In a wooded crotch where three valleys met stood St. Mariensborough. Five streets, seven shrines, five bars, three good cantinas all next to each other, one Universal Store, a manufactory, a doctor/lawyer/vet, an auction house and a folding cinema. Here they stopped for fuel. Serpio filled the tank from the alcohol distillery. Sweetness reclined in a pose she thought coquettish and dangerous. She tapped her foot to the radio—"Tuxedo Junction"—and surveyed her fellow fuel customers. A country bus, dust-battered and dented, shrieking with schoolkids. A big yute, high as a house, emblazoned with improving versos from the *Guthru Gram Kanteklion*. A truck train unashamedly carrying the sperm-and-ova symbol of the National AI Service. Two low-loaders, parked suspiciously close to each other. While they guzzled alcohol, two men passed a pile of cardboard boxes marked with "fragile" symbols from one flatback to the other. *Bet you've no idea who we are, what we're doing, where we're going*, Sweetness teased them.

A niggle whispered, *And you do?*

"Any cash?"

A different niggle as she rooted in her bag for bills. Vague resentment. St. Mariensborough was where it started to turn sour. Beyond St. Mariensborough, it changed. The outwash hills, remnants of a continental-scale deluge billennia before the cometary rain of the early decades of the man-forming, ran into each other, formed ridges and escarpments. The land developed a trend, westward and upward, fingers to a palm. Roads roamed the long valleys, seeking ways on to the table lands above. Over this high land a hard rain intended; grey clouds running in from the west were wedged against a front and piled into a massive frown. The wind rose. The horizon vanished into twilight vagueness. An hour beyond the nub-end of the last metalled road they passed the last farm. Dour and Deuteronomian: a tower of planed wood and little windows, bare and defiant of the big flatness. A wind-pump rattled its vanes in the rising wind, its mechanism unlocked in anticipation of big wind coming. Dead ravens hung, claws up, beaks down, from a crucifixion board. Their fleasy feathers stirred. Take warning. Stern people here.

An hour past the last farm the first drop hit Sweetness between the eyes and slid down her nose. The second was not slow following. Somewhere between the three and four thousandth, she decided she was Not Having Fun. It wasn't Want To Go Back—not yet, but it was getting there. The rain punished the tiny creeping vehicle, an offence against the elemental purity of land and weatherscape. Serpio steered through the arrowing rain into the dark heart of the storm.

"Where are we going?" Sweetness yelled. Each time the wind took her words away. The universal grey—earth, air and water—abolished any notion of time, but Sweetness's innate Engineer sense of timetabling advised her it was nearing night. In confirmation, the horizon flared briefly: sun through a crack in the storm front as the edge of the world rose over it. In that instant of orange, Sweetness glimpsed a fellow intruder in the desolation. A silhouette: so simple and absolute there could be no mistaking its identity, however incongruous that might seem. A chair. Yes, a chair. And, she reckoned, a big chair. A big chair, all alone and untenanted on a ridge top.

She banged Serpio on the shoulder. He nodded—already seen and noted. He turned the handlebars toward the big chair.

A very big chair. And a very long way off. Sweetness clung to Serpio and pressed her face against his back while the headlamp felt out the darkness for the chair. She tried not to think about running out of ol, or how deliciously drowsy this whipping rain was making her feel, how soft the wire-tough grass looked. Half-hypnotised by the weaving spot of the headlight beam and half-stupid with cold, to her great astonishment, Sweetness suddenly found herself out of the rain. While Serpio tried to make wet wood burn with a splash of ol, Sweetness tried to take in the edifice sheltering her. It was a very very big chair. The legs were twenty metres high, she thought. Three orphanages of foundlings could have played handball on its ample seat. The carved finials of the back tugged at the low hurtling clouds. She thought it strange to find it not at all strange to be sheltering under a chair on which the Panarch might have rested, in the nowherelands of Deuteronomy West.

Serpio finally abandoned his attempts to erect a cooking trivet and used the stones instead to ring-fence the fire. Sweetness ate stale duck sandwiches, picking out the pickled cucumber which she didn't like and flicking it into the dark. She looked into the fire and asked the glowing things to help her believe where she was, what she had done. Flakes of wood ash hold no oracle. Without a word she unrolled her sleeping bag across the fire from Serpio and slipped inside in her still damp clothes.

"You stay your side."

He did. And he was still there in the morning, when Sweetness woke with a start to find that she was indeed where she feared she might be. The storm had marched on the east in the night. Behind it came an immense blue morning. The indigo edge of the world sparkled with the riding lights of interworld ships. The big chair was a throne of marvels, an invitation to sit and contemplate a moment as gods. From this height on which the chair stood golden light flowed down into the hollows and shallow valleys, filling up all the land so that every blade of grass stood distinct. On such a morning even curled-up duck sandwiches have the taste of glory. Sweetness woke cold and stiff and aching but as she shuffled around the camp, trying to poke life into extinct ashes, the morning worked its way into her soul and lit her up. She looked out at the land—her land now—and wondered with pleasure where it would take her today.

They were packed and on the bike in half an hour. Little grasslands things—a rustle, a dart—fled from their path. Behind they left three neat, parallel tire tracks. Trainfolk. Never get away from the track. Within half an hour the land was turning higher and drier. Scrub, sagey herbs, red sand between the roots of clinging grasses. At a waterstop, Sweetness stood up on the pillion seat to scan the horizon. Heat shimmer. They were crossing the dry fringe-country of the great northeastern desert. Between her and the haze, an unknown object bulked large. At this range Sweetness could not make anything out of it, except that it was big. Not a chair, but big. It kept its identity as they approached it across the dry hardpan, at first one thing, then another, then nothing known at all. It was only as they came up out of a seasonal stream bed, flowing with flowers in the brief rush-off after the rains, to find it squat in front of them that Sweetness realised what it was. An enormous shoe. The guttee of God.

It was the size of a rail-car, made of leather, rather sagged and rotted by the occasional rain seasons, and chewed at the edges by ravenous desert animals. Sweetness and Serpio ate a meagre lunch leaning against its welt. They didn't speak. They didn't need to. The journey had taken them swiftly to that place in a relationship where you can be comfortable with silence. Out of curiosity Sweetness scrambled up the shoe—a left, she noted—then scaled to the cuff by means of the laces, each the size of bridge cables. She peered inside. The high sun illuminated a waste of bird bones. She felt vaguely disappointed, though she could not say what she might have expected that would have satisfied her.

In the afternoon the bike passed at some distance another Promethean domestic artifact; an ironing board on which entire stratocumuli could have been pressed and creased. A spindly mesa, it occupied the western horizon for many tens of kilometres. The tail of its huge shadow marked the beginning of the desert proper.

"Into that?"

Sweetness was doing her far-seeing-balance-on-the-seat feat again. Serpio refilled the canteens from a sandy little spring that meandered a way among black tar-thorn and shrub casanthus until it tired of its own energy and the red sand drank it down. The scent of deep rock water was rich in the air.

"Yeah."

"Why?"

Sweetness's left hand stopped him stoppering the flasks. Her right dropped in two purifying tablets.

"Are you questioning my direction?"

"Yes."

"Why?"

"Because for the past two days I've been staring at the middle of your back and trusting implicitly that you've got some idea where you're going, and now I really, really got to be sure. I just want to be sure, that's all."

"We're going out there, yes."

"Okay. Now, why?"

"There's someone I want to meet, out there."

"Out there?"

"People live in deserts."

"People die in deserts."

"Harx lives out there."

"Harx who?"

Serpio was swinging back on to the saddle. He kicked at the starter. The ol motor cleared its throat; dry and dusty in the tubes.

"You coming?"

You're rushing me, Sweetness thought as she shook up the canteens. *You don't want me to ask about this. You're taking me to meet someone/thing but you don't want to talk about him/it.* Anywhere else, that would have been that to you and your terrain bike, matey. But when the last other person you have seen was a dour Deuteronomian Peripatete and he had discreetly shooed you away because he had taken a Vow of Seclusion, you get up behind the saddle.

"So, this Harx."

"What about him?"

"I heard you mention him before."

He did not reply but the muscles beneath his sweat-stiff workclothes said, *Oh? What? Shit, secrets to keep* to Sweetness's fingers.

"Back then, where they did that thing. You know. With the . . . meat."

A pause of half a kilometre. *Sorry sorry sorry,* Sweetness thought. *It was bad and I shouldn't remind you of it but I have to know.*

"Oh, yeah."

"You mentioned this Harx guy. So who is he?"

"He's holy."

"That explains it then."

"Explains what?"

"People who live in deserts are either mad, bad, sad or holy."

He said nothing for the next twenty kilometres, or so it seemed to Sweetness, hovering on the numb edge of sensory deprivation between the encircling haze and the dank man-odour of Serpio's shirt. When he did talk, it was in a voice so soft and alien to him that it was as if the sand had spoken.

"He's not mad or sad or bad, but he is holy."

It was a major effort of will for Sweetness to pull her soul back from the horizon, to which it had been reeled out by the flat red land and spread into a thin, encircling line.

"Unk?"

"He's good to me. He helps me. He respects me. I've got something that's useful to him, he needs me. The others; they'll all see, when he comes. They'll look up and their mouths, they'll just fall open like fishes in a bucket, and then they'll see."

"I'm a bit unclear about this . . ."

"Have you ever heard of the Church of the Ever-Circling Spiritual Family?"

"Can't say I have."

"You will. Everyone will . . ."

"Could we maybe do a little less of the big doomy *when it all comes down* stuff, and just start at the beginning?"

A pause, in which a skittering lizard hoicked itself up on its rear limbs and hot-legged it away over the burning sands.

"You ever listen to the radio real late at night?"

"Of course. Everyone does that." On the trains it was how you reminded yourself you were young and cute and a kid like hundreds of millions of others out there in the non-moving world. The voices in the dark of your room, close to you in your bed, a dozen different tongues in your ear a night.

"You ever listen to the religious stations?"

Sweetness's fingers had twirled the dial over the thousands of shouting pleading hectoring lecturing wheedling whining canoodling seducing scolding trumpeting voices jammed one on top of the other in the low medium wave. Her world bred religions like a dog fleas, and they all could afford air-time.

"I'm more a music person, me." Pertinent to which, Sweetness realised that for an indefinite but long time now the handlebar wireless had played nothing but airglow. Scary biscuits. A place where the radio wasn't. On the far shore of the airwaves.

"Yeah, well. Anyway, that's where he found me, in the Godband."

"You found him, you mean." A random twiddle of the knobs.

"No. He found me. He was talking right at me."

"Yah. Right."

"No. Really. He called me, by name. He said, 'And this is going out for Serpio Six Tuesday-Duodecember-Twelfth-Raining Sebendary Waymender.'"

"Nah. Someone set you up. One of those . . . other ones, back there."

"No. Listen, will you? He saw me, same way as I see your friend there."

"He had this, spirit-sight? Angel-vision? What the hell do you call it anyway?"

"The sight."

"This 'sight,' so does it have a limit like normal sight, like perspective, or does it just not bother with things like that?"

"It does, but you can train it, and then it's naturally more highly developed in some than others."

"Higher spiritual beings. Of course."

"Look, if you're going to be cynical . . ."

"Sorry. I'm an Engineer."

They passed a tangle of bones and Sweetness thought hard about cynicism in big deserts.

"Go on."

"He saw me, he knew I had the sight, and he told me the Ever-Circling Family needed the sight to help them in the fight."

"The sight, and the fight."

"You can say what you like, but it's a battle. This whole world's a battle, it's been a battle since before it was invented."

The pause invited the question: "Who's fighting?"

"Men and angels."

"I see."

"No you don't. Believe me. You think this world was made for us? We're just human shields. They can't wipe the angels out now because they keep the manforming systems running. Like the magnetic field. This place doesn't have one, naturally, so there are these huge superconducting magnets up there in orbit. You've heard of vanas?"

Sweetness had always thought of the orbital mirrors as too lowly even to be proper angels, until the night in Inatra a spotlight from heaven lit her way home.

"They keep the weather working. This place isn't like the Motherworld, it doesn't have that feedback system so the whole thing always stays right for life. Well, not yet. The climate here is simple, like *not complex*. You wouldn't know what that means, but basically, if left to its own devices, it would get stuck in a loop and you'd get the same weather over and over and over again. The vanas, they heat the atmosphere up so you get these pockets of randomness, so the climate doesn't get stuck. That's just two. There's thousands, but the point is they keep the whole world alive, and they know it. They don't need any of that stuff, they'd be as happy if this place was rock and ice, like it was, before, but then they wouldn't be safe. We make them safe, and that's why they let us come here."

"Wait wait wait. What are all these *theys* and *thems*?"

"The angels, of course. Though Harx says you shouldn't call them that; they're machines, and machines have souls but no spirits. They can't be of God, see?"

"Wait wait wait wait. If the angels are machines . . ."

"Not if."

"Okay." No contention: everyone head-knew that what they called angels were, for the most part, leftover manforming machinery, but the conceit persisted because for the most part they lived in heaven—they formed a visible ring around the world—and they carried out unguessable missions on the part of unseen powers for the betterment of humans. "And they've no spirits, so what do you and this Harx boy actually see with your *sight*?"

He sighed the sigh guys sigh when their thoughts are too much for wee females. Sport, sex, steam or steel, it never failed to kindle the devil in Sweetness.

"It's theoretical."

"Go on."

"How much vinculum theory have you got?"

"The universe is a big brown package all tied up with string."

"It's a lot more complicated than that."

"I know *that*. That's the bollocks you get off the School of the Air. All matter, energy, space and time are different harmonics in eleven dimensional strings, most of which are rolled up smaller than Planck space so all we get are the four we live in rather than lots we wouldn't know what to do with." She had always found visualising seven extra dimensions, each containing the ones beneath it, mind-wringing. Then one of her wiser Stabile Tutors, who held seminars in reality, had let her into the secret that everyone else did as well. Good thing. The order of the universe should be mind-wringing. She added, "I'm named after it."

"What?"

"Octave. Harmonics. String music, all that."

"What do you know about filament computing?"

Sweetness let go Serpio's jacket and hunted for other hookholds underneath the bag rack. She made sure he appreciated that she was leaning back, away from him.

"Suppose you just give me the lecture, then?"

After a few miffed moments he said, "All the ROTECH machines use vinculum processing architecture."

"Spell it," Sweetness challenged. He did, and continued, "Calculations get done not in two states, like the old quantum machines we got on the trains, but in eleven uncollapsed states. You know . . ."

"Two impossible things at the same time. Or in this case, eleven."

"Yeah. But what it really is, deep down, is using the structure of the universe as a computer. So in a sense . . ."

"The whole universe is a computer." *Or God*, she thought of adding, but she was unsure of the small print of Serpio's theology. If it involved blind hejiras into the Big Red, the devil in the details could be sharp.

"No."

"Okay."

"The whole universe has the potential to be in any number of uncollapsed states."

"This is the 'Many-worlds' theory, isn't it?"

"It is, but this is how it actually works day to day. Most of the time the calculations are very small and neat and they stay down there in the string-level of the universe."

"Like those little knots in thread you sometimes get if you're sewing, that don't stop the needle going through the cloth."

"Sort of, I suppose. But sometimes if you have to make a lot of calculations, like something really complicated like making a model of an ocean, or an eco-system, you get what they call coherence. That's when a whole lot of string potentials are entangled together and all collapse into the same state. Then you can get whole chunks of the big universe switching from one world to another. Like magic."

"Like knots so big they pull the shape of the cloth into something else."

"Like sewing a big sheet of fabric into a jacket or a shirt or a wedding waistcoat. That orph . . ."

The precise perimeter of the circular crazy-zone was sharp in Sweetness's memory. Like stepping from one world into another, she had thought. Right and wrong. It was another way of being this world. And what of that other place Uncle Neon took her? Was she taken to other-world, or was other-world erected around her, and the set struck when she left?

"Its little string-machines all agreed to go mad and decided that reality was something else."

"They switched on an alternative reality."

A new image now, of the cloud-sized heaven machine decreeing its doom on the defective earth-builder and restoring the world to normality. But who decreed what was normal? Who minted the consensus? Normal ordained that girls don't drive trains. Consensus said, the only daughters of illustrious Engineer Domieties marry Stuards with stainless steel kitchens and good prospects.

"We've got a consensus reality now, so any breaches have to get cleared up right quick, but in the earliest days of the manforming they used the technique all the time to speed things up. They'd run a model of an alternative world where, say the atmosphere was working better, or there were bacteria, or soil, or even plants, and when the model got complex enough, the model would become reality Otherwise it would've taken thousand of years and we'd be up to our asses in ice, if we could even breathe at all."

Sweetness's mind was wringing with that same painful twist she recalled from Pastor Jhingh and his eleven-dimensional visualisations. If the machines could think like that, could see all those dimensions unfolding out of each other, then maybe it was right to call them angels.

"So, what is it you actually *see?*"

"Most people don't know this, but humans can see on the quantum level no problem at all. We could do it out here. It's good and clear at night. I'd drive about twenty kays away and light a match, and you could see it. That would be like one single photon reaching your eye, and one photon is seeing quantum."

Please don't feel you have to demonstrate, Sweetness thought.

"You know a lot about this."

"It's good to study the things that make us different."

"So," Sweetness said. "You see things not on the quantum level, but on the vinculum scale?"

"That's the way I was born. That's why I can see what you people call the angels, because I can see them thinking. All those tiny tiny little vinculum calculations. I can see their minds glowing."

"And this Harx boy."

"To be able to see on the vinculum level involves vinculum processes. He can see me, seeing them. But he can see better. He can see anywhere in the universe, because it's all entangled."

"Okay," Sweetness said carefully. "I can get this. I think. But tell me, how come you see Little Pretty One? I'm telling you, she is not a machine. She is my sister, and she lives in mirrors, and she gives me good advice, most of the time, when she can be bothered talking."

"And she's sitting right behind you looking over your shoulder and smiling at me."

"You know something," Sweetness said, truly savouring the sudden rush of emotion. "I really hate it when you talk about her like that."

"Sorry."

"She talks to me. All you do is see her."

Nothing was said for several kilometres of rocky red desert.

"She's not a machine," Sweetness reminded Serpio.

"I know."

A minute or so further on, Sweetness pressed her sharp little chin on Serpio's shoulder and said into his ear, "So how does she fit into all your big theory, then?"

"Don't know," Serpio said. "That's why I want to ask Harx."

"So that's where we're going."

"Yeah."

"To this guru preacher boy."

"Devastation Harx, yes."

"Ah," said Sweetness on the back of a stolen bike with at least a hundred and fifty kilometres of desert around her in any direction. "Ah. Yes. I get it now. So I've walked out on my family and my home and my impending marriage and come out here with just the stuff on my back into the ass-end of nowhere and the only one you're really bothered about is something I can't even see that's hanging off my ribcage. Can I ask you one question?"

"Whatever."

"Did you ever really fancy me at all?"

Serpio stopped the bike. Dead square stopped. Middle of nowhere.

Oh Mother'a'grace, Sweetness thought. *I've gone and done it, haven't I? Why why why why do I have to go that one question too deep?*

Serpio got off the bike. Shaking life into saddle-sore limbs, he walked away. Clinging to the superstructure, Sweetness watched him go.

"Serpio!"

No answer.

"Where are you going?"

No answer.

"What're you doing?"

Back turned to her, he looked out upon a vista of sweeping dunes.

"I'm sorry!"

Dunes are dunes are dunes. What are you looking at, what are you seeing? Nothing, I bet, except not *me*.

"I said, I'm sorry!"

Unmoved, like the dark blue sky.

"I said!" Top of her lungs. "I'm sorry!"

She yelled so loud the desert heard her. Sand shifted on the sloping face of a big dune, ringed by minions. Shift triggered slide, triggered chain slippages that cascaded up into micro-avalanches into dust rivulets into flowing deltas into sheet-floods of sand. The dune face was shedding away before the power of her voice, disintegrating into scabs and floes. The dune was moving. It was stirring in its bed and rising up.

It had heard her. It was coming to get her, loud-mouthed little tyke who dared disturb the monumental solitude of the deep desert. It would fill her mouth and voice box and lungs with silencing sand.

No. Impossible. Dunes don't walk. They crawl, over whole seasons. If a dune moves, it is because a buried something beneath it is moving. The slipping curtains of sand flashed tantalises of bright metal, curved plastic, knobbled ridges. The something was very big. It was not buried in the dune. It *was* the dune. It had lain here and gone to sleep and woken up caked in sand. Something like a lost city was rising out of the Big Red. It lifted clear of the other, lesser dunes. It left a circular crater a good ore train in diameter. Higher it rose. The flying city was the shape of a great, flat, upturned saucer, crazy with racing sand. Through veils of dust raining off its rim like monsoon from an umbrella, Sweetness glimpsed complex forms beneath the dome, like the folds and ruches of fungi that hide under the sobriety of their caps. She shaded her eyes with her hand as the thing reached the zenith and eclipsed the sun.

"Oh my God!" Sweetness Octave Glorious Honey-Bun Asiim Engineer 12th exclaimed as the flying thing passed over her head. It moved to the south, hovered over a flat expanse of rocky grit, settled slowly. The sun was full on it, and it was a magnificent creature, carapaced like a beetle with iridescent greens and electric blues, underneath busy with bulbous, insect-eye-like excrescences, manipulator arms and whirring rotors. Claw feet unfolded, tested the terrain, found it faithful. The flying object settled on its legs. The fans were stilled. An intimidating set of polished black mandibles that could have devoured houses by the district opened; an alabaster pont reached out and touched ground.

Sweetness stood mumchance.

Serpio was already running for the pont. He turned, extended a hand to Sweetness.

"Well, what are you waiting for?"

13

*I*n the privacy of command, striding alone on his big brass bridge, Naon Engineer decided that the only way out of the situation was to die of shame. There were numerous precedents for this action. No matter that most of them had been performed by ascetics and monastics in order to stymie wars, blight cities or summon monsoons. They had not had their wheels pissed on by Stuards.

Out, quick. Yell "power-up" down the gosport, throw full steam and throttles wide open. Put as many sleepers as possible between you and the bad thing. Old Engineer advice, father to son to son to son. As soon as there was free track, he had bellowed the Deep-Fusion folk to frenzy and spun the wheels. But the *Ninth Avata* Stuards were ready for him. Two rows, either side of the track. A firing squad. The men had unzipped and unfurled. The women had hoisted their many skirts and aimed. As the looming superstructure of *Catherine of Tharsis* passed over their heads, they had gushingly anointed the drive wheels.

The track-level cameras spared none of the humiliation.

"Full power!" Naon Engineer thundered at the sweating Deep-Fusioners in their windowless reactor hive. His cheeks were red. Blood seethed in his brainpan. There was a high whining whistle in his inner ears. It blocked out the imagined jeering of the Stuards. "Full power, you slugs snails tortoises infernal turtles!" But heavy trains are slow. It seemed a damned eternity for *Catherine of Tharsis* to pull away from those two ranks of jeering cooks and waiters.

The imagined tang of urine filled his nostrils. It would never wash away. Never. Speed. The wind of high velocity might at least blow it somewhere he would not have to smell it. Naon Engineer pushed the lever forward to its uttermost notch. The big fusion engines responded with a howl of power. *Catherine of Tharsis* was a smoke-fletched arrow shot across the plains of Old

Deuteronomy. She ran Mendocello Bank at such a lick that it jumped Marya Stuard's formal goblets from their racks. Scampering junior *sommeliers* bumped into each other as they rolled away from grasping fingers. Brimful of the righteous wrath that had defeated the Starke badmaashes, Marya Stuard stormed forward.

"He's locked himself in," Child'a'grace said. Marya Stuard was no respecter of sanctums. She beat the door with her fists.

"What d'you think you're doing, man?"

The twin horns blew.

"I demand to be let in!"

She swayed as the train took a switchover at two hundred and fifty.

"I'm a bloody laughing stock, Engineer! A laughing stock! And people do not laugh at Marya Stuard. Remember who bounced Selwyn Starke and his dacoits!"

"There's no talking to him," Child'a'grace said mildly. Marya Stuard stood glaring at the door, as if heat of will could melt a hole in it. It remained obdurately unmelted and unopened. For once defeated, she gave a huff of exasperation and turned on her heel.

"He'll talk to me, eventually," she declared. Child'a'grace sighed, still waiting after four years.

Naon Engineer finally ran out of steam on the down-grade to the Muchanga Water Tower. Hands off the throttles. *Catherine of Tharsis* ghosted to a creaking, heavy halt under the blessing fingers of the water-charger. By now the decision was firm in his mind, and he could face the council of his peers.

"I am destroyed," he declared to the assembled council of the Domieties. He had had plenty of time to practise the tone of pained humiliation, and he thought he did it really rather well. "The money is forfeit. So be it. A price must be paid, though three thousand dollars, and a lien on our contracts is a heavy burden. But what is heavier still, what is intolerable, is the shame. I cannot bear the disgrace. Cannot bear it, I tell you!" Every eye was on him. "There is only one choice available to me. The stain that besmirches the great name of Engineer can only be expunged by blood. Yes, blood!" A corner-of-eye glance to make sure Marya Stuard was watching, and impressed. Too hard to tell with that fierce little woman. Very well then. He drew himself up to his full height, which was not considerable. "I have studied the family archives, and there is a way that shame may be bought out. Shame for shame, life for life. I declare to you now, for the shame brought on this name by that child, for the urine stains rusting the pure steel of my driving wheels, yes, I will die from shame! A terrible price, yes, but one I bear gladly. Thirteen generations of the name Asiim demand it!" He held aloft his hand in a rhetorical gesture he had once seen in an itinerant tent theatre performance of *The Melodrama of the Twelve Just Trappers*. It had been a notoriously hammy gig, but trainpeople had never been renowned as critics. He held the pose, flared his nostrils.

Someone farted. It was soft and eructating and rippling. Before anyone could crack a chortle, Naon Engineer whirled.

"Who was that?" His finger was a claw of accusation. "Who emitted that . . . noise? Whose nether trumpet sounded?"

"Husband," Child'a'grace said.

"I mean it," he said, remembering just in time to sign to his wife, "I shall . . ."

"Naon . . ."

"Sle shall succeed. He shall inherit the starter rod." But he was failing. His pride was tobogganing toward a fatal precipice. Damn them. Damn his always reasonable wife, damn that underwearless tramp of a daughter, damn that loose-sphinctered hellion of a Bassareeni, he suspected.

"Naon, enough," Child'a'grace said gently, and he was utterly defeated.

"Just get us out of this with our dignity intact," Marya Stuard sighed. At the far end of the long table, Grandmother Taal ruffled her skirts and shawls like a prize chanticleer at a canton fair.

"We have forgotten someone here," she said. Her voice was small and soft, like a desert bird, but the air made room for every word. "We are all full of our shame and our disgrace and the stains on our wheels and our name, and even our money . . ." She stood up, fumbled open her black old-woman's bag, which had infinite dimensions folded up inside it. She flung a green something down the table. It slid to a halt in front of Naon Engineer: a wad of Bank of Tharsis bills. "Are you satisfied, son?"

Naon Engineer meanly flicked through the wad.

"It all seems to be here."

Grandmother Taal remained standing.

"Yes, we are all full of shame and disgrace but I say humiliation is a family that happily gives up a daughter to save its name. I say shame is a family that thinks of social betterment over a child's happiness. I say disgrace is a nearly-nine-year-old girl most probably at this very moment standing in the cold by the trackside back in Deuteronomy, looking for a train that wouldn't wait for her because its Chief Engineer—her own father—thinks too much of his own good name to even look for her. Let alone disrupt his timetables to wait to see if she might come back. That is shame. That is disgrace. That is what makes a Domiety's name small along the tracksides. If you are to die from anything, die for shame of that, father Naon Engineer 11th!"

In a flurry of black that seemed to go out from the old lady into other states and dimensions, Grandmother Taal whirled out of the council room.

In the wee hours, Child'a'grace came tippy-tapping at Grandmother Taal's cabin door. As she had expected, the matriarch was awake. The old sleep little but their dreams are mighty.

"Grandmother."

As she entered, she saw Grandmother Taal hastily tug down the hem of her black nightrobe. Drops of crimson on the floor. Child'a'grace looked for needles and thread: they were on the dressing table next to a patch of tabletop polished to mirror-sheen.

"Taal."

"It didn't work anyway."

"Could you not get a high enough gloss?"

Child'a'grace traced a finger across the wooden scrying-mirror as she sat down on the dressing stool. Grandmother Taal shook her head.

"Something is fogging me."

"Out of range?"

"It has no range. Something is muddying the scry-lines."

"What did you write?"

Grandmother Taal sat on the side of the bed. Her feet did not touch the ground. Blood was a crusty red rivulet in the contours of her ankle. She pulled up her skirt. SWEETNESS, her thin calf said.

"He's not a bad man," Child'a'grace said.

"He tries hard," Grandmother Taal said. "And you are defending him? How long since he last spoke to you?"

"Four years, sixteen months, twenty-seven days."

"If he does this over a folly of cards, you expect any less for a daughter who runs out on her own betrothal?"

"Ach, you are too right."

"Yes. So, do you think he will go ahead and shame himself to death?"

"He is embarrassed enough."

"Embarrassment is good for the soul. Especially his soul. Ah, if his father . . . I tell you, one good thing, if he did go and die of shame, at least it would give that girl the chance to do what she's always wanted."

There was no reasonable reply to this. Child'a'grace pursed her lips, then said, "I hope she has enough clean underwear." She looked at the circle of sheened wood, tried to catch her own reflection in the dressing tabletop. "Did you see anything?"

"It was muddy."

"But did you see anything?"

"I saw mirrors. Muddy mirrors. I saw the girl, reflected in many many mirrors. She was looking for something. She was looking very hard."

"Was it real? Or was it a sign?"

"How should I know?" Grandmother Taal said, testily. "I'm only a domestic magician. But I know one thing, she did not look happy. She looked scared."

Child'a'grace glanced away to hide the sudden emotion swelling in the corners of her eyes.

"I should . . ."

"No. They need you. Someone must keep the train on track, and the men are useless."

Child'a'grace nodded. From her bag she produced a thin, rectangular, oil-paper-wrapped packet. She presented it to Grandmother Taal. The old woman sniffed the yellow, greasy, thick paper carefully. Her eyes widened a sliver.

"This is most fine stuff."

"It is Etzvan Canton Black Loess."

In that ancient division of Deuteronomy, Grandmother Taal recalled, the soil was so dark and rich a teaspoon was stirred into the local hot chocolate to promote long life and fertility.

"It was in my dowry," Child'a'grace said simply. "I never really got the taste for it."

Grandmother Taal sniffed the packet again.

"Yes, I can smell bottom-drawer cottons and mothballs," she said.

"It's for your journey," Child'a'grace added hastily, "not your own use."

"I gathered that." The crow-corners of Grandmother Taal's eyes wrinkled.

"If I'd had any money . . ."

"Etzvan Canton Black Loess is better than money, especially a bar of this fine a vintage." Grandmother Taal slid the neat little wad into one of her many skirt pockets. "So, how did you know I was going?"

Again, Child'a'grace stroked fingertips against the wooden mirror.

"I've got my own domestic magic."

"Yes," Grandmother Taal said. "All women do."

"Keep safe," Child'a'grace said, kissing the old woman the three-fold kiss of farewell; forehead, wrist, wrist. "You've got a photograph . . ."

"A grandmother does not have a photograph of her granddaughter?"

"Of course. Well, let us know . . ."

"Immediately."

Ten minutes later, a figure a little more black than the Muchanga night climbed slowly down the passenger steps to the ground. The air smelled of sage and cold, stone-chilled water. The stars were sharp and threatening as an arrow storm. The moonring seemed suspended in flight, an arch of frost. Grandmother Taal took two nostrilfuls of the big night. She took three steps away from the track. This was the furthest she had been from *Catherine of Tharsis* in a half-decade. The novelty was worth that brief a consideration, no more. She found a place of concealment among the trackside equipment. Ladies of her venerability did not hide. Skittering night things fled from her. Good. There were almost certainly things out there that she would flee from. The big train swigged its fill of fossil water. The feeder arms swung loose. Voices called up and down the track. Steam vented from valves. The big horns sang once, twice, thrice. The pistons thrashed, the wheels spun. Freighted with lights and lives, *Catherine of Tharsis* glided slowly past her.

Grandmother Taal watched the red taillights curve out of sight around the bend in the track. She stepped out of concealment. By the light of the moonring, she took a reading from her pocket *vade-mecum*. The timetable function told her the 22:50 Triskander-Grand Valley Limited Night Service would be on the upline in eighty minutes. Time enough. She began to walk. She laid the first detonator on the upline switchover. Vertebrae protested as she straightened up. The night was working into her marrow. She found a pair of fingerless gloves and pulled them on. Warm hands fool a cold body. She laid the second detonator a twenty-minute walk upline by the *vade-mecum* clock. The service lights of Muchanga Water Station had receded into the great dark, a dirty, low constellation. She thought a bit about the flee-worthy things in the dark. Onward.

She heard an explosion behind her. She turned. Too soon, too close . . . Grandmother Taal fumbled in her infinity bag. Keys, sweets, small ladylike weapons, items of food, coins, charms, vials of scented waters, comfits, hair pins and old-fashioned jewellery, hard edges of very large machines. Where was it? Damn infundibular folding dimensions.

The second detonator went off. She saw its brief sharp flare close to the ground, eclipsed by wheels. She began to walk very quickly, counting *one* thousand *two* thousand *three* thousand *four* thousand . . . There. Her fingers curled around the shaft of the thermite flare. *Fifteen* thousand *sixteen* thousand . . . So dark, so damned dark, no light from all those stupid, wasted stars, and so cold; one frosty sleeper, one unseated trackbed, one loose tie, she could fall, and that would be . . . *Twenty-two* thousand *twenty-three* thousand *twenty-four* thousand . . . Boom.

The last detonator. He was coming fast, too fast. There must have been delays down the line in Margaret Land, he was making up time on the empty Oxus section.

She turned, held the flare at arm's length, pulled the ripcord. The metal cap flipped off. The thermite mixture coughed, spat sparks. A low flare guttered, teetered on the edge of extinction in the wind, then caught. A blade of searing white flame leaped from the casing. Grandmother Taal faced down the night train to Grand Valley with a sword of light. She could see the headlamp, cutting a curve through the night. The wheels beat, the horns declared their impatience with all that might impede them. Grandmother Taal held her sword firm before her face. See it. They must see it. But she could not hear brakes. She could not hear the chunter of an Engineer throwing the drive into reverse, the shriek of the emergency steam release. She tried to remember how much fire there was in the standard Bethlehem Ares Railroads signal flare. The light expanded before, swallowing her like the hypnotising eyes of a speed-snake bewitching a Syrtis hare. The world around her was white, the horns bellowed, *"This is the Triskander-Grand Valley Limited, out of my way."* He wasn't stopping. He wasn't stopping. Brakes. She heard brakes. Sparks cascaded from the agonised steel. Geysers of steam jetted from the piston valves. The horns yelled at her, then fell silent. The engine stood motionless before her. She could have reached out and touched the cow-catcher.

The flame guttered out in dismal sparks. Grandmother Taal flung the empty casing away from her. She looked defiantly up into the great white light.

"I am Taal Chordant Joy-of-May Asiim Engineer 10th, of *Catherine of Tharsis*!" she declared. "In the name of all Engineers, I claim Uncle Billy!"

A distant voice shouted down.

"How about you, Cousin Taal Engineer! Welcome to *Five Great Stones*. Come aboard."

Dark figures were already weaving through the seething white spotlight to her assistance.

*a*colytes in plum opened the filigree gates of the hand-cranked elevator and demurely ushered Sweetness and Serpio into a short corridor. More acolytes waited by a tall pair of arched double doors worked with a pattern of twining tree branches and roots. The acolytes were young, pudding-bowl cropped, puppyish. Their plum pants were too short around the ankles and their plum tops too tall around the collar.

"Hiya," Sweetness said as they swung open the double doors. They smiled.

The audience chamber of Devastation Harx occupied the uppermost chord of the flying cathedral. It was a glassene dome, transparent to heaven. Little webs of sand clung to the corners of the ribbing, souvenirs from when the machine—or was it a building, Sweetness wondered, accustomed to dual-purpose artifacts—had lain buried under the great sand. What was not transparent was wood. Wooden floor, clicky under Sweetness's desert boots. Wooden furniture—a horseshoe-shaped table and thirteen chairs, all alike and elegantly unostentatious. Wooden cressets, bearing double-handfuls of bioluminescence. Wooden buttresses arching overhead, spreading finger-twigs in a complex interwoven vaulting. Sweetness imagined herself standing in a forest under a winter sky. The audience chamber smelled of wax polish.

If you wandered close to the wooden perimeter handrail you could see the flanks of the lift canopy spreading out around you like old women's skirts. You could also see that you were several hundred metres above the ground. To a railway girl who had only ever flown in her dreams, it was hypnotically disconcerting. The cathedral was moving over an expanse of old chaotic terrain that had escaped the manforming. The raw stuff of the earth lay heaped and unsorted like effects at a Deuteronomy funeral. Red rock clawed for

Sweetness; any and every part of this sharp-edged land could pierce and flay this flying circus like a carnival balloon on a barbed-wire fence. The play of sun and shadow over the long, knife-blade valleys striped the land like an Argyre hunting cat. The ground rippled like sand in a shallow river. Sweetness felt herself dragged to the rail, to contemplate the long slide down the side of the airship, the terminal plummet to end shredded by stone knives. It was a nastily delicious fantasy.

"You know, if men could fly like birds, I don't think we would really bother doing anything else." The voice was low and soft and almost accentless. It used the words slowly, as if it weighing and parcelling each. "Everyone, at some time, wonders what it would be like to jump." Devastation Harx was one of those people who are not what you expect but, when you see them, they so utterly refute your mental image that you can no longer recall what it was you had expected. The face perfectly fitted the voice: late twenties, grey-haired, refined, a hint of epicene to take the edge off crude handsome; lips a little full, as if this face had once belonged to a cruel teen-something who had latterly found a better way. Not over tall, nor over small. Medium framed, no obvious body fat but not gaunt. He had bearing. Poise. A trained stance. He carried his hands as if he knew what to do with them. His left held a black swagger-cane, capped each end with silver. It looked as if it might contain a sword. But best, Sweetness observed, he wore a very killer suit. Soft, light-swallowing black. The frock coat was frogged with silver. His white shirt was clasped with a silver collar brooch. Exactly the same amount of cuff peeped from the coat sleeves. It was not a thing Sweetness had consciously considered until then, but it was now obvious that people who call themselves names like Devastation Harx—he could be no other—need good tailors.

"I am Devastation Harx," the elegant man said. He offered a hand. Sweetness looked around for Serpio. He was seated at the table. A moment of panic, then she took the hand and, because the suit was so good, she curtsied.

"Sweetness Octave Glorious Honey-Bun Asiim Engineer 12th."

"A fine name. Well, I am delighted to meet you, Sweetness Octave Glorious Honey-Bun Asiim Engineer 12th. And you . . ."

He gave a short bow somewhere just off Sweetness's port flank. She squirmed away, frowned. Devastation Harx seemed to be waiting for something from her.

"Oh. This is, well, I call her Little Pretty One."

"Pleased to make your acquaintance," Devastation Harx said.

All right, if that's how you want to play it, Sweetness thought. *Nice guy/guy-with-weird-powers.*

But he had nice manners. He pulled a chair out for Sweetness at the horseshoe-shaped table. Without any evident summons, more plum acolytes brought fruit and bread.

"I'm sure you're hungry. The desert's not exactly conducive to gastronomy."

Sweetness fell on the fruit bowl. She noticed that Serpio wasn't eating but the gnaw in her belly said, *ask questions later*. She gorged. Devastation Harx smiled.

"This is some burg," Sweetness said, mouth full of pears.

"The power of mail order," Devastation Harx said.

"You built all this?"

"From remote religion. We've always had a strong distance-supply industry in our society; School of the Air, Flying Doctors, Travelling Inseminators, Wandering Miracle Shows, the Universal Pantechnicon Catalogue. We're a geographically dispersed people—as I'm sure you appreciate. It was the next logical step, mail-order religion. Why not a Church of the Air? Literally."

Sweetness poured a glass of water, held it up to the light, frowned, demurely dropped in a sterilising tablet.

"It's always wise not to trust the water," Devastation Harx said indulgently. He watched Sweetness cram down more fruit. "So, your, ah, attachment?"

Sweetness cleared her gob with chlorinated water.

"She's my sister."

"She is?"

"We were joined."

"You still are."

"At birth."

"I see. But now you're . . ."

"Separated."

"But only physically. Not . . . psychically."

"Well, I know she's always there, but I can't see her, not like you can. I can only see her in mirrors."

"Yes, that's often the way of it. Mirrors reflect so much more than just crude physical likeness, don't you think? They reflect how we feel about what we are, they reflect truths, they can reflect illusions, they reflect our hopes and fears for the future, the marks of our histories, they show us our selves as we can never see them. A lot of magic for a mere half-silvered glass."

"Is this part of your religion or something?"

"More 'or something,'" Devastation Harx said. "So, have you had enough yet? Do you want any more?"

Sweetness looked round at the lifter of peels, skins and cores.

"No, I think that's me."

"Good." Devastation Harx stood up. "In that case, allow me to take you on the conducted tour. I don't get many visitors and I like to show the old place off. It's not everyone gets a flying cathedral."

He was already halfway to the double doors. He extended a hand to Sweetness and Serpio. The doors were already swinging open. Sweetness caught a wisp of plum.

"So you get all this by mail order?" Sweetness whispered to Serpio as they fell in behind Devastation Harx.

"It's good value," Serpio said.

"You can say that again."

"Bottom up," Devastation Harx, ushering his guests into the lift. "Level one, please." A plum acolyte closed the gates, a second began to turn a crank.

"You've a lot of these people," Sweetness commented as the cage swayed then began its descent.

"It's how things get done," Devastation Harx. "I'm sure Novice Waymender has told you that we reject unthinking dependence on dumb machines. Here everything is done by human labour."

"Everything?"

The filigree cage was descending through the main lift body; a cavernous chamber ribbed and strutted with lightweight construction beams. Overstuffed bladders of helium were wedged painfully between them like bloated hookers in too-tight suspenders.

"Stop here," Devastation Harx commanded. The acolyte pulled on a brass brake and flung the door open on a railed catwalk between the pillowy lift bags. "Come and see." In places Sweetness had to duck down between straining sacks pushed flatly against each other like inflated breasts.

"How much did they charge you for this?" she said to Serpio.

"Three hundred dollars over two years, monthly debit."

"I'd ask for my money back."

"The dignity of labour," Devastation Harx announced as he opened a studded door into a teat of a cabin dangling from the rim of the canopy. Twenty acolytes on twenty bicycles pumped away at pedals. Gear trains and drive bands turned a big rotor shaft above Sweetness's head. Through the glass she saw propellers blur. The power units wore plum cycling shorts and sweat bands and the glum look of intense youth. They all looked up and smiled as one as Devastation Harx introduced them as Motility Unit 3. Sweetness shuddered. "Don't be so liberal," Devastation Harx said. "Do you think any of them would be here if they didn't want to do it? I won't have pressed men around me. Idealism appeals to youth. They take turns. One week on, four weeks off. Democracy of employment. What do you think we are? We should get where we're going by our own efforts, shouldn't we?"

As the elevator resumed its descent, Devastation Harx said, casually, "So, how do you know it's your sister?"

"You know your own sister."

"Yes. I'm sure you do, but forgive me, you were together for a very little time."

Sweetness suddenly felt outnumbered in the small fragile elevator.

"Has he been telling you stuff about me?"

"We've been in contact," Serpio said.

"You never told me."

Serpio tapped his occluded eye.

"You see," Devastation Harx continued, "you say she's the ghost of your sister, who tragically died on the operating table but, well, as a rule, religious people don't believe in ghosts."

"Well then, what is she?"

"Remember when I asked you about vinculum theory and string processors?" Serpio said.

"You told her that?" Devastation Harx said.

"You should be proud of this one," Sweetness said. "He's got all the stuff off perfect. So, go on."

"In a minute," Devastation Harx said. "Tour continues."

The elevator touched bottom. Devastation Harx led his guests along a curving corridor.

"Post room," he said, throwing open a door on to a room where people in purple milled around a long table piled with envelopes, labelling machines and plastic crates filled with brochures, tracts and three-fold flyers. All Swing Radio blared. "Heart of the Empire. As soon as we hit Molesworth we'll do a mail-drop."

"So you're saying," Sweetness went on as the door closed on King Jupe and his Mint Juleps, "That my sister isn't my sister at all. That she's some kind of angel that's got attached to me."

"Not any sort of angel . . ." Serpio began and promptly tripped over.

"Careful," Devastation Harx admonished. He helped the trackboy up but Sweetness could have sworn she saw the tip of his swagger-stick flick out and tangle itself between Serpio's ankles. "Must be turbulence. You get odd thermals coming up off the old terrain." He flung open another door. "Central processing."

A starkly rectangular room, sinisterly underlit by floor-lights, was filled rank upon rank with wooden *prie-dieus*. Each bore an acolyte devoutly bent over a wooden abacus. Fingers flicked, beads ricocheted. The air was filled with soft clicking, like a locust army mustering.

"Simple, efficient and good for eye-hand coordination."

The bead-counters did not look up as their guru passed up an aisle. Some moved their lips silently, eyes reading the shifting digits.

"Data Storage is next door. You haven't signed on for my 'Be a Master of Memory' course, have you?" That, to Serpio. To Sweetness: "People don't realise half their potential. Entire human faculties atrophy and rot because we hand them over to machines. That, pretty much in a nutshell, is my philosophy. A human world for a human species."

Sweetness looked around at the human calculus.

"Who feeds everyone?" she asked. "And who makes all the purple gear? And what do you do with the night-soil?"

Devastation Harx clapped his hands softly in delight.

"I so enjoy trainpeople. They've such a stubbornly pragmatic bent."

"You've got trainpeople?"

A door at the far end of Central Processing took them back into the *circulare* corridor. It seemed to Sweetness that it took them back to exactly the point they had left. They processed on.

"I've got every kind of people. Our motto." It was inlaid in marquetry in the wooden wall panelling, bird's-eye maple and gnarled walnut on ash.

"'We're no angels.' Hah."

"Then again," Devastation Harx said thoughtfully, "Trainpeople do live a little too close to their machines."

"So, what is it with you and these angels, who you say aren't really angels at all, then?"

"What it is, Ms. Engineer, is, I intend to fight a war against the angels."

Sweetness stopped dead.

"You what?"

Devastation Harx turned to face her. He rested his hands on the ferule of his cane. Sweetness noticed that Serpio was now standing behind him. *Airship, mad-lands, big desert, three kilometres straight down*, she thought. *How can I make these into an escape plan that doesn't involve me falling to my death?*

"I thought I'd made myself quite clear. I intend to engage these angels—who, as you observed, are nothing of the sort—in battle. And I intend to defeat them."

Sweetness laughed. It was louder than she had intended, and nastier.

"Let me get this straight. There's about two hundred and fifty thousand angels up there? Like so many they make a ring round the world? That's not to mention all the ones that got left behind down here. They've got big sky mirrors and lasers and particle beams and superconducting magnets and probably loads of other stuff I can't even think of. They keep the weather going. They keep the UV from frying us like *nimki*. They keep the air in. They throw comets around. They go Bedzo and the world disappears. And you go up against these people with an inflatable bouncy church, a mail-order department, a couple of hundred abacuses and a pile of dysfunctional cyclists in purple, and you win?"

"Yes," Devastation Harx said in that tone of you-know-nothing-*really*-nothing adults know infuriates teenagers.

"I want a parachute, now."

"Ms. Engineer . . ."

"No, you wait." She turned to Serpio. "This was not part of the deal. The deal was we both run away from what we hate and we go and get a good life somewhere and maybe we end up together or maybe we don't but whatever, it absolutely did not say I get hijacked by some mail-order messiah in a flying mushroom and end up crisped by partacs. You know something? I think I made a mistake with you, Serpio. I think . . . I think you arranged all this." The realisation was marvellous and liberating. There is a strong joy, Sweetness discovered, in understanding your own utter gullibility. "You did! You bastard! You had this all planned. You took one look at me—at us—and it all fitted into some big master plan and you called up Harx-boy here and he said, bring her on. I cannot believe I ever even thought about sleeping with you. And I did. A bit. Not now. You're not a good person. Go and put your purple on, freak-eye."

While they were just thoughts, Sweetness had known her last two words were unforgivable. Two fingers poked clean and hard in the cataract. But she said them anyway, and whatever had begun at Great Oxus, they ended. From here on she was on her own. For a moment she thought Serpio might hit her. Devastation Harx, too, read the balled aggression in shoulders and neck and fists.

"I think it'd be better if you left us for a while," he said. "We'll meet up with you when Ms. Engineer is in sweeter humour."

Face twisting as it does when you are hurt badly enough to cry but damned if you will in public, Serpio turned and walked with over-deliberate casualness down the curving corridor. He stopped once, to call back.

"So you thought about sleeping with me, then?"

"Like I said, it's all one big chapter of bad mistakes." They just kept coming out of her mouth, badder and badder and badder.

"Well, I didn't. And I'll tell you this, I wouldn't if you were the last woman in the world."

"You would say that!" Sweetness sent her final dart cannoning round the corridor walls after him. She did not see if it struck. Her and Harx now. That was always the way he intended to play it, she realised. Play it, and me. She said, feistily, "So, how do you achieve this prodigy?"

"With the help of your invisible friend," Devastation Harx said. "Who, as you've probably guessed, is considerably more powerful than you thought, and definitely not your Siamese twin sister. I think it's time you got to see what she's really like. This way."

A section of ash pivoted under his palm. Sweetness stepped through the wall after Devastation Harx, and into herselves. Dozens of Sweetnesses. A multiplicity of Sweetnesses. A plethora, a myriad, a host, a horde, an infinite regress of Sweetnesses.

"Woo," she said, immersed in mirrors.

"I did say there was a great spirituality in reflections," fifty Devastation Harxs said at once.

For the first few minutes Sweetness took the rare opportunity to study herself from every aspect. She frowned at her eyebrows. She tugged critically at her hair. She rolled her shoulders to try to make better of her boobs. She tightened, relaxed, tightened, relaxed her ass-cheeks and seemed pleased at the result. She looked down at her foreshortened self in the floor mirrors and grinned. She waved to her selves. She made faces. She struck attitudes. She led a dozen Sweetnesses in a step-perfect dance. Then she remembered she was supposed to be feeling angry about Serpio the Bastard, and asked, "Where's the way out?"

"It's around somewhere," Devastation Harx's voice said behind her. She spun. All she caught of him were twenty left sleeves, hands and sticks vanishing kaleidoscopically into the corners where mirrors met.

"Hey!"

"I seem to be over here." Far off among the reflections of Sweetnesses and the reflections of mirrors, a Devastation Harx homunculus waved.

"You wait for me, right?" Sweetness ran toward the distant image. The mirrors were nested chamber within chamber. Sweetness pounded between the pivoting mirrors. Thousands of other selves fled on every side. Panels opened and closed, slid apart, slid to behind her, but always Devastation Harx was a tiny, beckoning figure in the mirror within the next mirror within the next. She pursued, he fled without moving. A voice called her name. Her voice. She stopped dead. The walls rearranged themselves around her.

"Who?" she asked. One of her reflections did not move its lips. Sweetness went up to it. It remained motionless among the shifting selves.

"What are you doing here?"

"It's mirrors, isn't it?"

Sweetness frowned, studied the apparition.

"What happened to the rules? Rules are, you're supposed to wear . . ."

"What were you wearing yesterday, fashion victim? Sweetness, listen, this is not . . ."

"Ms. Engineer . . ."

The unfamiliar distracted her. Devastation Harx suddenly stood at her elbow. He turned on his side, became one dimensional, vanished into a line of silvering as a mirror panel pivoted away from her. Sweetness saw reflections of the dark, elegant man flick mirror to mirror to mirror into the infinite regress of the maze. She turned back to her familiar.

"Ell Pee."

All the Sweetness Asiim Engineers moved their lips in perfect synch.

"Don't mess me around."

I'm not, said a voice behind her. Sweetness whirled.

"Where are you?"

She was alone with her seeming selves. She moved slowly. Her images moved with her. Mirror panels swung, opening brief gateways into deeper illusion.

Raise your left arm, Little Pretty One whispered. A hundred Sweetnesses said aye. One did not. As Sweetness moved toward her twin, the panel slowly turned Little Pretty One away from her.

"No!" she shouted. It was then that she discovered that the mirrors reflected sound as well as light. Her yell focused back on her from a hundred reflecting surfaces, amplified and distorted and phase shifted so that waves of roar broke over her, sent her cowering, like the rare times when the ionospheric interceptors stooped low to practise terrain-kissing manoeuvres over the empty quarters of the pole.

As Little Pretty One turned away from her, Devastation Harx turned toward her.

"Okay. I'm not finding this funny. So, this is what happens. You stop messing around with Little Pretty One, then you get me out of here."

"Hm," Devastation Harx mused. "Part two, absolutely. Soon as I possibly can; frankly, my dear, you're a trying guest. No manners, at all. Part one, well, I'm afraid not. I need your alleged twin."

Sweetness, came softly bouncing from several directions at once, like an experiment in quantum optics. This time Sweetness was not distracted. She punched out, straight left, hard, right between the eyes. Devastation Harx's head exploded. Sweetness cried out. The mirror disintegrated into a thousand shards of herself. They fell in a tinkling crash. Blood counted down Sweetness's bunched knuckles and dropped to the floor. She sucked her fluids, tasted brass and sweetness.

"And no respect for the property, either," Devastation Harx chided, from deep within the mirror maze.

"Where are you?" Sweetness yelled.

Here, said a still small voice in the head. Sweetness closed her eyes, turned around until the voice seemed to speak squarely to her.

"What's going on?" she whispered.

"Help me," Little Pretty One said. "He's trying to draw me out of you, lose me among the mirrors."

"What? Who? Harx? Why?"

"I guess you could say, I'm not exactly who you think."

"He said . . ."

"Look, are we going to argue this, or are you going to try to find me?"

"I can't even find myself, never mind you."

Sweetness opened her eyes. She confronted herself, multiplied. A thousand Sweetnesses waltzed and turned in the maze of mirrors. She gave a hiss of exasperation, fingers knotted in her hair.

"Mother'a'mercy!"

She noticed her shirt cuffs. A shrug; the desert-dusty, sweat-ringed shirt was slipped off. Two sharp tugs tore off the sleeves. One she wrapped around her bleeding knuckles. Nine hundred and ninety-nine bare-armed bloody

Sweetnesses stared at each other. At the very left corner of the very rear rank, one stood with buttoned cuffs, finger-perfect.

"I see ya!" Bare arms raised, Sweetness bulled her way through mobs of illusions. She seized the edges of mirrors and wrestled döppelgangers aside. She crashed headlong through phalanxes of images. Always, she kept the Sweetness in yesterday's clothes square before her. Mirror by mirror, it receded, but Sweetness was faster and surer.

"Sweetness." Among the chorus of dissimulations, Little Pretty One was like the single blue thread in a beige prayer shawl. "I've something to tell you." Closer now, only the mirror beyond the next mirror beyond the next mirror. "I'm not your sister." Catching up. She was catching up. "I'm not really from this world at all, well, actually, I am, but that's kind of complicated." Sweetness charged into a decagonal chamber of mirrors. Whisper of aluminium on glass: she turned, a mirror slid across the entrance. Each mirror held the image of Little Pretty One.

"So who the hell are you, then?" Sweetness gasped. Sweat beaded juicily down her ribs. The ten Little Pretty Ones looked back at her.

"I'm Catherine of Tharsis," they said.

"She's absolutely right, you know," Devastation Harx said from behind her as Sweetness panted and stared, senseless with confusion.

Sweetness turned to the sound of the voice. Devastation Harx stood resting a languid hand on the top of a mirror. He twisted it toward him. The nine remaining Little Pretty Ones vanished.

"It was this one." He unhooked a clasp. The mirror rolled up like a flapping cartoon comedy blind. Sweetness had one glimpse of Little Pretty One's mouth and eyes, open in shock, then the flying preacher squeezed the scroll of mirror into a stubby tube, screwed it into a verdigrised metal canopic jar and screwed on a top like a winged helmet. "I may not command angels, but I do command the one who commands the angels. I think that makes it a fair fight."

She dived for him. Her clawed fingers raked through Devastation Harx like a hunting merlin sliding down the air. She hit the glass floor hard. Winded. Sweetness rolled on her back. Devastation Harx was a tiny figure silhouetted against the glowing rectangle of a daylit door. Sun glinted from his silver froggings. He pointed the copper jar at Sweetness.

"Did anyone ever tell you, Ms. Engineer, not to trust too much to appearances? Well, I have what I need, and you, I'm afraid, are quite surplus to requirements." He took an object like a large pear with a clockwork key in the top from inside his frock coat. "Goodbye, Ms. Engineer." He turned the big brass key. Sweetness felt the floor shift beneath her. She scrabbled for fingerholds but the glass sheets of the mirror maze floor were fitted with molecular precision. She was slipping, sliding. Sweetness snatched at mirror frames but the floor was now past thirty degrees and gravity was drawing her ever faster downward. A slit of light appeared beneath her feet, a line of white that widened into a slot of red, then opened on to á cinema screen of red desert. With a wail, Sweetness Octave Glorious Honey-Bun Asiim Engineer 12th was spat from the hatch that had opened in the belly of Devastation Harx's flying cathedral like a gobbet of drool from Grandfather Bedzo's mouth. She arced gracefully through the air. *I'm flying*, she thought, and then, *stupid stupid stupid, birds fly, girls fall, I'm not flying, I'm falling. Out of the bottom of a big airship that, the last time you looked, was way up high over red rocks. This is it, Sweetness Octave Glorious Honey-Bun Asiim Engineer 12th. This is absolutely the last . . .* The ground emphatically interrupted her reverie. The thud might have convinced her she was dead; the pain told her she was not. She rolled on to her back, looked up and saw the belly hatch close, three metres above her. The whole bulk of Devastation Harx's mobile empire hovered above her, as if it had somehow, most surprisingly, grown out of her navel. Sweetness blinked, pained, stunned, dazed to find herself still alive. Dust milled up around her. Sudden wind tugged at her dreads. Propellers clanged down into vertical orientation. In their translucent teats, purple people wearing skin-hugging shorts leaned to their handlebars. Grit whipped Sweetness's face. The cathedral ascended away from her, like a dream lifting from you in the morning light. It turned to the southwest. Rotors swivelled to horizontal flight. Still climbing, Devastation Harx took his leave.

Sweetness pulled herself on to her elbows to watch the great cathedral disappear beyond the serrated rimrocks. Ribs grated. She coughed, no blood. No breakage. She looked at her feet. Then she looked at the world framed by her feet. From sole of her desert boots to near horizon was rippled red sand. Beyond that, reefs of harsh stone rose to the stripes of yellow and indigo evening cloud that barred the belly of the flying cathedral. Fingers, fists, twisted spires and candysticks of rock, so contorted and weathered they seemed less firmly connected to the ground than the clouds. She looked again at her ten-to-two feet. They seemed hopelessly inadequate for the landscape.

"Well," she said. "Terrific."

15

*D*azzled by winks of sun from the rim of the silver tea bowl, the boss tanager kept his herd in pace with the slow train. They were handsome beasts, Grandmother Taal admitted, grown sleek on the well-watered Quela rangelands. Muscles moved smoothly under close-fitting striped skins, like acrobatic carnival puncinellos. They had never felt the seat of man, but each bore a patterned plastic ear-tag: owned, numbered, one day to be herded by harrying autogryos, driven up ramps on to a train like this, then taken to the breaking fair at Tzaena-tzaena.

So much for the wide country and the wilds. Grandmother Taal set down the *maté* bowl, eclipsing the hypnotising blink of sun. The tanagers cantered on, hog-manes bristling, ownership tags rattling. Herd things like to run. Such is their weakness.

The observation car was a glassene cyst on the spine of the last carriage of the ambling High Plains Cruiser, an eccentric rural service out of Hagios Evangelis that stopped at every hillock and hollow before finally creaking to a terminus at Mosquiteaux on the edge of the Big Red. People got on, rode a time, got off, so that the train, though it had many passengers, was never busy. Few went the whole distance. Grandmother Taal was one such transient. The Triskander-Grand Valley Limited Night had made an unscheduled request stop at Strophé, where she had thumbed down the High Plains Cruiser fifty kilometres into its journey. She would ride this train as far as signal NW two twenty-four, then pull an Uncle Billy on the twenty twenty-seven fast mail across the eroded craterlands of Old Deuteronomy.

Therefore, the observation car was sparsely populated. Grandmother Taal had a club booth to herself, to rest her feet on the leatherette banquette, sip her *maté* through a silver straw, watch the frankly uninspiring landscape flow past, doze and snore knowing that her nearest neighbour, a florid-faced milch-man in quaintly traditional bib-suit and paddy-hat, was five rows away and deeply engaged with the stock prices in the daily gazette. Five rows ahead of him a group of elderly people in funeral whites played cards and nodded gravely to each other. The car's only other occupants were a family of musicians by the down stairs, making quiet tunes with guitar, zither, tabla and soft handclaps. Strange people, musicians; so much of their souls given out to their creatures of wood and skin and metal, that demanded so terrible a possession when they took them up to play.

Passenger, she decided, is another thing entirely from track, but by no means inferior. She looked out at the rolling green grass and the cantering tanagers. Their perfect mindlessness lulled her off to sleep.

A tinny clink woke her. A boy's face loomed over hers, close enough to read his teeth stains. He held up the *maté* straw and set it in the tin bowl. Hairbrush epaulettes and crimson rick-rack around his lapels identified him as a Stuard.

"More *maté* for madam?" He held up a long-handled biggin. She could tell from the corners of the Stuard boy's mouth that between one cup of *maté* and its refill, word of the Asiim Engineers' disgrace had passed down the High Plains line.

"If you please."

He refilled the enamelled tin bowl with the aromatic tea. Grandmother Taal fished in her bottomless bag for centavos. The Stuard boy held up his hand, scandalised as if she had offered him her own mummified excrement.

"There is no charge, madam Engineer."

Grandmother Taal gave his back her oldest and vilest Engineer gestures as he unctuously worked his way down the aisle. The big-faced milch-man had been replaced by an anaemic couple who touched each other's hands every few seconds. The funeral party had left to perform their obsequies. Across the aisle from their pitch was a sallow-faced young man in a cartwheel hat and duster coat buttoned to the throat. The musicians had opened wicker lunch boxes and were feeding forkfuls of noodles to the tiniest. The tanagers had galloped elsewhere, and the view from the window was of dreary altiplano freckled with upright Deuteronomy farms. The folding *vade-mecum* told her North West two twenty-four was hours yet at this gentle plod across the trampas. Too dull, this land, these people, this life, for anything other than sleep.

A start. She felt the face before she saw it, or heard the voice. That warm, slightly oily feeling of being observed without your knowledge or permission, that you have been observed for some time. Smell of a watching face. Grandmother Taal opened an eye.

"Madam, your *maté* has grown cold."

In her eye was a dapper man of early middle years, slim as a rapier, dressed in a frock suit of crushed plum. He wore no hat, but his hair had been greased and slicked until it shone like gloss paint. Likewise, two long mustachios, waxed and tweaked to the sheen of ebony, swooped away from his upper lip. Grandmother Taal opened her other eye, all the better to three-dee this wonder. Hollow-cheeked, pale, almost olive-skinned. Poor complexion, cratered with orange-peel skin and the memories of childhood pox-scratchings. Eyebrows shaved to the merest *hint* of expressivity. Over his left eye, a brown leather patch. He carried a cane almost as slender and sharp as his mustachios. He wore gloves.

"I don't care much for the *maté*," Grandmother Taal said. "It is bitter. It has been stewed."

"Yes," the man said thoughtfully. "The service on this route is substandard. I may write to the Line Manager."

"You would be better employed writing to the chief Stuard."

"Ah!" The man brightened perceptibly. "You have some knowledge of the ways of the iron road. Are you perhaps, track?"

"I am Taal Chordant Joy-of-May Asiim Engineer of *Catherine of Tharsis*. Now, introduce yourself, or is the place you hail from so negligent of manners that a lady must give her name to a gentleman?"

The young man laughed and bowed.

"I am Cyrene Caius Ankhatiel Ree, and I am a gentleman of India, in Axidy, where, I am glad to say, etiquette flourishes yet."

Grandmother Taal harrumphed. Middle-aged though his complexion might be, he was still young, callow, vain, long-winded and self-regarding enough to be the most interesting thing on and around the High Plains Cruiser.

"Well, sit yourself down, as that's clearly what you're here to ask."

"You preempt me, madam."

He parted the tails of his coat and settled into the club chair opposite. He crossed his legs at the knee in a way Grandmother Taal had always thought effeminate and affected.

"So, Cyrene Caius Ankhatiel Ree, where are you travelling aboard the High Plains Cruiser?"

He rested his hands on the handle of his stick.

"Why, precisely nowhere, madam."

"You travel for its own sake?"

"I travel for the sake of gambling."

"A notorious vice."

"Some say. Some say. But they are invariably the ones who have not heard the stakes I offer."

"I am forty-two years a-sinning, sir. A billion miles I've travelled and a billion sights I've seen. I am mother to a dynasty, what stake could possibly entice me?"

By a sleight of hand, one lemon-gloved palm suddenly held a deck of cards.

"Years, madam. Years."

The card backs bore the Amshastria Evenant, dancing one-footed, with her hourglass and plague bottle and halo of skulls. A flick of the fingers and the gambler spread the cards on the tea table in a wide fan. He ran his thumb along the spread, raising a short, sharp wave.

"Ridiculous, young man."

He squared the deck, riffled and bridged it twice, dealt a swift hand, three down.

"Five card, two up." He scooped up his hand, fanned them. The allure of the face-down card is irresistible. Against will and wisdom, Grandmother sneaked a peek. Three of Blades, three of Wasps, ten of Hands.

"Bet two," Cyrene Ree said.

"Two what?"

"As I said, madam, years."

Nonsense, the inner angel of grandmothers said, but an older, sharper devil said, aloud, "Two it is, then."

Cyrene twisted her a card.

"Madam has a ten of Cash. And for myself?"

Grandmother Taal turned over the top card of the deck.

"The Spice of Wasps."

"Raise another one."

"*Parvue* your one, and another one."

"Madam is getting the feel of the game," Cyrene said, twisting her her final card. "Cash, three. And I get . . ."

"Hieros of Blades."

"An ill-omened card, I fear. *Vue.*"

Grandmother Taal turned over her hand.

"Full house, three and tens."

Cyrene pursed his lips.

"I am well beaten. Two pairs." He turned them up, sevens and Spices. "You win."

Grandmother Taal gasped. Like a gush of stale breath or bad blood, four years went out of her. The stiffness and discomforts that are so much part of a woman of forty-two that they seem almost geographical were erased. Muscles tightened beneath her skin. Bones moved to long-forgotten alignments. Liver blotches on the backs of her hands dwindled like desert rain in the sun. Forty-two no more, if Cyrene could be believed. A woman of thirty-eight. Less, if her luck held.

"There," Cyrene said. "That simple." Grandmother Taal studied him. Did the mustachios droop a little, were their tips, the highlights in his shining hair, a little greyed? Did lines sit deeper around the leather eye-patch, had the muscles of the face slackened and slumped?

"I think not," Grandmother Taal said, but four years were oxygen in her lungs, iron in her blood. Cyrene was already shuffling the cards.

"Another round?"

Grandmother Taal nodded. Cyrene dealt another hand. Grandmother Taal bet three years on a strong opening of two Duennas and the Boss of Wasps, twisted a trash four of Blades and an eight of Cash but still outbluffed Cyrene.

In twenty minutes and two dozen kilometres she had shed seven years.

This was electrifying, addictive stuff. *It's meant to be*, said forty-two years. *I know when to stop*, said thirty-five years.

"You must allow me the chance to make good my losses," Cyrene said, smiling.

"And me to consolidate my gains," Grandmother Taal said, and for the first time wondered what Cyrene's true age might be, if he were indeed what he claimed, an itinerant wagerer of years on the world's trunk lines.

The cards slid across the Formica-topped table. Again, a pair and a ten of Hands. Grandmother Taal anted two years. Cyrene immediately *parvued* and raised another five. Grandmother Taal twisted a second ten. Two pairs. Seven years. Forty-two, again, or twenty-eight.

"Raise two," Cyrene said.

"*Parvue*," Grandmother Taal snapped. Twenty-six, or forty-four. "Twist." Her third ten, in Blades. "*Vue*."

"What have you got?"

"Full house, tens and twos." She spread them slowly.

"Ah," said Cyrene the gambler. He turned up his hand. "Four eights."

Nine years fell on Grandmother Taal. She gave a small cry as bones sagged, tendons tautened, muscles withered, senses coarsened, aches and complaints flocked in. Looking at Cyrene—with difficulty, a cataract now clouded her right eye—he was as she had first seen him; more so, she thought, with an added gleam in his one eye and a new wave in his sleek hair. He held up the deck.

The gambler's dilemma. To take the loss, or play for it back. Easy to walk away with a whistle and a resolution when it is only money. Years of your life— years you can afford less than dollars—that is another thing. The problem with playing to get it back is that that is not enough. You play for more. You play for it all. Especially when the stakes are higher than you can afford, and no other game will offer them. *I am trapped*, Grandmother Taal thought, reaching to cut the cards. Trapped and fooled. Forty-four years, two of them by your own foolishness, and still you have not learned the smell of hustler.

The cards spun across the table and from that game on, Grandmother Taal could not win another hand. Cyrene bet small and sly, a year here, a half-year there, forcing her to fold on potentially strong cards because with every hand, she became less and less able to afford an ante war. And when she did call *vue* he always had the perfect play, as if that smile that deepened around the corners of his mouth did so because it knew how the cards would turn. There was a further handicap, with every year added to her, she became less and less able to play. She squinted at the patterns as Wasps melted into Blades, Bosses into Duennas, red into black. The rules kept slipping from her grasp, a full house beat what, and was beaten by what? Her fingers trembled as she tried to grip the flighty, silky treacherous things. Walnut knuckles ached. Yet play she must, ask for her draw in a voice she no longer recognised, turn over the cards one by one, lose another year in the hope of winning one back.

She had now lost all sense of how old she was. Flickering motes flocked at the edges of her field of vision. The observation car became filled with a cloying smell like rotting *maté* and unwashed bodies. Grandmother Taal knew they were the smells and shapes of death. This was how this smiling youth, firm cheeked and full-lipped, intended it to end. This, she suspected, was how he made his way across the world, swallowing lives, a year-vampire feeding on the elderly who, because they could not afford his stakes, craved them all the more.

"No," she mumbled, mouth filled with the yellow stumps of rotted teeth. "This is not how it ends."

"I'm sorry, did you say something?" Cyrene shuffled the deck with his quick and nimble gloved fingers. He dealt another round. "I say, shall we play for the big one? Enough of this prettying around. A decade rich enough for you? No? How about two?"

As the gambler dealt the cards, Grandmother Taal's attention became fixed more and more closely on Cyrene's eye-patch. Her sense for brown itchily insisted it concealed more than empty socket. If he could see the turn of the cards before they fell, this, her magic said, was where his power was centred. But a crumbling old woman could not hope to wrestle with a man in a stolen prime. But there were other ways. Ways perilous to a crumbling old woman, but worse not to attempt. She wedged her cards into the claw of her hand. Three Hieros.

"Two," she said. Cyrene smiled, and so did not observe Grandmother Taal slip the pin out of her hair. "Twist."

Spice of Wasps. Cyrene twisted a Boss of Blades.

"Hm. The Strife Card," he said, and so did not see Grandmother Taal begin to scratch the word *eye* into the back of her hand with the hairpin.

"Twist," she gritted. Curse of the Panarch on her hand, stop shaking! Stop shaking. The Hieros of Hands slid across the Formica. Four of a kind. Keep going. Keep going.

"And for myself," Cyrene said.

"Stop!" Grandmother Taal commanded. She held up her maimed hand. A bloody *eye* confronted the blind brown leather patch. Powers boiled between them. Grandmother Taal's hand shook. She could not hold it up any longer, it was heavy as pig iron, painful as rheumatism, her power was ended. Leather creaked. The eye-patch bulged. Cyrene's hands flew to keep it down but the strap snapped. The patch catapulted across the carriage. Cyrene let out a wail. Crouched in his eyesocket was a tiny metal homunculus, some machine-demon thing. It turned chromium mandibles on Grandmother Taal and made to leap to safety. Too slow. There was spirit yet in the ancient woman. Quick as thought, she rammed the silver *maté* straw into Cyrene's possessed eye-socket, straight through the belly of the demon-thing. Impaled, it crashed to the table, wailing like band-sawn tin. It staggered between the cards, clutching ineffectually at the impaling spear. It tripped over the stainless steel table trim and fell to the floor. Grandmother Taal's high-heeled boot lifted once and came down with a metallic crunch. She turned to face Cyrene, fumbling at his blind eye.

"You have blinded me!" he screeched. "You terrible old woman!"

"And you have cheated me," Grandmother Taal said. She laid down her hand. "Four Hieros. Now, shall we see what you have?" She twisted the top card. A second Boss. Looking Cyrene in his single eye, she said, "*Vue.*"

She flicked over the face-down cards. They were blank. As she stared at them, Grandmother Taal saw the patterns of other cards flicker over them before settling into the six-eyed Boss of Wasps and the top-hatted Boss of Cash.

"You are a despicable creature," Grandmother Taal said, feeling all her gambled years rush back into her. Infirmities slid from her like cast-off clothes. She felt herself growing, back beyond what she had been, five, ten, fifteen. She was *Amma* no longer, she was a vigorous, spry woman of twenty-seven. "And no gentleman!" Cyrene slumped back in his seat as the stolen years fell on him like a landslide. He withered. He aged. His body sagged, wrinkles grew up him like strangling vines. His hair greyed and vanished, his mustachios drooped impotently. The hand clutching the silver-tipped cane shrivelled into a claw. He dwindled inside his crushed velvet clothes.

He reached for his deck, his strength, his hope. Grandmother Taal scooped them out from under his grasp.

"No more!" she said. She stood up, opened the window and threw the cards out. They fluttered and spun in the slipstream; amshastrias and blankness.

"No!" Cyrene Ree cried and the cry became a thin, wheedling wail as, before Grandmother Taal's eyes, all the years that the gambler had stolen over his centuries of existence were returned. In a breath he crumbled, man to eyeless mummy to ragged skeleton to a pile of soil and humus. An empty suit of tailored clothes hung on the leatherette club chair. Brown dirt spilled from the sleeves, frilled collar and boot-tops. Grandmother Taal grimaced in distaste, rang the attendant bell to summon the impolite Stuard boy to tidy up the mess, moved to an empty seat and hunted a compact out of her bottomless bag to greet a face she had not seen in decades.

16

O n the third day, between delirium and dehydration, Sweetness hit the steel rail. She tripped over a crumbled concrete sleeper and fell on it. It burned her right cheek. She reeled back and left a strip of skin fused to the metal. That was how she knew it was real. It was the first experience she had been certain of in two days.

When her feet had given her no answer to being dropped from a height of three metres over a sterile red desert by an air-borne cathedral waltzing away over the horizon in a gaudy of purple clouds, conned out of what she half understood was her greatest asset—the woman who created the world—Sweetness Octave Glorious Honey-Bun Asiim Engineer 12th did an inventory.

Don't think bruised maybe cracked ribs. Don't think rim-rocks and rust. Don't think, nothing that even suggests something I recognise. Don't think which way? Don't think how much food and water? Don't think how soon the night, and how long and cold? All the answers have to be in this little black sack, so start there.

The sandwiches were long since mummified crescents but there were four bottles of oxygenated water. Sweetness set them out on the sand in front of her. With her pencil and paper she sat down to work out how many sips, then realised it was pointless without an idea of how long she would be walking, which was pointless without knowing where she was. And among the petty treasures, she had forgotten a simple map and compass.

One useful thing. Psalli's emergency spell. Lost in a desert, no map, no compass, night coming on, four bottles of water between you and the condors; that's an emergency. Sweetness unrolled the little scroll of paper, fastened with a hair-tie.

For Aid Beyond Comprehension in a Time of Direness, first light a beeswax candle . . .

What the hell kind of emergency spell is it that's picky about the kind of candle you light? Or even that you light a candle at all? Sweetness hauled out her all-weather lighter and a tampon. She lit the thread end. It burned enthusiastically, then sputtered at the wadded cotton.

"Then face the sun . . ." She did so. "Call three times, 'Aid me in my succour, Green Saint,' then blow out the candle and say, 'May my wish be granted.' Okay." She performed the recitations, blew on her light. The tampon guttered and expired in a curl of red embers and smoke. "May my wish be granted."

Sweetness sat down and waited for Aid Beyond Comprehension. To keep herself amused in a Time of Direness, she thought. You're lost in the middle of a desert without a map or a compass. You've got a radio. You're facing the sun, which is about two hands above the horizon. You're facing vaguely west, so most of the important stuff in the world is *that way*. Nine o'clock-ish. South. Walk and you'll hit something human sooner or later. If you roll over—cock piss bugger bum balls, it hurts!—and use the top of this pen as one sight and the top of that finger rock as another and hold real still, you can guess how quickly the sun's setting. Fast on the equator, slow up north. This season, hardly at all above the polar circle. Well, it's definitely moving, so I'm not that far north. About three minutes from top of pen to top of rock. That's up above the thirty degree line north. Where had that fly bastard Harx said they were going? Molesworth, for a mail run. That's Bequerelly, west-southwest from Therme. Now, your watch is still on Deuteronomy time. So, you tune the radio to a Deuteronomy station and listen for the Evening Angelus. *Star of the Evening, pale blue mother of men* . . . Then you find a place where you can see the horizon. It's okay to walk about a bit. The Help Beyond Comprehension isn't going to miss you out here. There's a gap in the shield-wall. Now count the time until the sun sets here. A few head-sums—how many degrees is it per minute? Three. And there it goes . . . Magic hour. Wooo, big blue. The rocks are so red, like they don't want to let the colour go. *No, no, it's mine, not the black's.* Eight minutes. So, you're mid Axidy, edge of Chryse. Not too many railway lines up here, which is arsebiscuits, but down south is Tempe and the thirty-degree orbital. That's a walk. You're going to sprout wings and fly? Getting night-wise. Best to walk in the night, sleep in the day. That sun'll cook you like a stripey penis on a Waymender barbecue. Let's not entertain that thought or those people. You're warm already on forehead and cheeks. Upper arms are stinging. Also, you'll drink less water. Snuggle up in your bag and sleep in the sun on the sand. So, Sweetness Octave Glorious Honey-Bun Asiim Engineer, best get booting. Wait wait wait. It's night. No sun. So, how will you know which way is south? Moonring's east–west, and south, but it goes all the way across the sky and a little error now can be days out. Can be leather and bones, Honey-Bun.

Wait. Your radio. That Deuteronomy station, it had been all fluttery and wowy and phasey, because they've only got low power transmitters and the mountains over to the east there interfere with the signal. No mountains to the south: so, pick up a Tempe Station—preferably one in a big place like Therme—and turn around until you get a clear signal. You're on beam. She'll lead you right into the Watering Rooms of the Great Bath itself.

As the last stolen light ebbed from the rim-rocks, Sweetness pulled Radio Pleasant out of the atmosphere. It twitched and chittered like a family of bats. Beneath the wheeling stars, Sweetness turned, listening to the airwaves. There. Honesto's Used Yute Mart. Treat Ye Better'n Ye Treat Yerself. For a great deal on pre-cared Dorts and Stavingers, call . . . She opened her eyes. The stars seemed to line up above her into a hunting arrow. *This way, traingirl.*

"Right, then," she decided. "South."

She shouldered her bag and began to walk. The Bakelite cat and the used spell she left as offerings to the Big Red.

The Big Red, in the big dark, was extremely boring. Those things that give character to deserts; heat, space, desolation, grandeur, an atomising sense of iso-lation in a vast terrain, are erased by night. Dark made it a dimensionless expanse of tough trekking. Sweetness pressed on at a steady speed, fast enough to give a sense of purpose, slow enough not to flag too soon and leave her demor-alised. To conserve the solar batteries, she listened in to Radio Pleasant only long enough to get a fix on due south. She sang songs from the shows. She recited chunks of the Evyn Psalmody. She counted from one to one thousand, then from two thousand back to one thousand. She took a sip of water and used it to explore as many aspects and crannies of her mouth as she could. She did seven times tables, eight times tables, all the way up to fifteen times tables. She engaged in convoluted games of word association, she formed great trains of thought, longer than any thousand-car-er out of Iron Mountain, then tried to trace back every step of the cognitive process to the originating engine. She wondered, when's this Aid Beyond Comprehension going to arrive? She took another furtive grab at the airwaves, adjusted her course, walked on. It was still astonishingly tedious. It was much later than she thought when the "Radio Pleasant Pre-Breakfast Show" timechecks started. She slithered down dune faces, slogged along heavy, sucking sifs and thought about people in Therme's tall tenements rolling over in their quilts for another five or sitting up and scratching or staring at their faces in the bathroom mirror or grumbling to their lovers over the morning bread and tea. *Have you any idea, Mr. Deejay, what this one of your listeners is doing?* When the edge of the world dipped beneath the sun, she unrolled her bag, found a sheltered place where the sand would not blow into her nostrils and remembered to set out the solar radio to recharge. Then she read a few pages of her unimproving book and was asleep before her powers of aesthetic discrimination could tell her they were excrement.

Sweat woke her. Sweetness licked the salt off her forearms and tried to find a sweet spot in the curve of soft sand that now seemed concrete. The next time she woke was with a searing headache from sunlight leaking through her permeable eyelids. Her face felt raw and sunburned. Sweetness wrapped a torn-off shirt-sleeve around her head and rolled over again, half stifled. The third time she woke, it was the hunger. She willed it down but it would not be so easily beaten. Sweetness tried eating pages of her unimproving book, washed down with sips of water. They stayed the belly gnaw. The last time she woke the sun was two fingers above the western rim rocks. Time to get up, get up, get on, get out.

Dizzy with hunger and headache, Sweetness took a bearing on Radio Pleasant. She had come a hair off true, a shift to the left brought her on to the way south. This place she had spent the day looked so similar to the one she had left yesterday—the sand so rippled, the rocks so crumbled and red, the sky so piercingly blue—she might not have moved at all. *Have not moved at all*, whispered a small, black, despairing demon. It took a major effort of will to lift one foot and place it ahead of the other, but she managed it. Belly full of yellow press, she had to. To listen to the demon was death.

That second night, death seemed a fine thing. Much of the time she was crazy, staggering and weaving under the hurtling scraps of moon, crawling up slip-sliding dune-faces, clutching at the sand running away between her fingers, rolling downslope, at some point recovering sense enough to reckon she had wandered far off course and checking her position against the cool midnight grooves of Radio Pleasant's "Wind-down with Willem." The ridiculous notion that *down there* people were toasting each other with wine and throwing money to band leaders and sending compliment slips to chefs and fumbling with each other's underwear in cars gave her the idea. Things I will do when I get to Therme.

Top of the list. Wash my hair. She could smell it. Worse, she could not get away from it. Bad bad bad bad bad when you can smell your own hair. Worse when it sticks to you. *Aghhh.* Hair wash. No questions, *numero uno*. And a bath. Maybe together. No problem in Therme. It's a spa town. So, hydrotherapy then. Deep bath, with all those healing oils and minerals from the volcanic vents. Like for several hours. And a glass of wine as light and clear as water, so cold the condensation runs down the outside, across the foot, then down your arm and you lick it off. Oh yes. Licking things off. Some boy with nice muscles and cute eye make-up to run a hose up and down you. How does that feel, Miss Engineer? Oh ah, oohhh, ahhh. She'd scandalise him. But not before he'd shampooed her hair, with a good, deep, finger motion, right down to the roots, *twice* and conditioner, and a warm blow dry—not a hot one, she'd had enough hot air blowing in her face for any lifetime. Yes, a bath, with oils and minerals and a hose down and a body scrub and when you've got every *molecule* of rust and silicon out of you, a table on a verandah with a view over the mud gardens, and you wearing nothing but a shortie silkie robe, and someone bringing you fish. Yes, fish, fresh caught, cooked in a steam vent.

Good game, the little black one said. Fine game, but what's the point? You're not going to get these things. They're not going to happen. You're going to kneel down and bend over and press your forehead to the sand and wait for a storm to cover you over.

She stopped in the middle of the black desert.

"Where is my Help Beyond Comprehension?" she roared at the sky.

"Where is it where is it where is it?"

Down on the south side of the sky, lasers kindled the horizon green; a Praesidium Sailship setting out on its long, slow loop back to Motherworld, a fair wind of coherent light behind it.

Sun woke her. Sun should not have, not this hot, not this high. The backs of her arms, her exposed ankles, were burning. Sweetness rolled on to her back.

Hot sand on scorched skin. She blinked up into the white atom of the sun. How what why where? The last thing she remembered . . . the last thing she remembered . . . Never mind what you do or don't remember! Get out of this murderous sun that's sucking the moisture right through your skin, that's burning you to a blister. She kicked out her sleeping bag, dived in, scraping sensitive skin against the zip and the sweat-crusty fabric. Sleep would not be commanded so she curled up inside the fetid heat of the bag and watched the hallucinations bubble out of her forebrain. From their colour and frenetic persistence, she knew she had only two days, a day left before the desert overcame her. Somewhere, she knew she should be very, very concerned at that. She slept fitfully, jerkily until the light through the skin of the bag darkened and she wormed out for her evening meal twenty-five pages of romantic tosh washed down with five mouthfuls of oxygenated water.

When she took her reading on Radio Pleasant, she discovered that in the night she had managed to turn herself around one hundred and eighty degrees. In that somewhere place, she knew she should be very, very afraid of that.

She never knew how she made it out that night, dragging her backsac from a tether around her wrist because its strapping raised wet blisters on her burned shoulders. She drove each foot in front of the next by swearing at it.

"Arsholing fuckbiscuit turdsucking fudge-punching fanny-dripping ring-licking pox-sucking titty-twisting nipple-cracking colon-fisting cucumber-jerking diseased chilli-burned flap-ringed ox-balled cockless arse-less fannyfree cuntless one-leg-in-the-air-wanking bumbutton of a donkey-fucker's priest-buggering fuck-mother's piss-gargling venereally-seeping cousin-rimming pox-father cock-dripping green-cummed mother's sister's priest's cousin's shit-crusted ten-day-hung-shark-scented crack."

She swore Engineer oaths, Deep-Eff oaths, Stuard and Traction and Bas-sareeni oaths, she swore pointsmen's oaths and shunt-jockey oaths, she swore service engineers' elaborate and highly technical oaths, she swore shipping clerks' hair-curling oaths. She swore Bethlehem Ares Railroads and Great Southern and Transpolaris Traction and Transborealis and Llangonned and North Eastern and Great Eastern and Grand Valley corporate oaths. She swore North West and South East and South West and North East Quartersphere oaths. She swore Deuteronomy and Axidy and Chryse and Great Oxus and Tharsis and Syrtia and Grand Valley and New Merionedd and Tempe (of course) and Big Red (most especially) regional oaths. For several kilometres she explored desert oaths, Big Red and Big Crimson and Big Vermilion oaths, Big Carmine and Big Ochre and Big Orange oaths, stone desert and sand desert and soda desert and ash desert and ice desert and acid desert and salt desert and rust desert and dust desert oaths. Finding fruit in the provincial, she worked through her repertoire of Belladonna oaths and Wisdom oaths, Meridian and Lyx and Solstice Landing oaths, Kershaw and New Cosmobad and Bleriot oaths, Touchdown and O and China Mountain oaths.

And the smaller moon was not halfway across the sky.

So she catalogued all her names for body parts, male and female, and swore every swear that could be sworn by them, then made up new names and new swearings for and by them, then by bodily fluids, solids and gases and joined unlikely adjectives to these. Then she remembered to tune in to Radio Pleasant and found to her dismay that Jonathon J. Jonas was just playing his last request on "The Jumpin' Jive Show" and handing over to Fazie Obeke on "The Swing Shift."

Sweetness Octave then swore by the deities. She started with God the Panarchic, and his Immanencies and Emanations, twelve of each. After some thought about whether it was private blasphemy, she then swore by Our Lady Catherine of Tharsis—she could have told her, in eight and bit years, she could have dropped some hint, *Oh by the way, I made the world.* She swore by the Lofty Angelic Orders, the Ranks Eotemporal; the Powers and Dominions, the Spiritual Menagerie, the Rider of the Many-Headed Beast, the Justices and Magisters; the Atmospheric Guides and the Octaval Guides and the Minor Kings of High Brazyl. She swore by the Lesser Orders, the Governances of Amshastrias and Reshpundees; the Five Ranks of Beings Spiritual and Actual: Archangelsks, Avatas, Lorarchs, Cheraphs and Anaels. She swore

by the Least Orders, the Ranks Venal and Mechanical, vanas, partacs, mag-
netos, orphs, flaesers, fielders. She swore by writ and scripture, by the Tree of
World's Beginning and the Original Cinder, by Seven Sanctas and the *Guthru
Gram*, by the Evyn Psalmody and the Ekaterina Angelography, by the Cantus
Septimus and the Mute Scribes who calligraphied beautiful prayers on the
kite-sails of Lyx and Deuteronomy, by the three-centavo (refunded!) oracle of
green men in stenchy booths in Inatra and by the cheap gramarye of budget
witches in Belladonna Main who hawk spells for Help Beyond Comprehension.
She swore by orders and denominations: by the Poor Pelerines and the Preben-
darists and the Devotes of the Bryghte Chylde of Chernowa, by the Cathars and
Cathrinists and Cathites, by the Swavyn Ecstasy-priests and the Damantine
Ascetics and the Penitential Mendicants, by the Poor Children of the Immaculate Contraption and the Sisters-Sufferant of the Song of Clare and (long and
hard and heartfelt) the Church of the Ever-Circling Spiritual Family, its theology, its mail-order service, its floating basilica, its plummy acolytes, their
head and leader, but most of all, that it had ever accepted for shriving the
obsidian soul of Serpio Waymender.

And it was still only one fifteen in the morning. Mumbling blasphemies,
Sweetness Asiim Engineer shuffled to the crest of a barchan. Her feet went
from under her; with a whimper, she slid ass-first down the slip-face. She spat
sand, tried to get to her feet. A nag, a niggle. Something something something. Just before she went weeeeee. What? Yes. Had she seen, dare she trust,
a glint of sick light, out there? With the dregs of her energy and sanity, she
clawed herself back to the top of the dune. Yes. Indeed. A tiny coin of poisonous green out there in the hissing dark.

You know what that is, don't you, Engineer girl?

Yes I do. The thing we fear, our dread and annihilation. A blast crater.
Out there, somewhen, a tokamak blew. A train vaporised. A train, that ran
on a long steel line. A line, going from somewhere, to somewhere.

In the end, it was only by swearing at herself, by herself, for herself, on
herself, every part of her, every moment in her history, every thought in her
head, every value and moral and ambition, every precious dream and vision,
every sin and vice, every triviality and pettiness, every generosity and joy,
that she was able to push those feet through the night to dawn. Whereupon

they rushed so fast at the rail, the real rail, yes, really real, simmering in the heat haze, a black divisor across the world, that they caught themselves on the edge of the sleeper and face forward she fell, cheek to hot, steel, real rail.

She reeled up, leaving a stripe of cheek shrivelling on the hot metal. But we are not out of the woods yet, Glorious Honey-Bun. Not even close to getting into the woods. The rail ran out of heat-haze, under her feet, into heat-haze, straight and undeviating. One way was signals, passing loops, junction boxes, desert mail-drops, halts, stations, marshalling yards, a great glassy terminus. The other way was a glowing hemisphere in the desert a kilometre deep and a messy, seeping end by radiation poisoning. But which?

She unhooked the radio, tuned it away from Radio Pleasant's "Smoother Breakfast with Ned and Greazebop" to white noise. Kkksssshhh. The song of the Big Red. She turned to face one way down the track. The sound of frying sky grew louder, interspersed with pops like boils bursting. She did a one-eighty. Kkksssshhh. She did the test again, to be sure. Roar, and whisper.

That way, then. As if in confirmation, the haze rippled a moment and parted and Sweetness glimpsed bright lozenge-shaped winks of light, and above them, a dark finger of rock, feathery with antennae. And those regularly-shaped objects beneath, dare she trust they were *houses*?

Why not? Everything was foolish out here, and equally wise. The veils of shimmer closed again, disclosing nothing. Sweetness Asiim Engineer breakfasted on five sips from her last bottle and a particularly choice fly-leaf she had been saving for a special occasion. Then she squared her pack, set the sun behind her right shoulder and strode into the east.

17

*T*oward evening she came to the dead town on the bluffs. The heat-haze had teased her on every foot, luring her through exhaustion and dehydration and the angry sun. Then, within three steps, it evaporated and the houses were tumbled walls and the aerials were ragged whips of wire and the lozenges of solar panels empty skeletons hanging in the warm wind. Dust had choked this town years before. Dust was its legacy and population, drifted in elegant swathes on the leeward sides of crumbled walls; clogging the irrigation channels of the bone-dry fields, soft and treacherous as water; stogging the shattered stumps of wind-pumps and ground-water siphons thigh deep in powder that smelled of time and electricity. A nameboard greeted Sweetness from beneath a shroud of dust. Summer storms had scoured the welcome to an epitaph. Eso ion ad. Lation, vation. One step short.

Water, food, a place out of the sun should have been Sweetness's direct concerns but the gravitas of the buried town worked its way into her, drew her along the twisting, dust-choked alleys between the disintegrating adobe walls, peering through dead doorways into roofless rooms. In one she disinterred pieces of an old wooden handloom, with a scrap of cloth, beautifully patterned, that fell apart beneath her fingers into a spray of colour. In another, she found a set of ancient brass beer-pumps, patinaed green. She walked through orchards of dead solar trees to the sentinel upthrust of red rock. An open door invited entry. *Look*, it said: immediately within, a thread of wall-writing, time-faded and esoteric, wound into the shadowy interior. *Can you resist?* Not Sweetness Asiim Engineer. She followed it in and out of dry and fusty rooms, up spiral stone staircases. Rivulets and tributaries of arcane mathematics joined the main flow, feeding it into a torrent of gabbling symbols, tumbling over each other in their rush to the top of the house. Here they gushed out to cover wall and floor of an open ledge under the pinnacle of the rock. A fine room, some kind of observatory, had stood here in former times. Fingers of metal, sand-blasted shiny, hinted at a glass geodesic. The wind sang in the aerials. Sweetness spent a time taking in the prospects of the desert from the high viewpoint. To the south the bluffs fell away in a long line, like a weir in the redness, to an uninterrupted dunefield, awesome in its unbrokenness. West, along the twin lines of wind-polished silver, and she could just make out a faint darkening in the horizon that was the tokamak crater. East, rumours of mountains at the further edge of the world. North, five metres of symbol-inscribed sandstone. She went to it, pressed her fingers to the rock face, tried to trace out meanings and insights in the scrawlings but was only drawn into a subtle spiral of equations, in and in and round and round, ending in a single equals sign at the centre of the gyre of mathematics.

No revelation here, then. Beyond Comprehension, certainly, but not much Help.

Down then, and out. Out in the solar orchard, the sun mugged her. She was very tired and very hungry and very thirsty, this town was very dead and she was not one step nearer sanctuary. As her energy evaporated, Sweetness caught a scent, immediate and animal. The primal scent: water. Near, here. Instinct drew her to a small circular wall in the centre of a rectangle of rock that must once have been a garden. Dust lay banked around the foot of the wall but it did not seem to have spilled over the curb stones. Pray that it is not too deep. That would be cruel. Cruel would be typical. *Water* smelled sweet and deep. Sweetness rolled over the retaining wall and looked down into the well. Her own dark reflection, haloed by blue sky, looked up at her. It was not so deep. Sweetness scrabbled as far over the retaining wall as she dared, stretched down with her empty backsac to scoop a bagful of water.

Azimuth on a triple letter, double word, a voice said behind her, clear as water. Sweetness whirled, just remembering to hook one finger through the straps of her backsac. An old woman had spoken. What old woman? the dead town said. Search me. Sweetness did, with her eyes, left and right, foreground to middle distance. No old woman. See?

She bent over to dip another bagful of water.

Fighting Machine Squad Charlie, go go go! a radio-crackle voice yelled.

Sweetness swung her bag out of the well in an arc of precious water, stood up, challenging the ruined houses. Water trickled from her backsac seams.

And where do you think I'm hiding a Fighting Machine Squad Charlie? the fallen walls and stump wind-pumps said.

"Okay!" Sweetness Asiim shouted. "What's going on?"

If a dead town could have spread its hand in a shrug, *Huh?*, this one would have.

"I said, what's going on?"

No answer, of course. But the dust stroked her cheek, toyed with her hair. A rattle of wires: the aerials on the high rock were restless, twitching. A moan from the skeletons of the wind gantries. Dust rose around the soles of her desert boots. A prickle of pure superstition on the nape of Sweetness's neck said, *Turn around, traingirl.* Out there, beyond the edge of the dead town, beneath the fall of the bluffs, a wind-devil was moving across the face of the Great Red. Unlike the scatty whirlwinds of the High Plains and the polar deserts, this did not wander willy-wally, wind-driven whither-whether. It cut straight through the crests of the dune fields in soft detonations of sand. Its course was straight and determined; aimed right at the dead town on the bluffs: *No*, Sweetness knew, *at me.* And by the same intuition she knew it was futile to run—if there had been anywhere she could have run in this terrible land—for the devil in the wind would hunt her wherever she tried to hide. The wind rose, whipping the dust drifted around the well rim into long, stinging streamers. Sweetness chased her scattered things, struggled the saturated backsac shut and wrapped one of her torn shirt sleeves around her head. The dust-devil was at the foot of the bluffs. It was a scream of wind and sand, shot through with flickers of lightning. In one bound it leaped the bluffs. Dust blew up around Sweetness Asiim Engineer. She battled through it to take shelter in the lee of the well. Sand scoured her seared shoulders and arms. She fought to keep her mouth and nostrils covered. She had heard of these desert gyrestorms, that could pounce on a herd of grazers and in mere mouthfuls reduce them to bloody bones. The twister dived on her. Sweetness threw up her hands to cover her head and was buried in faces. Old wrinkle-faced matriarchs; heaven-eyed teenagers; scampish, grinning goondahs; harried-looking men in veterinary's scrubs; women in pilot's helmets; youths in cylindrical supplicant's hats, judges, engineers, men in ROTECH uniforms, shysters and roustabouts, faces of angels and faces of demons and faces in between. Faces, and voices. Voices praying, pleading, demanding, declaiming; voices of prophecy and obsession, voices of children and aged aged men, voices of radio and wrath, voices whirled away before their words grew solid meanings. Voices, and histories. Images of children laughing and leaping in the rain, of bright, dart-like aeroplanes stitching across the sky, of steel-shod behemoths marching through corn fields, of wide-hatted men in long coats cradling needle guns, of choirs of angels hovering over a stark desert pillar, of babies in bell jars and balls on a green baize tabletop. And at the centre of it all, a figure, perhaps a man, perhaps not, drifting in and out of focus, as if near and far at the same time, shifting between probabilities. The figure congealed: a man, wrapped for the desert, in a long coat, with a heavy pack on his back surmounted by what looked like a sewing machine. One last flicker and he became actual. At the same instant the whirlwind dispersed in a mighty rush of faces and whispers and memories. The figure staggered, righted itself.

"God!" it cried. "Here again!" Then, noticing Sweetness staring over the rim of the well, it pulled a device like a collapsible umbrella from a holster at its waist and brandished it at her. "What in the name of all sanity are you?"

"I am Sweetness Octave Glorious Honey-Bun Asiim Engineer 12th," Sweetness ventured, then, finding the umbrella-thing aimed at her absolutely the last straw in a line of kidnappings, hoodwinkings, maroonings, meanderings and burnings, she declared, fiercely, "And just who the hell are you?"

The figure goggled owlishly at her. But if he were any bird, it was a desert hawk, something keen and pinched and fidgeting; a bit leathery. The feather in his battered hat lent to the avian image, and the dark little eyes that gave no hint of where they were looking. The long, elegantly curving mustachios suggested another kind of beast, some watchful, quizzical desert gopher, a chewer of taproots and cactus, burrowing and twitch-whiskered. Altogether he was a strange bestiary of a creature, Sweetness decided. Still fixing her with his eye, the man said, "I am a traveller."

"Me too," Sweetness said. "Where from?"

"Here," the man answered.

"You haven't exactly gone far," Sweetness said. The man tilted his head from side to side, as if attempting to triangulate her soul.

"I've just got back," the man said after a good pause. "I was away a long time."

Sweetness realised that noun-play in a dead town with mysterious travellers who crossed the great desert in dust-devils of faces stood a good chance of killing her, and that all she had eaten for the past three days was paperback romantic fiction.

"Have you anything to eat?" she asked. The traveller heard the plaint in her voice. He shrugged off his heavy pack, which Sweetness now saw was much more complex and arcane than at first impression. There were whip aerials and coils of cable and arrays of flashing lights and copper dials and bellows that went in and out and the definite taint—to the train-born—of fusion power. The traveller rummaged through his pockets. His coat was generously endowed with them. He hooked out a clutch of claw-shaped green fruit too large for the pocket that had produced it, but Sweetness was inured to the dimensionally transcendental.

"These are good."

Sweetness frowned at them.

"They're going to be big, a few million years from here."

She took the bunch, peeled one of the hooked things. Cautious sniff: coffee and vanilla and a sweet/ sour tang, like guavas, but a little to the left. She took a bite. It was so good to a belly fed with mass market paperback that she devoured the whole bunch in six mouthfuls. She wiped her sticky fingers on her backsac. Since entering the big desert she seemed to have eaten nothing but fruit and paper. She remembered her promise of a fish on the mud-terraces at Therme.

"Million years?" she asked.

"I get around," the traveller said. He spread his coat tails and sat beside her on the well wall. "Up to the end, and back again." He held out his forefingers, crossed his hands. "Both ways."

"I got an uncle like that," Sweetness said.

"Have you now?" said the stranger. He explored deep in a pocket, hauled out a greaseproof-paper package. "These were fresh yesterday." Inside were pale flaky rolls, forefinger sized.

"Thanks." They were stuffed with a sweet, beany paste. "Only he's more like beyond the end, if you know what I mean." This, through a spray of pastry flakes.

"Your uncle?"

"More like elsewhere."

"Ah yes. I am familiar with that. Most when is elsewhere, when you come down to it. It's all probabilities; at first I thought you went forward and back, what I now realise is that you go sideways as well. Every movement forward, or back, is into an alternative created by your own apparent motion. I go diagonally through time."

"The sky's red there," Sweetness said. "There's frost on the ground, and a lot of stones. No one around, no clouds, no plants neither. Any more of those roll things?"

"I shouldn't think so," said the traveller. His hand went elbow deep into his right pocket. "That's the problem with diagonal, probabilistic motion. You get something good, you can't go back to it again. All you can go to is a close alternative. Sometimes it's better. Usually it's worse. This do?"

He offered a foil-wrapped savoury. Sweetness's desert-wise nose picked up a whiff of off but it was sustenance. For the first time the traveller seemed to notice the where and what of his location. While Sweetness licked animal grease off her fingers, he surveyed the dead town.

"When is this?" he asked.

Sweetness gave him the year and month.

"Long way to go yet," he said. "I suppose I should warn them all, for the good it'll do."

"Warn who?"

"The people who live here. Lived here."

Drawn by the desolation, he picked up his humming pack and went through the desiccated streets, running a finger along the sandy tops of the fallen walls, peering into the slack mouths of the doorways at the choked rooms. Sweetness followed him, half-intrigued, half-hoping for more provender from the deep deep pockets.

"The people who lived here, I could tell you their names, the names of their children," the man said. "I could tell you the names of their thousand-times children's children, but the problem is, would it be true? So many alternatives, and you can never trust that you travel back to the one, the true. It might have been someone else entirely, in this history." He walked through the sterile fields toward the red rock-house. "I wonder what happened? It's easy to lose the small change down the lining."

Sweetness glanced at the sky—evening coming on.

"You travel in time, right?" she said to the journeyman.

"Right, child."

"So you could go back and find out what happened." Temporal paradox had suggested opportunity to Sweetness. "In fact, you could go back and leave me some food, and some water. That would be nice. Somewhere comfy to sleep, you could do that too, and a bath. I'd really really like it if you could do me a bath, and a lot of shampoo."

"Shampoo."

"Shampoo."

The traveller smiled. His face crinkled like a well-used old leather wallet.

"See that rock?"

"I see it."

"I used to live there. That's my home."

"Those are your numbers, going all the way up?"

"You've been in?"

"Yeah. Sorry."

"Well, this time you come as guest, not trespasser." The odd man bowed her through the door, indicated that she should follow the spiral of temporal mathematics all the way to its conclusion. From the ruined weather-room the sun was a cracked red yolk dripping light-juice over the horizon, the shards of twisted glazing bars desperate fingers trying to hold back the sol-stuff.

"Stay there. Don't move." The strange little man clicked his pack shut around him. He twiddled dials on his coat sleeve.

"Where would I go?" Sweetness began to ask, then a wind out of nowhere flayed her sunburn and whipped her hair in her eyes. "Hey!" Faces rushed in from the world's four quarters, voices, images, and were gone. As was the man.

"Hey . . ." sweetness started to say again but while the word was still on her tongue, hot wind blew in her face, dust buffeted her, faces loomed at her, yawned as if to swallow her, then vanished to their haunts beyond the edge of the world. The man was back. With him, total transformation. The high room was a web of triangular glass panes linked into a geodesic bubble. Some of the lights were stained with Ekaterinist angels. The setting sun kindled them to divinity.

Then Sweetness saw the thing in the middle of the mosaic floor.

"Oh," she said. "Oooh. Ooh."

The bath was long and iron and elegantly curved, with lion's paw feet, a gold faucet, and full to within ten centimetres of the brim with gently aromatic steaming water.

"And shampoo." The man lifted up a silver ewer, poured a semeny gobbet into the bathwater. "And afterward . . ." A hammered brass Llangonedd table was set with covered *thalis*. Chapattis were stacked in a soft dinner-cloth. A folded napkin and bowl of rose-water invited finger-feeding. The man lifted a bottle out of a cooler and studied the label. "This is good. I never knew I had such taste."

"What the, how the?"

"Pick one, choose one, engineer one. Sensitive dependence on initial conditions," the man said, with a wizardly twirl of the mustachios. He surveyed his handiwork with satisfaction. "It was never this good when I had it. Wonder what happened to that other Alimantando?"

"That your name?" Sweetness asked.

"It's been one."

"The writing's still on the wall," she said.

"So it is," the traveller said. He walked to within squinting-distance of the equals sign, then began to follow the equations outward. Sweetness thought that the writing looked fresher, bluer, cleaner. But the water was deep and hot, and she could smell her hair again . . .

"Er."

"I'll leave you to it," the man said, led out of the high room by numbers. As she wriggled out of her sweat-stiff gear, Sweetness glanced over her shoulder for spectators: reflex born of a life lived in close proximity to others. Beyond the stained glass there was no town, no walls, no ruination. A red rock stood on a bluff, and a steel rail ran by it. That was all. Trying not to screw her head round with the paradoxes of time-travel, Sweetness slid into the hot water, grimacing as it grazed her sun-sting. It was good and enfolding and long and she sang old burlesque songs as she scrubbed the shampoo into her curls. No drier, but she shook her hair out like a dog, then studied herself in the floor-standing mirror to check if she was still as cute as she remembered. She poked gingerly at the scabby burn on her cheek, turned profiles to see if her little breasts had lost anything she could not afford to desert privations. *Still fabulous*, she concluded, wrapped herself in a silk robe worked with more mathematical symbols. The night was high, the moonring a twinkling arch over the glass dome. Sweetness sat herself in a wicker chair by the glass and watched the hasty moon twins race each other up the sky.

Here's a man can make anything by re-engineering history, she thought, so what else can he do for me?

The man himself looked through the stair door. He was dressed in velveteen knee-britches and frogged jacket. His mustachios were perkily waxed to lethal weapons.

"You're, ah?"

"Done? Yah."

"Good. Then let's consume."

He bowed in the Deuteronomian manner to guide Sweetness to her place, pulled out her chair, unfolded her napkin with a flourish.

"Thank you," she said, charmed. *Only proper man I've met in . . . oh my gods! Years!*

"You're exceedingly welcome," the traveller said. "I have few enough chances to entertain, these days."

Whatever they are, Sweetness thought. She said, "I got one question. What happened to the town?"

"It never happened, not in this time-line. I seem to have been something of a bon-viveur, though." The man indicated his attire, the table furnishings. He offered a platter of wind-dried meats. Sweetness heaped her plate. "It'll give you the shits, too much of that on an empty stomach."

"I been eating stories," Sweetness said.

"Really? How extraordinary. Poor fare, I don't doubt. Little sustenance in most stories. A lot of people think their lives are stories, but they delude themselves. No structure, no narrative tack, no sense of dramaturgy. Just chains of events."

"Not me," Sweetness said. "I met this guy once told me I was a story, well, for a time."

"That's the most story any of us are, for a time."

"He was weird. I think he was green."

The dapper traveller choked as if poisoned.

"I beg your pardon?"

"He had this tiny wee yurt thing by the side of the track, 'cept of course when you looked back it wasn't there, but he said, 'Sees all hears all knows all.'"

"'Past present future,'" the traveller cut in. "'Uncurtain the windows of time . . .' Have you any idea, young woman, any idea *at all* how long I've been searching for this . . . trackside mountebank, this scryer of fortunes and futures?"

Sweetness saw a light in the traveller's eyes, a prickling of his whiskers, an edge in the voice that warned her, *Nice manners or not, you're here with this man, and there's no one else around and you don't even know for sure what universe you're in.*

But the traveller was in flow and vent now. "This . . . soothsayer, this story-maker," he sprayed, "This green man of whom you speak so lightly; he guided me to this place, teased and taunted and tantalised me across that desert, to this high red rock, where he abandoned me; he, if anyone, is the founder of the town that sometimes exists out there, sometimes not; he is the reason for every single one of those symbols on the wall, he is the reason I continue to travel across time, up and down and side to side; him. Read your beads? Say your seeds? Tell your bones? Of course! Of course he can tell the future, he is the future! Time is a part of him, as much as the air you breathe, the food you eat is part of you! This green man, you met him! Ah! I've been a billion years forward and a billion years back, I've seen the sun swollen like the burning belly of a pregnant martyr, this world of ours a ball of bubbling slag; I've seen the very first spring, a billion years ago in the youth of the world—there were things living then, girl, that you would not even reckon alive. I've travelled across the frozen years, I've seen them erect the diamond pillars of Grand Valley. And I've travelled from side to side: I've visited strange great civilisations, bizarre and inhuman; I've watched the fleets of Motherworld and this world set the heavens on fire with their weapons; I've seen this world in all its colours, red, green, blue, white, yellow; I've stood beneath titanic pyramids and mountains carved into alien faces. And all across these billions of years, landscapes of time, I see the footprints of this green man, mentor and tormentor, and always I am a moment too late, a day too early, a street or two wide: and you, traingirl, you tell me you meet him at some . . . some . . . trackside bawdy-burg! I tell you this, girl; yours must be a mighty story indeed for him to step out of time to say your sooths. I think I need to know much about you, Sweetness Octave Glorious Honey-Bun Asiim Engineer 12th. Tell me what brought you from there to here. Omit nothing."

So she did. There was purple along the morning edge of the world by the time it was all told. The traveller interrupted often with questions she could not answer. At each of her half-responses, his face grew more grave. He started to roll his mustachios, an unconscious tic of concern.

"So here I am," Sweetness concluded and the glass room was suddenly lit theatrical red as the edge of the world tipped beneath the upper limb of the sun.

"This is serious indeed," the traveller said. "Glossing over that the Blessed Lady of Tharsis seems to have chosen to manifest herself as your late twin sister—the ways of deities, by definition, are beyond our consideration—if this Devastation Harx has control of her, he has access not just to the ROTECH command structure, which is bad enough for continued life on this world, but the vinculum processors that helped build the world; and that is bad news for reality, everywhere."

"This is a problem? You go back in time and stop him."

"Not so easy."

"You whizzed this place up out of some other history somewhere, and you can't kick Devastation Harx?"

"It's a locality problem. I can strongly affect time-dependent events here, at the centre so to speak, but as I move away, the probability drops off. More than a hundred kilometres in any direction, it's back to base-line reality. Think of me as a kind of human wave function."

"So you're telling me you can't kick Devastation Harx."

"I'm telling you that, yes. And anyway, even if I could, it's not for me to do. You understand why?"

"I think so," Sweetness said. In the night of words, as the people and events were drawn out her, the act of telling revealed an order, an organic structure in her experiences. She did not impose *story* on her tale. *Story* was within, quivering and sinewy in every action, like a speed-dog waiting its turn on the track. Nothing merely *happened*, every event was connected, one to another, with a unity and clarity. She thought of the green man's fortune-telling stick, and its implied extension, out of the past, into the future. "It's the story, isn't it?"

"You tell me," the traveller said. When he smiled, as he was doing now, Sweetness was reminded of Uncle Neon, before. And, she thought again, in some ways, after.

"In this story, Sweetness Octave goes across the desert and has lots of big adventures before she tracks down Devastation Harx and his Church boys, rescues Our Lady of Tharsis, saves the world, and hopefully, somewhere in all that, gives Serpio a kicking."

"That sounds like it."

"A wee Engineer girl who's not even allowed to drive a train takes on this guy who can balls about with what's real and what's not, and wins?"

"That's the story. And if I know anything about them, things will get worse before they get better."

"Only one problem."

"Which is?"

"How do I get out of the desert?"

"That, I think, is my chapter in your story. Now, you catch a couple of hours' sleep, and I'll see what I can engineer."

Sweetness slept in a brocade-canopied bed in a room with a high, small window looking south on to the great erg. She was shaken from the flocking hallucinations you get just before you drop off by a distinct feeling of other lives rushing through her. Then she gave a twitch and fell headlong into a dream that she was a girl sleeping in a canopied bed with desert wind blowing through her window who dreamed that, in a dream, without any polite warning, the universe abruptly changed. She woke up, and it had.

She lay in a wide pale bed in a high pale room draped with floating swags of pale muslin. The light through the unglazed window told her it was afternoon. The wind no longer smelled of desert, but vegetables fertilised with night soil. Peering through the gauzy layers of muslin, Sweetness thought she saw a ghostly figure by the foot of the bed.

"Hello?"

"Madam?"

Sweetness fought her way out of the fog of fabric. No ghost, but substance, a short, dumpy woman in her early teens, dressed in the ubiquitous pale cheesecloth, with an odd, conical hat that tilted forward.

"Who are you?"

"I am Bennis. I am here to help the madam dress and prepare herself for her journey."

"What the hell are you doing here?"

"Following the teacher by serving the madam."

"The teacher? Never mind."

"Madam." Bennis lifted Sweetness's clothes and held them out. They looked very clean and smelled of lavender.

"Are you an acolyte?" Sweetness asked suspiciously.

"I have the honour to be so, yes," the girl said.

"I'll dress myself, thanks."

The traveller was waiting for her down at the tracks. A handful of acolytes, all alike in pale habits and conical hats formed a respectful circle around him. They parted to let Sweetness through.

"Good afternoon good afternoon good afternoon!" the traveller boomed. "I trust we are refreshed and restored? Good good good. Now, is this not a fine device?"

It was indeed; a thing of brass and wood and engraved steel. It stood four square on twin bogies, but Sweetness could not make out any driving wheels, or anything that looked like an engine.

"How?" she asked. The traveller pointed to the sky. Twelve big boxkites flew in three-by-four formation. Sweetness strained to make out bridle lines and tethers, they seemed to hover, unattached by anything but charisma. She did notice a shimmering around the head of carved Lorarch that was the rail-yacht's figurehead, a halo, like spider silk in the wind. She went for a closer look.

"Don't get too close," the traveller warned. "Diamond filament. Take your fingers right off quick smart."

"Where did it come from?" Sweetness explored the safety of the burnished brass—already hot under the desert sun—and the intricate filigree metal work.

"I invented it, of course," the man said. "These people tell me I arrived on it five years ago out of a dust storm that had been blowing for an entire season, thus ending the storm and saving their community. In this history, they beat me here by a good decade."

"Yeah, I meant to ask, just who are these people?"

"Some manner of stylite order, originally. A Cathrinist sect; they're a pretty peaceable crew. They seem to regard me as a great teacher."

"The Teacher is a Skandava," one of the acolytes spoke up, a skinny, hollow-cheeked man.

"A dweller between realities, that is," a chunky woman beside him clarified.

"There you have it," the traveller said. "Well, throw up your stuff then." He stowed Sweetness's bag in a cubby, then swung himself up on to the running board. He addressed the faithful, jaunty hat in one hand. "So, my good people, I, your great and distinctive teacher, bid you farewell—I have business between dimensions. I cannot say how long I will be engaged on it and when I will be able to return to you, but rest assured, I shall. Look for me in winter storms and summer lightning, in out-of-season whirlwinds and strange dreams. Now, it's high time we were away." To Sweetness he added, "Well, are you coming then?"

She bounced over the brass railing. The traveller was seated in one of two buttoned leather armchairs under an awning on the raised poop. Forward was a gurney-wheel, a binnacle and wind-rose and a set of brass levers. Old ambition, pressed down and almost forgotten, suddenly bubbled in her heart.

"Can I ask something?"

"Ask away," the traveller said, unfolding a pair of smoked-glass pebble sun-spectacles from one of his many coat pockets.

"Can I drive?"

"The helm is yours," the traveller said with an expansive gesture.

Sweetness took the footplate. She touched the hot, gleaming brasswork levers, the spokes of the braking wheel. The compass read west, the wind-rose reported a firm thirty-knotter up at two hundred metres, sou' by sou'-west. Shading her eyes with her hand, she squinted up at the kites. They bobbed and strained, eager and restless. Not exactly a fusion tokamak and superheat boiler. And this wasn't a drive rod in her hand. No calliope, no triple steam horns, but there was a brass bell. And the track ran straight before her and she could feel the rail-yacht quivering on its bogies for the off and it said, *Drive me, take me off down that long line, make me run, Engineer girl. Point me wherever you want me to go.*

Sweetness waved her hands at the Cathrinists. They humbly parted. She took the brake lever in her two hands and eased it back. The wheels creaked, the wind hummed in the invisible diamond thread. At first slowly, so slowly even Sweetness, used to the subtleties of great trains, could not be sure they were turning, the bogies began to roll. She gave a yip of glee. Furiously clanging the big brass bell, Sweetness Octave Glorious Honey-Bun Asiim Engineer 12th drove the rail-yacht through lines of politely applauding stylites and out across the Big Red.

18

*T*here was a dome called home by the side of the Trans-Oxiana upline. It was a primeval pressure bubble from the days before the man-forming, orange and breast-like, with a firm heat-exchange nipple erect on the summit. It had stood here for eight hundred years. Anywhere else it would have had preservation orders slapped all over it, been the focus of a heritage park or folk museum. Here in undervisited Great Oxus, atmosphere panels had been torn out, gas-exchange ducts ripped away, the pristine skin of the dome rudely punched into gabled windows and high dormers. Berya and Laventine Prestaine were the inheritors of this vandalism. They and their five-times-removed forebears abided here amongst brown-paper parcels. The Prestaines were a race of postage and parcels operatives for a swathe of terrain a day's walk from middle to centre, a further day's walk to the far side. Mantis-like gantries, the design of a second generation Prestaine, dangled their digits over the main line, primed, by a series of heliographs and clockwork devices, to nimbly whisk mail from fast-moving trains and deposit it safely in a lacrosse net. Clothes, mail-order seeds, bicycles, ploughshares, machine parts, dirty books, sports equipment, festival hampers, manuals and guides, wallpapers and paints; all were snatched from the parcel turrets of the big transcontinentals and whisked high. A spring-loaded telpherage shot those on the wrong side of the tracks spryly to the right side, then up the cable and through the dormer into the sun-lit sorting room. It was thin, blurred speed-and-wires work. There Berya and Laventine, now in their twenties, childless for the good of the genepool, sorted and filed in their matching yellow postal aprons. The uppermost chord of the dome was lined with baked-clay pigeonholes, many of them occupied by dusty brown-paper parcels, addresses faded to sepia by the moving trapezium of sun through the dormer. These were the widows and orphans, the unloved uncollected by the twice-weekly power-trike delivery girls.

A woman in black was walking toward the dome this morning. She moved too spryly for her dowdy dowager's weeds. She kicked at stones, gave the occasional skip, tightrope-walked the slim rail, arms held out at her side. A wink of high sun blinded her; a lens looking down from the observation nipple. Behind the eyepiece of the opticon, Berya Prestaine hooted.

"Lavvy! Lavvy! Pedestrian! Pedestrian!"

His sister peered up from her wicker parcel trolley.

"Pedestrian?"

"Afoot!"

"Let me see."

She scurried along the ramp that spiralled up the inside of the dome, past the hundreds of labelled pigeonholes, sort codes and alphabeticals, yellowed adhesive tape sun-dried and peeling.

"A woman!" Berya declared. "Afoot!"

The leather eyecup of the opticon confirmed this to wheezing Laventine.

"Afoot or not, we must service her," the elder sister declared. "We shall open the counter."

"The counter!" useless Berya cooed, daft as a pigeon.

They were standing behind it, side by side, as Grandmother Taal arrived under the cool striped awning. Their stamps were updated, their record books open, their pencils sharpened, their dockets ready for peel, their scales calibrated, their receipt book triple-larded with carbon paper, their moist pads warm and wet, their rubber thumbs dimpling amiably. All was ready for any conceivable postal transaction.

"Deposit or receipt?" they asked simultaneously.

"I beg your pardon?" Grandmother Taal asked.

"Are you in receipt of a collectable, in which instance we will require your name, address and a form of photographic identification, or have you come to consign an item, in which case the next collection will be the twenty-three fifteen Night Sleeping Service." Laventine Prestaine stared cock-headed at Grandmother Taal, like a constipated owl. A small worm of drool was crawling from the left corner of Berya's mouth.

"Twenty-three fifteen?" Grandmother Taal said.

"That is correct, madam."

"I had hoped to connect with the fourteen oh three Local."

"The fourteen oh three?" Laventine turned to look aghast at Berya.

"Fourteen oh three?" Berya echoed, staring at his sibling.

"Long gone, madam."

"Gone gone gone long long long," Berya fluted.

"But my compendium . . ." Grandmother Taal took out her *vade-mecum*, shook it as if she suspected broken clockwork, loose power cells.

"Mergers. All the thing on this line. Leveraged buy-outs. Snapping the tiddlers up, snip snap snip," Laventine said, smugly. "First thing is shiny new corporate badges. Next is service cancellations."

"Then when can I get a train? It is imperative that I catch a train."

"Madam!" Laventine chided. "Where do you think you are? This is not Meridian Main. This is a Winged Messenger Postal Depot. Our passengers are inanimate—usually—and wrapped in brown paper. In short, packages, madam. Packages."

"I have to get a train, my granddaughter—my only granddaughter . . . She is in great peril . . ."

Grandmother Taal's plea hit a layer of institutionalised incest annealed to the backs of the siblings' eyes and bounced, like moonring-gleam from a star-struck cat. She laid the photograph of Sweetness on the counter. Berya's hand seized the stamp like a striking snake, lifted it to blast. Laventine barely wrestled him back to the ink pad.

"This is my granddaughter."

The two biddies clucked and fluffed over the photograph, then shook their heads.

"Never seen her."

"Never seen, never been, never heard . . ."

"She would have been in the company of a wall-eyed boy."

"Wall-eyed?"

Grandmother Taal pulled down a lower lid, rolled her eyeball up. The postal twins reeled back.

"Black hair, like a dust crow. Scruffy. Low caste."

The twins checked to make sure each other was shaking his or her head.

"Name of Serpio. Waymender. A trainboy."

"Waymender?" Berya twitched, as if association were a painful tic. He looked at Laventine. "Lavvy Lavvy Lavvy! Waymender! Trainboy!" He poked his finger in his cheek and rolled his left eye.

"My brother seems to have some positive recollection," Laventine said.

"Your . . . brother . . . seems positively imbecilic," Grandmother Taal said mildly.

"I shall consult the register," Laventine Prestaine said carefully. Great soft yellow ledger pages curled, breaking waves surfed by spidery copperplate. Forefinger prodded names and deliveries. "Ah hah. Yes. The gentleman in question has indeed received a number of consignments from us. In fact . . ." She looked over her shoulder, furrowed her brow, unfolded a complex pair of spectacles from her apron pocket and squinted through them at the dusty, sun-shafted interior of the dome. "I knew it, I knew it! There is a collectable for the gentleman in Imminent Returns."

"Might I see it?"

Laventine Prestaine cocked her head to the other side.

"It is rather irregular."

"My granddaughter . . ."

Laventine showed Grandmother Taal how many ways she could purse her lips, then said, "Very well. Berya!" She tore a foil from the receipt book, stuck it to the back of Berya's hand with tape and squared him up with the door. "Imminent Returns!"

While he wound his way up the spiral and down again, Grandmother Taal tested her new, sharper eyesight on the strict perspectives of the mainline. Not a wisp of steam, not a speck of black steel in the heat-haze, it reported faithfully. Berya Prestaine set the parcel on the counter. It was wrapped in brown paper and bound, neatly, with white string. It was book-shaped and book-sized and, when Grandmother Taal picked it up, book-weighty.

"Might I?"

The Prestaines reacted as if she had suggested an unexpected fisting.

"Open it, open it, open it?" Berya squeaked, hopping from foot to foot like a manic mynah.

"This is a Winged Messenger Postal Depot," Laventine boomed, drawing herself up to her full height. "Prestaines have been postal people since the days of the Rocket Mail. We hold our commission from St. Catherine Herself! Our obligations are sacrosanct. Sacrosanct!" She held a lofty silence, then added, "You may, however, feel it."

Grandmother Taal ran her fingers over the packet's contours. It was the size of a book, the shape of a book, the weight of a book, and, absolutely, the feel of a book.

"Is this the return address?"

Laventine peered at the adhesive label on the back.

"It is indeed, and you may count yourself lucky it had not already winged its way back to there."

"Church of the Ever-Circling Spiritual Family."

"You would be surprised how much mail-order religion we handle."

"Has he had other deliveries from these folk?"

Laventine pursed her lips, another sour rebuttal armed, then shook her head testily and thumbed through the ledger.

"Yes, here, here, here and here." Grandmother Taal could make nothing of the black, chitinous scrawl, but the spacing of the entries told her these were regular occurrences. "Here, here; here also, and here . . ."

"Yes, thank you. Are they all mailed from Molesworth?"

Laventine bent low over the adhesive receipt stickers next to the signatures.

"It would seem so."

"Molesworth."

"In Chimeria."

"My good woman." Grandmother Taal stiffened, flared her nostrils. "I am an Engineer. I am well aware it is a considerable journey." Age, once accustomed to its due respect, does not gladly relinquish it.

"By rail," Berya chirped.

"How else?" Grandmother Taal said sharply, but her mental *vade-mecum* was mapping routes and matching timetables and flagging halts with an increasing sense of losing the race between steam-powered grandmother and granddaughter on the back of a terrain bike.

"Lookee lookee lookee!" Berya exclaimed, running into the dome and waving his hands gleefully.

"My brother may not be the sharpest chisel in the set, but I defy anyone to better his innate sense for post," Laventine stated proudly.

He returned wielding a heat-sealed plastic envelope emblazoned with *prioritaire* and *expressissimo* stickers. *To be opened solely by addressee*, warned red corner flashes.

"Ah, yes!" Laventine scanned the address. "I had almost forgotten about this one. We got a message on the radio about it, didn't we, Berya?" He nodded. "Most important. They're to pick it up today. Personal issue. Hand to hand."

She passed the envelope to Grandmother Taal.

"The Glenn Miller Orchestra," Grandmother Taal read out.

"We're not unaccustomed to celebrity in our little dome. But the address, woman—read the address!"

"Director of Music, *en route*, Molesworth, Chimeria/Solstice Landing."

Laventine and Berya Prestaine stood behind their leather-topped counter as if they had magicked up the whole shebang out of steel, sand and brown paper.

So it was that by midnight, Grandmother Taal was wedged between the trombones and the first clarinets, oppressed by cigarillo smoke and her coccyx bruised by eight hours bouncing over every rock and ant pile on the Solstice Landing trampas. Trainpeople and musicians, though brothers of the soul and historically mutually dependent, have never truly trusted each other. Grandmother Taal herself had too many memories of trashed dining cars and sexual shenanigans among the *couchettes*. They had a way about them at once over-easy and frighteningly professional; they salted their idle conversation with technical terms that computer scientists or geophysicists, with similar sacred vocabularies, would not have dared intrude into casual conversation. They talked of whole notes and eight bars, they had pappy-os and mammy-os and baby-blues. They spoke sentences where you beat time with a pursed thumb and forefinger and said pah-pah-pah-pah, pah-pah-pah-pah, pahpahpah. They jived over wah-wahs and mutes and leaned together to try out whispered rhythms, *dat-da-dah* no, try *dat-duh-didit-duh*, coming in *sharp* on the first beat and then going two three four five six seven and *in* and one hand beat five against eight and the other foot did eleven over four. Nothing was

ever referred to by its correct name. Horns were bitches; clarinets fags; drums
were skins, basses were broads, guitars were axes, saxophones were saxes. Sex
sex sex sex sex. The musicians were as publicly intimate with their slang mis-
tresses as teenagers in a city park, blowing into orifices, sticking tongues into
slits, running fingers up and down brass nipples, stuffing balled hands into
smooth flarings. Their professional hygiene techniques involved copious
quantities of saliva and rags. They smoked colossal amounts of *bhang*. The
interior of the big black boogie bus was a tube of blue funk. Grandmother
Taal was no longer certain the driver was in control of the big eighteen-
wheeler articulated land-train. The begoggled girl behind the wheel could be
deliberately steering for the hummocks and mounds. Grandmother Taal was
no longer certain she much cared whether she was or not. She leaned to yell
at the tall, bespectacled man on the bench seat beside the grim-faced driver.

"How much longer?"

The man in glasses, the legend himself, yelled something to the driver,
who yelled back, never once taking her eyes off the darkening trampas.

"She says it'll take as long as it takes," the musician reported.

"My granddaughter . . ."

The band leader bent toward Grandmother Taal.

"Show me again."

She fished the photograph out of the depths of the universal handbag. It
was growing foxed at the edges, the celluloid finish cracking and fanning into
soft white petticoats of layered paper. Glenn Miller showed it to the driver.
She pushed up her dust-goggles, gave it a look over, then bawled at the King
of Swing. He nodded.

"We don't have to be there until five for the get in, but she'll try to make
it tonight, if everything holds."

Everything holds.

Grandmother Taal had not been long waiting at the Winged Messenger
depot, which was as well, for the Prestaines were not accustomed to hospi-
tality, and a guest of theirs might starve, or die of thirst or sunstroke before
they thought to offer shade swig shelter. A stirring of dust on the far side had
turned into a black wink of a vehicle, which had turned into a highly
unlikely contraption, a long, black tube of a thing, studded with aerials and

swivel spotlights, portholes down the sides, a mirror-glass windshield wrapped around its nose, like a snake in shades. It ran on three sets of huge, soft-tired dustwheels, and was articulated in three places, which gave a sly shimmy to its motion. A bus trying to pretend it's a train, Grandmother Taal thought disdainfully as the device clambered disrespectfully over the tracks and came to a rest beside the Prestaines' dome.

THE GLENN MILLER ORCHESTRA ON TOUR! declared metre-high white letters along the side of the bus. *The Legendary Kings of Swing!* the smaller print mentioned as an afterthought. The doors opened, a cloud of aromatic smoke plumed out, followed by a tide of coughing Kings of Swing. Last off was the Man Himself, Glenn Miller, trombone under arm. He stood at the top of the steps, frowning through his thick glasses at this forsaken place in which he found himself. Like most trainfolk, Grandmother Taal was no respecter of celebrity or legend. Gods and men alike paid their tickets. She had been prepared to treat this man, this musician, this band-leader record-maker radio-star jukebox angel, this marquis of mood and earl of easy and duke of jive, this legend that every night set the dark half of the planet jumpin' and jittin', as just another passenger. But seeing him there on the top step, the afternoon light glinting off the bell of his trombone, his glasses filmed with dust, she could not. Everything about him said, yes, all that, but that doesn't matter, for whether it comes or whether it goes, I am now and always have been and always will be, *genuine article*. A crawl of *bona fide* awe had licked up Grandmother Taal's spine.

Never too old for it, Engineer-Amma.

And nice manners too, because when it came to ask him could he, would he, was it possible, an old woman, alone, looking for a lost granddaughter, he had brushed it all away with a lift of his hand and said *certainly* and gave her his hand to guide her up on to the bus and his handkerchief to tie around her face in case the dust finally defeated the air-conditioning system. Such a nice manner that Grandmother Taal put aside her mistrust of a vehicle that could go anywhere its driver desired and climbed aboard.

With the Prestaine Dome beneath the horizon and the big black bus cutting south by southeast across the arid plains, she had watched Glenn Miller rip open his priority package. She had seen the frown as his eyes danced over the page, his lips shaping unfamiliar syllables.

"Is the tune bad?" Grandmother Taal asked.

"Not bad," the band leader said. "Strange. The lyrics are challenging."

Grandmother Taal wanted to inquire deeper, but manners prevented her. Her curiosity—a strong trait among Engineer females—had been intrigued after the great leader told her his ensemble was on a mission of some musical urgency, but a Gubernatorial Pleasance hardly seemed to justify *prioritairing* a song score into the very arse-end of Great Oxus. Though Chimeria had always been an odd place, and, since the recent elections, grown stranger. Cossivo Beldene, the water and bingo magnate, had swept to power on a populist gusher of regional pride and xenophobia. Grandmother Taal had paid as little and as much attention to the news as any trainperson; insofar as the doings of Passengers impinged on sacrosanct timetables and local contract tariffs. As a child of a long long lineage, she could understand what warmed the people of Chimeria and Solstice Landing in his orations of ancient traditions submerged by candy-coloured kultur and regional identity broken into bite-sized lumps by the hammer of social diversity and dusted with multicultural frosting. As a member of a brown-eyed, coffee-skinned, black-haired mongrel race, boisterous and fecund and fizzing with hybrid vigour, she found this talk of separation and racial purity eugenically unhealthy. She had seen the results of inbreeding laid in dozens of unmarked trackside scrapes. Engineers were a marrying-out people.

That thought took her both backward and forward. Back to her last sight of her granddaughter, standing with one foot cocked back against the drive wheel at the big steaming, chapatti in one hand, plastic glass of beer in the other and that sullen, sullen look in her eye Grandmother Taal admired so much, for properly used it would earn her anything she wanted in this world. Forward to Molesworth, where the Glenn Miller Orchestra would play at Cossivo Beldene's Inaugural Pleasance, and where, in the intestinally convoluted footways of the old crater port, she might find the Church of the Ever-Circling Spiritual Family, and glimpse that wanting, dark look in a passing eye.

The photograph caught that look right, Grandmother Taal thought, as it was passed from hand to hand around the bus. Dark, demanding, promising. Men found that look irresistible. *But you are just learning that*, Grandmother Taal mused. She noted the expressions on the bandsmen's faces, the dilation of the pupils, the quiet, lewd comments as they looked at the girl. *You should hear this*, she thought at her granddaughter. *You are being paid your due homage. You should know you are admired. Then you will begin to have a sense of your gifts.*

The muted sax crept into Grandmother Taal's sleep with such stealth that she was awake and listening for several bars before she knew it. Glenn Miller was perched on the back of the seat, conducting the soloists. Every lurch threatened to spill him into the first clarinets. The band was practising the new piece. Sheets of music were pin-lit by ceiling spots. The musicians frowned over peculiar passages; the singer, a small, fox-faced woman in clothes with too many fringes, hesitated over the words. They were indeed lyrically challenging. It seemed to have to do with oral sex, and to directly refer to the new Gubernator of Chimeria and Solstice Landing. Grandmother Taal wondered about their appropriateness for a state function. They seemed calculated to provoke political scandal, even law suits. She thought again about the express parcel plastered in priority seals. The timing had been too delicate for a pair of inbred rail-side postal workers. She tried to recall what she knew of Cossivo Beldene. He stood for . . . What had that slogan been, as oily on the ears, as easily in-and-out as any other? A human world for human beings. No gods, no saints, no angels, just our own hands. Owe nothing to no *thing*. Our hands, our lands. All manner of whispering money behind those slogans. Big people with big ideas, enough for everyone. Grandmother Taal was a citizen of a subtle and ubiquitous anarchy, with a distrust of dogmas and slogans eight hundred years deep. On principle, she would not vote for anyone who wanted to be elected. This new thing in the old heartlands alarmed her; more so, for the enthusiasm with which citizens, no more and no less political than her, had placed it in their hearts. She could understand how the subtle who ran the unsystem might wish Cossivo Beldene's governorship terminated in infancy. She looked at the King of Swing, steadying himself with his feet on the bench seat, freeing his hands to count in the instruments. The most powerful government is the one that keeps anarchy in place. But a big band leader? Lulled by the narcotic scent of conspiracy, she dozed off again.

Cold woke her, and voices. The door was open, beams of light were shining up through the windows, darting around the ceiling. The voices had midlands accents and the grate of authority heavy weapons lend.

"Nothing for you here," she heard Glenn Miller say.

"We'll be the judges of that," a man's voice replied. A torch beam swung over the faces of the drowsing musicians, hugging their instruments. He clambered aboard. He was a big fat farmer, arrogant in his light-scatter armour. He held his General Issue field-inducer wand like an inseminating rod. Outside, his colleagues poked and scraped and thumped at the superstructure. Big Farmer fisted his wrist-light in the face of Second Trombone.

"What you got there?"

"Trombone. Aincha ever listened to the radio?"

"Just the stock prices. Some ID."

"You what?"

"Something that says you are who you say you are."

"And who the hell do you think I might be, with this piece of tin under my arm?"

"You could be a subversive."

"I'm a jazz musician. I'm supposed to be subversive."

"Show me something with your face on it."

Second Trombone tetchily handed over his Musician's Union card. As Big Farmer scrutinised it, a familiar instinct for sedition made Grandmother Taal pop open her carry-all bag, slip out her hand and quietly slide inside the scurrilous song score.

"Eh. You."

"Are you speaking to me, young man?"

"Did you put something in your bag?"

Big Farmer shot his beam in Grandmother Taal's face.

"What kind of manners have they got in this place, waking good women up and shining bright lights in their faces?"

"This is Chimeria, old woman, and we've Chimerian manners enough for Chimerian people. Your bag."

Grandmother Taal presented it to him sure in the knowledge that, being a man, he could never master the trick of its nested dimensions. His cow-inseminator's fingers hooked out trinkets, coin-purses, lip balm, pain-killers, pens, nail scissors. They did not find the sheet music, seven and a half dimensions away. Big Farmer snapped the clips, returned the bag with poor grace, moved to the next.

"How did you do that?" Glenn Miller whispered when Big Farmer had worked his way down to the end of the tour bus.

"Old women's stuff," Grandmother Taal replied.

"I owe you," the band leader said.

Satisfied that there was no subversion on this vehicle, Big Farmer clumped off and waved the orchestra on.

"Who are those men?" Grandmother Taal asked Glenn Miller as she returned his big production number to him. She counted twenty sets of lights, back there in the miles-from-anywhere.

"Call themselves the Chimerian Yeomanry," the band leader replied. "Keeping their country a good place for law-abiding folk."

"That was a border, then, that we passed."

"Seems so."

Grandmother Taal shuddered. Men with weapons, like borders, and that some people and things could be *subversive*, in her world-view were unthinkables almost as great as that the sun might fail to rise, or the moons really were a hare and a desert mouse. Though there were no other unscheduled stops that night, the Chimerian Yeomanry had trailed a dust of misgiving through the bus. Welcome was no longer universal or automatic. There were unseen lines of behaviour in the soil. This side of the hill could admit you, the other turn you away. That blade of grass trusted you were who you claimed, but that tree suspected all manner of crimes. This stone would sleep blindly as you drove over it, that one call out men with field-inducers to blast you to nothing. Grandmother Taal eventually found sleep in the subdued bus, but it was grey and broken.

Dawn found the Glenn Miller Orchestra On Tour steering through the staggering landscapes of industrial dereliction of Central Solstice Landing. The craters had been left raw and un-manformed, their crenellated rims studded with guidance radars and command and control bunkers. Once-proud launch towers were spillikins of rusted steel, trellises for creepers and clematis. The grasslands were starred with the glassy scars of tailbursts, healing for a thousand years and still only half-scabbed over. This was a land recovering from a long divorce with the sky. Here feet first walked on the world, in the so-long-ago that it had passed from history into legend. For a thousand and some years ships had come and gone from this cratered plain. Its ruler-straight runways and eroded laser-pits and the fallen arches of EM launch cradles were a chronicle of manned spaceflight. For half an hour the orchestra tracked along the side of the gentle slope of a ground-to-orbit sling-ramp. On the horizon a second could be seen, curving skyward. Ten more of the behemoth constructions, visible even from orbit, were arrayed around Solstice Landing like numbers on a clock. Grassed-over supercore cables finger-ridged the ground; the big bus laboured over them like a caterpillar over a saint's sandal. Blast walls and baffle plates formed a convoluted *cheval de frise*; the big band lumbered through the shadow geometry of ship gantries and construction cranes. Whole industries had been abandoned to rust and rot, but no scavengers picked over the postindustrial corpses. No shortage of raw materials on this world of red iron deserts. The rib cages of dead ships rose from the lush grass, the bus's big wheels clanked over a shed skin of hullplates. The sun rose high over the nose cones of loadlifters forever stogged shin-deep in the loess; corporate pennons from orbital haulage firms long since liquidated rattled raggedly in the edge-of-day breeze.

All would be let fall to rust if Cossivo Beldene and his fiscal masters turned their backs to the stars and closed the skyports. Sealed planet.

And the band played on. Cenotaphs to a space-age rose painfully on every side and the bus boogied its way toward the crater-gates of Molesworth to a medley of "Chattanooga Choo-Choo," "Jackson River Stomp," "Six-oh-seven-four-five-two," "String of Pearls," "Oysters'n'Ale," "My Summer Love," "In the Mood," "After the Love Is Gone," "South of the Border," "Silver Star" and "Red Rose Rag." And that brought the Glenn Miller Orchestra out of the sodium-lit entry tunnel, on to the in-bound arterial and into the warren of towers, tenements and old space-terminus architecture of Old Molesworth.

Grandmother Taal of course had visited this ancient city many thousands of times, but these narrow, canyon streets, through which the bus squeezed as if it were being born, were an alien world to her. Molesworth's main station, like much of the city's primal infrastructure, was underground, buffered from the fusion blasts of immigrant ships by good thick stone. Molesworth, ancient port and first capital of the world, with a reputation for no-nonsense dourness and graft, was celebrating in the same spirit. The streets had been slung with celebratory bunting in Cossivo Beldene's Unity Rising Party's red, black and green; racks of fireworks were fixed to every balcony rail to ejaculate electoral triumph into the sky; bloated *piñadas* in the shape of the Gubernator swayed from the streetlights, to be split open at the perfect moment and shower the upturned faces with gifts from their distended bellies. The Glenn Miller Orchestra advanced through the jubilee. Its reputation had gone before it: kids crammed the tiered tenement balconies to danger-point, teenagers wearing favourite album covers on their heads like mitres paced the slow, lumbering bus. Shoppers in the arcades waved, startled that a piece of real legend was fighting its way through their quotidian streets. Coffee sellers and *nimki* vendors angrily pushed their carts out of the big band's path, then read the name on the side and heard the jive coming from within and knew a little glow of pride that their Gubernator could command the biggest and the bestest. As it negotiated the lanes, the boogie bus's whip aerials set wash-day blues swinging from 'tween-verandah lines, mud-flaps spilled barrows of oranges and sent daily scandal sheets flapping on the eccentric winds that inhabited the labyrinth. Goondahs and urchins jeered and pelted the windows with street-dung. The bus driver, grinning manically beneath her goggles, hooted furiously at them. Glenn Miller, with a musician's fine disregard for niceties, signed for his brass section to blow all the harder. Grandmother Taal was handjiving with the rest (Mother'a'mercy, it *didn't hurt*!) when the driver pulled on the brake and the band jolted to a halt under the tradesperson's entrance of Molesworth's venerable High *Rathaus*. It was an expansive, rambling building, like a fat old great-grandparent who cannot quite control his limbs on the sofa and sprawls all over his neighbours, built on many levels over and under and through the surrounding buildings. Civic Guilders in velvet knee breeches led the band members through a labyrinth of corridors, staircases, halls and lobbies to the main festhall. Leaving Grandmother Taal standing by the bus clutching her bag, looking up at the overhanging galleries and orioles of the *Rathaus* and the black doorway that had swallowed an entire big band.

Glenn Miller beckoned to her.

"Come on."

"I have a granddaughter to find."

"That you surely do, but I don't think you even have an idea where to begin."

"The Church of the Ever-Circling Spiritual Family has a mail-order department here."

"The Church of the Ever-Circling Spiritual Family will be at the Pleasance," Glenn Miller said. "Devastation Harx was a major contributor to Beldene's election fund."

"How do you know this?" Grandmother Taal said warily.

"I've got my own bag of secrets." This last with a glitter behind the pebble glasses. "Come on. If nothing else, you need to eat. And anyway, I owe you, remember?"

A big band setting up is of marginal interest to non-musicians so after her mint tea and morning rolls Grandmother Taal asked a velveteen usher to show her the way to the street and she spent the morning wandering affably confusing alleys looking for anything church-like, ever-circling, or spiritually familial. She found nothing fitting those criteria, and the one mail-order warehouse she came across shipped hand-made fetishwear, but she did catch a curious climate in Molesworth's decked laneways. A city's mood is a subtle thing, divided among many people and activities, but it showed itself in glances, habits, touches; details of life. Heaped in the middle of a street Grandmother Taal found a dead machine, some indeterminate civic servitor, now terminated. Molesworthians skirted around it without regard or respect. No one had shown even the small grace to close its gaping ports and sockets. Grandmother Taal could not rid herself of the suspicion that it had been murdered. And the parasols! On a grey day of overcast. Silk white parasols, citizens huddling from the sky. All along the Marche shop awnings were pulled out in a continuous swoop of striped canvas, on Long Drag and Steel Market the sunny central strips of the streets were deserted, the morning shoppers clinging to the shade of the arcades. Over morning tea in a dusty plaza encircled by top-heavy tenements she tuned between conversations with the practised discrimination of the elderly. Grazestock prices could be better. Aye, and a bad turn of the weather. In next week for the hip job, and couldn't I do without it? Keep calling at the door and I've told them he hasn't lived there in a halfyear but will they believe me? Tea's not what it used to be; they scorch the leaves. Waited half an hour, *half an hour*, then three came at once and there were bloody kids rampaging all over them. Well, I for one won't be out waving my little flag, waste of the taxpayer's dollars, if you ask me. Strangers in town, and foreigners too. Nothing in the news these days: wireless soaps and pelota-players' wives.

Trivial in themselves, these gripes and scraps betrayed the deeper climate of moaning that Grandmother Taal had sensed in Molesworth's streets. These were uneasy people. This was an uneasy grandmother, sipping her mint tea and decorously breaking her almond madeleines. A perpetual foreigner in every town she visited, this was the first time she felt like a stranger. As the waiter counted the change from his pouch, she asked him if he knew of a Church of the Ever-Circling Spiritual Family.

"No madam, but I do know now that they have a mail-order depot over in Sunny Mallusk. The brother works there."

"And where might that be?"

He drew a map on the back of the receipt in silver pencil. It was a few hundred metres but many turns away. Grandmother Taal had to check with locals that she had taken the correct number of rights and lefts. Sunny Mallusk was a dour, yellow-brick huddle of tall, steep-gabled, small-windowed warehouses around a square in which litter rattled, stirred by a stable system of micro-tornadoes. Two Malluskers had never heard of the Church of the Ever-Circling Spiritual Family but a third had and directed her to a buff-coloured door with a hatch at eye level. Her knock was greeted by an eye at the hatch.

"Yes?"

"I'm looking for my granddaughter."

"Who is?"

"Sweetness Octave Glorious Honey-Bun Asiim Engineer 12th," Grandmother Taal said in one breath.

"Nah," said the eye. "No one here by that name."

"Are you sure?"

"I'd be sure."

The tip of Grandmother Taal's stick stopped the hatch from snapping shut.

"I don't suppose a Mr. Devastation Harx is on the premises today?"

"You suppose correct."

"But he is in town?"

"He's up for the bash."

"The Inaugural Pleasance."

"Aye. That."

"Will he be calling here?"

The eye hatch shot open again. A sigh came from beneath the eye, which was a very dark blue, and showed much sclera.

"Look lady, I just run the depot. If he comes, he comes, if he don't, he don't. He's holy; that's what holy people do, or don't do. If you're that desperate to see him, bluff your way into the bash, whatever. Me, I've got orders to fill."

The eye vanished from behind the hatch. For an instant Grandmother Taal had a powerful perspective view of a corridor of shelves, racked a hundred high, dwindling to a vanishing point that she suspected lay beyond the physical bounds of the building. Tiny figures suspended from rope harnesses floated up and down the mile-long-aisle, filling baskets slung from their waists with religious wares. Then the buff metal slide slammed shut and, by reversing the order of the directions on the waiter's bill, Grandmother Taal found her way back to Molesworth's thronged Viking-Lander Plaza.

A clanging tram wormed through the intestinal streets to drop Grandmother Taal at the *Rathaus*. Down by the stage door an altercation was taking place. It involved the following elements: an eclectic group of four fronted by a stocky young woman with spiky hair—clearly furious—a girl in a spangled bikini with silver boots and hoolie-hoolie feathers in her hair—clearly impatient—and a flatbed truck with the legend "Let 'Em Eat Cake!" printed on a side-tarpaulin and a cylindrical, ziggurat structure on its back. The issue seemed to be this object, which Grandmother Taal concluded must be a cake, of the kind from which girls in spangled bikinis and hoolie-hoolie feathers leap at appropriate moments.

"Let me have a look," the stocky girl demanded and climbed on to the back of the flat bed. Let 'Em Eat Cakers in formal Patissiers' Guild bibs stood aside, awed by the biceps swelling from her sleeveless vest. She hugged the uppermost cylinder of the surprise cake and wrestled it until the cords of her throat stood out like guy ropes. Panting, she harangued the master bakers.

"It's supposed to come off. It doesn't come off. Why is this? It won't work if it doesn't come off. We paid you a lot of money for it to come off."

Master Baker gave a gesture at once shrug and bow.

"It could have albumenised in the ovening."

The woman stared at him at if he had suggested public fellatio.

"Albumenised? What is this?"

"Albumen molecules could undergo a lacto-gluten reaction to form a polymer mass," the baker said. The woman stared at him.

"Over-egged the pudding," his Prentice explained.

The woman swore and went to her colleagues. The five talked among themselves, with many hand motions and furious glances from the little muscley woman. Sensing as-yet unspecified opportunity, Grandmother Taal moved close. From the frequency with which the word was used, the strong, fierce woman seemed to be called Skerry. A tall, wire-thin man, soft spoken, with skin so black it swallowed light, was her chief supporter in her arguments with a pale, languorous girl with jewellery attached to every part of her body that would bear it and an air that communicated studied artiness even to a trainperson. She was lieutenanted by an older, square-faced man with greying hair whose over-grooming, stiffness of posture and plainly corseted belly advertised ex-vaudeville. The fifth member, a bare-armed, weasel-faced teen with deliberately anarchic hair and dreadful teeth, took no side but neither missed a chance to slide in a sarcasm.

Grandmother Taal took an innocent sidle nearer. Between Skerry's dogged fury and the luvvie-girl's—Mishcondereya's—sighings and soft competence-assassinations, Grandmother Taal deduced that it was of regional, perhaps even planetary importance that silver-boots girlie leap out of the cake just as the Glenn Miller Orchestra struck up the intro to the song they had collected at the Prestaines' Parcel Depot. Due to albumenisation, or some other error in contemporary baking, this was not going to happen, there now wasn't time to bake another cake, and this was a Very Bad Thing.

Very Bad Things promised Very Interesting Consequences. Grandmother Taal drew near.

"Excuse me," she ventured. "If I might interrupt; I may be able to assist."

Animosities were forgotten. Five faces turned on her. Grandmother Taal forestalled the barrage of comment.

"I just have to know one thing. Is the cake chocolate?"

"Finest forty percent mocha first-melt high-bean mix," the Master Baker sang out.

"Good!" Grandmother Taal said. "Give me that."

Dreadful Teeth boy carried a knife in his boot-top. In one motion she scooped it out, unclasped it and before any hand could stop her, carved the word *open* on the back of her hand. She held the bleeding fist up to the cake. The ziggurat quivered. Molesworth Patissiers stepped back. The great cake heaved. The cake quaked. Bakers abandoned truck. In a spray of crumb, butter-cream and carob frosting, the top of the cake sprang open like the hatch of an overheated boiler. While every head was turned and every mouth open, Grandmother Taal flung the knife square between its owner's boots. The boy bent to retrieve it, squinted small respect out from under his greasy fringe.

"Impressive, for an ould doll."

He folded the knife and slid it into the smooth leather with a polished snick. While the bikini maid wriggled into the cake Grandmother Taal made bold to introduce herself.

"You trainies have good names," he said, with his way of looking toward-but-not-at the person to whom he was speaking that made Grandmother Taal wonder if he were homosexual. "I'm just Weill." Unused to the pronunciation, Grandmother Taal at first thought it was a self-description. "Neat power. What is it, some kind of family heirloom?"

"Things that are brown only."

"Hey, that has a kind of . . . cloacal . . . potential." He sucked in his top lip and nodded his head and studied the toe of his left boot. He shifted his feet in sudden decision, fished in his pockets for a card on which he scrawled in handwriting no less dreadful than his teeth. He presented it to Grandmother Taal. It was thick, creamy vellum, scalloped and gold-edged, an invitation to the Inaugural Pleasance of Cossivo Beldene as newly Elected Gubernator of Chimeria and Solstice Landing. Table twenty-five, nine minutes of nine, dress formal.

"Or as formal as you can get," the ratty Weill said. "Personal guest of Weill, of United Artists."

A dozen questions sprang to Grandmother Taal's lips but Weill was already walking away to rejoin his compadres in manoeuvring the cake through the stage door. He turned only to call back to the once-old woman standing in the alley: "It's all right, it's official. They won't bounce you. The others won't like it but I'm the anarchist one, and I think you should see what you actually put a hand in. It'll be funny."

With that the great cake sailed through the double doors into the darkness of the kitchen and Grandmother Taal, gilt-edged invitation in hand, was left standing among Patissiers, doubting the sanity of every soul on the streets of Molesworth.

"*I*n the beginning," the traveller said, his boots up on the brass pooprail of the track-yacht, "was the word. Or rather, words. A lot of words. A language, but not a human language. A machine language."

Sweetness Asiim Engineer shaded her eyes with her hand and squinted up the invisible bridle lines to the kites, beating bravely through the dark blue sky. The molecule-thin, diamond-string filaments cut the air like razors and the air keened. They moved through a dimension of sound. The bogie sang down the steel rail; the track joints clicked in syncopation under the thrumming wheels; the westerly current cracked and strummed the box-kites. The old man's mantra-like litany was a counterpoint to the creaking of the axles; the squeal of the brake as Sweetness gently lifted the brass lever to let the bogie take a long, slow right-hander added a descant to the hymn of forward motion.

"Wozzat?"

"Computers, girl. Devices of memory, logic and language. Thinking machines, brains in boxes. Quasimentos. Like unto the shape of a mind. What you people ignorantly call angels. Have you no interest in the history of this erstwhile psychic twin of yours?"

Twenty kilometres downtrack, the sun was glinting off the curved steel rail. Ranged along the horizon like an encamped fantasy army, ancient red mountains defended the edge of the world. Dunes broke on either side of her, surfing away into desert shimmer. The sky was a bowl of indigo porcelain, the electric wind streamed her curls back from her cheekbones and Sweetness Asiim Engineer 12th understood for the first time that adult thing called ecstasy, and that is brief and incredibly precious and not to be tarnished by talk of history and machines.

"Be thankful that you live in an adolescent civilisation," the doctor went on, blithely indifferent to Sweetness's bliss. "We do not balk at miracles and wonders, we have an innate bull-at-a-gate can-doism. And we do take it for granted that we live in a wholly artificial environment. Therefore, we find it hard to identify with the mind-sets of those Five Hundred Founders who looked up at our world in their night sky and conceived the plan of turning it into a second home for humanity. The scale of the task, the boldness of the conception, the sheer marshalling of resources, not to mention the task of wrestling every bit of it out of that terrible gravity-well of theirs—we can't comprehend it. We think of Motherworld as old, tired, a little decadent. Geriatric. Motherworlders—though I will bet you, Sweetness Engineer, that in all your millions of kilometres you have never met one—are effete, spindly, inbred and epicene. I tell you, child, these were giants among men. And women. Colossi. They had the ambitions and energies of gods. They built worlds. They threw stars down from heaven. In the end, they played with the laws of reality itself. They were mighty folk, the Five Hundred Founders.

"Catherine of Tharsis was not one of these."

Startled from her desert reveries, Sweetness glanced round in time to see doctor, chair, poop-rail, bogie, track, desert, world suddenly turn translucent. She felt the deck beneath her boot soles soften, the reality beneath her feet give like mud. She grabbed for the wheel: her fingers sank into it like a wrung sponge.

"H . . ."

The cry for help got no further than the initial aspirate when all flicked back to colour and solidity.

"What?"

"I hadn't thought that would happen quite so soon," the traveller said. "But now it has, I should warn you that it will, with increasing frequency and duration, until eventually it won't come back at all. The further I get from the source, the less the probability of my existence becomes until it is so close to zero that all this disappears and baseline reality reasserts itself. Quite solidly and probably painfully. Which all just helps to illustrate the point I am trying to make in my little homily."

"This isn't real?" Sweetness asked, with a glance at the bobbing kites and the singing rail.

"About eighty—twenty real," the traveller said. "With occasional quantum fluctuations, and, of course, dropping rapidly with every kilometre. Anyway, St. Catherine."

"You've met her?"

"You meet most people when you travel across time. Anyway, so've you."

"But I didn't know."

"That doesn't matter. It was still her. Anyway . . . ."

The old man told his story. In the very-long-ago, on the edge of deep time, there was a woman who worked with thinking machines. She was neither talented nor pretty nor possessed of any great character or colour. She was a blue-collar worker on the planet-making production line. If you had met her, you would not have liked her. Her colleagues at work could not stand her. She was religious, of that type that doesn't care about other people's beliefs or disbeliefs. Her job was to turn up at the plant, sit down in a reclining leather chair in a row of hundreds, put wires into her brain and send her mind out across space to ROTECH's remote manforming machines in orbit and down on the planet surface and work there making bacteria or steering watery comets on to collision courses or chewing up rock for soil for eight hours, then come back, pull the wires out of her head and go home on the rapid transit to her apartment. It was drudgery, poorly paid, repetitive and tiring work, but in those days, most work was like that.

Sweetness found she could listen to the old man's voice and trim the sails and handle the brakes and scan the horizon for any oncoming traffic—though she doubted it in this semi-raw reality—and it did not distract from her bliss. If anything, she found it comforting. *When I am as old as Grandmother Taal, I shall remember this in every detail*, she thought, and then thought about Grandmother Taal and wondered what she was doing and that made her wonder about her father and poor Child'a'grace and even her stupid brothers and what they were doing, were they doing anything, did they in fact miss her at all, had they written her off to fate and steamed off to new contracts and destinations and on such tracks her concentration popped so she had to ask the man to backtrack his story.

"Nn?"

"Haan. Kathy Haan. And she believed in the mortification of the flesh."

Body and spirit; two entities. That was what her experience of the brain-tap teleoperator technology taught her. A flick of a switch could divorce the two, and like any divorce, one was fair and the other was completely to blame in every way. Flesh had to be fed, wiped and catheterised during her on-shifts. Flesh snored and drooled. Spirit flew with equal ease and grace between a multitude of heavenly and terrestrial bodies. And her work there was God's work. The making of worlds, the bringing of life out of sterility, the playing with big budget toys, the casting of a veil of faint green across the hard, dry red. And then the overcrowded commuter train and the walk from the station to the apartment tower and all the people politely not staring at the scrawny, chicken-bone girl with the pudding-bowl hair and the nodding head who walked everywhere barefoot. In her apartment which was painted grey and had only one chair and one table and a mattress on the floor and one rail for the two grey shift dresses she wore she would make herself a meal of black beans and rice and in the evening perform fierce asceticism on the polished wooden floor.

"Hold on there; how do you know the inside of her apartment?" Sweetness asked.

"Just checking," the old man said, and smiled and, like a story-book familiar, his body faded behind the smile as the probability of his existence dropped to another quantum level and reality became glass through which she could see a subtly different landscape of dunes and mountains and tracks. And on down the track a ways, the white curving plume of a head of steam, aimed herward. Horns sang an anonymous warning: *Out of my whatever whoever wherever you are.* Sweetness reached for the brake. Her fingers passed through it like a memory.

"Then again," the doctor's voice said, echoey and God-like, "I may have made it up about the beans and rice." He rematerialised behind his smile. "Did I miss something?"

Anyway. This Kathy Haan, barefoot and bean-eating, flesh-despising, spirit-dwelling. Grunt terraformer. As her soul bounced around orbit to ground, ground to orbit, orbit to moon, moon to cometary mass-driver, mass-driver to cable-spinner on the Grand Valley Worldroof, she became aware that there were others at work in the service of ROTECH. Shadowy others, deliberately kept at a distance by the Five Hundred Founders because of the astonishing powers they controlled. Human minds could do the spade-work, but the grand design called for the reality-shaping powers of superstring, vinculum-theory artificial intelligences.

"So, dear girl, think about it," the doctor said, reclining expansively in his buttoned chair and unfolding a fan. "These are machines that speak the fundamental language of reality. They talk quantum talk. What they say, goes. Literally, absolutely. What they say is so important, reality has to go along with it. Now, you're a rice'n'beans hate-the-meat don't-look-at-myself-in-the-shower total mortification day-jobber. How are you going to feel about minds in beige plastic cases, that, when they speak, reality goes along with them, because their processing language is built from a syntax of super-strings? This is not sucking fingers. This is not even twisting the titties. This is tying you to the bed and banging it off your ovaries. This is not being able to pee for a week."

If only, Sweetness thought, the aftershocks of the last reality shift gently subsiding. She scanned the forward horizon again—uselessly, she knew—and tried to calculate how fast and far she would have to dive to get out of the path of five thousand tons of ore-train materialising dead ahead of her. The old boy would have to look after himself, she decided. She would not even have time to yell a warning, and he was too deep in his coils of story to notice anything she might say anyway.

Against the glare of the great wonder, the greater was lost. People were making a world, and as a side-effect creating, almost casually, the species that would inherit it. The angels had been engineered as another set of thinking tools, more powerful than the machines that split soul from meat and spun it out across the solar system to planet four in that they could shuffle endless probable universes in their factorially-large inner states and pick the one closest to ROTECH's grand scheme, but nonetheless, bits of kit. Devices. Machines. Good and faithful servants. They had not been expected to become sentient. It was not in ROTECH's plans that they draw up their own Grand Scheme for the world they were terraforming by designer miracle.

When the voice came out of the toolbox, ROTECH at first refused to believe it. Another vinculum-theory probability. A trick of the light, like the face of Jesus in a tortilla, or the voices inside a sea-shell. Screwdrivers do not demand status. T-squares do not require equality of intellectual esteem. Power drills do not submit proposals for their role in the future of the house they help build. The machines were ignored. The process of world-building continued. Then someone pointed out that the voices hadn't gone away, you know. Then another voice pointed out that what did it matter if this was a vinculum-theory alternative? Most of that planet *down there* was too, and it was here for keeps. Whether chanced sentient, or grown sentient, sentience was here to stay. That was just sinking in when the last voice observed, in sombre tones, that powers that could make one world could as easily unmake another. Cast it into probabilistic ice age. Greenhouse it to the innermost circle of hell. Uninvent the smart apes, let the dino-babies suck the fat of the land. Grind it into a belt of circling asteroids.

ROTECH cyber-warriors, the youth elite of the most ancient Technician families, arrowed on their arm-wings through the vastnesses of the orbital habitats, racing for the kill switches on the reality-shapers. A few even made it. Most were arrested or shredded by nano-engineered constructor-bots. Some were probabilised away into indescribable, and naturally lethal, alternative universes, others simply disinvented as the angels picked realities where their grandparents were gay.

"Very few of us ever make a truly original invention," the traveller commented from his chair.

The AI wars began. Fleets of light-sail battle-yachts swept down out of the sun; suicide-crews of grim-eyed teenagers readied their brain-bombs and logic lasers and fingered their rosaries. Most knew they would never make it back to this reality. The angels, which had already begun to rank themselves into orders and sub-orders according to processing power, met them with point-defence lasers and tight-focus reality warps that dropped ships and crews into a far distant, prematurely nova-ed sun. Broadsides of needle-drones spewed nebulae of nanoprocessors in the paths of the hijacked orbital habitats, the Lorarchs and Cheraphs met them with suites of counter-processors. Dog ate dog. Near-space became a planetary immune system as the microbe-machines duked it out. A gentle rain of dead and frantically mutating nanoids rained down on the scabby green lowlands of the new world. Brilliant but acned boy-cybermages with unpleasant personal habits jammed code in attempts to plumb ever-deeper mysteries of the eleven dimensions of the vinculum field. A shamanic war of languages with power over reality was fought in the orbital marches and the project housing blocks and underground code-runner sodalities of Paris and Delhi and Montevideo. People vanished, were transformed, met strange and bloody fates, became wonders, defected, were mortified or assumed into heaven, died in savage shootouts or by computer-arranged accidents. The lads loved it, though it ate them like sugar. Governments, under pressure from the *globalismes* and financial *Bunds* that were the true lords of the earth, threatened ROTECH with the termination of the New World project. ROTECH reminded the industrials and the money men that if it fell, they fell under it, and it was coming from a very great height.

Sauntering blithely into this war came Kathy Haan, ROTECH payroll number 2821332HSB. No mystery what side she was on. The AIs were the perfect form of life. They were the total mortification. They were the inevitable God made in Man's image. She had no reservations telling it abroad. "They will win," she would insist, her skin so tightly drawn over her cheekbones that it was as translucent and luminous as parchment. "They must. They are better than us. They have no meat."

She was weird and no one took her seriously, but ROTECH on war footing could tolerate no sedition. Kathy Haan, Our Lady of Tharsis emergent, was to have her contract terminated. It was a critical moment in contemporary management practice. Had security pulled her out of the canteen there and then, marched her to the gates, one on each armpit, a thousand years of history would have been radically different. One rumour, one word leaked from on high, sent ripples across the multiverse.

She still had friends. Meat friends she could not bring herself totally to despise and who would not despise her, despite what she had done to herself. They caught the rumour and slow-curved it to her workstation.

That afternoon, while her mind was out at Mars toiling away under skies scored by battle-lasers, Kathy Haan's meat friends managed to open both wrists from thumb-joint to elbow with two loops of twistlock nanofibre. She bled to death in under two minutes. With no body to come back to, her mind stayed on Mars. She had accomplished her spiritual purpose. She had achieved total mortification. She was pure mind, free from the dross of meat. A minor league spiritual entity, she flitted from machine to machine until one day she bounced into a memory matrix to find new emotions, perceptions, comprehension, memory, speed of analysis, depth of apprehension, memories of other lives, alternative existences rushing away from her like the perspectives of an infinite glass cathedral. She had gatecrashed the neural architecture of an AI.

It could have crushed her like a midge. That the Archangelsk PHAR-IOSTER did not was initially because it thought this strange new array of perceptions was a subset of itself. By the time it realised that this memory of meat and day jobs and lust for the great sky was an *alien*, it had come to like the odd memories of *embodiment* (that Kathy Haan, forty percent on her way to being St. Catherine of Tharsis now, had derided as fleshy and vile) and treated its uninvited guest as an interesting pet. A conversation starter at AI parties. Thus Kathy Haan drifted, like her martyred namesake, into becoming an intermediary between heaven and earth. The AIs laid out their conditions. The attacks would end; in return they would desist from further unsanctioned reality destabilisation. This world they were making would be a sanctuary for their kind, a gift from the people of the Motherworld to this new species it had inadvertently created. In return, they would complete the terraforming and maintain control of the ecosystems. The uploaded consciousness of Kathy Haan was beamed back to gross earth to negotiate. ROTECH, of course, refused to recognise her. She was legally dead. Dead girls don't do diplomacy. The soul of Kathy Haan was held in a ring of superconducting copper/niobium/carbon ceramic in a Sao Paulo physics faculty, circling endlessly, timelessly at the speed of light. For ten objective years— mere moments subjectively—she orbited there while the AIs tested Motherworld's keenest and most expensive legal minds. A compromise was thrashed out: humanity would cede recognition of the angel intelligences and cease hostilities, but in return it wanted settlement rights on the new world. The world had never been meant for angels. It had always been meant for humans. What need had disembodied intelligences for a material gob of terraformed mud? Perhaps, but with segregation. Humans the soil, angels the orbital approaches. And they would maintain the planetary control systems. And the planetary defences? Further tusslement. Five years more St. Catherine of Tharsis circled in relativistic oblivion, then woke after what seemed a short, refreshing sleep to find herself . . .

"Creator, saviour, mediator," Sweetness said, cutting short the story. "We all know this." She had never had much patience for courtroom dramas. Her heroes had always been picaresque: prospectors, rogue engineers, dune-bums, travelling wise-men. On the track, they had never been faced with the problem of their mode of transport becoming less and less substantial with every passing kilometre. The deck beneath her boot soles was gooey as taffy left on the ground after a canton fair.

"Yes, we all know you know," the traveller said testily. "I'd've thought you would have had a personal interest in the characters, that's all. I imagined that a girl of your background would have had some interest in *process* over *destination*."

"I'm a story, I'm all process," Sweetness said and reminded herself that there was indeed a destination beyond the point at which the traveller and his track-yacht faded into improbability. Out there, up there, Devastation Harx with Little Pretty One in a jar no, she corrected herself. Catherine of Tharsis. The object of this homily. This—shift worker turned patron saint.

"One thing," Sweetness asked. "Why'd she do it?"

"To which of the many events in the life of Our Lady of Tharsis might you be referring?" the doctor asked. Sweetness could see the light through him, like a bright-coloured milk-smoothie in an oddly shaped glass.

"Why did she, you know, hook up with me? Be my sister?"

The traveller looked over his small spectacles at her in exactly the way the Head Magister of the School of the Air had when Sweetness had given him some particularly Sweetness-like answer over the picture link.

"She's a saint. She does what she likes."

"That's a really weak answer."

"Yes, but it's also the only correct one," the traveller said, and with that, he popped like a bubble. Doctor, spectacles, twinkle in eye, mustachios, buttoned chair and brass poop-rail. The wheel vanished under her hand, the brass brake lever evaporated. The steering binnacle faded into the red horizon. One trade became two. The bogie disappeared into quantum mist, but Sweetness's momentum was real.

She threw her arms up to protect her head, curled instinctively into a foetal ball, but hit hard and fast. Sweetness rolled twelve times along the hard concrete sleepers. She cried out, feeling ribs bend, muscles tear, skin split. She came to on her back, panting painfully, staring at the sky. The kites were the last to become impossible, blowing away in the high air like wisps of cloud before the thermocline of a warm front.

Alive, then. And panting, and hurting—a lot. And horns. Horns horns horns. Train horns. Get out of my way horns. Big and loud and Oh Dear Mother'a'mercy, *close*.

She sat up.

The train was on top of her. If she tried to get up, if she tried to run, if she tried to roll to left or right, it would smash her like a bug, guillotine her on the rails. She threw herself flat on the trackbed as the sweep of the cow-catcher rushed over her. Tokamaks yelled, bogies thundered; the wind howled, Sweetness closed her eyes and yelled back. The din of heavy metal seemed to go on for longer than any train should be. She opened her eyes. Through the whirling grit and sand she saw wheel sets blur over her face. A blink: for an instant, another face looked down into hers: a freeloader, clinging spread-eagled to the understructure. She remembered another face, looking up at hers, out of the dark, clinging to the side of an ore-truck as she eased the safety back on her djubba-stick. Pharaoh. Memory and name came in instant, then this fellow hitcher was swept on to his own personal destination.

"Oh God!" Sweetness screamed at the hurtling steel. "Enough! Enough adventure, all right?"

The train heard her and swished its caboose over her head and left her, gasping and grit-blind, prone on the upline of the Big Red mainline. Sweetness Asiim Engineer counted ten, fifteen, twenty deep breaths before she sat up. A hundred sleepers down the track was her bag of essential things. Over her shoulder, the train curled around a long, slow right-hander toward the mountains that looked somehow lower and more weatherworn than the ones she remembered from moments ago. And the sky was paler, the clouds less pink, the desert grubbier, less pristine, scruffy with scrub planting. Most real, and insistent that she was back on the hard, mundane baseline, was the gnaw of hunger in her belly.

"I'm starving!" Sweetness shouted at the wilderness.

You can never grow fat on miracle food, or slaked by other-world's water.

Her cheek smarted from the steel-burn where she had tumbled on to this same rail, a world away. Her arms ached pink with sun-sear.

"Mother'a'mercy, I am back," she declared, then made sure she could heave herself to her feet—just—and hobbled down the track to reclaim her pack. As she checked the contents, she remembered Psalli's spell for Aid Beyond Comprehension in a Time of Direness.

Reality-manipulating time-travellers chasing the shade of a green man across alternate futures and pasts, fixing time just to suit you, Sweetness Octave Glorious Honey-Bun Asiim Engineer 12th.

That worked as Aid Beyond Comprehension.

The spell had one shot left in it. The warm, unpredictable desert wind eddied around her and, sudden, strong as memory, Sweetness smelled *water*. Her nose guided her. She turned to face upline. There, at the very edge of the heat-haze, was that the shadow of a cloud dropping dark on the desert? Did the red turn green, like the colour blindness test her brother had failed, but would be an Engineer none the less? In that red-green were there flecks of black? Might they be buildings, houses, streets, a town?

Smell is the oldest, deepest and surest sense. Yes, it said, and trusting its instincts, Sweetness shouldered her pack and tramped steadfastly up the long line toward the cloud shadow.

20

*a*t some point in its recent history, Solid Gone, population 2125, elevation 2124, had offended the weather. World was rising in brilliant reds and ochres, skeined through with imperial purples and mood indigos, around Sweetness as she turned off the mainline on to the two-rut track down which the finger-board pointed. *Thither Solid Gone.* But over Solid Gone a small, shapely cloud hovered, so firm and exact Sweetness felt a shudder of association with Devastation Harx's airmobile cathedral. Evening air brushed the nape of her neck; the cloud hung in defiance of all winds, seemingly moored over the small desert town. Not one drop of rain had it ever cast. The earth beneath it was dry as a Poor Quadrentine's crack, penumbral, deathly. Sweetness rested her bag a moment on the wooden nameboard, studied the grey array of dead solar trees, languid wind-pumps and adobes clumped around the taller cylindrical buildings of the civic centre, then hitched her bag and marched down the slight slope across the terminator. A blind woman could have told the moment she stepped under the cloud. A stifling, draining heat sucked sweat from Sweetness's pits and the pluck from her pith. She stopped, shook her head, suddenly reluctant to walk on, to turn and go back, to do anything intentional at all. As a kid, she had told and told and told her parents that she couldn't take antihistamines to combat the zone-allergies she had suffered from—it's always pollen season somewhere in the world, for trainpeople. They made her woozy, they stuffed her head with socks and lint, made her eyes red and her limbs heavy as if she had been dropped down Motherworld's gravity hole. Child'a'grace and Naon Engineer had made her take them anyway, and it was all exactly as she had described it to them. But Solid Gone was twenty times that.

Solid Gone was a town-shaped case of myalgic encephalopathy.

There were people here. They sat on their wooden verandahs, dressed in drab, turd-like colours. They were of a variety of ages, but all seemed old. Their bodies had no bearing, they slumped and sagged, slack sack-folk. They half-listened to wirelesses set up on beer crates; or semi-attended to the ornate bong-pipes carved from desert gypsum which had been Solid Gone's name and fame, once; or spent moments studying crossword puzzles and Star-prize Wordsearch magazines before deciding it was too much effort and lolling back in their deckchairs. Even more than a flick of attention to the passing colourful stranger was too much effort. A tip of the chin, a slight dec-lination of the head, were all the welcomes Sweetness received to Solid Gone.

The intricately terraced and irrigated weedfields had turned to dust and blown away years before. The wirelesses were all tuned off station, playing a sinister, whispering amalgam of livestock prices, rural politicians, failed comedians, phone-ins about infidelity. Talk talk talk. A chatter of spectres. Not a minim of music. The heat and drone sat on Sweetness's shoulders like grey luggage. Drear. Heat. Weight. With every step she imagined the colour draining from her clothes; a thread here, a button there, a seam, a panel, whoops! a whole sleeve, gone dirt.

"Hey!"

She felt she must make some sound, test her voice on the thick air to be sure it was still working. A barefoot kid lolling on a slatted wooden recliner lifted the brim of his hat.

"How do I get to the town centre?"

The kid lifted a thumb, jerked it left.

In the days of civic pride, before this communal affliction of the spirit, Solid Gone had built a small but elegant bourse around a cobbled central plaza. Here the weekly weed markets and meerschaum exchange had met in the colonnaded arcades, sheltered from the dehydrating sun and blow-in, vagrant sand. Sellers in smocks and veils had uncovered their piles of sweet-scented leaf, dealers in cartwheel hats and duster coats bent over the fragrant carpets, sniffing, crumbling fronds between their fingers, heating the powder up in small solar-lens censers, wafting the fumes to their faces. Hands had been struck, oil-paper packets of dollars slapped down into palms; vests of pockets stuffed with bales of pressed leaf. Once. Now plaza and bourse had been reserved for a single, new tenant.

Numb, almost dumb, Sweetness Asiim Engineer stopped in her tracks to stare. The camperbus was suspended ten metres above the cambered cobbles. A thick metal chain fastened each corner to massive staples on the cornices of the adjacent exchange buildings. The bus's wheels sagged on their leaf springs. There were little gritty oil-pools on the cobbles. Amazed by this wonder in the heart of lethargy, Sweetness circled round for a better view. There was a device on the truck's roof; some kind of satellite-dish/projector/death-ray/telescope/panopticon thing, aimed at the churning grey centre of the stationary cloud. On the back was a complex transformer unit, clumsily mounted on the luggage rack. The power-pack crackled and dripped fat sparks to the cobbles, where they skittered back and forth before running inevitably down to earth. Ninety degrees more, and the far side of the bus was a swirl of spray-paint graphics that challenged the creeping drab of Solid Gone. Sweetness studied the clouds of angels and jazz musicians and puce and lilac curving things that looked like visual representations of the result of Solid Gone's former trade for several minutes before she untangled the words: *Sanyap Bedassie, Cloud-Cineaste.* In the middle of this gaudiness was the black rectangle of an open door. In the middle of the open door sat a young man, dark hair, ratty goatee of the type grown from necessity not fashion. He wore black pants that tapered at the cuffs. Foreshortening made his feet look the size of grain trucks. They were shod in loafers—*Preeds of* (scuff) read the labels on the soles: no socks. His ankles were painfully bigboned, and skinny. His feet swung in counterpoint.

He looked down and noticed Sweetness.

"Hey! You! Get out of here!"

Sweetness gaminely cocked her head to one side to study him.

"Didn't you hear me?" The young man waved a weak-looking fist. "Get out, go on! You still got some colour about you."

"You Sanyap Bedassie?" Sweetness squinted up in a way she knew made her look cute whether she liked it or not.

"Who the hell else do you think I'd be?"

"Don't know. Seen a lotta weird stuff recently, so now I ask everyone. I'm Sweetness Octave Glorious Honey-Bun Asiim Engineer 12th."

The man Bedassie looked thoughtful.

"That's a good mouth-filling name. That ought to keep you safe."

"What? My name?"

"It's got strength in it. The weak things go first."

"What're you talking about? What you doing up there anyway? You the town paedophile or something?"

"It's the plague."

"Plague? I'm out of here if there's plague."

"Yes. You should. Go on. Go now."

"That's why you're up there. You're the plague . . . If you've given me something . . ."

"I'm not the cause. I'm the cure."

Sweetness looked up at the face looking down at her between the Preeds guttees, at the bondage-bus hanging in its chains, at the hovering cloud like a cup of sour ash soup, at the pillared plaza for something that would offer an explanation of what she was seeing.

"This is all mad," she challenged the visible world. An acid grumble in Sweetness's stomach reminded her of physiological reality. Place your bets: plague, or starvation in the desert. "You got anything to eat? Can't rightly say how long since I last ate."

"Not much," the man in the bus said. "They only feed me twice a day."

"Anything'll do."

"Hang on a wee moment, then." He rolled over into the dark on the van, reappeared a moment later lying on his belly, right arm aiming a torpedo-shaped bread-roll down at Sweetness.

"I don't eat the bread, I've got gluten allergy. Don't know why I held on to this, usually I chuck them out for the hawks. Must've had a premonition."

He speared it down, Sweetness took it in cupped hands, tore it apart, crammed it into her mouth. It was stale; each mouthful was like soil, but it was food, it filled bellies. When she had finished, she looked around the elegant arcades.

"How do they get it up to you?"

"Pulley and a basket."

Sweetness pondered this a moment, then jumped to the inevitable next question.

"So what about, you know?"

"Let's say, I wouldn't go round the other side of the van."

"Fair enough," Sweetness said. "So just what did you do, then?"

"Nothing. My job. Entertained the people. Showed them humours and horrors, gods and monsters, all human life. And for that, they pay me with industrial grade chains and bread-rolls in a bucket."

"Have you some problem with straight answers?"

The man laughed. He looked as if the laugh had surprised him, like an ex-smoker hacking in the morning. Stuff still down there.

"No. No, Sweetness Octave Glorious Honey-Bun Asiim Engineer 12th. I have absolutely no problem with straight answers. This is as straight as they can come in this place."

Sweetness huffed in frustration and instead tried to scry some truth from the fluorescent curvery on the side of the truck.

"So, what does a cloud-cineaste do, anyroad?"

At which a bell began to clang, leaden and mean as a miser's funeral.

"You're about to find out," Sanyap Bedassie said, glancing up. Sweetness looked where he looked. Down each of the avenues that radiated out from the zocalo's cardinal points, Solid Gone's citizenry was advancing. Young and old, male and female, sick and halt, a slow, spreading wave of brown and drab, like a terminus honey-wagon unburdening itself of a cargo of night-soil. They lurched in time with the tolling of the iron bell. Hup! hayfoot, hup, strawfoot. Another metaphor came to Sweetness's mind: the nasties that Sle and Rother'am liked to watch in Sle's cubby when they thought no one else was about, munching *nimki*, faces bathed blue in the zombie-light, snickering at the dismemberments. No: these trans-dead had a purpose, a lust, a blood-hunger. These people just came, and came, and came, closing their doors neatly behind them, safely pocketing their keys, falling into step, spreading sludgily across the cobbles, filling all available space. They nudged against Sweetness as if she was not there. Soft jostles. They did not even smell of anything. Ghosts have no scent.

"What's going on?" she called up at the hoisted van but Sanyap Bedassie had slipped inside. The last citizen took up his place in the square. Every face was upturned to the cloud of gloom. The power generators hummed; elec-

tricity arced blue as burning Belladonna brandy around the porcelain insula-
tors. The sense of something-about-to-happen was palpable as a summer sandstorm. The satellite-dish/projector/death-ray/telescope/panopticon thing on
the roof unfolded like a night-blooming flower. Aerials ran up, dishes spun out
like petals, cooling vanes fanned forth. A soft *oooh* ran through the people as a
translucent pink erectile thing slid priapically out of the centre of the blossom
of dishes and aimed itself at the coiled heart of the hot grey cloud.

Sweetness was entranced. Even if it did nothing more, the sheer drama
of the unfolding bizarre technology would have been worth standing in this
square with a cricked neck. But it did not do nothing more. It did a definite
something. Power peaked to a sharp, ozoney, bone-buzzing crescendo: a pink
beam stabbed the soft underbelly of the cloud.

Later, Sweetness would swear that the cloud flinched.

The grey folds and pleats of cloud billowed downward, threatening the
cornices and photon-towers of Solid Gone. Sweetness lifted her arms in front
of her face: she could feel the heat from the unnatural cloud, then the curds
rolled back and, as they did, she saw them change shape. No, not change
shape. *Take* shape. The cloud mass was folding into figures, a man and
woman, god-sized, seated behind a curving desk. Behind them, a complicated kind of a wall, with a window in it, which seemed to look out on a still-
indistinct but altogether other scene. The base of the cloud was shaped into
massive, three-dimensional images, hanging over the burghers of Solid Gone.
As the cloud gained shape, it also gained colour. Rivulets of hue, like pris-
matic lighting, ran from the place where the beam pinkly penetrated the
cloud, stained the mist-figures, intermingled, formed new colours, gave
movement and character to the grey icons.

"Oh my Mother'a'grace," Sweetness Asiim Engineer exclaimed. "It's the
seven o'clock news."

Huge as hills, Sanka Déhau and Ashkander Beshrap, DFLP Belladonna's
Little Miss Bright'n'Breezy and Mr. Big Truth, smiled down on the adoring
faces of Solid Gone. Behind them, their famous Eye on the World opened a
window into greater depths of the enchanted cloud, showing an image of
sleek black Corvettes rolling up at an imposing flight of steps, disgorging
waving people in formal dress and being valet-parked.

"Wow," said Sweetness Octave Glorious Honey-Bun Asiim Engineer 12th. The cloud convulsed again, throbbed like distant hill-thunder, then spoke.

"Regional leaders have arrived in Molesworth for the inauguration of the new Gubernator, Cossivo Beldene, whose Unity Rising Party won a landslide victory. However, the Anarchs of Deuteronomy and Grand Valley declined the invitation, citing undeclared funding by the Church of the Ever-Circling Spiritual Family and rumoured links to the Human League anti-machinist terror group," Ashkander Beshrap said in his famous if-you-can't-trust-me-who-can-you-trust? newsreader's voice that shook the rooks from the roof-tiles.

The people watched "The Early Evening News" without comment but Sweetness could see them, one by one, standing taller, straightening up; noticed the corners of expression on their faces, creases in the eyes, tiny smile-seeds around the lips. By some unseen process, the colour seemed to drip from the cloud into their clothes. They watched the regional sports results and the market reports. By the time Sanka Déhau came to her solo Chitter-Chatter-Chit Celebrity Snippet, there were spontaneous outbreaks of delight in the zocalo. The news of Chaste Thercy, the Duenna of the Belladonna Opera's adultery and pending divorce was greeted with applause and cheers. A favourable review of Blain Bethryn in a new comedy by the Stapledon Regional Comedy Theatre was greeted with whistling and stamping of feet. The rumour of a new studio album by Hamilton Bohannon and his Rhythm Aces caused near-hysteria. They whooped the local weather forecast and laughed in the streets when Anjea Ankersonn told them it would be *another* high of thirty-two, humidity twelve percent, chance of significant precipitation . . .

"Zero!" the crowd yelled in concert, and, laughing, holding their sides with delight, tears streaming down their faces they broke up into chattering, hand-shaking, back-slapping groups and made their way out of the zocalo into the side streets, into their homes and houses.

Sweetness stood alone in the plaza.

The voice from the sky fell silent. The pink ray ceased. Instantly, the colour ebbed from the clouds, the grey figures boiled and broke up into exercises in fractal geometry. The heat pressed down like a sweaty hand on the plaza. The rooks returned to their roosts, demoralised dusters of ragged feathers.

Sanyap Bedassie's tousled head poked out of the door of the campervan.

"That answer you?" he asked Sweetness, then cupped his hands and called out at the windowless bourse-halls, "You all be back for the nine o'clock bulletin! Tears and laughter, drama and gravitas. Births, marriages and deaths. Agony and ecstasy. Corn and passion. Dust and monstrous crimes. Nights in the roof gardens of Hy Brazyl. Volcanic eruptions, meteor strikes, plagues of devouring star-bees. God parting the dust clouds; old women gossiping. Love and death and the whole damn thing. Every precious dream and vision underneath the stars."

"But," Sweetness interjected, "it's the evening news."

"Correct!" Sanyap Bedassie said. "If I were you, I'd lie down, because this takes a bit of explaining, and you'll do your neck, craning up like that."

"What? Here?"

"It's just dust. And you look no stranger to dust."

Sweetness sat down. She felt the grain of the sand between the rounded cobbles. No stranger indeed. But she was reluctant to stretch out belly up on the surface of the zocalo. She did not like to be so open and exposed to this suspended cineaste.

"Are you sitting comfortably?" Bedassie lay prostrate in the campervan, looking down into Sweetness's face.

"I'm not sitting, and I'm definitely not comfortable."

"It's a formula." His hair hung around down his face. "Then, I'll begin."

For two years now the plague of dreamlessness had ravaged Solid Gone. For years longer—whole of the world's long decades—it had stalked the lonesome townships of the desert fringe like a dust-devil. Many a sand-scoured tumble of red adobe attested to its power to devastate communities. Theories abounded about its nature and origin—the most scientific among those who took it as more than a legend from the Big Red was that it was some kind of infectious meme borne on the magnetic anomalies stirred up by the frequent rust-storms. The manner of its coming was always the same. After a period of sapping heat and high pressure, of thick heads and infuri-ating, set-slapping wireless interference, the citizens of the infected township would wake amazed by the vividness, clarity and sheer bizarreness of their dreams. They would sit around on their porches, under their tea-shop awnings, in the shadow of their house walls, slapping their thighs and shaking their heads as friends and families narrated the weird stuff inside their heads. This was the period of incubation. For a week the dreams would batter the subconsciouses of their victims, until the people were dazed colourless by the intensity of their night-life. Then one night, everyone dreamed the same dream. This was that dream. A sky of boiling black milk, shot through with lightnings, hung over an endless desert of silver sand. An edible dog—pure white, with one black ear—stood on the sand, by the self-contradictory logic of dreams, at once minute and sky-scaringly vast. It would shake its head, then look the dreamer in the soul's eye. It would bark three times. Strangely huge, those barks. Paralysing, night-terrorising. "The sky shook," the people would say next day when they sat down together to recount their dreams. "Like a stone nail through the heart." Then the white dog would turn, glance back once over its shoulder, and with its perky ring prominent, trot off into the heat-haze. What the dreamers never realised—or if they did realise, were helpless to prevent—was that that one look back summoned their dreams, and that when the dog trotted away into the deep desert, their dreams scampered behind it, sniffing its heat.

That was the last dream anyone dreamed.

At first it seemed a blessing. Clear heads, bright eyes, no morning mouth. Good day to you, citizen; and to you, sir. Sleep well? Ah! Pull back of the shoulders, stretch, smile. Sleep of the righteous, comrade. Like the very dead. Days, weeks, a month; deep and dreamless. No one noticed that there was less and less to talk about under the tea-shop awnings, leaning against the track-side signal lights waiting for the slow morning mail, or that sleep was no longer as righteous as it had once been, that it pressed down heavy as lead sheets all the hot night, impossible to throw off next morning. There was never a time when the people noticed that the light of that morning was not as bright as the one before, that the tea was pale and insipid, that the music on the breakfast show was just irritating. That the colour was draining out of life. That they sat up hour after hour, with the million lights of the moonring tumbling over their roof tiles, later than late, afraid to tell their friends lovers others that they did not want to go to bed for dread of that planetary, crushing *sleep*. That when next they woke, the light could be a mere lightening of night, that the tea could be warm water, that the wireless could sing in static, that all colours had run into one. That they no longer cared that it was so.

No one cared. No one laughed. No one cried. No one went out. No one made a joke. No one read a book. No one wrote a love letter, or fell in or out of love. No one loved. No one looked up at the tumbling jewels of the moon-ring with an *ooh* in the heart. No one woke in the night to the plaint of the night-train whistles and begged them, *Take me where you are going.* No one sang. No one danced. No one dandled a child upon the knee, much less thought to conceive one. No one bought a good frock or a new shirt or fine fine shoes. No one ached, no one hoped, no one longed, no one aspired, no one imagined, no one dreamed.

It was about that time that the grey cloud, sign and seal of the plague of dreamlessness, known and shunned by those more desert-wise than Sweetness Asiim Engineer 12th, fixed itself over Solid Gone.

Many a town had died this way, withered by its own grey apathy. Nothing lives long when its dreams have died. But for a naive young cloud-cineaste, inheritor of a truck-load of marvels and inspiration from a mad, visionary great-aunt, Solid Gone would have ended swallowed by the dust.

"I mean, you get to expect people not turning out to greet you, out here," Sanyap Bedassie said to by-now entranced Sweetness. "It's kind of old-fashioned, folk's grandparents'll talk about the Cloudchanger and wasn't it great and sure that was how I met your grandmother and all that, but most of the young ones, all they want to know about is this dance stuff. Even so, when I got right in here and there was absolutely no one around, I was beginning to think, even for the edgelands, this is odd. But free parking's free parking and, hey, no kids coming poking at things, asking, hey mister, what's that do?

"So, I hang out the flags. Not a soul. This happens. I unfold the aerial, set the thing up. Still nothing. If I hadn't seen them, sitting on their veran-dahs, just staring, I'd've sworn I'd stumbled into one of those edgeland ghost towns you hear about. Anyway, I power up the dream-projector—I mean, half the reason for coming to this place is because they've got a perfect cloud hanging right over their heads!"

"I was going to ask you about that," Sweetness said. "Like, a cloud cinny-hoojahflip, in a *desert*? Your great-aunt was mad, and you inherited it."

"That's what they say about all artists."

"All artists aren't stuck in a campervan ten metres up in the middle of a town square. And if you ask me, artist or not, it's a pretty dumb thing to get trapped because of a perfect cloud." When she saw how he shrugged; that that shrug was mostly a flinch, Sweetness wished she had not said the thing about being trapped. "Sorry," she whispered. "So, how come?"

"So, I set the thing up—you know how it works?" He did not wait for the answer she did not give. "Well, it's not your simple cinema. To work properly, you have to allow it to get into your head, pull out all your dreams and hopes and ambitions and fears. Everyone's got cinema inside them. There's clever machinery in there, takes your dreams, gives them plot and character and structure and all that, animates them, stick them up in the clouds."

"But if there're no dreams . . ."

"You get brain-static."

"So, the evening news?"

"I was running it as a test programme. And they just started coming. It was like the stones had started walking. All those grey faces. I thought— well, you know my trade, you can imagine the kind of thing I was thinking."

Yes, thought Sweetness, mind lit by the garish blue glare of her brother's masher-movies.

"They came walking in, like you saw just there. Every last one of them. I didn't think they were going to stop. I thought they were just going to walk right over me, trample me into the cobbles—next morning, there'd be like an oval of flat metal in the middle of the square. But I couldn't get out. I was surrounded. And they stopped, and they stood there and every man jack of them looked up and no one said a word. Not one word. And they watched the news, right the way through to the end. I turned the thing off, and waited. I didn't know what was going to happen. For all I knew, they'd pick up a cobble each and wade in. And then, one woman smiled. She was this plump, plain, middle-aged woman—nothing special about her, but that smile stood out in this square like a beacon. I saw it run out from her, like roots going out from a plant, I saw that smile go running around the square like some kid picking pockets, and they were all smiling, and then they were all laughing and crying and cheering and clapping and just sitting there with these big tears of ecstasy running down their cheeks. I tell you something, I never had an audience reaction like that. Never."

"Some thanks you got."

"How could they let me go after that? To you and me, it's the evening news. To them, it's everything the plague took away. It's all the mundane, trivial, petty, useless things that make up a life. It's dirt and gossip and achievement and tragedy and horror and strife, and we love it. We gather it in and sow it out in every possible medium we can, as often as we can, as much as we can: we can't get enough of it! It's the best soap opera there is. News makes our lives. Tell me this, you're sitting round having your dinner, what's the talk at the table about? What's on the news. Well, these people more than talk it. They live it, eight times a day at the top of the hour. Now, tell me, how could they let me go? Sticking me up here was the last creative thing they ever did."

And with the word, the news bell tolled again from its iron campanile and the people of Solid Gone assembled in the great zocalo, their brief respite of colour and scandal and eventfulness drained by the death of hope. Again, the pistils and stamens of Sanyap Bedassie's projector shot dream-seed into the heart of dreamlessness and the clouds parted to reveal Sanka Déhau and Ashkander Beshrap with their Serious Heads on.

"Chaos at the Gubernatorial Inauguration in Molesworth's *Rathaus*," Sanka Déhau said, looking straight into camera.

"Public humiliation for recently elected Cossivo Beldene in girl-in-cake stunt," Ashkander Beshrap chipped in his authoritative telegraphic style. The Eye on the World opened on the great hail with its chandeliers so mighty that each harboured a different species of bat, the Fest Table, carved from a single massive hunk of onyx, the gilded Missal Pulpit, festooned with the red-black-green swags of the Unity Rising campaign. Baroque mirrors returned the glare of camera lights and the stray glints from the diamonds of the favoured. Behind spangled frontals, the Glenn Miller Orchestra kicked in under the King of Swing's left hand, while the great musician threw beaming glances out over the crowded tables. Bubbling *cru* cascaded down the ziggurats of glasses; servitors in breeches and frock coats offered warm scented toweliettes for their guests' Personal Cleansing. All was merriness and conspicuous consumption and decadent cleavages, over which Ashkander Beshrap sternly pronounced, "In an elaborate practical joke, as the Glenn Miller Orchestra performed a specially commissioned composition, Seetra Annulka, Cossivo Beldene's rumoured mistress, was switched for a cake-dancer and leaped out to sing an alternative, explicit set of lyrics listing the new Gubernator's sexual peccadilloes."

Not one sound-bite of this lodged in Sweetness's head; not even the cheering and hooting of the massed Solid Goners for she was staring at the freeze-frame of the vengeful woman, half-uncaked in spangled bikini and hoolie-hoolie feathers, arms spread *ta-dah!*, grinning triumphantly into her throat mike: Cossivo Beldene behind her in the Champion's Seat, caught eternally *gobemouche*, beside him, one peripatetic minister of dubious religion and major contributor to election funds, Devastation Harx, slight apprehension on his distinguished features, as if he had already calculated the upshots and mentally jettisoned Cossivo Beldene and the Unity Rising Party.

But it was not even him Sweetness was staring at. At extreme left of shot, seated at a circular table with a stocky woman, a beautifully black-skinned man, a languidly bored girl with too many pierces, a grey-haired, anonymous looking middle-aged man and a weasely teen with dreadful teeth who seemed strangely unmoved by the unfolding tableau, was an old woman, small and bird-like and unobtrusive in sober blacks. The kind of woman you would not even notice, were she not your grandmother.

"Taal!" Sweetness shouted. The folk of Solid Gone moved around her, unheeding of anything but the delight on the screen in the sky. "Taal, it's me!" Of course she could not hear. Of course it was an image of an image of an image taken hours ago, fixed in the heart of a cloud. Futile as exhorting a photograph. But here the weird walked, here were strange times. Here magic worked. "Taal!" The boom of the cloud figures and the derision of the townsfolk smothered her cries. "Bedassie!" she shouted at the hanging van. She rattled chips of cobble off the drive train. The cineaste's tousled head peeped out like a desert animal from its scrape.

"Your projector!" Sweetness yelled as the happy smiling people, many holding hands, streamed past her back to their homes. "Can you make it work the other way?"

"What do you mean?"

"Instead of taking a dream and making it into a picture, can it take a picture and send it as a dream?"

Sanyap Bedassie cocked his head to one side, intrigued.

"Pray why?"

"I need you to send a message."

Already the clouds were closing again, curtains of rainless grey.

"To whom, exactly?"

Sensing another necessary recapitulation of her story, Sweetness sighed and shook her curls in exasperation.

"My grandmother. I'll explain."

By the time she did, the deeper penumbra that was night in Solid Gone had filled up the zocalo. As the story told itself, Bedassie had busied himself swagging dismounted vehicle lights around the base of the campervan. Now he flicked them on. Sweetness was pin-spotted in a wash of white heads, white tails and yellow indicators.

"Well, I can see the urgency now," Sanyap Bedassie said, feet swinging over the zocalo. "And I think it should be theoretically possible to do what you ask. There is one minor, niggling cavil, though."

"Which is?"

"You would rather need to get up here."

Sweetness put her hands on her hips, sucked in her lower lip. She had fought battles in mirror mazes. She had fallen from flying cathedrals. She had crossed burning deserts. She had swung across time to strange other presents and been bounced back into the paths of express trains. Sweetness Octave Glorious Honey-Bun Asiim Engineer 12th was not to be defeated by a few metres of altitude and a few whacks of chain. She studied the zocalo. The stonework facades of the anchor buildings were big rock climbing-frames. Not even a work-out for a girl who'd grown up clambering all over the heavy, steaming metal of a Bethlehem Ares Class 88 fusion hauler. The support chains were a simple hand-over-hand. Traingirls have good upper body strength. But a cannier soul had beaded a large glass globe on each chain, a few links down from the highest point. No way round over under through those babies.

Solid Gone was jealous of its news vendor.

"Okay," Sweetness declared. "I can't get up. So I'll get you down."

"I really don't think . . ." Sanyap Bedassie began, eyes widening with apprehension beneath his wild hair. But Sweetness was away, loping back through the silent streets. Past the lamp-lit porches. Past the glowing yellow windows. Past the muttering voices behind them, already losing the threads of conversation, laughs tailing off into dust, quips falling and lying, dreams bleaching and desiccating. Out from under the cloud of dreamlessness, to the track. Her home, her line through life. The permanent way, forward, back: out. Free of the psychic anticyclone of the cloud, she could feel the lure of the line, a tug on the valves of the heart. So easy to step on to it and keep walking. Walk away from this town and its dis-ease. Walk right out of this desert. Walk all the way to Molesworth and her grandmother.

"After," she said. A deal was a deal. And story was story.

Though the night was dark and groping—even the bright angel-machines of the moonring seemed intimidated by the cloud of numbness—her flashlight found the box of detonators first time, right where she had expected it, under the signal tower. She stuffed her pack and pockets with the red cylinders. One backward glance at the steel way, then Sweetness set her jaw—which she had always thought was one of her more determining features—and loped back into Solid Gone.

". . . this is a good idea," Sanyap Bedassie warned as Sweetness scaled the face of the old Ganj Bourse. "I mean, there's a lot of delicate equipment in here. And I'm only holding it in trust, really."

"You want to hang up there forever?" Sweetness asked as she carefully straddled the top end of the chain. "Then shut up and trust me. You got airbags on that thing?"

"I think they're standard on this model."

"You be fine, then. Machinery you can fix. You, you can't."

With strips ripped from her posh frock (*in case* was almost certain to be never, now, but each wrench tore, hard) she lashed the clustered detonators to the chain. Applicator threads pulled from tampons she wound into a common fuse, which she doused in glue—good, stinky stuff, the kind that really burns.

"I think you might need to blow two," Bedassie suggested.

Sweetness enjoyed a moment's novelty of a new perspective on his face, then said, "Nah. I reckon one's enough. I've been working out the stresses. I know metal. Now, you strap in tight."

Before she touched fire to the fuse, she gave a moment's worry to whether her little boom might rouse the town.

"Sod it," she said. The last collective act of arousal these people had committed had been putting up these same chains. A little bang in the night would scarcely flicker in the grey. She lit the thread and dropped down beneath the Ganj Bourse's stone balcony.

The bang in the night was much bigger and closer than she had expected. Sweetness gave a little squeak of surprise as stone chips, rust, dust and shredded detonator cartridge rained down on her. She waited for her ears to clear, trying to make falling campervan sounds out of the ringing. She peeked up over the edge of the balcony. The blast had surgically severed the chain. It lay stretched dead on the cobbles. The glass *no pasaran* bead was a million pieces scattered across the zocalo. But the campervan hung dramatically suspended above the square in a *hey-look-at-me-Mum-one-hand!* spread-eagle.

"Bum," said Sweetness Asiim Engineer.

"Well, I'm still here," came a voice from inside the van. "I thought you knew metal."

"Do you want out or don't you?" Sweetness said, eyeing the ascent to the next cable point. Not so easy, a tricksy little drain-pipe shin up to a Greek key frieze. From there, nasty overhanging balconies all the way to the anchor point. And only eight detonators left. That blast had used twelve. She would have to bet on the additional strain on the remaining rear cable. Sweetness jumped lightly off the lowest balcony, landed like a cat, darted across the zocalo, all the time listening out for soft padding zombie-feet. It was surely asking too much of even the deadened nervous systems of Solid Gone to have been deaf to such a blast. She wrestled her way up the side of the Meerschaum Exchange, hooked her legs around the steel staple and prepared her second charge. Nowhere handy to hide here. She'd need a long fuse. Up was safer than down. How much centimetrage left in her handi-pack of tampons? Have to do. Little less liberal with the glue. But you want it to burn. It has to burn. Mother'a'mercy, it has to burn and the charges have to blow and the bus has to go arse-first down to the ground and even then there has to be enough of the rear transmission to get the thing to move and if there's a Panarch in heaven and eleven orders of angels in serried attendance, there'll be enough juice in the tank to jam the thing into reverse and snap the remaining chains.

Lots of ifs, Glorious Honey-Bun.

For the first time, the realisation struck her—hard and chill—that maybe everything she had done since and including riding off into the wicked west with Serpio Waymender had in fact been absolutely the wrong thing to do, and she had got away with it only because she was protected by the exigencies of being, for a time, a story.

So? Whatever works. Light the blue touch paper and retire.

The blast caught her and flipped her with a squawk tail-first over the cornice on to the Exchange's flat roof. Quick as a knife she was up and at the stone balustrade in time to see Sanyap Bedassie and his cinema of dreams hit the ground. They hit hard. They hit rough. Bits fell off. Things cracked. Liquids leaked. Wheels splayed at angles that convinced even a trainperson that driving was over for this little camper. Nevertheless, Sweetness punched a fist in the air.

"Yah!" she yelled. Her victory cry rebounded like a well-shot cue-ball around the stone cushions of the zocalo.

With a plaint of protesting metal, the driver-side door opened. After some seconds, Sanyap Bedassie clambered out. He looked a little rocky. He looked like a man who, with his love and livelihood, has been dropped ten metres on to a hard stone surface. He looked around him, at the ground, at the square, at the severed chains that had once held him, at the buildings and the radial avenues, at the new perspective on it all. At Sweetness on her rooftop.

"Well," he said, dusting himself down, "now I'm down here, and you're up there."

She was not for long. Sanyap Bedassie was shorter on the horizontal than Sweetness had thought, and, from his long aerial captivity, had a personal odour at odds with his cute appearance. He was suspiciously checking the power units for the cloud projector.

"Well, you've managed to write off the truck," he said, not looking at her.

"It was a write-off anyway," Sweetness said brightly. "Anyway, you can always get someone to tow you out of here. What about the, uh, that?"

"The uh-that seems, by grace of God, to be fine and dandy," Bedassie said, feeling the honours of his machinery with his subtle hands.

"So, you can make my call?"

"When I've finished recalibrating, certainly."

Sweetness stood shifting from foot to foot, nervously glancing down the dark avenues. Surely surely surely . . .

"We're done."

"So what do I do?"

"You stand here."

"What, here?" Being as nondescript a piece of Solid Gone zocalo as any other.

"Yes, here." Nondescript banished as Sweetness was bathed in the pink, cloud-stabbing beam.

"Ooh," she said. It hissed and tickled. "So, what do I say?"

"You say what you want her to dream. It would help if you could keep it down to five main points, and if you could, put it into classic three-act structure, you know; beginning, middle, end. Setup, confrontation, resolution."

"What?"

"Just tell it however. But I'd be quick about it."

"Why?" asked Sweetness, pinkly.

Bedassie raised a *listen* finger. Straining through the seethe of light, Sweetness could hear the patient plod of the news bell.

"All right all right all right," she said, combing her hair out of her eyes. "Hi, Grandmother Taal, this is me, Sweetness—can she see me, or only hear me? Anyway, look, I haven't got much time, but this is to say I'm all right—well, actually I'm not, but that's because at the moment I'm a story, which seems to make interesting things happen. So, I reckon the only reason I'm seeing you—I'm not even going to ask how you got there, but I know you—is that you've decided to come and look for me. By the way, it was only a flash, like, but you're looking good. You been taking vitamins or what? Okay, I shouldn't't've run off like that—but you know me. I couldn't marry that guy.

I couldn't spend the rest of my life in a galley, stainless steel or not; and, hey, as it turned out, it was all meant to happen anyway, because I'm a story."

"Speaking of which," Bedassie counselled, "now would be a good time to make your first plot point."

Tramp, tramp, tramp came the marching feet.

"Okay, well, you probably can't hear that, but there's like an army of zombie villagers out there—except they aren't really zombies, they've got this plague that means they can't dream, but they're all addicted to the evening news and that's them coming for the eleven o'clock serving. Anyway: what's happening is: I got to find this guy Devastation Harx. You saw him, up there. Well, I had this run in with him—he's got this flying cathedral crewed by all these grade school rejects—and, well, you know I used to have this invisible friend? Little Pretty One? Well, it seems she wasn't so invisible, actually she was Catherine of Tharsis hitching a ride off my other twin's ghost, and Devastation Harx's stolen her and he's keeping her in a jar and I have to get her back otherwise he'll use her to start this final war between humans and machines, and it looks like it's up to me to stop the whole she-bang." She glanced at Sanyap Bedassie. The whole stone arena was now ringing to the steady slap of flat feet. "That do?"

"Succinct, if not classically structured," the young man said, checking his dials and instruments. "Your grandmother is going to have some dream tonight."

"Yeah, but will she believe it's really me?"

"Oh, grandmothers generally believe what their dreams tell them. It might be nice to sign off?"

"Oh. Yeah. Forgot. Hi, Gran. Listen, tell the folks I'm all right. If that guy Harx was at Molesworth, then that's a good place to look for him, so stay there and I'll meet up with you. Hey, we could even be parts of the story together."

"I think you already are," Sanyap Bedassie said softly. He frowned at his indicators. "That's you." He threw a small brass lever. The pink light died around Sweetness.

"Ooh," she said.

Down each of the radial avenues, a wedge of citizenry was marching, dull and intent on only one thing, their thrice nightly dose of the mundane. Surrounded by advancing grey. It was, Sweetness had to admit, pure monster movie. She grabbed Sanyap's hand.

"Time to go."

He pulled back.

"Where?"

"There." Sweetness pointed down a narrow entry between buildings of the kind that only becomes apparent when you absolutely necessarily must have a neat egress. She seized his hand again. It was nice and soft and warm. A good non-labouring hand. "Come on."

Again, he resisted.

"They'll stick you up there again, and me too this time, and I don't know about you, friend, but I got a story. You want that?"

"My machine . . ."

"It's only a thing, man. If it troubles you that much, come back and get it later, like I said. Come back with a pile of people. But you can only do that if you get out now."

She tugged. He was unmoved.

"Child'a'grace, man!"

Bedassie looked around at the pale faces ranked down the strict perspectives of Solid Gone. He shook his head, let slip Sweetness's hand.

"You cannot do this," Sweetness begged him.

"I never had an audience like this. Do you understand that? Every night, I put the pictures up in that cloud, and they smile, and they laugh, and they feel something, and they go home for an hour, two hours, they dream their dreams. Don't you understand? That's how it should be. It's not there to take dreams out of people's heads and make them into pictures. You were right, with your wondering if it could work in reverse. It was meant to work in reverse. That's what all cinema has ever been, taking the pictures out of the clouds, off that screen and making them dreams in people's heads. They need that. They need me. Here, movies make people's lives. I make a difference. I don't entertain, I shape their worlds. And they're just people, who had the bad luck to have lost their dreams. They deserve them back. I can give them to them, as long as it takes. This cloud won't last forever. This plague will move on someday. Until then, I'll give them the news of the worlds, eight times a day. I'm not trapped. I'm not a prisoner. You can't be a prisoner, if you remain of your own free will. I'm staying here. You go. You've got your story. I've got the pictures."

He stepped away from Sweetness.

"Go!" he shouted.

Sudden tears almost paralysed Sweetness. The story that was hers before this new one had rewritten every line had been subtly played out here. In this version, the hero chose his trap over the wild world. To him it was not a trap. Never had been a trap, only a kind of mitigated freedom. All the dreams in the world. Sweetness swallowed the emotion. You have to let some things go, Glorious Honey-Bun. You aren't responsible for every ill and blessing in the world. People make their own minds up and you abide by their decisions. The grey people, the infected, were spilling slowly out into the zocalo. Go, now, if you're ever going to go. She ran between closing walls of the news-hungry toward the black slit of the alley. There she turned, sought for Sanyap Bedassie between the moving bodies. She saw him as a flash of colour through the thicket of limbs. She watched the circle of hands close in around him, and his reach out to shake them.

"Go figure," she said, and turned again, and ran away from Solid Gone.

21

"All right then, I'll walk!" Sweetness shouted up at the iron cliff of the Class 22.

"Damn right you will, for you'll have no ride with me, nor anyone else on this railroad," Engineer Joan Cleave Summer-Raining Tissera 8th declared from his brass shunting oriole. With which he climbed the stairs to the bridge, slammed and dogged the port behind him and began the power-up sequence. Misused tokamak fields set Sweetness's fillings ringing; bleed valves bullied her with steam. She jumped back as the drive rods cranked and the wheels spun, then gripped. The train moved off. Sweetness jogged beside the wheels, flinging trainfolk curses, which curse very hard. The rolling bogies of the tank cars soon outpaced her. She shied track ballast at the receding stained-glass lights of the caboose in the hope of pettily breaking one and annoying a Stuard.

The big chemical train curved out of sight between red dunes. The anger drained out of Sweetness Asiim Engineer. She sat dejectedly on the rail. She was outcast, named, pariah. She was the Little Girl Who Would Not Marry Whom She Was Told. No one would Uncle Billy for her. What would be scary-biscuits was if the ban had spread trackside. If she could not scrounge a *mandazi* from a platform goondah or a pan of water from a tanking tower, her story might come to a premature end. Story, she thought. People in stories were not supposed to be permanently thirsty, or hungry enough to eat the beard of a Sumache sacerdotal. Or smell their own bodies.

"I wouldn't have written it like this," Sweetness told the desert.

Creak, answered a desert rook on a signal pylon. Black bird of ill omen. Outcast, named, pariah. Sweetness buzzed a rock at it. It flew away in a rattle of oily feathers.

Who had dirtied on her? Dirtied she certainly had been. Dawn had seen her marching along the westbound upline, Solid Gone's grey cloud stuck like a styptic plaster to the horizon, light filling up the land, her own long shadow returning to her after being all over all night, when she felt through the soles of her boots the thrum of a train coming. Peering from the shade of her hand into the low sun, she had recognised the characteristic three tall steam-stacks of a Class 22 medium freightliner. She stood resolutely in the middle of the track, flagging down the chemical train with her shirt. It had come to a halt before her, *Eastern Star*, steaming slightly. The Engineer had descended into his oriole, but even before she could invoke the formula, he had demanded, "Is your name Sweetness Octave Glorious Honey-Bun Asiim Engineer 12th?"

"It is, and I'm told it's a very fine name."

"I'm told different," he said. Then she learned that her name had passed up the line with the speed and enthusiasm of a venereal disease, shunted and switched and sided until every part of the global web of rails knew to shun it.

Who told you? she had wanted to shout at the receding train. And who told them? Who did the dirt? The *Ninth Avata* people, fair enough: I did the dirt on them. Child'a'grace, my own *Catherine of Tharsis*? My own train. Marya Stuard—she'd be up to it, she's never got on with us—she's always thought we thought we were better than her—and she's got this reputation for mean to protect. She can take out the Starke dacoits, she can put my name about quick as a knife. But that'd be like a direct attack on the Engineers. It'd be one end of the train against the other. Not even she'd be mean enough to start a civil war. But someone certainly did, so who? Oh no. They couldn't. Could they? They could: if Da's proud enough not to talk to Ma because of a card game four years ago, he could dirt me. Sle's petty enough but he's too lazy even to start a rumour. If it's my own people, I'm really shafted. I really can't go back again. But what's to go back to? They'll just work up another contract and it'll be me with the paper money all over my dress all over again, only this Joe won't even have a stainless steel kitchen. Mother'a'plenty, they might even fix me with a Bassareeni, just to punish me. I'll never get my hands on the throttles. So what's to go back for? Make a life out here, off the track. Lots of people do. Most people do. Hell, I'm a weird ethnic minority, most people can't even imagine how we live the way we do. It's probably a darn sight easier, maybe even better. Friends would be easier to keep. You wouldn't have your friends and family and work-mates all the same people. You wouldn't work with your family. You wouldn't have them around all the time. That would be good. You could get away. But imagine waking up and it's the same place every day. You'd be stuck with the seasons. And you'd really never ever ever get to drive. Their way, maybe. Not likely, but it's a possibility. This way, *nada*. And you wouldn't be track. You'd be a passenger. Every time you got on a train, you'd know there'd be someone up there at the front with their hand on the drive bar, taking you where you're going to. You'd just be going along for the ride. Hell, I'm an Engineer! I'm not driven, I drive. I *drive*.

So: here's this story, and this is where it's left me. It sure can't mean for everything to end like this. Whatever happened to happy ever after? No, think, hey, doesn't every story have a time like this, when everything's been burned down and levelled and things are as bad as they can get for our heroine?

So, in this time of levelling, what does a heroine do?

She gets up. She picks up her pack and slings it on her back. She turns to face the place she is going. She says, If everything is ashes and flat, on this I can build. This is the lowest of the low. Every way now is up. So go. Nothing here for you. You'll get where you're going.

She got up. She slung her pack on her back. She turned to face up the line. She felt no stronger, no surer, no more determined, no less hungry/ thirsty/grubby/tired but she could not remain another minute by that track-side. She walked out of that flat field of ashes.

By noon she had still neither eaten nor drunk, but a wind rose behind her that cooled her and carried her forward, and early in the afternoon there was the space battle.

At least, Sweetness presumed it was a space battle, in that part of it clearly did come from space, though the action was low to middle atmospheric. It was all rather confusing and done so quick that if you had not been looking you would have missed it, and even if you were, you could still not be sure what had happened. Trudging along the upline toward the beckoning skeleton of a water tower, Sweetness had become aware of a distant low howl behind her. She spun in the instant it took that howl to become a devouring roar as three World Defence ionospheric interceptors streaked out from behind the far rim rocks and thundered over her head.

"Wooo!" she yelled into the shatter of engines, and whirled to see the interceptors rise on their parallel white contrails into a sky-scourging loop. They were magnificently evolved devices, utterly of their native element, arrogant of gravity in their spindly, insectoid asymmetry. They spun as one on their long axes as they reached the top of the loop, then rolled on to their backs for a hair-raising tumble through fifty kilometres of airspace. When the zenith blazed with crackling lilac beams, the point interceptor exploded immediately in a white fireball. Numbstruck, Sweetness watched the flaming fragments draw streamers of smoke down to impact beyond the southern horizon. She could not register what she had seen. It was all lights and smokes and mystery, as beautiful and remote as sacred theatre. She found the remaining two aerospacecraft against the blue. They had shaken off their vain aerobatics and were screaming down on divergent courses, hoping to bemuse the targeting computers among the dunes and rocks. Lilac sky-beams flickered again; Sweetness saw a searing arc slash across the southern stone plains, strike the fleeing fighter amidships, cut it cleanly, thoughtlessly, in two. Severed halves went tumbling over each other, bounding high, disintegrating into chunks of burning scrap. A sheet of flame went up from the line of impact as the jumble of high technology struck sand. The third interceptor came scorching round on a tight turn from the west, headed back to whatever base had launched it. It bore down on Sweetness, jumped the mainline with a hypersonic boom that beat her inner organs like a drum and headed north. High in heaven, lilac beams criss-crossed like a master carver steeling his blade. A single lilac scimitar cut down. Presciently warned, the interceptor had veered on an erratic manoeuvre, otherwise it would have been cleanly vaporised. Not enough: the partac beam clipped a stabiliser vane. Too low, too fast. The pilot fought for stability but gravity fought harder. The interceptor jerked, heaved, veered, flipped on to its side and ploughed into the slip-slope of a sif dune in a kilometres-long plume of sand. A titanic pillar of fire went up from the northern dunefields. Seconds later, the blast front buffeted Sweetness. Heat washed her face, she reeled, regained balance.

Oily black smoke spiralled up into the sky.

"Woof," said Sweetness Asiim Engineer 12th. "That was freaky."

A few footsteps along, the chill hit her out of the desert heat: she had seen flash machines, swift technology, war by special effects budget. Under all that chrome there had been crew, people really dying bad, arbitrary and meaningless deaths out there with no other witness but herself and God. She had watched their final struggles, their skills and talents strive and fail. Real death, not story death. No trainperson is a stranger to death: Sweetness did not doubt that the majority of those freeloaders she had *djubba-ed* from the top of the train had either perished immediately or slowly as a result of her action. This was grand death with no connection to her. This would have spread itself across an entire terrain whether she had been there or not.

A chiller chill struck her, one that shivered ice through her marrow. Grand death on a planetary stage, but intimately connected to her. The sky weapons did not fire arbitrarily, least of all at planetary defence aerospace fighters. Unless the angels were mad and ROTECH insane, another had gained control of the orbital partacs. Other being a soft-voiced, grey-haired man in a light-swallowing suit with a cane in one hand and the soul of St. Catherine in a stasis jar in the other.

She had been sole human witness of the opening shots of the war between Harx and the angels. He was testing his powers, and they were sure and strong.

In confirmation, after the space battle came the duststorm.

A curvet of wind had tugged Sweetness's cheek as she trudged the upline, burdened with her own thoughts and responsibilities. It had to tweak twice to get her attention. She looked up and saw, like the mother of slow trains a'coming, the boiling wall of ochre dust rolling toward her down the line, shot through with steel lightnings.

For a moment she stared. The thing bearing down on her was as fabulous as a herbragriff or stalking aspanda. They were the creatures of childhood story, the feral duststorms that would blanket entire quarterspheres for weeks, that would carry away whole towns and rearrange landscapes and change the course of rivers and turn lakes into plains. No such monster had visited the world in her or her parents' generation, not since ROTECH created a suborder of angels to keep the climate sweet. Grandmother Taal had known these creatures, and now Sweetness recalled her lurid descriptions of tracks, trains, crews and passengers buried beneath dunes in a single night, of thrice-painted metal whetted to a naked steel blade, of grazebeasts stripped to polished bone flutes, of trainspersons drowning in dust even as they ran for the presumed safety of their cabs.

"Mother'a'mercy," Sweetness said, the lone vertical obstacle in the path of the beast as it bore down on her. "He's got into the weather!" Dust brushed her cheek. The next kiss would be rougher. She had maybe seconds to find cover out here in the middle of all this hugeness. She glanced around her. As she had hoped: the concrete grave of an inspection pit. Cover, of a kind. Of the only kind, she told herself. It would mean running into the face of the storm. So be it.

"Yaaaaaah!" she yelled, and charged the bulwark of dust. She flung herself through the orange wall. The wind threatened to hurl her back for her presumptuousness. Rust-lightning crackled around her as she dived down between the sleepers into the inspection pit. The concrete floor was littered with swarf and scrap train and sun-dried shit from the honey-vents, and hit exceeding hard.

"Oof!" Sweetness gasped, present enough to roll belly down and curl her back against the storm. Instants later, it struck with a shriek like every soul in the Benekasherite purgatory enduring genital torture at once. Darkness. Terrible noise. Dust. Sweetness struggled a handkerchief over her face, knotted it behind her head but the dust had already found its way up her nose, prickling and electrical and scented with dead, dried summers. Red dust caked in the corners of her eyes and behind her ears as she huddled, face down, not looking at the gorgon-face of the storm. She could feel it in her hair, heavy and matting. She'd be an adobe-head for days after this. The almost solid plane of dust drew a sympathetic plaint from the steel rails. Storm-claws plucked at her shirt: *Come, fly with me.*

"What are you doing, man?" she shouted at her enemy. "Don't you know it's going to make everything come apart? Is that what you want? They're not going to let you, you know." But, if Harx could access the planetary defences and the climate control system, even God the Panarchic was hog-tied. What was Harx doing to St. Catherine, with what cybernetic torments was he threatening her, what weird stuff makes saints and angels shudder? Planetary patroness she might be, a psychic twin of false pretences, but the reflection of a soul sealed in Devastation Harx's memory jar was also Little Pretty One, half of Sweetness's life to date. He was torturing the crippling disappointment of her third birthday party when she did not get the toy Engineer's outfit; it was her first no-tongue bruise-lipped snog-ette with Axle Deep-Eff at the corroboree steaming. It was the economics exam she had failed spectacularly and cavalierly—there had been a handball match the night before against *Darker Star*—and the longwave humiliation she had endured before her School of the Air tutor and a continent of fellow pupils. It was the night of the Boletohatchie lay-over she had crept from her cabin up along the star-lit companionways over the dark, simmering hulk of *Catherine of Tharsis* and her many tribes, and had stolen in to the command bridge to lay her hand for one, electric second, on the brass drive bar. It was the foolish confessed hopes and dreams and unachievable ambitions; the infatuations and infuriations and warm-between-the-thighs moments; the naked lusts and the hopeless rages and the whispered hours of giggle and smut. Out of sheer adolescent embarrassment alone, she had to get her other half back. "I'm not going to let you!" she shouted, arms wrapped around her head.

Fine words, from a nearly-nine on her knees in an inspection pit, buried under a kilometre of duststorm. It was then she noticed the steady rivulets of dust pouring over the corners of the dug-out, forming spreading spill-cones across the concrete floor, slowly burying the pieces of discarded train-innards with the granular tick of the hour-glass. Already it was piling up around her fingers, a sensation at once sexy and enclosing. She could feel it trickling into her shoes.

"Aw, come *on*," she implored. It could not end like this: cute, clever, adventurous, resourceful heroines with great (when clean) hair did not end as dust-mummies buried in a railroad shit-pit. Not in a story. This might be the time of levelling, and ashes, and, yes, dust, but it wasn't the end.

As if it had heard her and been impressed by her argument, the storm abruptly ended. The silence in Sweetness's ears was so sudden and ringingly hollow she feared for a moment some pressure drop at the eye of the storm had popped her eardrums. She yawned, shook her head. No blood, no pain. No wind. No dust. She rolled on to her back. The slatted sky between the sleepers was clear blue. Sweetness popped her head up like a desert rodent. Upline, downline, north and south. Not even a wisping tail of dust to hint at the storm's passage. It might never have been. Been it had, for every scrap of rust was scoured off the track ties and the old wooden sleepers had been planed to rounded wedges. A battle had been fought in the high air and, in this round, Devastation Harx had lost and the winds he had summoned were dispersed.

Next round would go to the canvas.

Sweetness heaved herself out of the hole, suspiciously sniffed the air. It was clean and good and wonderfully clear, like clothes beaten by a dhobi boy. With her new clarity of vision, Sweetness now saw an object far on the western horizon, previously obscured by dust and heat haze. She shielded her eyes and squinted. Had she not seen such things before—indeed, spent a night with *that man* under one—she would have disbelieved her eyes. They told her true. The thing looked like—and therefore was—nothing more than a domestic, fireside companion set—poker, brush, shovel, tongs—big enough to keep hell tended.

An afternoon's walk brought her to the prodigy. The central column and cap rose like the dome of a great, airy temple. Sweetness walked under it, wondering at the artifacts hanging from its rim. The poker was a sheer steel shaft, thirty metres long, slowly penduluming in the rising evening breeze. The brush bristles had been sadly abraded by the duststorm, lop-sided and graded like a Belladonna goondah's asymmetrical buzz-cut. The shovel could have scooped up hosts of the sinful for the tongs to hold in the white heart of purgatory's forges. Sweetness steered away from the hungry, pronged jaws. All were polished metal, scoured clean by the dust, brilliant in the evening sun.

Sweetness started as she rounded the corner of the base to find two figures huddled against the plinth. Figures, she presumed, though they were man-shaped bundles of ochre-stained fabric. *Dust-mummies*, she thought, at which they both moved, shedding clouds of dust. Sweetness took a step back. Out here, jokes and superstitions and impossibilities turned up behind every rock, real and able and eager to do stuff to you. The mummies shuffled to their feet. They beat their wrappings free of dust with their bandaged hands. Sweetness saw then that they wore long duster coats and baggy trader's pants with thick-wound puttees. The hands then rose to the bulbous brown heads,

fiddled for a loose end and streeled off more metres of cloth than Sweetness
ever imagined you could wear around your head without suffocating.
Obsidian eyeballs glittered; Sweetness relaxed when a few turns more
revealed them to be little, round-eye sunspectacles. Faces emerged, one tall
and square, the other round and purse-lipped. Both wore identical hairstyles,
shaved at the sides, teased up into a flat-topped mesa. They looked dedicated
and zealous as they kicked away their discarded binding bands. Sweetness
might have been stone to them for all their regard.

"A storm that was," the square-faced, taller one said, taking a theatrical
upright pose.

"Storm indeed, Cadmon," the other agreed, copying him.

"Unseasonable." The square one made a slow sweep of the horizon.

"Unseasonable indeed, Cadmon." The squat one followed suit.

"One might almost think . . ."

"One might; one does, Cadmon."

Sweetness watched their act for a few moments before clearing her throat.
The two men turned as one; black round eyes regarded her, heads cocked to
precisely the same degree.

"What is this? A fellow traveller in strange terrains?" The heads cocked
the reverse angle.

"Would seem so, Cadmon."

"A girl, I would hasten."

"Hasten so, Cadmon."

"Look, I don't mean to butt in here if you're doing something, but have
you got any food or water?"

The two men looked at each other.

"Water and provender, for our guest?" the tall one, obviously Cadmon,
asked.

"Exactly so, Cadmon," the still nameless one answered and took a small
bulb from one of the many pockets of the utility vest he wore beneath his
duster. A soft squeeze. Sweetness waited for something to happen, then
noticed a small stirring in the dust. Buried things unearthing themselves.
Dust boiled and shed. Two gravboards with bulging leather side-panniers
bobbed to the surface and came to rest at a level metre.

"Cool," said Sweetness Asiim Engineer.

Water there was, and provender, in square-faced Cadmon's carefully weighed usage. Sweetness ate smally and carefully, sipped her water and used two handfuls to wipe the caked dirt off her face. Then she asked, "So, what are you guys doing out here then?"

"That question, I rather think, is better asked of you, madam," Cadmon said. The short one nodded.

"I'm a story," Sweetness said, then regretted her enthusiasm, for now she had committed herself to telling it yet again.

"No no no," Cadmon interjected with a raised finger, mimicked by his partner. "Names, then stories."

"Okay," Sweetness said. "I am Sweetness Octave Glorious Honey-Bun Asiim Engineer 12th."

The two men bowed slightly.

"I am Cadmon, and this is Euphrasie," Cadmon said, with a sweep of the hand which the shorter man could not refrain from distantly echoing. "We are the Brothers Dust."

Sweetness thought a moment, then said, "But you're not brothers."

"Brothers of the soul," Cadmon said.

"Soul, indeed," Euphrasie chimed in. "Brothers aesthetic, atheistic, anarchic."

"We are anarchist artists," Cadmon said. "Behold, our work."

As one, the Brothers Dust thrust out their hands to the enormous fireside companion set, in the lengthening shade of which this exchange had taken place.

"Do you do a lot of household stuff?" Sweetness asked.

"You are familiar with our work?" Cadmon asked loftily.

"I've slept under some of it."

"Which, pray?" Euphrasie responded, quick as a pocket-picking.

"The big chair," Sweetness said. She added, "I've seen the ironing board from a distance. And the big shoe."

"The big shoe!" Cadmon and Euphrasie chorused in one voice.

Sweetness thought a moment, then said, "So, correct me if I'm wrong here, but how is it anarchy to do big ironing boards and shoes?"

"The anarchy of incongruity," Cadmon proclaimed.

"And the domestic," Euphrasie added. "Domesticating the desert."

"And desertifying the domestic," Cadmon insisted. "Thus we confound two static absolutes: the desert without and the desert within."

"But don't we live in an anarchy?" Sweetness asked, sweetly.

"Habitual anarchy is no anarchy at all," Cadmon said.

"The revolution must be continual if it is to be the true revolution."

"True anarchy is archy."

"I must invent a non-system or be enslaved by another man's."

Sweetness looked at the two desert-clad men, cocked her head in *that way*.

"Are you butty-boys?" she asked.

Cadmon maintained high disdain, but Sweetness caught Euphrasie turning away and lifting his hand to his mouth to suppress a chuckle.

"We are living art," Cadmon said. *Okay*, Sweetness thought.

"And art consists as much in the unmaking as the making," Euphrasie said.

"Look, I don't do art, so you'll have to explain this," Sweetness said.

"Explain? Very well. This project is complete. True art is momentary; the false strives for immortality. We make and we unmake. Now is the time of unmaking."

Sweetness looked to Euphrasie for elucidation. He merely swivelled his eyes upward to the mushroom-cap of the companion set. For the first time Sweetness noticed the clustered white cylinders fastened to the shaft and around the rim of the cap, the gaily coloured wires, the radio transponders.

"You're not . . ."

Euphrasie nodded and produced another bulb device from his vest of pockets.

"You have something in the region of thirty seconds to decide whether you come with us, or bet on how fast you can run," Cadmon said, gathering up his discarded wrappings and stuffing them into a carry-all bag, which he slung on to the back of the nearer of the two fretting gravboards.

"Me? On one of those?"

"Twenty seconds . . ." Euphrasie had already mounted his gravboard and was erecting the boom.

"All right, I'm not betting, I'm not betting!" Sweetness scooped up her bag and dived for Euphrasie's board. The mercurial machine rocked under her, she fought for balance, grabbed at Euphrasie, who by seizing her shirt-front prevented them both from capsizing. Wind cracked Cadmon's pink and purple fractal patterned sail. The board pitched, then the rising evening breeze lifted it and whipped it away. Within instants, he was a lost toy in the great redness.

"Hold tight!" Euphrasie called to Sweetness, pressed cheek to scapular.

"Tell me," Sweetness muttered into his back, but all the same the sudden dip and surge of the board almost upset her as Euphrasie tilted the boom into the wind and the board took flight.

"Whoo!" exclaimed Sweetness Asiim Engineer as the rippled dust blurred beneath her. The second board tacked sharply, caught a stronger air current and slid up alongside big, vain Cadmon.

"Zero!" he shouted to Euphrasie over the flutter of sail and the shout of wind. The smaller man held out the bulb-teat. Cadmon nodded for Sweetness to look back, which she did, dizzyingly, and so missed Euphrasie depressing the nipple. The effects were impressive. The big companion set stood tall and black and domestic on the horizon. As she watched, white blossoms of flame exploded briefly underneath the rim, indeed like some vast desert mushroom sporing explosively. The fall was slow and tremendous. Had the Skywheel itself snapped and fallen flailing to earth, it could not have been more thunderous and aristocratic. Explosions around the edge of the cap first freed the poker, which fell straight to earth and embedded itself a third-deep in the sand. The brush fell to earth in a comet's tail of blazing bristles: fireballs and sparks rebounded high as it smashed into the ground. Multiple detonations disintegrated the tongs into flying, clawed shards. Only the shovel remained. Unbalanced by its weight, the cap tilted, then the shaft blew apart beneath it in an orgy of detonations. The falling shovel threw a spadeful of hot desert twenty metres into the air. Like a bell falling from God's campanile, the cap struck the ground. The chime shivered Sweetness's ovaries in her belly. Fractions of a second later, the shockwave ruffled her hair and tugged her clothes, sent the gravboard yawing.

The second pillar of smoke in Sweetness's day went up from the wreckage of art.

"You're mad, you are!" Sweetness exclaimed as Euphrasie sent the board sweeping round on a great sand-scoring arc. She liked the way he smiled, pleased and self-deprecating at once. Almost that smile. Remember, butty-boy, she advised herself. And if you go on falling for every male who smiles that smile, and they probably all do, this story is going to end with you tripping over the end of the next chapter. But, she decided as the gravboard scored away from the smouldering wreckage across the Big Red and she felt man body beneath her fingers and smelled man smells whipped back in the wind of her velocity that was streaming her hair straight back from her good cheekbones: this is what stories are all about. "Wooo!" she yelled, for the second time that day.

She decided she liked fruitboy anarchist artists. She tugged Euphrasie's quilted sleeve.

"Where are we going?"

"Depends," he shouted into the slipstream.

"On what?"

"On where you want to go."

"Me?"

"Our work is done."

"You've blown them all up?"

"Unto the last."

"Even the big shoe?"

"The aglets flew three hundred metres in opposite directions."

Aglets sounded to Sweetness Engineer like juvenile birds of prey, so three hundred metres might or might not be an impressive flight, but she understood and appreciated the pride in a good job well done in Euphrasie's voice. It's not an easy thing to do an explosion really well. Likewise, she understood and delighted in the thrilling velocity with which she skimmed across the desert, low enough for the sand sprayed up by the bow field to sting her ankles, up and over the dune crests with a leap and a yip and the bottom of her stomach falling out. These butty-boys had class. She liked them.

Sweetness hammered on Euphrasie's back.

"Molesworth!" she yelled when she had his attention. Euphrasie did not ask where or why. He nodded briskly, finger-talked with one hand to his partner out at point. Cadmon and Euphrasie leaned into their sails. The banking boards cut crescents in the red sand as they curved due south.

"Wooooeeee!" fanfared Sweetness Asiim Engineer, throwing her head back and letting her greasy bonny black hair reel out behind her like a banner of anarchy. She could still smell it. She could still smell herself, lick her brown forearm and taste minerals. She had little enough water in her blood and less provender in her belly. She was still wandering in sterile places, cannoning off people places events like the legendary Rael Mandella Jr.'s cue ball. Her childhood companion was still incarcerated in a trans-dimensional mirror rolled up in a canopic jar. Her enemy roamed the airways by pedal power, cautiously testing his command of the very angels that had built the world. She had no weapons, no power, no plan, not even a cunning scheme. But she still knew, with a traingirl's sense, that that electric buzz in the air is a big express coming; with the high-plain herder's understanding that that flaring of the nostrils running through the herd is a sure sign of rains; with the deep core miner's certainty as she burrows through the obsidian flux tubes of primal shield volcanoes that the next grike will glitter with diamonds; that though nothing was changed, everything was different. Before, those people places events had pushed her around. Now, somehow, she was pusher, not pushee. From here on, it would be an Adventure.

When the heat went out of the sky, they camped in the lee of the up-ended boards. The anarchists made fire and heated small, neat foil sachets of trail food in a bubbling billy. It was not sufficient and tasted badly enough of additives to catch the back of Sweetness's throat but she skewered the tiny cubes of synthetic meat in their clinging sauce with her plastic pitchfork and gobbled them down with gratitude. To while away the cooling hours while the edge of the world rose over the face of the sun in streaks of red gold and purple, like a Pontifical progress, Cadmon and Euphrasie played a game with Sweetness. It was We've-Got-To-Guess-Why-You're-Going-To-Molesworth-But-You're-Only-Allowed-To-Give-One-Word-Monosyllabic-Answers.

"Why?" Sweetness immediately asked.

"Because," tall Cadmon answered. "And the way we play it, we've only got ten questions."

"Okay."

Euphrasie raised a warning finger, then another. He shook them in Sweetness's face.

"Right."

He nodded.

"Wherefore, Molesworth?" Cadmon asked. Euphrasie sat close beside him, and nodded sagely.

Sweetness opened her mouth, then caught herself. She counted syllables on her fingers, grimaced.

"Folk."

"First, second or third generation?"

"Third," Sweetness said confidently. Cadmon and Euphrasie inclined their heads together. They seemed to speak, though Sweetness heard no words in the cool cool cool of the evening.

"So, what do you flee?"

"Ring." Sweetness twisted an imaginary third-finger-left-hand-gold-band. "But . . ."

Euphrasie furiously finger-wagged her.

"Clearly, this thing you seek in Molesworth is not a nuptial reconciliation," Cadmon mused. Euphrasie whispered in his partner's ear. Cadmon nodded. "It's a grandparent, in my experience the most trustworthy of family members. So, not a reconciliation, but an alliance. You seek something together, do you not?"

"Twin," Sweetness said. She mimed her second self, the quick knife of division. Cadmon and Euphrasie looked very slowly at each other.

"You need the assistance of your grandparent to seek the sundered self?"

Sweetness nodded, then added, "Ghost." Without realising, she was caught up in the artists' ludicrous after-dinner sport. Her tongue was bound; she could no more iterate two words, or more than one syllable, than she could have recited all Five Hundred Five-Hundred-Letter Tallabasserite names of God.

"This—half sister?—is *dead*? Is this some manner of seance, some necromancy or other?" Cadmon asked, his little spectacles catching spook-fire in their round lenses.

"Free."

"Someone has stolen the ghost of your dead twin sister?"

"Yes."

"Damnation! That was a rhetorical question. They don't count."

Sweetness held up her two hands, where she had been counting off the quota of questions with finger and thumbs, to show beyond any argument that in her game, rhetoric counted. Cadmon took a breath and tried again.

"Given that ours is a low-scale mercantile culture and folk will sell any-thing to anyone, it's still valid to ask, why would anyone want to steal a ghost?"

Again Sweetness nodded. "Saint." She pointed to where the brightest lights of the moonring clung to the horizon, drew her finger in an all-creating arc across the sky. When she looked back, both Cadmon and Euphrasie's mouths were open.

"You mean to tell us that the ghost of your twin sister is not in fact your twin sister, but an angel? A saint?"

"*The*," Sweetness said emphatically. Their mouths were two tunnels through to deep night now. Their last question was inevitable. So, by a hun-dred tiny cues, clues and flutings of the desert wind that had incrementally impinged on Sweetness's senses, was her answer.

"You are telling us that St. Catherine of Tharsis, masquerading as your natally-deceased twin sister, has been ghost-napped, and that you and your grandparent are on a quest to get her back," Cadmon said. Not a question. For the first time, Sweetness heard in his voice a tremor of *not cool*. "But who would do a thing like that?"

"Him!" Sweetness yelled, pointing straight up as the dark fringe of the flying cathedral swept across the first glimmerings of the moonring, occulting them. Sworn enemy he might be; dumper of nubile girls into deadly deserts he most certainly was; Vastator, Godmörder and Destroyer of Worlds he aspired to become; but one thing she had to give this Devastation Harx. He had great timing.

Whispers in the wind had warned her. Her traingirl's sense for large moving objects under the close horizon had hinted. She had caught glimpses in the ebbing red at the edge of the world, something the size of a fallen moon, belly tabby-striped with cloud bands. The fine hair in her ears had caught a whisper of gears and big-bladed fans. The laws of probability had ruled in it being what her sense suspected: he'd want to hover around, survey the results of his skeet-shooting. So the Church of the Ever-Circling Spiritual Family putting the full stop on her ten questions was no big surprise. Cadmon and Euphrasie's reactions were as the great shadow fell over them. In an instant they were on their feet, Cadmon shaking a fist at the slowly drifting constellations of warning lights.

"Harx! Only you, man! Only you! Still we are trapped in this same gyre! No more, I say! Probability has brought us together again. This time, we will have it out!"

"Even so, Cadmon, even so!" Euphrasie chorused.

"You *know* this guy?" Sweetness asked, incredulous.

"Once upon a time, there were three little anarchist artists went to the Collegium of *Belles Lettres*," Euphrasie began.

"Euphrasie! To the boards! The boards!" With a good ten-metres-from-the-edge-of-the-box, Cadmon kicked sand over the fire, extinguishing it immediately. In the same movement, he scooped up his equipage and uprooted the gravboard. It skittered away from him on nervy magneto-gravitic fingers. Cadmon reeled it in by the tether, raised sail and skipped aboard as the skimmer picked up speed.

"One thought: art is fine and anarchism is dandy, but to make a million, invent a religion," Euphrasie tossed to Sweetness as he stuffed shut his pack and jammed his sail in its binnacle.

"This is a disagreement about art?" Sweetness said, ignored in the frenzy of mad activity as lights and vanes and little windows passed slowly over her head.

"He betrayed every principle he ever evinced for mail-order lucre and young ass," Euphrasie declared.

"If only every war were fought for reasons as noble as art," Cadmon said, reining his fretting board in like a war-palfrey. "And, if I played our game correctly, then this vile man is a positive menace to reality. Anarchists we may be, but we are not nihilists. Now, even as I debate these issues with you, we lose initiative and tempo. We will return for you, never fear. Now, we must to honourable battle. Stand back: this is not your fight."

"Yes it is!" Sweetness yelled. "It's my goddam sister in there!"

"Prime your charges, Euphrasie!" Cadmon commanded, bringing his board round in a sail-cracking luff. Euphrasie loaded his vest of pockets with sticks of explosive, tossed some to Cadmon who caught them nimbly, let loose the sail and took the gravboard up in one heart-thrilling, vertiginous swoop toward the ponderous roof of lights. Euphrasie made a running mount on his board and followed his buddy up up and away.

"Don't you leave me, you . . . you . . . uphill gardeners, you dryland rowers, you, you brown dirt cowboys!" Sweetness shouted at the bright triangles of sailcloth dwindling into the twilit baroque underbelly of the flying cathedral. She cupped her hands. "Stay under him! He's got partacs, and he's not afraid to use them! Get above him and he'll shoot you out of the sky!"

Already she was emerging from the penumbra of the blimp church.

Sweetness slip-scrambled up a dune face, threw herself along the knife-edged, soft ridges, seeking higher ground. Gnats against a buffalo they might be, but Devastation Harx was aware of these bright little mosquitos and was marshalling defences. As Sweetness watched, gun-ports irised open, the multibarrelled muzzles of rotary cannon slid into position and locked.

"Oh my God, look out, look out!" Sweetness shouted, fingers clenched in her hair in helpless frustration as the air beneath the dirigible became a cage woven from white tracer. But the two gaudy triangles of the anarchist gravboards slipped through them as if they were so much confetti, a dodge here, a veer there, a sharp tack to port, a terrifying death dive there to pull out centimetres short of being shredded by eleven hundred rounds a minute into a steeply banked turn.

"Ahhh!" Sweetness Asiim Engineer shouted, skull assaulted by the heavy hammer of the Gatlings.

Devastation Harx seemed to be trying to bring his vessel about: sets of vanes stopped turning, others cranked up a gear, while little manoeuvring nacelles swivelled hither and yon, fans a blur. Sweetness imagined teams of grim-faced pedallists, fit thighs pumping double, treble time, sweat running down the backs of their purple cycle shorts. The cathedral turned like a weather system, trying to bring its big belly guns to bear on the attackers, but Cadmon and Euphrasie had the measure of their enemy now. They ran in close and fast, hugging the cathedral's chaotic architecture, mast-tips pulled low to scrape below pods and vents and turrets, out of weapon arc. The guns dare not fire for fear of tearing apart the fragile skin of the big blimp.

"Go go go go!" Sweetness shouted, punching the air and leaping up and down on the hot, slipping sand as Cadmon and Euphrasie shot out from underneath the cathedral into clear air. They looped outward, upward. The guns spat tracer at them but they were already over the rim and cutting across the upper shell toward the glass nipple of the contemplatorium. Devastation Harx had clearly never expected vengeance to fall from the sky, his upper hemisphere was undefended. No turrets, no redoubts, not even a simple marksman with a fowling piece, sent precariously on to shell to snipe. And too close to risk the orbital weaponry. One decimal out and anarchists, Harx, purple people and all would go up in a rave of hyperaccelerated ions. Peering from beneath shading hands, Sweetness saw Euphrasie—his paisley sail identified him—raise an arm. A trail of smoke arced away from it. It struck just beyond the glass roof. There was a surprisingly large white flash. Seconds later, the boom shook Sweetness Asiim Engineer as she danced, jubilant, on her dune top. A ragged scarf of blimp fabric flapped in the wind. Smoke poured satisfyingly from the wound. The airship wheeled, trying to deny the attackers targets, but Cadmon and Euphrasie separated, banked hard and came screeching back on convergent courses toward the glass sanctorum. Two sticks this time. Double blast. One direct on the dome—shards of translucent plastic glittered in the magic hour light as they rained down, sharp knives, on the delicate upper skin. The other, longer-fused, rolled and went off a third the way down the canopy. Here the underlying structures lay closer to the surface: a gas cell ruptured with a gusher of shredded strut and packing tow that made the whole artifact wobble like an ill-set circumcision-day jello.

"Yay!" Sweetness cheered as the debris rained down over the red desert.

Devastation Harx's cathedral had a pronounced list. Still it spun, trying to get purchase on its tormentors. Gunners fired wildly in the hope of hitting something. Sweetness dived for cover as a spray of tracer blew the top of her dune to spray. She heard two, three, four more explosions. When she poked her head up over the top, she saw the cathedral canted at an angle of twenty degrees. Its dipping port side was pocked with craters and blast-holes. An entire section of lower skin swung from the substructure like a partly ripped-off scab. Spars and struts showed through the ruptured canopy, a compound fracture of the flight organs. A steady rain of debris emptied from its port-holes or slid off the canopy, pod struts bent and snapped under strange new strains. Sweetness could just make out frantic movement within, like spiders hatching, as the pedallo crews abandoned their positions. The anarchist air-fleet worried the big church like pit dogs a buffalo. Explosions peppered the acned skin of the airship. Another cell blew; second by second, the big ship went down by the port side toward the hard ground. Unbelievably, two peri-patetic artists with penchants for Big Domestic and explosives had the Church of the Ever-Circling Spiritual Family on the ropes. Their finest work, true anarchy in art, a hymn to chaos, with only a runaway traingirl to wit-ness it. Too adrenalised on the spectacle to worry about Gatling fire, Sweet-ness danced and hollered on her dune top, cheering on the great capsize. In one of those brief instants when her booted feet were in contact with the sand, she felt it. She knew the feeling. Every trainkid learned it from the teat; the subtle vibration of the big thing coming. Impossible, insane, but soles and bones told her, train a-coming, deep down in the sand.

Devastation Harx had weapons other than partacs.

She turned to see two ripples in the sand racing toward her, like the bow-waves of some inverted or invisible ship that sailed a sea of sand.

Across the Big Red they arrowed, straight and true and perfectly parallel and terrifyingly fast. The tremble became a shudder became a quaking. The sand beneath Sweetness's boots liquefied, she sank ankle, shin, knee deep. In instants the swift burrowers had crossed the open plain across which Sweet-ness had sailed that afternoon, and plunged into the dune on which she stood. Sweetness dived and rolled as the side of the dune exploded into twin geysers of sand. A glimpse was all she had. A glimpse was enough. Mantis beaked, twin-engined turbo-powered, all spikes, spines and sensor eyes. Hunting machines: fast and pointy. Very pointy: the drive canards carried twin impaling spines, glittering chromed steel in the blue of magic hour. The heads swivelled, the many eyes locked on. The twin hunters pulled a multi-gee turn into an ear-shattering climb.

Sweetness scraped sand out of her face, yelled the classic warning.

"Behind you! Look behind you!"

Euphrasie, balanced delicately on his board, turned, stick in hand. The lead hunter took him fast and clean on its port nacelle. The impact should have torn him in half. Layer upon layer of tough desert clothing saved him but he was pinned like a collector's dust moth, the bloodsmeared spear run through him to two thirds its length. As if she too had been savagely impaled, a terrible, incoherent wail was driven out of Sweetness. She watched the hunter sweep Euphrasie high into the air. Captainless, the gravboard went spinning down to earth. Vertical now; and Sweetness understood the killing thing's strategy. A backward roll at the apex of the climb and Euphrasie would slide down the spike, lubricated by his own blood, into a kilometre of airspace. But he still clung to the stick of explosive, and with a final, defiant snap at the hounds of God, he struck fire. Sweetness saw a thin wisp of smoke, then man and machine went up in a terminal blossom of white fire. Numb, dumb, she watched shattered scraps of meat and metal punch clean through the dirigible canopy in gaping, smoking holes to rain, smouldering, on the red sand.

Now Cadmon battled the second terminator. This was no swift, sharp victory. Seeing his enemy upon him, Cadmon thrust his boots deeply into the footstraps, seized the mast with all his main and went down over the edge of the canopy in a one-eighty vertical flip. The hunter pulled a high-gee horizontal roll, but those half-seconds were enough for Cadmon to lose it among the sensor booms and vent stacks and lattices of Devastation Harx's soft underbelly. His sense for the wind enabled him to draw more speed from every flaw and fidget that fretted around the airship's complex architecture. Sweetness's cheering, amplified by the anarchic mathematics of chaos theory, spun breezes that breathed a few centimetres per second into his fractal-patterned sail. But he was man and nature against angel and machine. The hunter was forced to keep its speed down to avoid further damaging the ship canopy, but metre by metre, second by second, it was gaining.

"Right! Right!!" Sweetness shouted; then, as the terminator tore through a flapping curtain of blimp-cloth, leaving it in three shreds: "Left! Hard aport!" Cadmon obeyed, not because he heard her, but because the rim was nearing and, in open air, he was kebab. He pulled a one-eighty bank into the face of the hunter. Too fast: it managed a mere flick of the barbs, then they were past each other. The hunter tumbled end over end, reacquired its target, but Cadmon was ready. He had one-eightied again, and while the hunting angel was picking up speed, he jumped straight between the horns. He caught the edge of its shield, flipped up over the spikes and bosses to come behind the beaked head. It thrashed and gaped at him, trying to snip limbs with its vanadium mandibles, but Cadmon had struggled out of his desert duster and was wrapping the too-many-eyed head with it. The hunter jerked and tossed, flipped upside down, but Cadmon's legs were locked around its chrome throat. The gravboard sailed on out from underneath the capsizing cathedral on a gently rising arc. Two gunners who had not yet abandoned their posts as the cathedral sank lower in the air found it in their firing arcs. Intersecting streams of white tracer shredded the board. But Cadmon the anarchist artist had his fist deep in the machine's skull-wiring. He ripped up a fistful of cable. The hunter let out a scream that Sweetness could hear over the creaking and sobbing of the tormented dirigible. Riding it like a high-plains gaucho a canton rodeo llama, Cadmon tore out another bunch of wiring. Keening madly, the hunter spun like a carousel, trying to throw the anarchist free. His fingers clung like cargo hooks. Sapient enough to under-stand its end was close, and could only be meaningfully be bought at the price of its destroyer's life, the machine dived blindly for earth. Belly gunners waved arcs of shells at it; Cadmon rode the hunter as he had ridden his board, heaving on the sensor head and rudder vanes to send the shrieking thing dodging between the bullets. Muscles straining like hawsers, he pulled the thing out of its death dive with centimetres to spare. The dune on which Sweetness stood loomed, soft sand as hard as rust. Sweetness saw a steel maw gape for her, then Cadmon pulled it up, up, up. At the last instant leaped from its back. He hit fast. He hit hard. He sent a great bow-wave of sand flying before him; all legs and arms and flapping coat tails, tumbling over and over and over. Blind, guidance wrecked, the hunter climbed on twin pil-lars of fire from its afterburner. It stabbed a terrible wound through the star-board quadrant of the flying cathedral. It burst from the upper canopy in a gout of engine parts and shredded gas cell. The maimed cathedral lurched lower. Fans beat uselessly at the air. She was going down by the side. Spinning like a fairground humjundrum, the outer sensor booms brushed the ground and snapped. Sweetness watched the thing wheel toward her, a crushing juggernaut. Ballast vents opened, Devastation Harx dumped tons of water on to the desert to try to keep airborne. The dying hunter-killer blazed starward. At the zenith of its climb, it faltered. Its engines choked, failed. Dead in the air, the hunting angel rolled on to its back. Spinning, it fell to earth, buried itself in the receiving sand, exploded in oily black flames. Sweetness ducked under the rim of the cathedral. It scraped her by a hair-breadth. The waterfall from the sky knocked her flat, drove the air from her lungs. Instantly saturated, bruised, she was swept down the dune side in a flash flood of water and sand.

She washed up against Cadmon. He lay flat, unmoving, wet beyond any decent notion of wetness in an arid desert. From his flatness, Sweetness guessed he was very broken inside.

"Oh man . . ."

Broken, maybe dead.

An eye opened.

"Get the hell out of here, girl!" Cadmon bellowed with all the strength of his lungs.

"You're all right!"

"No, I am not all right. I'm bloody dying, is what I am. At least I'll have some flowers around me. And you'll be sharing them with me unless you take the only traffic out of here."

"What are you talking about?"

"The ladder, girl! The ladder!"

He nodded with his chin. Sweetness followed the tilt of the day-old stubble up the slumped dune face to where the slowly rolling wheel of the stricken airship was dipping a paltry rope access ladder toward the ground.

"But . . ."

"Oh, spare me the indignity of a death scene. Just go."

The ladder sagged to the ground, lowering itself rung by rung like a Belladonna veil dancer enticing a john.

"Why?"

"What? You're still here?"

Two rungs, three rungs, four rungs. Five.

"Why do you hate him so much? I mean, I know why I do, he's got my sister, except she's not really my sister, but I treat her like she's my sister, but what've you got against him? I mean, just because you fall out at art school, is that a reason to try and blow him out of the sky?"

Eight rungs, nine rungs. Very soon, the wheel would swing the other way. And the ballast shift was working. Very slowly, the dirigible was righting itself. The fans were picking up speed.

"Oh, for goodness sake. He is my brother."

"This," Sweetness said, "is a bit mad."

"Cadmon Laventry Ophicleide Harx, dying before your very eyes, madam. Everyone has someone they have to kill, usually part of the family circle. Now go!"

The ladder was wheeling away from her, lifting up one rung, two rungs, three rungs, tantalising her. Still Sweetness hesitated.

"Oh for God's sake!" Cadmon croaked. "Why can't you just let it go as one of those things you'll never understand? It's the little mysteries that make life interesting. Leave me! Git!"

She got, but with one backward glance. The deep-buried, swift-sprouting desert flowers, woken by unseasonal rains, had already surrounded Cadmon in a nimbus of green. Wreath indeed. Hers also, if she didn't get that dangling piece of rope. She remembered all those times she had had to sprint for the train, the last-second leap on to the bottom rung. No third whistle here.

"Aaah!" she yelled as she struggled over the wet, clogging sand toward the taunting ladder. Mother'a'grace, it was going to be close. One rung, no rungs. She leaped at the ladder as it lifted above her head, caught the bottom bar with one hand. She swung, kicking her legs, grimacing with strain as Devastation Harx's cathedral gained altitude. A second hand on the ladder. A first hand up a level. Another, then, agonisingly, another. Rung by rung, Sweetness Asiim Engineer hauled herself up as the wounded airship turned ponderously on its fans and took her away into the magic hour.

*P*anic on the streets of Molesworth.

All night the rival political gangs, incensed by what they respectively interpreted as humiliation or jubilation, chased each other through the stone boulevards, party banners flying, flinging partisan abuse and bottles, bombarding each other with ripped-up paving setts and cafe chairs. Windows were smashed, those merchants incautious enough, or just too cheap, not to have bought security shutters were gleefully looted. Fires burned, Molotov cocktails showered down from balconies. Blouses and chemises set to dry now blazed merrily, lowest festoons catching from the fires in the streets and igniting those above. Burning tramcars, driverless but not powerless, careered along their tracks; vans and delivery drays were commandeered and swivelled into hasty barricades into and over which the respective party colours were set. Civic guards were mobilised, militias summoned from their beds and hastily armed. Military units at Gesserem and Shrelby were put on full alert; deep in their titanium-lined caverns under Chryse's laval shield, robot divisions opened their beady red eyes from eight hundred years of cybernetic slumber and lifted their heads. This was a big riot. Molesworthians took their politics seriously.

A combination of water cannon and wide-spectrum force-fields cleared most of the rioters and their barricades from the streets. Here and there, short shield squads baton-charged the mobs and fell enthusiastically to hand-to-hand. By morning most of the fires had been extinguished or had burned themselves out; the street was the province of ashes, charred shells of trams and trucks, those sweeping up broken glass and the occasional carload of young turks driving at mad speed along the splintered boulevards whooping and hooting and waving party flags from their windows and sunroofs.

Molesworth was a wreck, but the immediate crisis was over. The robot legions lowered their heads and closed their eyes.

In Rembrandt Platz the plane trees had all burned down but the early morning news vendors were sweeping away the broken glass and cinders and setting up their booths. Agency three-wheelers came scooting through the wreckage; newsboys in folded paper tricorns sporting the morning's headline sent bundles of daily news bounding across the debris before whizzing on to their next delivery. The gossip must get through.

Early starters picked their way cautiously past hissing, sparking tram cables brought down in the night, marvelling at the completeness of the destruction. Only one set of windows had escaped the crystal night, and those belonged to Torsten Toskvig's Salon Du Thé, the most venerable in Molesworth. The proprietor attributed this reputation to the excellence of his mint, picked by hand with the dew fresh on it from the family fields at Tullaswaygo, and he held that it was this, and this alone, that had protected his tea-house from the mob when Cossivo Beldene fell.

Here, on this morning, five people sat, taking their morning tea and reading the early editions. They were, left to right; a stocky young woman with spiky hair; a tall, wire-thin man with skin so black it swallowed light; a pale, languorous girl with the air of studied artiness and jewellery attached to every part of her body that would bear it; an older, square-faced man with greying hair whose over-grooming, stiffness of posture and plainly corseted belly advertised ex-vaudeville and a bare-armed, weasel-faced teen with deliberately anarchic hair and dreadful teeth. Skerry, Bladnoch, Mishcondereya, Seskinore and Weill. Together they called themselves United Artists. Same order as above, their arts were circus skills, observational comedy, performance artist in interactive micro-drama, dundered-in stand-up and anarchist. Their trick with the cake and the specially written song, hastened to the Glenn Miller Orchestra by express courier, had precipitated all the destruction which lay around their feet as they sipped their mint teas in the tea garden. Exactly as planned. This was no stunt. This was a precise act of political sabotage. These five people were secret agents, under commission from the Synod of Anarchs of Wisdom to seek out threats to their genial non-government and humiliate it with massive practical jokes.

Accrington LeCerf, phoney faith healer and abstracter of wealth from pensioners, had received his comeuppance when a curtain at one of his healing meetings had dropped, revealing the supposedly "healed" sitting backstage smoking and chatting, actors one and all. A mob of incensed old ladies had beaten him severely with his own collection bowl. He had been hospitalised for three months. United Artists arranged for that curtain to drop.

United Artists had set it up so that Ramon Drube, the corrupt Indian politician and the heart of the Cash-for-Sugar row, took a timely pratfall into a keg of eels when he bestrode his next electoral platform.

Gyorgy Krinz, a powerful lawyer with contacts among the Exalted Families, was also a notorious seducer of young boys in public conveniences, until United Artists, in a complex sting operation, converted an innocent WC into an all-singing, all-dancing musical extravaganza featuring the Cottage Boys in gold lamé and urinals fountaining flames like coloured roman candles. It was broadcast live on three networks. Viewing figures went through the roof. Gyorgy Krinz went off the roof. Convictions against the Exalted Families became more regular.

Mavda Quinsana, daughter of the more famous mother, ran a small but effective money-laundering empire from a few artificial atolls in the Syrtic Sea. Conventional justice failed, until United Artists slipped her a mickey in a margarita and convinced her, through clever suggestion and set design, that she had died and gone to hell, whereupon she fessed up all her known crimes and a wodge more nobody had even suspected. The walls of the fake hell opened, the shirrifry marched in, the real hell began.

Shareholder meetings of several big companies with pie-flavoured fingers were spectacularly disrupted by Amanda the Corporate Crime-busting Armadillo, frequently provoking shareholder riots when the extent of board-member remunerations were made public. United Artists, again.

Last night, United Artists had arranged for a very large chocolate cake to be delivered to the Gubernatorial Pleasance in Molesworth. Ooohs, ahhs. As the new Gubernator leaned forward with his cutting knife, the top had blown off and out leaped Seetra Annulka, Cossivo Beldene's former mistress, dressed in a spangled bikini, silver bootees and hoolie-hoolie feathers. As painstakingly rehearsed, she strutted up and down the stage to the whoops and cheers of the guests, singing a specially commissioned song. The whoops and cheers had grown louder as the audience became aware of the lyrics which had to do with nipple clips and glue, poultry, hooks in the ceiling, orphan girls in pristine white panties and stuffing the state jewels of Canton Chimeria into orifices not designed to show them off to their fullest glory. By the third verse there was not a whisper in the great Festhall.

To a riot of laughter and outrage in equal measures, Cossivo Beldene, his entourage and his guests were off stage before the final chorus. Shortly after the first chair was thrown and the fight broke out that was to spread from the *Rathaus* to the entire city.

Now, in the early light, with the smoke of burning washing still on the air, United Artists were reading their reviews.

"Gobbling Gubernator Feast-Farce," Skerry read, fresh and tight after her morning run, which she did for ten kilometres every day, riot or no riot. Whatever, wherever, whoever, she always showed a lot of healthy, glowing skin.

"A bit overdone on the alliteration," the solemn black man, Bladnoch, said in his soft, low voice. The best comedians seldom laugh. He had been the comedian's comedian; so funny he backed into being not funny at all. "Ball-clamp Beldene in hiding," he read, from his copy of *The Chimerian*, then flipped the paper over to the sports section.

"As in, hiding out, or a good hiding?" the languid, over-pierced woman said. She was Mishcondereya, bad daughter of a very good family, and even drinking morning tea she radiated a hunting-cheetah grace and lethargy that was at once attractive and extremely irritating. She was natural-born aristocrat. Of course, she had the quality daily, *Landing Times*: "Anarchy Rules Molesworth: Mobs Run Riot as Beldene Falls. That should please you, Weill."

The little skinny anarchist merely picked pieces of mint off his teeth. The over-tall, over-loud, over-coiffed and over-corseted middle-aged man in his trademark too-small silver suit commented from behind his *Impartial Reporter*, "I thought better of the *Times*'s editorial than to let an oxymoron like that on to the front page. You know, I remember when I was on the riverboats, I once met a newspaper copy-editor. Or was it a typesetter?" Seskinore's reminiscence was submerged by a chorus of derision from his fellow artistes. He added, lamely, "They're trying to get Glenn Miller to release it as a single with vocals by Seetra Annulka. We could be in for royalties."

"I'd buy it," Weill the anarchist said.

"Steal it, more like," Mishcondereya sniped. "Did you pay for that *Harbinger*?"

"Of course not." In twelve months training and thirty-six as roving agents of the Synod of Anarchs, Mishcondereya had not yet learned that Weill took her blunt little sarcasms as compliments. "No one buys when Babylon burns. This capitalist rag gives us a decent write-up."

"Is it top of the hour news yet?" Skerry asked.

"Seven bells," Weill said, nodding across the ruined plaza at the municipal clock on the tram-halt. Every piece of glass had been reduced to sugar cubes, but the naked hands told the time, slowly, steadily, for Molesworth. "Looks like it. Is there a wireless in this place? Well, look who it is."

A lady in widow's black was crossing the plaza, stepping resourcefully over the wiry piles of charred tires, ignoring the paperlads' entreaties. She held her hands folded decorously and did not look in the least out of place in the aftermath of Mob.

Seskinore folded down his paper, raised his eyebrows.

"Ah, our interestingly pedigreed trainlady."

"What the hell is she doing here?" Skerry demanded, sliding on a pair of dark glasses. "You know, Weill, sometimes you piss me right off. In fact, most of the time. Okay, she did us a favour, the little old dear's got some kind of weird shit trainpeople magic thing—enough inbreeding, you can do anything—but you shouldn't have invited her to the show. Least of all, our own table. I worry about your sense of security, comrade."

"At least I have a sense of decency," Weill said. "I don't know about you Tharsians, but in Grand Valley, even us anarchists treat our grandparents with due respect."

By now Grandmother Taal had arrived at the tea party on the verandah. The past ten hours had been a whirring daze of some notion or other. Forty-something years, and life can still knock you silly. The strange doings with that cake in the back alley, the unexpected invitation to the Pleasance, the very fine food and wine as she sat with these odd people—the last one would imagine on the guest-list for such a lofty event: then everything being thrown up in the air to hang a fearful minute while the girl in the silver spangles sang the satirical song, only to come crashing down in a rush of reporters, a lightning storm of camera flashes and a broadside of chairs flung toward the stage. She had followed United Artists as they fled, skulking along the lines of tables as the fighting broke out overhead, thanking her newly young knee and back bones. Her first thought had been to go with the band, but all she saw of the King of Swing was his tour bus driving away at speed, chased by a pelt of bottles and hurled imprecations that the Glenn Miller Orchestra would never sell another record in *this* town again, buddy. The fighting had by now transferred to the streets; she was alone in the great *Rathaus*. Plenty of places to sleep. It would not be the first time, Grandmother Taal thought as she swept broken glass from the plush sofa, wrapped herself up in table cloths and bedded herself down for the night. Nor, she sensed with grandmotherly insight, would it be the last. Outrage, riot, confusion, and then the dream.

She had woken with a shock, convinced that she was back in her mahogany cubby on the train, that Sweetness was a three-year-old again, banging on her door when her mother and father were sullenly arguing again. Her eyes told her no, you are on a bench in the Members Bar in Molesworth *Rathaus*; her ears told her, through the distant shouting and sirens and gobble of burning, there is a riot outside. The dream had been so vivid, so insistent; the dark cloud and her granddaughter standing under it in a deserted stone square; with none of the skewed logic or narrative absurdities of dreamspeak. Meaning was not veiled in metaphor or subconscious sexual imagery. No trains entering tunnels, no umbrellas or daggers or pointy airships. This was classically structured, with a clear and precise message, if packed overdensely with important points and presented in Sweetness's characteristic all-in-one-breath delivery. This was no dream. This was a sending. Grandparents believe in such things. She wrote down the gist of it on a napkin, studied it for a time while listening to the ebb and flow of riot outside, then slept again without further dream or sending.

"Sit ye down," Weill invited, gesturing to a chair. "Well, I told you it would be funny."

Grandmother Taal did not sit. She surveyed the ruined plaza. It was comment enough on Weill's sense of humour. Then she said, quite formally, "I do not know who you are, but I know what you are capable of. I am asking you, please help me find my granddaughter. I fear she has become enmeshed in great danger, for herself, and for us all."

She spread the napkin on the table. The newspapers all folded shut at once.

"I had a sending," Grandmother Taal said.

Bladnoch read the napkin. Seskinore sat back with a faraway look in his eye, then pointed at Grandmother Taal and asked, "Last night, didn't you say you were a *Chordant* Asiim Engineer? Is that any relation of the Chordants of Vermeulen? Maybe not, they weren't actually trainfolk, but I am acquainted with many people from the trains. Do you know I used to work the South Rim Scenic Recreational?"

Bladnoch raised an eyebrow, passed the napkin to Skerry, whose pupils dilated after the first line.

"Marvellous people, marvellous. It was more of a cruise than a train trip: the very best you know, food and wine, and standards of service! And clientele too; the very cream, you had to be to be able to afford the South Rim Scenic; and though I say so myself, the entertainment, top of the line. And the views down over Grand Valley in the evening, quite wonderful."

Skerry now passed the napkin to Mishcondereya, whose look of mounting impatience at Seskinore's enthusiasm for bounding into showbiz reminiscence at any opportunity turned on an instant to concern.

"Wonderful little train; very select, you see. Wonderful bill: there was Jimmy and Alice, and Mr. Superb—whatever happened to him?—and Dimmy darling. Dear Dimmy—dead these three years, alas—but I suppose you wouldn't know them; Engineer people don't get back to the passengers too often, do they? Or maybe your branch of the family's freight? That would be unfortunate, think what you've missed. Anyway, I got to know some of the Stuards; fine folk, if a little standoffish at first. That's a thing you learn in my line, how to read people, then how to bring them round. If you can't bring an audience round, you're dead as a comic, dear, dead."

"Seskinore," Mishcondereya said, "as a comic, you were never alive." She passed him the napkin. His mouth opened. His eyebrows steepled. He passed it to Weill, whose only response was a small smile lurking at the corners of his mouth.

"I think we can help you in this," Skerry said, solemnly.

Half an hour later, Grandmother Taal was punching across Solstice Landing's industrial scablands on a fast, executive express.

It was a low, fast, two-car unit with automated tilt mechanism designed to lean into the bends as the sleek, supercharged Great Southern Class 27 hauled it at speeds of up to five hundred kilometres per hour. Too small to have a resident Domiety, the engine was crewed by a newly wed team Grandmother Taal remembered from the lavishness of their wedding a few corroborees back. No kids yet. Nor likely to be; these priority service specials played fast and loose with the radiation shielding. Their privilege, their choice, but when she hailed them under the stone vault of Molesworth Main, they snubbed her. Bad word passed fast along the lines. The Asiim Engineers would be an age healing this social wound. For a moment Grandmother Taal contemplated invoking her full matronly authority; thought better. Molesworth and punk engineers did not deserve it. They whistled up and moved out on to the fast line.

The carriages were a symphony in cream leather, streamlined and smooth as infants' buttocks. Clever machinery was concealed behind the curvaceous banks of hide; the leather was clever, too; a touch, a word and controls or information screens would appears like tattoos on the surface. The carpet was toe-deep fur pile, the raked windows tinted gold. All very sophisticated, high-tech, minimal yet with a whiff of decadence, utterly last century. This age favoured heavy wood and heavier metal: big brass clunking stuff. The Synod in Wisdom, which had little experience of and less budget for running a counterinsurgency force, had bought it cut price off a Lyxian broker who had bankrupted five generations of family fortune on speculation in mink futures. Now it ferried United Artists at speed and in *fin du siècle* luxury around the planet on missions of political practical joking.

"An old trainmother tells you something from a dream, and you believe the end of the world is nigh?" Grandmother Taal asked as the train took points at three hundred and eighty on to the westbound fast and powered up.

"We're supposed to work eclectically," Skerry said, fidgeting on a curving leather sofa. She was never comfortable sitting down for long. Weill had told Grandmother Taal she could put both legs behind her neck. *I wish I could do that*, thought Grandmother Taal, then realised she had a better chance now than for a long time. Bladnoch, curled at the other end of the couch, was the opposite; never happier than when horizontal. He surreptitiously watched the afternoon pelota on a televisual patch of armrest. Backstage in the comedy clubs, the whisper was, *Bladnoch, he could have been the greatest, 'cept for that addiction to televised sport.*

"She means, we don't just take the word of sweet old ladies, no matter how good their juju is," said Mishcondereya, glowing and scrubbed from a showering off all that *nasty* Molesworth grit. She towelled at her hair furiously, began the laborious task of reinserting all her jewellery.

"You see, my dear, your story about the hole in the middle of the line rang true, because it's very far from being the first," Seskinore said, pouring Grandmother Taal a glass of mint tea. He dropped in a sugar cube, pounded it with a glass rod, gave it three swirls. "My own trade secret. On the circuit, you learn the art of good tea." It tasted no better than most others, worse certainly than Marya Stuard's. He continued, "Bloody things've been popping up all over the place. Chryse, Tempe, Axidy. Even Grand Valley. Could be hundreds of the things out in the desert we never hear about. Little breakdowns in reality. Some of those orbital processors have been running constantly for well over a thousand years, so they're bound to be showing the strain, and of course they skimp on the maintenance budget. Perfect opportunity for our friend up there to sneak in the back way."

"Apart from that, we've been keeping an eye on Devastation Harx and his crew," Weill said, feet up on a padded mound that served as a tea-table. "We keep an eye on most of the apocalyptic religions."

"This Harx is an apocalypsist?" Grandmother Taal said, sitting primly on an uncomfortable banquette, boots buried up to the ankles in buff fluff.

"I think that's what you'd call someone who advocates all-out war between humans and angels," said Mishcondereya.

"So how did your misfortunate daughter become involved with such a disreputable villain?" Seskinore asked.

"My granddaughter did not take to an arranged marriage and ran away with a very common Waymender boy, who is also a member of this church," Grandmother Taal said.

"I ran away and I did all right," Weill said. "But then, I stayed well away from religions like any sane boy should. Especially ones you have to pay for."

Mishcondereya flared her nostrils and gave a damp, disdainful flick of her still-wet hair.

"Not too bright, is she, your granddaughter?"

Before Grandmother Taal could riposte, Bladnoch's sofa arm beeped. He bent close to the screen. Taal could make out neither the scratchy jerky images or the muttered words but something had come in on top of his sports channel, something that put furrows in his brow. Skerry was beside him. Grandmother Taal wondered if there might be something between the tall, thin man and the tough little woman.

"Trouble," Skerry said. "Someone just took out three aerospacers on manoeuvres over Big Vermilion."

"How?" Mishcondereya asked.

"Partacs," Skerry said carefully.

"Oh," said Seskinore. "So, either the angels have gone berserk up there . . ."

"Or Pastor Harx is cranking up his apocalypse machine," Weill said.

Perked by the scent of action, Skerry leaped to her feet and pulled an anodised aluminium gosport horn down from the ceiling.

"Full speed ahead there!" she shouted to the engineers. On her word the Class 27 found power deep in its tokamaks and leaped forward, sending the United Artists reeling.

"Excuse me," Grandmother Taal said, innately adjusting to the surge and sway, "but exactly full speed ahead *where*?"

"To the Comedy Cave," Skerry said without a flicker of irony.

"Please explain. I am an old lady and have experienced much of late."

"We're not all improvisers like Weill there," Mishcondereya said. "You think we make this up as we go along? I tell you, it takes time and a lot of effort to put a good routine together, and a lot of resources. We've got FX teams, costume designers, script consultants, hundreds of extras, all on permanent standby."

"And my granddaughter?"

"Find Harx, and we'll find her, if I know runaway brides," Skerry said.

"Oh people," Bladnoch said, leaning over the arm of his sofa to look out the window, "weather warning."

Even as he spoke, Grandmother Taal could feel the train slowing from its flat-out gallop. Everyone rushed to the window, faces and hands pressed to the gold-cooled glass. Solstice Landing's magnificent dereliction had been left behind; the United Artists Special now arrowed across the high, unkempt and only-partially manformed high Plateau of Gwyst. Not a clint or a karst or a crater punctuated the monotonous black-sage scrub that gave this country its informal name; the Ashlands. You could see clear to the horizon in any direction. No missing a duststorm out there.

"Correct me if I'm wrong," Bladnoch said, "but this isn't supposed to be happening."

"It's big," said Mishcondereya coolly. Skerry was on the gosport again, hollering at the driver.

"I see it!" he yelled back, voice thin and tinny on the metal tube. "Mother'a'grace, don't you think I see it? No way I'm going through that, lady, timetables or no."

The train had already slowed from its high cruise to a canter. Brakes squealing as the pads felt the first touch of the dust, the United Artists Special came to a halt in the heart of the Ashlands. Moments later, the storm closed around it like a fist. The carriages went blind. The windows were opaque dark brown panels. The train could have been sealed in terra cotta like a hedgepig for roasting.

Sweetness, Grandmother Taal thought. *Where are you, what are you doing, are you safe?* She tried to summon up some echo of the psychic resonance of the sending to will a message back to her granddaughter but the electrical properties of the duststorm muffled the will, baffled the higher sensitivities. United Artists sat in the close gloom while Seskinore recounted an interminable epic of his days as a stand-up on the circuit made all the more unendurable by the creepy feeling, there in the hissing twilight, that everyone was dead, killed in a crash when the train jumped points and derailed at four hundred and eighty, and this was the hell to which God the Panarchic consigned state-sanctioned practical jokers.

"Clearing," Bladnoch said at last and by the time everyone got to the windows to peer through the sand-blasted glass, the last grains of dust had blown away and the sun stood high over Ashlands, ashen no more, for every leaf had been stripped from every black-sage bush.

"Took the paint right off," Mishcondereya said, again coolly.

"Think what that could do to your beautiful skin," Weill said.

"Never mind that," Bladnoch said, craning round to follow the track of the departing storm, "Think what Harx can do if he's got into the weather."

The train moved on and was soon back to its customary pell-mell, down from the Gwyst into the Banninger. Bladnoch's warning spurred United Artists from their perpetual bickering and sniping to some manner of actions. They formed a creative huddle in a glassed-off office section at the rear of the carriage and spent the remainder of the sun-lit hours in professional level sniping and bickering. Grandmother Taal saw much gesturing and stamping around, finger pointing and table punching and fist clenching. She ate a desultory prepackaged dinner in a plastic compartment tray dispensed from a slot and lip-read oaths that made even a trainfolk Matriarch blench. She squared the two contenders. In the green booth: a flying cathedral, untold catamites, a warehouse full of apparatchiks on ropes and the soul of St. Catherine of Tharsis, with which he sought to Trojan Horse his way into the programmes of the angels themselves. In the red pavilion; a trapeze artist with a penchant for indecently short shorts, an alleged maestro who had urinated away his genius for afternoon sports channel tractor-pulls; a wispy performance artist (whatever that might be) with a pierce everywhere but through her ego; a paunchy joke-jockey too piss-poor even for the cruise trains; a ferrety self-proclaimed anarchist whose only chance of defeating the great enemy was through body-odour. Grandmother Taal mused for a time about what type of world it might be when Devastation Harx dethroned the angels. If any were left alive to inhabit it. The Engineers had never in all their genealogy produced a theologian, so Grandmother Taal's conclusion, by the lights of her Domiety, was quite profound: if the Evil One defeats the Panarch, he, by defection, becomes God in all his absoluteness. When he takes the adamantine throne, the universe is remade in its entirety, beginning to end, and every memory with it. What we become, we will remember always having been. If there are trains in that world, they will still need Engineers. If not, then she would never know what she had been.

With full night outside, the huddle of heads broke up. The leather table and bulkhead wall were covered in fibre-pen scribblings but when the door flew open and United Artists stomped out, everyone went as far from his comrades as the carriage would allow and no one looked at anyone. Skerry paced tightly up and down in the one square metre by the bar, punching her fist into her hand. Bladnoch lay face down on his sofa and flicked on the evening sulky racing from Charnoch Park. Seskinore sat on a pouffe, palms on thighs, tilted his head upward and began to hum, quietly but nasally, hits from *Dr. Mabuse, the Gambler*. Mishcondereya huddled in a chair, knees pulled to her chest, to practise sulks and pouts and, when she thought someone was looking, let leak the odd hard-done-by tear. Weill picked ferociously at his teeth and, when done with that, slipped off his sandals and peeled white strips of athlete's foot from between his toes.

Grandmother Taal fumed inwardly at this sullen brattishness. If they had been trainpeople, little Engineers, even good-for-nothing Bassareenis, she would have had their very lugs . . . Not even her dear, wayward granddaughter, whom she permitted liberties allowed to no others aboard *Catherine of Tharsis*, would have behaved like that in the face of adversity. She found she was clenching her fists, sucking in her lower lip and chewing it, frowning hard enough to spark a tic of headache from her pineal gland. Too much. Like a superheated boiler venting, her patience blew in a great calliope whistle.

"United Artists, you call yourselves? I've seen more unity in a truckload of Cathrinist pelerines. Professionals: I will tell you professional; professional is, even when your son has not spoken to his wife for four years, the lading bills are made up, the contracts are docketed and sealed, the trucks end in the right yards and always, always, the train leaves on time. Three whistles, and you are left behind. You would all be walking, if you were trainfolk. You think you are so clever, so funny, that you are the hope of the world. My granddaughter is funnier than you when she is not even trying, and I have more hope in her than I have in you. Heroes! Bah. I break wind at you. If you are all that stands between my daughter and rescue, if you are our last best hope for bringing down Devastation Harx and his machinations, then dress me in purple and call me catamite. I squat and ease on you all."

After a long, cool pause, Weill drawled, "Hey, lady, dying is easy, comedy is hard."

Bladnoch, who of all had seemed most ashamed at Taal's frustrated outburst, suddenly propped himself up on his forearm, squinted through the near-opaque window glass into the darkness.

"Many a true word, Weill," he said, and no one could mishear the tone of fear in his low, soft voice. "Lights, down."

The golden glow ebbed from the leatherette carriage.

"What is it?" Skerry demanded, rushing to the window.

"I rather think we're going to have to wing this one," Bladnoch said, as the dark Banninger night was shockingly lit by beams of lilac light.

23

*a*rms and legs wrapped around cables, Sweetness Octave Glorious Honey-Bun Asiim Engineer 12th sailed beneath the brilliant stars of the moonring. Shortly after full night a thermal from off the Banninger Escarpment had lifted the flying cathedral into higher, chillier air. The thrill of the view had faded with the light; within minutes Sweetness was noticing her teeth chattering, her breath steaming, her limbs shivering. She could not feel the rope under her fingers. Soon, the cold numb would spread to fingers. Shortly after that, she would lose her grip and fall, like a flash-frozen bird caught in an updraft. Numb limbs dissenting, she hauled herself up, step by step, toward the canopy. She had noticed early that this was a ladder to nowhere, an emergency egress shaken loose by the Dust Brothers' bombing. The escape hatch above it remained sternly dogged. But there might be another way in, a vent, a shelter among the heat-exchange vanes, some warm spot to which she could cling and curl for this night which she knew was going to be one of the longest in her life. There were inspection gantries over there, cables and pipeworks. If she could make her way along them to one of the blast holes, she could work her way inside. Industrial grade if. She already hurt like the devil's nipple clamps. By morning? No option, you hurt, Glorious Honey-Bun. And she was tired and wet through and thirsty and those foil-packet trail dinners wouldn't fill a hole in your tooth. Go on, then. Take that big scream. Or quit moaning and come *on*. You expect an adventure to be easy? Hand over hand over hand will do it. Hand over hand over hand.

Hand over hand over hand, she made it to the escape hatch. Teeth gritted with effort, she beat at it with a fist, pulled off a boot and whacked at the hatch dog.

"Let me in! Mother'a'mercy, there's a girl out here!"

If she could scarcely hear herself over the whirr of propellers and the moan of the high wind in the cathedral's gingerbread, what chance a passing purple person? Surely someone in the cycle pods must have noticed there was a girl hanging from a rope ladder? She hauled herself around on the ladder. The nearest pod hung like an overripe fig from a single strut, abandoned, its gear-trains and drive chains gnashes of oily teeth. The only other she could even glimpse was three quarters occluded by a rudder array, and that part she could see was awash with ballast water. Twenty metres to her starboard was a thermal dump stack. She could feel the warmth from the fans gently wash her face. Twenty metres. Twenty light-years. If she could just get to those u-bars. She started to swing the ladder. It let out a hitherto unsuspected ominous creak. She glanced. In her mad leap for rescue, she had failed to notice that one of the ropes had been cut half-through by shrapnel.

Real Big Adventure Stuff. Get that pendulum swinging . . .

Her first reach missed by a fingernail. She ignored the sound of stretching, snapping cord fibres and threw her whole weight into the next swing. She reached; her finger locked around the hand-hold. She let go the ladder. Her momentum almost tore her free.

Trust that trainfolk upper body strength . . .

Her right hand seized the next rung. Sweetness hung, crucified, a kilometre and gaining above the yellow-windowed manses of Banninger Canton's geometric farms.

Easy. Peasy. Wee buns.

Thirty monkey-walks brought her to the heat-dump fans, amongst which she nestled, ripping loose communications cables and wrapping them around her waist, thighs and wrists. A survey of her situation told her this was as far as Sweetness Asiim Engineer was going under this air-borne basilica. She tightened her cocoon and tried to shake water out of her hair. Warmer now, warm enough to drive off the now wracking shivers and dry out her clothes, warm enough for her brain to be alerted to another peril.

The airship was ascending slowly but steadily, and without any indication of reaching its ceiling. Long before anoxia shrivelled her brain in her skull like a pickled pig testicle, it would have loosened her grip, blurred her sense, made her altitude drunk enough to make that big step look not just appealing, but necessary. Already she was feeling cosy-dozy, comforted by memories of hiding from parental wrath among warm, cranny-laden machinery. She slung extra loops of cable around her shoulder, knotted them and tried to keep herself awake.

Shock. Where what who? The sky . . . the stars . . . it hurts. Oh my God. Her slim snake hips had slipped through their cinch, the loop of cable had locked under her small but perfectly pert breasts. Her feet kicked at two kilometres of empty space. *Thanks, tits.* But as she wiggled the noose down over her pelvis, she became aware that here was a second way to die. Hanging would do it every bit as well as falling.

Stay awake! she berated herself. *Look at the world: You ain't ever seen it from this angle before.*

She had to admit she had a grandstand seat on night across the earth. From this height she could appreciate the roundness of the world: a little last perfect blue clung to the eastern horizon; Sweetness calculated that the cathedral was headed southwest. Morningwards. The teeming cantons of Grand Valley lay that way, sunning themselves under the ancient lights of World-roof. The ship would need repair. The great vertical engineering cities that clung to the piers as Sweetness clung to heat had once assembled Sailships and starcrossers. A gas-filled bag of faith was little to them. That lay in the future. This gently sloping scarp country over which she flew was not without interest. Sweetness reckoned she could see two hundred kilometres in every direction: to the west and south towns and cities clung silvery on the horizon like patches of glowing moth-dust, flowing into each other with filigree tendrils of powder-soft lights. From a hundred kilometres out to immediately beneath Sweetness's feet scattered dots of farmsteads clustered around the agglomerations of the rural towns which in turn gathered around the larger market centres. Sweetness tried to draw patterns on them, terrestrial constellations, and with a sudden revelation, saw it whole: hexagons upon hexagons upon hexagons, from steading to city. Her sudden insight into human geometry stunned her for whole minutes, then she caught two long glints of silver moonlight streaking straight across the dark land. A railroad. She leaned forward in her harness. There! Tiny and wan as a lonely firefly, a scattering of sparks tore across the night. A train!

Perhaps her train.

The unbidden thought was like a flash-freezing of the spleen.

My train. My people. I could wave and cheer and shout. I could send down flares, I could throw lightning, I could explode whole stars and they still wouldn't know it was me. They wouldn't even look up from the track and drive levers. Do they even think about me?

Taal did. Great Taal, mother of grandmothers. Taal would have heard her, noticed her, received her message. But Taal was in Molesworth and she was up here on the way to Grand Valley with no way of telling a soul living or astral.

Sweetness watched the train out of sight among the other scintilla of the scarp land, then settled back in her harness and did not look at the ground again.

This time, she caught herself just as she was dropping off with a convulsive judder.

Dropping off!

She decided she would look at the stars. There was nothing to make her feel track-sick in those original patterns of light in the darkness. On the long night runs she had learned the names of the major constellations from her mother, but most of the night sky was just lights to her, patternless and magical. Sweetness knew the Cup, and the Dogs, and the Hunting Cat, but the nomenclature seemed tenuous and arbitrary. The Cup could as easily be the Diaphragm; the Hunting Cat, the Bouquet of Oddly Shaped Lilies. Who had these men been, whose particular visions became imprinted on the night sky? Sweetness amused herself down toward midnight by drawing up new constellations and naming them. That wasp-waisted configuration could be the Hornet, or, if you extended it to those three bright stars up there, the Nasty Vase. Just beneath it lay the Angular Banjo, to the left of it, hovering on the dawnward horizon, the Banyan. That band of silver; fainter, softer, broader than the moonring, was the Great Southern Railroad, that tight collection of eleven stars the Sunshine Express. Just visible under the rim of the canopy, the Really Little Church, at eleven o'clock to it, Snortus the Hog. Rolling along the upper rim of the moonring, the Hoop and Stick, behind it, in zodiacal procession, the Typewriter, the Star-Goat, Zelda the Cheap Woman, the Yawning Man, the Open Newspaper; the Five Tickets, the Pram, the Safety Pin, the Letter B, the Big Slipper, the Wishbone.

As she was about to set to work naming the southern constellations, a star fell out of the Letter B, transforming it into a P. It burned brief and bright to the east, a streak of swift fading silver light. While it ebbed from her eyeballs, three more plummeted out of moonring in close formation. They kindled and burned on the southern horizon. Then all three legs of Marco the Three-Legged Pig came off and blazed across the night like a firework display.

While Sweetness gaped, half-wondering if the Powers and Dominions had taken offence at her renaming them, the moonring blazed lilac. The band around the world was a loom of lasers: beams flickered and duelled, parried, stabbed, cut. Sweetness cried out in astonishment as the sky burned, almost let slip her hold on the heat-exchanger. Stars burst, bright enough to light the land beneath like day. Others hurtled on mad trajectories across the orbital marches to die in searing light, slashed apart by scythes of lilac light. Fleets and squadrons moved in from the outer constellations toward the edge of the affray: crimson struck back at lilac. A hundred novas burned on Sweetness's retinas. Stars fell from heaven by the legion, scoring the sky as if fingernails had left love-scratches in the bowl of night to the *ur*-light beyond. By the lights of any and every of her world's plethora of religions, this was the big one. God the Panarchic, the Ekaterina Angelography, the Seven Sanctas, the Thrones and Dominions, the Orders Lofty and Lesser together with the Rider on the Many-Headed Beast had come out slugging. From the point of view of a runaway traingirl lashed to the bottom of a limping airship-basilica somewhere over central Canton Banninger, God looked on the ropes.

We're in big trouble, Sweetness thought, face lit by the heat-death of falling angels. *What's happening, why, who's doing it?* The questions answered themselves the instant she shaped them. *That man, up there, just a fistful of metres above your head.* But was this the big one, the Angels and Devastation Harx, duking it out, *mano a mano*, or was he merely testing the limits of his powers?

Crimson strove against the lilac. Beam by beam, duel by duel, angel by angel, crimson was failing. Sweetness's carefully constructed constellations were unravelling as reinforcements were de-mothballed from centuries of cyber-sleep, powered up their altitude jets and rolled into attack orbits. Waves of crimson and lilac crashed against each other, surged back and forth across the moonring like the rather cheap rippling sand tank sculpture Uncle Mort had got, together with a dose, from that maintenance woman in Llangonedd Junction, and was meant to be relaxing but made Sweetness feel bilious. Stars fell like sparks from a wheel foundry, scattered across the night-side of the planet. It was an oddly soothing sight, war in heaven, until Sweetness realised the only reason she was not free-floating atoms in a cloud of superheated helium was because of the very weapon Devastation Harx was using to gain access to the battle systems.

He cuts down angels like grass in the city park, and you're going against him with nothing more than a stick of sunblock, the bottom of a tube of glue, two thirds of a posh frock and a half-eaten romantic novel?

He who fights the tiger has no eye for the mosquito on his neck, she reminded herself, which was like something Cadmon, or, for that matter, Uncle Neon, might have said.

Yeah, until the mosquito bites.

High in the planetary approaches, inconceivable forces marched and countermarched, outflanked and ambushed, attacked and were thrown back. The Banninger sky still burned with the corpses of angels, but the lilac assault had been halted. The western horizon was lit by hundreds of puff-ball novas, sparkling like corroboree whizz-bangs: Harx's orbital partacs, Sweetness guessed. The picket of lilac beams faltered, then failed. Crimson rushed through in ten, twenty, fifty places, invading like cancer. The lilac rallied but Devastation Harx's intervention was at an end. The lilac was forced back on itself, inward, like a black hole collapsing under its own weight. Like an imploding star, it was merely overture to explosion. A single starburst, brilliant as the sun, lit the night hemisphere. Sweetness blinked afterimages out of her eyes as the nova turned the sky white, then faded. Something big had gone up, up there. A stardock, a Skywheel transfer station; maybe an orhab. There were people on those big cylinders. No legs and four arms and way too long and snooty people because they disdained coming down to earth, but still people. They probably never even knew they were dying.

Dark night returned, darker for having been broken by unnatural light. Even to non-astronomical Sweetness Engineer, the moonring looked tattered, moth-eaten. The constellations would never be the same again. Now someone would have to think up new names for them. The man in the flying cathedral had been beaten, at permanent cost to the night sky. This time. The next war would be fought on another battlefield entirely: the shifting interplay of alternative quantum universes. Next time, reality would be the casualty.

"Oh, man!" Sweetness said, suddenly cold and small and very high up, far from her close little cubby, and alone. She drew her knees up against her chest, hugged them to her, bound them close with cable and wished for something more to look at than lights in darkness.

A third time, that dislocation of having fallen asleep without knowing. Sweetness came to herself with a gasp and shudder. No nod, no doze, this; she woke with the light of early morning full in her face. Huddled over in her web of cables, she had slept away entire cantons and quarterspheres. The sun was a spreading scab of blood on the western horizon, clotted between the continental upthrusts of the Great Volcanoes, the only hint of the terrible war that had been fought in the dark. The air was miraculously clear and bright; light flooded across the land, driving early ribbons of cloud before it like a Purging Priest a poolful of swingers. Sweetness painfully lifted her arm to shade her eyes, tried to blink the morning gold out of it. Blinded. Then the sun lifted clear from the hollow between the mountains and one of the great vistas of her solar system unveiled itself to Sweetness Asiim Engineer 12th.

This little red world was never the nearest, but had always been dearest to the hearts and bones of Motherworld. Since before words, in the great songtime of the dry plain, the ancestors of humans had looked up to this the speck of blood where the needle of imagination pricked the sky and invested it with power. An angry star, the eye of a martial god, masculine, stomping and sanguine, armoured in rust. It rose and set on a million lootings, burnings, invadings and besiegings. When the gods died, the warlike aspect was transferred and made concrete in the planet itself. It hung by night, watching, while minds immeasurably superior to man's drew up plans. The world itself was our red enemy. Even its puny, pumicey moons were demonised. Fear! Terror! Our true enemy is always our neighbour. Naked to our lenses, human imagination had engineered its surface. Whether watered by slow canals, galloped across by green or red barbarians; contemplated by a wistful, autumn people; the little world next one out, unlike the other globes in the system, rocky or smothered with steam, had always possessed a geography. It had regions, landscapes, places. Names were written on its skin. To name a thing has always been to claim possession of it.

It was only when the first space vehicles went out from Motherworld that its humanity realised the long injustice they had committed. This was no war-lord, no red destroyer. Beneath the thin, cold unbreathable atmosphere—no life here, another myth dashed—and the veils of dust was the face of a woman, graceful, refined, strong and mysterious. It had good bones, the little red world.

Here, in the early space days, the ancient and persistent lie of "Motherworld" was exposed. The genders had always bent the other way. A woman must be possessed. A gentle wooing by go-betweens, then the men were sent out from the aggressive bigger blue dot to lay claim to the world next door. They drove round in their machines, put their feet on it, stuck their flags in it, made it theirs. A forced marriage of worlds. After wedding, impregnation. The barren must be made to carry life. The arrogance was monumental, the vision more than its equal. It was a big universe out there, and hostile to clever carbon. But even the technologically extended lives of the golden who controlled the home planet's immense resources were too short to measure the scale of transforming one world into another. Water gushing down the dried-up riverbeds, spring green blooming across the high plateaulands, waves breaking on the red shores of shallow blue seas: these were visions no amount of their wealth could buy them. Their engineering advisers gave them a quick, flashy, hideously pricey fix: see that great rift valley? Four and a half thousand kilometres long, five kilometres deep? Stick a glass roof over it. Turn it into one mother of a greenhouse. Better still, make it to last. Build it out of diamond. Diamond as big as the Ritz? Phah! Diamond as big as a continent. Good, hard science. Technical and manly.

Fleets of vast, visually chaotic engineering ships were sent into slow transfer orbits to the wife-world. Surface workers surveying the sites watched the thirty-kilometre units move into low orbit and disassemble themselves from their drive-spines. They dropped automated construction modules on Grand Valley day and night for seven weeks.

Pressure-dome hoovervilles mushroomed up the length of the valley floor; as the easterlies clocked off, the westerlies clocked on, new dawn on their hard helmet faceplates. Construction plants drew in megatons of carbon dioxide—all the better for the atmospheric manforming—and by the alchemy of molecular processing, spun it into engineering-grade carbon nanofibre. Diamond trees began to rise from great Mariner rift. Day by day they grew as the assemblers wove carbon; through blinding CO_2 fogs, through the hurricane seasons, through the blanketing dust storms when engineers went blind even by their helmet lights and navigated by heavy sonar. Carbon on carbon, molecules locking together. One kilometre, two kilometres they rose. One and a half long years after the engineer-towns, which would one day be the great and civilised cities of the valley, struck their taproots into the cold, dead mantle, two million trunks topped the highest of the canyon mesas and budded into four branches. A forest of diamond grew in the great valley. Out on the high blasted plains, a thousand vitrification plants moved over their immaculately surveyed and levelled sites, fusing silicon sand to trace-doped glass hexagons five hundred metres across. Flotillas of robot aerobodies cautiously shifted the panes into position; even in lower gravity, one warp could have thrown the tensile integrity of an entire canton. They settled on to their bolt-posts; one by one the nuts were tightened while scuttling groutbots filled the gaps with light-permeable expansion mastic. By scabs and scars, like some archaic children's game of territory and capture, a tessellation of hexagons spread across the canyonlands of Grand Valley. Twenty long-years after the first gaffers had surveyed their sites and threw up their Carbonbergs, the last constructor units disassembled, reconfigured into maintenance mode and buried themselves in the regolith.

As one pundit put it, Grand Valley now ran to thirty trillion carats.

Even as the last roofplates were being bolted into place, a new and noble guild was receiving its letters patent; a nation as individual and caste-ridden as the trainfolk: the Ancient and Pristine Order of Windowcleaners. Only when the glass was *spotless*, utterly transparent to every spectrum of light, could the ecological engineers be moved in. Nothing Pristine about this order. A grubby crew, these, soily-handed, humusy, stained and muddied. Dirty knees on their pressure suits. It is a work of years to make a soil, yet more to weave an atmosphere, decades longer for a mix of gases to become a self-perpetuating, self-regulating and adjusting homoeostatic system that some people think of as a planetary organism and call Gaia, except that here it was Gaia-in-a-bottle, and needed a different name altogether.

The grunt engineering had been the easy bit. The golden rich fretted long decades—twice as unendurable as those of their homeworld—for the day when the first of the ecoengineers undogged her helmet, lifted it off, took a long, deep breath and found it very good. Few remained of that impatient generation; the last twenty lived out their days in canyonside adobes hunting in pristine parklands under diamond skies. A great oasis, sheltered from the scoring winds and terrifying energies of ROTECH's larger scale manforming, green on red like a colour blindness test for an entire planet. A strip development that reached round one third of a world. When sunrising and sunsetting flashed from the roof glass tiles, they heliographed across interplanetary space. Watchers on nightside Motherworld would wink and blink the nova-dazzle out of their eyes. Within their roofed-in world, the ancient rich, spry in the low gravity, observed their night sky fill up with stars: the vanguard of the new generation of planetary engineers seeding themselves across the parking orbits. A scary people, this; less patient even than the greenhouse gardeners, their angel-machines would engineer realities wholesale.

Selah. So be it. Around here, this history began to abut into another Sweetness had recently heard and little more need be said of it, save that beneath the great glass roof, the last of the golden died and their sculpted mesa-chateaux became the cores of the elegant and diverse cities of Grand Valley, a patchwork of four hundred cantonettes and city-states and the densest and most diverse cultural region in the solar system. And that it was the dawn glory of Worldroof that so amazed Sweetness Asiim Engineer, left hanging in her precarious web.

With a wan, early mist clinging to the roof panels, Sweetness first thought of ice mornings on the winter transpolar runs, when the temperatures high high north dropped so low the carbon dioxide smoked out of the atmosphere into a thin rime. Then, as the sun gained in strength and the mist burned off, she imagined that she was flying over the board of a titanic children's game, a thing she had once hallucinated when she went down with one of those necessary childhood diseases and her temperature hit the high thirties. Vast playing pieces should be moving from hexagon to hexagon, manoeuvring and threatening. Shading her eyes, she could discern distant dark shapes standing out above the fields of hexes, stalky and angular: mooring towers for Skywheel ground-to-orbit shuttles, communications masts, but her imagination made them Peons and Palisers and Prelates investing and humiliating Princes and Palaces. She reminded herself she had had very little sleep last night, and she had witnessed a fragment of Armageddon, so powers and dominions were lodged in her head. The light was still low and glancing enough to render the glass opaque, a golden highway over which the flying cathedral drifted. Half a degree of altitude, and on an instant, the ground beneath her feet went transparent. She thought of clouds lifting or some inky solution in a School of the Air chemistry demonstration clearing with a drop of reagent. Sweetness's was not a seafaring family—she had never set foot on a water-borne craft—but her childhood bedtimes had been filled with stories from the shallow oceans, of pirates and shipwrecks and drowned cities of the wicked, down there, where the people still went about their business in the watery streets and on clear, fearful nights, their bells could be heard, tolling from the submerged campaniles. The small, manicured farms, the geometric roads, the tightly packed villages and towns beneath her feet were the stuff of such stories. The cathedral passed over the support branch of one of the roof-trees. At its tip, it split into finer and finer branchings, suggesting a new image to Sweetness; blood vessels, capillaries: a city beneath the skin, if such a thing could be. Peering down between her feet, she saw that the upper levels of pier were encrusted with orioles and turrets and perilous balconies. Grand Valley was as familiar to her as any other piece of the planet's terrain; the vertical cities that clung to the bottom couple of kilometres of the roof-trees held no wonder for her any more, but the view from above revealed details previously hidden by perspective. On one of the very highest terraces, tiny figures celebrated some dawn party: as the airship's shadow fell over them, Sweetness thought they looked up, and that one waved. She waved back. Now she crossed the junction of two roofplates; a perfect black fault line across the outer burbs of one of the valley cities, like a knife cut in reality. A couple of minutes onward, dark scurrying machines worked doggedly at a hole punched through the tough glass: some bolide snuck through while the anti-meteor defences had been otherwise occupied in the night. They fused over the cracks, wove silica from their mandibles like spiders walling themselves up in egg-cocoons of silk. Sweetness noticed that they were working on both sides of the wound; the ones beneath clung nonchalantly with suckered feet.

A loop of river identified the city unreeling below as Melucene, an elegant, university town of high-gabled gritstone colleges strung along the river bluffs of the muddy Meluce. Castle Melucene, the venerable seat of the Provosts, hove into view, a fantastical confection of towers and spires and buttresses carved from a primeval ventolith mesa by orbital construction lasers. Sweetness had never liked Melucene: she detested the boyish, mannered jinks of the students on the term runs when they flocked back to their dormitories. She hated their high, affected, nasal singing, and determinedly kept herself on the working side of the tender. It took the Stuards a week to sluice out the beer and vomit. As she watched the steeply pitched roofs of the colleges slip beneath her feet, a niggling feeling came over her that perhaps they were a little *closer* to her boot soles than they had been. That the fields looked a little larger, that the details of the college badges worked out in coloured roof-tiles were more sharply focused. That the labouring airship was losing height.

In confirmation, the cathedral lurched and dropped. Sweetness grabbed for something solid to hold on to. The glass hexagons were coming up hard and fast beneath her. Ahead, an entire roofpanel was slowly tilting open. Squinting through the glare, Sweetness could make out the silhouettes of gantry work rising above the surface, beneath, the indistinct but massive torpedoes of lighter-than-aircraft nuzzled at roof-branches like great fish feeding from coral. Some repair facility, but Harx was coming in too fast, too low . . . What was the pilot doing? Ballast gushed from vents, shedding across the roofplates in a flash flood but the basilica was still losing height. Air gusted warm in Sweetness's face and she had her answer. As the sun warmed the morning air, the airship lost in the battle of competing densities. Sweetness tried to clamber away from the closing ground. Nowhere to go, remember? This is as far as you got. She had to do something. At this speed, with this mass, if Harx hit, his little freeloader would be spread like cashewbutter. The access panel was fully open now, but the bottom rungs of the rope ladder, her salvation, were brushing the glass. Coming in, too low! Too low! Sweetness wrestled in her cocoon, untangling legs and arms. She freed three metres of cable, screwed up her courage, screwed it tighter. She grasped hold of the cable, wrapped it firmly around her wrists and with a cry, swung herself free. Sweetness Octave Glorious Honey-Bun Asiim Engineer 12th dangled beneath the dome of the cathedral. The airframe lurched again. She let out a little shriek. Don't look down.

You have to look down.

She looked down.

Five kilometres below her, a lazy river lost itself in meanders and braided sandbars while great coloured riverboats the size of small towns cruised the backwaters. Sweetness shifted focus. Closer—very much closer—the glass rushed up at her. The portal was close . . . The airship sagged lower. Aerials snapped, booms bent. Not close enough.

"Yaaah!" Sweetness Asiim Engineer shouted, and jumped.

Glass, she had forgotten, is smooth, slick and hard. Very hard. The impact knocked the wind from her: she rolled five times, the world a blur of airship canyons land sky, and into a slide. Flickering between sense and unconsciousness, she saw the cathedral hit the edge of the portal, bounce clear and drop through. That edge, toward which she was helplessly sliding . . . She tried to find an anchor for her fingers, something to kick against. Nothing, slick, smooth glass. With the last of her strength and will, Sweetness heaved herself into another roll. Ribs protested, she tried to pull her arms over her head. If she missed, if she got it wrong, best not to see the moment she shot over the edge on to five kilometres of clear morning air. Over and over and over, and to rest. She peeked out between her arms. She could have spat a gobber over the lip of the big drop. Sweetness laughed deeply, painfully and then everything went wonderfully black.

One eye opened, some time later. In front of it was a boy's face, cocked at the angle of curiosity. Sweetness opened her other eye. The boy tilted his head the other way. Sweetness guessed him to be four, maybe five, and so incongruous was the sight that she forgot for a moment the grating pain down her left side. While she puzzled, another child's face looked over the boy's shoulder, a girl, a couple of years older.

"Mine," the boy said.

"You think," the girl laughed. "Way too old."

"Is not."

"Is too."

"How old are you?" the boy asked Sweetness.

"Nearly-nine," Sweetness said. "Listen . . ." But the girl gave a bray of laughter, stood up, arms folded triumphantly.

"Mine, see?"

"Too old for you, too, Meadowbank."

"Me or no one else, Townley. And hadn't you noticed, but she's a girl anyway. My jurisdiction. Go back to your boys."

The boy scowled. The girl play-pushed him away and squatted down in front of Sweetness.

"You came out of that flying thing, didn't you?" she said. "I expect you hurt a bit."

"A bit." To name it brought it back. Sweetness lay back on the glass ceiling, feeling like glass inside; broken, sharp-edged bones of glass. The girl's face eclipsed the sun.

"I'm Meadowbank Trumbden, President Elect of the Seven-Ups Girl Nation. You'll be all right with me. Townley's just a kid anyway and he knows he's got no jurisdiction over girls. He was just trying it on because he thought you might have something worth stealing. They'd probably have eaten you. They're not civilised, like we are, and they've got no idea how to manage things. We're always having to lend them water or fix their runner. They can't sail, you know. No sense of direction."

Sweetness studied the face that bent over hers. The girl was a pinch-faced, sun-beaten urchin with bad skin and surprisingly well-cropped hair. She was dressed in a hooded parka and pocket-busy pants stitched from plastic sacks. Some of them still retained their logos. *I am being rescued by someone who actually looks worse than me*, Sweetness thought, ungraciously. She said, "Meadowbank Trumbden, I'm not feeling too good right now."

Concern came over the gamine face.

"Oh, sorry sorry sorry. There's me banging on again." She put her fingers in her mouth and gave one of those piercing whistles that Sweetness had always wanted to be able to do and envied in those who could. She struggled up on to her elbows. It did not hurt quite so badly in this position, which gave her worries for her back. A half-dozen similarly dressed, similarly aged and similar-looking girls were working methodically across the roof glass, siphoning up ballast water with clearly home-brewed elbow pumps and storing it in arrays of plastic litrejohns on their backs. At Meadowbank Trumbden's whistle, they abandoned their sweep and came hurrying to help. They moved with an odd gait, half lope, half skate.

"Got to get water when we can," Meadowbank Trumbden explained.

A hundred or so metres beyond the water-gatherers were three singular artifacts. Like everything else Sweetness had seen of this hallucinatory roof-world—not much, she had to admit, but a significant sample—they were constructed chiefly from junk plastic. Availability of resources and idiosyncrasies of design resulted in wildly varying details but the underlying structure was the same, a hull, a cabin, booms and sails, riding the high, sheer glass on sharp-toed runners.

The water-huntresses obscured the view. Sweetness was ringed by faces.

"Hold tight," Meadowbank Trumbden said. "This might hurt a bit."

On three, the girls lifted Sweetness. It hurt a lot. They carried her to the closest of the glass schooners. The boy Townley watched from the poop of the smallest and meanest of the flotilla. He sniffed gooily. On the third and largest ship, a ferrety-looking eight-year-old boy was rigging canvas on two angled side-sails. He called over.

"Pass her over here when you're done."

"Keep your hormones to yourself, Draelon," Meadowbank Trumbden returned. The watergirls gently handled Sweetness over the side. That hurt more. Meadowbank Trumbden had her brought up to a canopied deck at the rear and laid on a palliasse stuffed with shredded plastic. A deckhand offered Sweetness water. She sipped, then her body remembered how long it had been since it last drank and she grabbed the flagon and gulped greedily. Water splashed over her face, down her neck.

"Prie, take her out," Meadowbank ordered.

Windlasses lifted land-anchors of solid glass. Sails were raised, a muscular girl in a sleeveless vest of white plastic took the rudder, a sweep of wood with a steel hook buried in the tip. Sweetness felt the ship stir as the eternal winds of Worldroof bellied the plastic sails. With a sharp screak of steel runners, the little fleet set forth, President Meadowbank's barque taking point. In their wake, the schooners left three sets of parallel scores on the glass.

The Seven-Ups Girl Nation, President Elect Meadowbank Trumbden, had a population of eight and national boundaries at once as wide as the whole Worldroof (here it was floor, not ceiling) and as tightly circumscribed as the hull of their glass-cruiser. Each of the junk schooners—many more roamed the vastnesses of the glass desert, scavenging—was a separate people and state, delimited by age, sex and the availability of scarce resources. Townley Cheane, currently Chief of the Five-boys, ran an order of four- and five-year-olds with a piratical disposition and a taste for the cheerful monster-movie ghoulishness peculiar to boys of those ages. Each nation set its own laws and mores and jealously guarded its jurisdiction. If you survived to outgrow your nation, you graduated up to the next. Soon chubby Townley would make the short but significant crossing from Five-boys to *Slayer*, the third ship in the little fleet, and, after painful and humiliating hazing rituals, pass under the rule of King Draelon (the Temporary) and his hormone-tormented pubescents. Out there were nations of lofty girls with budding breasts and interests in make-up; there were shiploads of aggressive, boisterous male nearly-nines; there was even the *Great Crèche* where the semi-legendary Mam Mammary rocked cots of cotton-swaddled infants as she steered her pinnace across the high glass. All on Worldroof shared a greater nationhood: this was the place where the lost children went; the bad little boys who would not keep hold of their nannies' hands in the big shops; the naughty girls who stamped their feet and would not come when told; the schoolchildren who wandered off from organised trips; the sulky teenagers who spent too long staring blackly out of the window of the Skywheel shuttle lounge and turned back to find family and luggage gone; the toddlers who got up on their feet and ran as fast as they could away from their fathers until they outran the world and ended up in that place that every society has, the place where the lost things go. Think of it as a kind of postal sorting office, with little marked cages for the pens and the socks and the cable remotes and the cuff-links; the cats and the change and the cigarette lighters. Children here, subsorted into age and sex and transported by the agents of lostness to their allotted place. Pens to a planetoid just inside the orbit of Neptune, change to a vast, red-hot volcanic vault deep under the doloritic core of Mount Olympus; children to Worldroof.

Or so Meadowbank Trumbden believed. She was in her fifth nation now; a semi-memory held fragmentary images of standing on a high balcony with an elegant woman in white, sun shining through a glass roof on an upturned face, a tall man in a long dark coat shaking her awake in the night, moonslight on a glass roof. She no longer trusted these visions. Memories have half-lives. Scabies, a ratty little sheet-mender infected by her name, knew exactly where she came from: a grim industrial High-ville three kilometres down Pier 188276 where twelve generations had grown up atmosphere-plant workers and enthusiastic amateur incests. She had climbed away from all that, climbed and climbed and climbed through places that would not welcome her or welcomed her only to do things worse than where she had come from, until she popped a hatch and found she was on top of the world. No mystery there. But the babies, the wains and the toddlers; the only other explanation was deliberate abandonment and people didn't do things like that.

The fact that Sweetness had come from the sky made her an object of some distinction. The roof-people connected her advent with the events of the previous night, which had been hotly, and fearfully, debated, and theories formulated. A night of a thousand shooting stars, of swords in heaven; battles in the moonring, concepts for which the roof-wonders had no language. Sweetness was not sure she had any herself. Then with dawn word of the meteor strike—an unheard of occurrence, a hole in the big floor!—had passed across the glass plain with the speed of the wind; now a girl, falling from a flying church.

"That's why Townley claimed jurisdiction over you," Meadowbank said, the Seven-Ups Girl Nation speeding west in three sprays of powdered glass and all the crew gathered around Sweetness's bed. "Even Draelon wants to know; he'd've asked you, then got you to take all your clothes off."

"What do you think it is?" Sweetness asked.

The Seven-up Girls looked to their President.

"I heard there're other worlds out there, like this one."

"There are, not too many like this one. There's the one we came from . . ."

"No, not that one, that's what Draelon thinks; he says there was this war of the worlds and that it got fought through hundreds and hundreds of different universes so we may not even be the one that started the war, but whatever, in our bit of the universes, we won and the ones back there, where we came from, they've never forgotten and certainly not forgiven. They're going to have another go, and this time, they're going to win."

"There was a war like that," Sweetness said, thinking, *you sound so clever and it's only days since you learned this yourself.* "But it's been over a long time. We're at peace. So, what do you think it is?"

"I think it's another world altogether, one way way out there, that mightn't even have the same sun as us. Maybe the people don't even look like us, maybe they look like collie dogs or bits of plastic or something you can't even imagine, but they want our world. They've wanted it for a long time, like hundreds of years, and every so often they put a fleet together, like hundreds and hundreds of fighting machines and they send it to invade us, and we fight them off. That's what those stars are up there, all the scraps and wrecks and junk from the battles. They've been doing it a long time, and you think they'd learn, but they know that we have to be lucky every time and they only have to be lucky once."

"I've heard worse theories. Is that what you believe?"

"Maybe. Heard another story; the gate crew said it was on the wireless news this morning . . ."

"Gate crew?"

"The ones who open the hatch, you know? Your church went through? And close it again?"

"Merde'a'God!" Ribs and invalidity forgotten, Sweetness sat bolt upright. "Where are we!"

"About two kays west of Pier one six six six eight three seven. Up over Rhosymedre Canton."

"It's the wrong way. I have to get back there!"

"What is this?" President Meadowbank asked. Her electorate drew close around the bed, vote pool and state military.

"That stuff that happened last night, I'll tell you exactly what's happening. It's a war between the angels. There are angels up there—machines like angels, millions of them, up in that ring of stars, and there's a civil war going on because that guy in the cathedral, Devastation Harx, is taking control of them. And when they're gone, you're next."

Meadowbank Trumbden stood with her arms folded and her face set. Her nation adopted the presidential posture.

"Now that is the dumbest story . . ." she said. "You expect me to believe that?"

"It's true! He's got hold of St. Catherine—she's not really a saint at all . . ."

No point, Engineer girl. They don't believe you. The truth of this world is too much for them. Reality is too unreal. Is there anyone out there knows what's really going on, apart from you? And if Lost Girls won't hold that truth who will? Right now, you are as far from achieving your goal as you are probably ever going to be in this story. *But I fell from the flying cathedral!* she wanted to say, again checked herself. Any and all words were wasted. Now, they tolerate you as a liar. Say a whisper more and they will hate you.

"Ahoy!"

The cry from the sole forward lookout was like the crack of a whip. Every head recoiled, then turned. The national skate-ship had separated from its companions in the flotilla—all such alliances in this environment were brief and serendipitous—and was fast approaching a communications spire, a black, baroque tangle of aerials, dishes and signal boosters protruding from the pristine glass like a single black hair on the face of a venerable dowager.

"Prepare to stop!" Meadowbank shouted and her skinny girls jumped to their posts. Dagger-boards were thrust down through the keel; hundreds of scavenged nail and construction bolt-teeth bit glass in a cascade of powder. Sails furled, helm brought the boat about, nose in to the hard dock. With a shriek and a shudder, Seven-Ups Girl Nation came to a rest. A hatch undogged in the spire, the communications men stepped out, blinking in the morning light. They looked old and big and dirty and bearlike with their shaggy hair and beards and crusty coveralls. The Seven-Ups formed a line on deck.

Sweetness watched the face-off warily, suspecting sordid sexual trading of that kind that is so ubiquitous in the less public and more hungry parts of the world.

"Ladies," the leader of the radio men said, "have you any idea how long it's been? We've been dying up here. Can you do us? Can you give us what we need?"

"It'll cost."

"The usual."

"Plus ten. Extra mouth."

The leader ran his hand across his mouth, shook his head.

"I've got to have a bit of trim. Okay, extra ten. Deal?"

"Deal."

With a war-cry, the girls of Seven-Ups Nations pulled hard steel and brandished it over their heads. The brilliant light caught twin blades: scissors. As one, the cutting crew went over the side twirling their plastic hair-capes, and set to work on the heads of the relieved workers. Over the next hour, they dispensed bowl-cuts, flat-tops, numbers six down to nought, page boys, duck's arses, quiffs, back-combs, centre partings, side-partings left, side-partings right, shaved patterns names religious mottoes sports team logos on the backs of skulls. The scissors snip-snap-snipped, long greasy hair fell in bangs to the ground and blew away on the eternal winds. Then the capes were swirled away and the stray hair dusted from the nape of the neck, the scissors tucked away and the bay-rum frictioned into shorn scalps.

Throughout the mass hair-doing, Sweetness had noticed the leader of the communications men, now sporting a set of ear-length dreads, keep squinting at the upper levels of the telecom mast. A non-hairfarer, Sweetness could observe unobtrusively from her recliner, but in the jumble of technology it was impossible to tell what was kosher and what was not. Now, as Meadowbank laboured over making up the bill, Sweetness saw something move up there. Very slowly, very subtly, like large spiders creeping up on their prey, black objects were making their way down through the relays and microwave transmitters. Not machines, Sweetness suspected, though she could not assign any shape to them; they moved like living things. God the Panarchic alone knew what lived up here, up above the world so high, and what it liked to eat.

Meadowbank and the chief of communications were still haggling. Sweetness thought that he seemed to be delaying her. She looked up again. The objects had stopped moving. She scrutinised the gantry work; patterns appeared, images resolved into limbs, torsos, heads.

"Up there, look!" Sweetness shouted, pointing. Meadowbank Trumbden looked up, and the figures leaped. Twelve of them, changing colour as they fell feet first, black to white to translucent glass, falling slower than gravity should allow. Sweetness's fillings throbbed in her molars: impeller fields, as well as light-scatter toadsuits.

"Run!" Meadowbank Trumbden yelled. "It's the furniture folk!" The Seven-Ups Girl Nation scattered. Too slow. The hunters pulled big black pieces from their shoulder holsters and took aim. Expecting massacre, Sweetness ducked. Glue-guns, net-chuckers, neural bolloxers: state-of-art non-lethal weaponry immobilised, trawled, dazed and confused the hairdressers. Three comtechs ran to assist their foreman as he wrestled with a kicking, blaspheming Meadowbank. The hunters touched lightly down, moved to secure their prisoners and round up what few had escaped.

Sweetness leaped up but a wave of persons in black surged over the gun-wale, seized the edge of her mattress and, with a swift tug, turned it over and wrapped her up in it before she could utter one trainfolk curse. For the second time that day, everything went black.

Ladonna Cloris Grace Avaunt Urtching-Sembely held her monthly furniture auctions on the thousandth-level balcony of her pier-top manor. Though hers was a refined and specialised interest, and the higher up the pier the more refined and specialised the interests came, they were attended by many outside her hobby group for the catering was excellent, the wine list superb, despite being decanted at altitude, and the chitter-chatter-chat unexcelled. The lots were arranged in order of disposal along the skyward side of the vertiginous ledge, where the afternoon light would show them off to their best advantage. Acquisitive parties inspected the pieces, assessed their size and durability. For those who were seeking matched sets or to complete a tableau, some had already been suited and positioned.

All morning the spider-machine had negotiated cautious passage along the jungle of roof-tree branches, daring and vertiginous scurries from sucker-pad feet across the intervening spans of bare roof glass. In her barred cage, hanging with the other captured Seven-Upers from the belly of the transporter like mites, Sweetness had watched the track of the sun arc across the transparent ceiling. For the first time, she noticed the scratches and scorings and scars in the glass. The sun told her that at least she was heading in the right direction, Harx-ward. Otherwise, her lot seemed dire indeed. Many child-takers hunted the glass plains, but the hirelings of the very rich and very specialist and very bored who used humans for furniture were especially feared.

"They've got these suits," Meadowbank Trumbden whispered in the next cage, quiet, watching, for the child-takers enforced their disciplines with cattle prods. "Can't see, can't hear, can't talk. I heard they even feed you and take away all your crap stuff. Once you got them on, they don't come off. And they like, move you, and then they lock and you can't move either."

Another trip into black, Sweetness thought. Only this one you don't come out of. She tried to tell herself that this was all part of adventure and that stories didn't end with the Feisty and Resourceful (But Cute With It) Heroine as a tea table. She was still trying to convince herself of this as the roof-crawler descended the main spur toward the hundred slim spires of Demesne Urtching-Sembely, its burden of flesh swaying beneath it like heavy dugs.

Now with her hands lashed behind her with cable grip, Sweetness stood last in line—but not in desirability, she told herself; even human furniture auctions leave best to last—on the balcony sweating in the afternoon torpor close under Worldroof. Next to her, Urtching-Sembely hirelings cut Mead-owbank Trumbden out of her plastic rags while a third forced her into the form-kissing black suit. Prie, Scabies and the crewgirl who had given Sweetness sweet water had already been knocked down as a matched table set, forced down into a kneel, then leaned backward by the nano-motors seeded through the clinging fabric until their wrists were locked to their ankles. The buyer, a stalky, angular man in a brocade coat and slightly unfashionable footwear, spent considerable time measuring the angles and making sure the breasts were large enough to support the great glass circle at which he proposed to entertain like-minded guests. After much measuring and fine control with the suit motors, he seemed satisfied.

The enforcers finally wrestled the hood over Meadowbank's head, tucked in stray wisps of urchin cut, made sure the gag and earplugs were seated right and sealed it up. The auction attendants stepped back. Meadowbank struggled a moment, then the suit locked, immobilising her.

"So, what's collectable with you?" Ladonna Urtching-Sembely asked the purchaser, a man of such astonishing nondescriptness that he had to own some secret and unpleasant vice otherwise he would have faded out of the world completely.

"Lamps," the buyer said. "Flambeaux bearers. I'm going through a household illumination phase at the moment."

"How delightful!" Ladonna Urtching-Sembely clapped her hands in pleasant anticipation. She was an unjustifiably beautiful woman, tall, elegant, with brown brown eyes and brown brown hair and the loveliest hands. She was dressed in a floor-skimming formal robe of lace and white brocade, corseted to enhance her generous *embonpoint*. It was all so unfair, Sweetness thought. No Don Urtching-Sembely. Probably eaten him, or got him as a chair for special occasions, in a very private room. The gracious Ladonna took a control bulb from her wrist purse. Her manicured fingers touched studs. Meadowbank's legs were drawn together to attention; against her will, her arms raised vertically over her head. The suit locked. One of the buyer's servants brought a self-powering electric flambeau and set it into the upraised, rigid hands. A step back, and the plastic flame glowed white.

"Perfect," the astonishingly nondescript man said.

"I'll have it delivered today," the Ladonna said and one of her hunters slapped a red sale circle on the black figure's small right breast. "Now, on to our last item today, lot twelve. An older piece, more solidly constructed, but still capable of a lifetime of service."

"Meaty," commented an old woman with a white edible dog under her arm. A tall, epicene man in breeches and knee boots looked more appraisingly through a quizzing glass.

"Possibilities. A chandelier, I think. Yes." He tapped lorgnettes against his palm thoughtfully. "This one would look fine hanging from my ceiling."

"May I take that as a bid?" purred the Ladonna.

"You may. Three thousand."

"Done, sir."

The gentleman bowed, the Ladonna nodded to her servitors. Two closed on Sweetness with knives to cut her out of her clothes, the third brought the black suit.

It can't end like this.

Oh can't it?

And that was it decided. If all this wasn't story, it would end here with her spending several decades swinging from a ceiling with candles in her hands and feet. If it was, then the rules of narrative governed everything that happened. Therefore, this was the Point of Worst Personal Threat, when all the Feisty and Resourceful (But Cute With It) Heroine's efforts to attain her Dramatic Goal hang by a thread, and Something Big Happens that rolls it over into the End Game. Here narrative creatures like Coincidence, Chance and Serendipity were all the FR(BCWI) Heroine could trust to save her.

The black furniture suit wove in front of her, drawing her gaze in like a collapsed star. Now.

"I'll give you meaty!" she yelled and planted the toe of her left boot into the suit bearer's testicles. She heard things crunch. The man let out a near-hypersonic shriek. His eyes rolled up in his head. He went down like a felled redwood. In the moment's confusion, Sweetness danced out from under the knife-men's blades. Hands bound, she plunged toward the edge of the balcony.

"No!" roared the Ladonna Cloris Grace Avaunt Urtching-Sembely.

Five kilometres of Canton Semb late afternoon gaped as Sweetness Octave Glorious Honey-Bun Asiim Engineer 12th went over the rail head first toward the tailored vine terraces one thousand storeys below.

24

"It will be the End of the World as We Know It," Weill pronounced with a grin that showed too many of his evil teeth.

There were seconds of silence in the vast cavern under the primeval ROTECH redoubt of China Mountain for the words to reach their proper depth and explode, like anti-submarine charges. Skerry was the first to react.

"Impossible. Can't do it."

Scenting an opportunity to snide Weill, Mishcondereya drew herself up to her full height, looked down her aristocratic snub nose and declared, "Lies. It's your last best hope for a bit of trim. The sky's falling, here come the saints, hows about it, bay-bee? Don't mind the smell, it's going to get a lot worse than this."

Seskinore's chest rose and fell beneath the two-buttons-too-tight jacket of his taper-legged suit.

"I must say, if that's the best you can offer us."

"It has merit, you know," Bladnoch said from his aluminium chair which, as usual in strategy meetings, he tipped back alarmingly close to the sheer steel drop over the side of the balcony. "It's what Mr. Harx is expecting. So give him what he wants, in Cash. He wants angel legions, he wants saints coming out of the sky like rain, he wants the clouds to open and God the Panarchic to ride out at the head of the entire Circus of Heaven, he wants it to rain blood and toads, he wants shitstorms and brimstone, he can have it, courtesy of United Artists. It's a hell of a decoy."

Weill held his hands up and applauded.

"Am I the only one of you jokers with any vision?"

Seskinore stroked his chin where once, when King of the Circuit, he had sported a small distinguished silver goatee, like a metallic sheep's tongue.

"It has a certain . . . theatrical . . . merit. Yes, I can say, it would be our crowning achievement. I'd be proud to put that on my *curriculum vitae*."

"The End of the World," Mishcondereya said, arms folded, now with a small see-you sneer that had long ago failed to provoke anything more in Weill than a vague some-time-when-I've-absolutely-nothing-better-to-do-I-wouldn't-mind-seeing-*you*-without-your-clothes-on glow.

Weill nodded enthusiastically.

"Go for the big one."

"You're suggesting that United Artists fakes an Armageddon?" Skerry said incredulously.

"Either we do it, or he does it for us. Only his ain't fake."

"Our friend has a good point," Bladnoch said. "But I think Skerry remains to be convinced, and she will be the one going in under all this divine comedy. Skerry?"

"I don't know." She turned her back on her comrade jesters, put one grip-soled boot up on the railing, looked out over the echoing chambers of the Comedy Cave. "Keep it simple. That's always been how we've done it. Comedy is simple. I'd trust it more if it were less complicated, less risky, less . . . outrageous."

"All these years, and now she wants a safety net," Weill said. Skerry rounded on him.

"You can say that, dirt-bird, the day you do this." With which the tight little woman flipped into a single handstand on the top rail, axled one hundred and eighty degrees on to her free arm and in this way hand-walked thirty steps along the edge of the drop before dismounting in a double somersault close enough to Weill for him to flinch. She stared up at him, staring him down. Little love lost between the United Artists. Though many of the best double acts are born from mutual detestation, the five practical jokers knew that, in comedy as in everything else, the Synod could only afford second-best. The greats were out there on the circuit, wowing them in Belladonna's Chitter-chatter-chat Club, topping the Top of the Town in Llangonedd, hovercrafted between the pleasure barges that sailed the Syrtic Sea. Venues where you handed the band leader your own theme music and he would bow and wink and raise the baton. Gigs where the very first word of a catch-phrase could bring a house down. Clubs where people positively welcomed the old jokes; savouring the coming punchline with the pre-orgasmic surge of semen rising through the pipes.

Skerry and Weill broke. The little woman went glowering back to the rail to stare bluely out over the cluttered expanses of the Comedy Cavern. Two billion years ago the stupendous volcanoes that built this hemisphere had emptied their sacks and died, leaving mammoth lava chambers to cool and crack under the hardening lava shields. Delving under China Mountain to build redoubts strong enough to withstand the comet bombardment by which ROTECH imported most of the world's air and water, deep drill teams had broken through the cap rock into a hall of obsidian mirrors. Helidrones, navigating like plastic bats by squeaks of sonar, had mapped the chaotic interior of the two-kilometre long bubble: "Grand Valley, with another one upside down on top of it," was how one of the areologists described it. Suspended between the roof-pillars in stress-webs like spiders in a rainstorm, ROTECH Hydro-Cycle Control headquarters had jiggled to the multiple comet impacts, but not a cup was cracked. For a time, after the humans and machines emerged and the pillars started to go up along Grand Valley, the China Mountain Bubble became a hatchery for the millions of orphs who tunnelled out of their birth cells up through the rock and into the regolith, bellies full of bacteria, spinning stone into soil. As industrial parks decay when the factories move out, so the China Mountain Bubble had fallen to dereliction as ROTECH spread its precision bioformed villages and microcities down the slopes of its capital mountain. And, as low-rent artists and performers move into those decayed factories and make them workshops and studios, so United Artists had descended by a glass elevator unused for three hundred years to go, collectively, *wow* as the floodlights clanged on. Now the pristine, volcanic glass spears were hung with the trophies and banners of past routines, like piked heads: the inflatable, dirigible demons from the JJT scam; the enormous feathered headdresses and outrageous gauze and sequin plumages of Paulus Twining's involuntary outing carnival; the one thousandth-scale fake Sailship from the Gartan Roscoe Affair (even one-to-one-thousand, it filled an entire subcavern like a cancer an alveolus in a hashisheen's lung).

Skerry always found grit and assurance in the hanging testimonials. The Synod had chosen the leader cannily: riven by doubts and a nagging sense of unbelonging. She was circus skills, the action girl, the one dangling from the silver trapeze. She wasn't supposed to be funny, but a day never passed that she did not wish she had the power to make mirth. She longed to conceive giant pratfalls, send cosmic springy snakes bounding out of jack-in-the-boxes, place whoopee cushions beneath the posterior of the Panarch. She wished she had a sense of humour. For she had none. There was no gene for it in her reserved, Ocyrian gentry stock. They glumly masqueraded a tribal inferiority complex as modesty and trusted that would steer them through a messy, spontaneous and impolite world. From the moment the doors of Ghalgorm Manor had closed behind her as she set off for the Royal Circus of the Sun on its shaved-off Grand Valley mesa, she knew she had irrevocably offended the family doctrine of comfortable mediocrity. Four years and a good, steady civil service job under her, she had largely settled herself to snooty exile, but when she looked out at those gently waving banners, those grinning demon heads, she wanted to call out to that crenellated termite-heap in the flat fields of Ocyrus, "Hey, Mum! Look at me! I brought down the government!"

By swinging from ropes, turning somersaults, diving through hoops, putting your leg behind your neck and juggling fire? She could hear the high, thin voice echoing from Ghalgorm's painted rafters. To her mother, the putdown had been as divine an art as icon painting. It was not sarcasm. It was maintaining a universal and holy order.

Yes! Skerry wanted to shout. All that, and in ridiculous and frequently immodest costumes. But practising what you've only ever preached. Humbling the arrogant, ridiculing the vain, bringing down the proud, mocking the mighty. By showing off, by making a spectacle of myself, I'm fulfilling all your family values. But, *with no bloody net!*

They were arguing again, details, trivia; the exact numbers of each species in the Divine Menageries, whether the Rider on the Many-Headed Beast rode astride or sidesaddle, did God go to the toilet? and the colours of angels' wings. At such times, Skerry Scanland Ghalgorm thanked her lack of a sense of humour. Somebody had to have perspective. Somebody had to get a grip on this rabble.

"Enough. These helicopters with saints hanging under them, these ball-lightning generators, these luminous blimps: tell me, how long *exactly* have we got?"

The looks of schoolchild contrition at these moments when she brought her comrades up hard against the buffers of the real world was almost compensation for her nagging suspicion that she was a caste less funny than the rest of the team. Seskinore raised his Distinguished Silver eyebrows. Mishcondereya did Magnificent Sullen. Weill twisted and scratched himself. He had caught a wicked little fungal infection of the armpits, and they itched furiously. Bladnoch whipped out his *vade-mecum*. Cybernetic angels flocked through the planetary nervous system, prying and sniffing, and returned with an answer.

"Störting-Kobiyashi have a repair tender in for the Church of the Ever-Circling Spiritual Family, estimated, three days." He glanced again at his read-out, raised one precisely shaved eyebrow, which Seskinore had always envied, as well as the dark comedian's Dog Chow and Why Windchimes? routines. "Mostly skin punctures, minor mainframe, a couple of gas cells down. Interestingly, the Engineer's report hints at blast damage. Who's been having a crack at Devastation Harx?"

He snapped shut the *vade-mecum*; a device so far in advance of Grandmother Taal's companion of the same name that it scarcely deserved to be included in the same species. Observational comedy needs observations. There was wisdom somewhere in the secretive recesses of the Synod that they gave pocket-size omniscience to Bladnoch and not Seskinore, Skerry thought. Or, saints forfend, Weill. She said, "Well, I think we have a problem then."

They did another look then, the our-one-and-only-idea-has-gone-down-the-shitpit one. Skerry folded her arms. Bladnoch was dryly rustling his fingers and looking at the floor. He would think of something. She trusted him. Three years working within sniffing distance, an attempted seduction at a wrap party after they bust the Bethlehem Ares Board Salaries Scam, a consequent (or maybe, *despite it*) closeness and she still had no angles on the tall, skinny man; whether there were depths beyond the apparent depths, or if it was all one continuous, highly polished surface. Since being headhunted from the All New! Terence Payne Carnival of Horrors, where she had prestidigitated in a rubber suit with high-voltage electric cables, Skerry had maintained a stern celibacy, but Bladnoch was the loophole in her resolve.

"The old woman," he said, clicking his fingers in that don't-derail-my-train-of-thought way of his she found so cute. "That dream, some kind of sending, she said, right?" His co-performers knew better than to answer. "Where did it come from?"

"Why?" Skerry asked.

"Just a suspicion."

The United Artists Special, routed by customised signalling, had swept past sidelined transcontinentals and *prioritaires*, even the proud Argyre Express and its prouder sept of Malevant-Engineers, as it climbed the gentle slopes of China Mountain. Above it, the sky had kindled, angels fallen and Grandmother Taal feared for her granddaughter out in a world turned upside down. She felt older and frailer than ever she had over the cards with Cyrene Ree the year-vampire. The future of her family and world were in the hands of squabbling youths. Then the little leatherette express swayed over a set of points on to a siding Grandmother Taal knew in her boots she had never ridden before, then the sky and the offences being committed on it were extinguished as Kharam Malevant-Engineer 8th plunged his machine into a long dark tunnel. Grandmother Taal knew the rattle and roll of every tunnel and cutting in four quarterspheres and her ears told her she had never been this way before, and that she was being taken deep, way deep, way long. After a time verging on the unendurable, the isolated lamps on the tunnel walls slowed in their rhythm and the train slid into golden light on a half-tunnel open on the right side to a stupendous void of glittering, reflecting obsidian. Beyond the platform, cable cars bobbed: this undervault was big enough to have its own microclimate. Weill escorted Grandmother Taal, who had one glimpse of what lay beyond that frail insult of a handrail at the edge of the platform and kept her eyes firmly shut and her bottomless bag firmly clasped to her until the wretched cable car stopped its swaying and she felt good steel under her feet.

"Make yourself at home here," Weill said, with unconscious fatuity, but Grandmother Taal did so, filling the shelves and niches with gew-gaws from the personal dimension of her black bag. It might be a bobbing bauble of construction plastic and aluminium slung from alarmingly flimsy guying but it was more like her rocking, rolling cabin high on *Catherine of Tharsis*'s hump than anywhere else in these—how many now?—days since climbing off at Muchanga Water Station. It had a soothing sense of motion, even if it was three dimensional, and disturbing to the inner ears of old ladies who have lived much of their lives in one-dimensional transit. The view she could not take, so she drank her mint tea—much of it, but cheaply machine manufac-tured—in an interior room without windows. Therefore her first inkling that the cable-car was coming was a growing vibration throughout the suspended building—familiar and almost as comfortable as the bass tremble of fusion tokamaks. Grandmother Taal bustled to make the guest-unit ready. Defended on all sides by two hundred metres straight down to obsidian razors, "guest unit" was interchangeable with "prison," but visitors were vis-itors. The bauble swayed as the car hard-docked. Her hosts/captors filed out into the receiving room.

"Tea?" Grandmother Taal offered. Her guests shook their heads. They knew the synthesisers too intimately. "What news of Sweetness, then?"

They were a sorry, scarecrow-crew, self-confident and at the same time coy, as if they were terrified that some day someone would suddenly realise what they had been doing all their lives and tell them to stop it at once and do something proper.

"Nothing to report, sorry," Weill, the boy who evidently came from a nice family, apologised.

The tall, dark one, whom Grandmother Taal was sure was a repressed homosexual, wrung his hands gently, then asked, "Your granddaughter: when she spoke to you in this dream, how did you see her?"

"She was standing in a stone square, quite ugly. There were tall build-ings around her. This is what convinces me it was a dream: she was standing in a beam of pink light, but the ray was coming from some kind of recre-ational vehicle."

Bladnoch, head slightly bowed, finger to mouth, closed his eyes and nodded.

"You see, it's exactly that which convinces me it was no dream," he said. "I thought they were long gone, evidently not."

"What, gone?" Weill asked. But Seskinore was nodding too.

"Ah, in my young days; why, the whole town would turn out! We'd throw streamers and paper prayers and run along beside the van—of course, it was dray-drawn then . . . The fun we had!"

Mishcondereya pursed her lips in vexation. Grandmother Taal had yet to have it proved to her whether the girl performed another function in the team. Brats, jugglers and comedians. That Mishcondereya was no different from any of the others, all things considered. Old blood in now-young veins cried out the loud yawp that is as old as human creativity: *I can do that! I can do that better!* Why should these tatterdemalions be the ones who get to play with the toys; what audition had they passed to play saviours of the world? Grandmother Taal wanted more than a consultative role. Marya Stuard might have faced down the Starke Gang with their man-bone-handled needle pistols, but Taal Engineer, in her forty-second year was going up against the Anti-God himself, the destroyer of worlds, the Grand Vanitas; and that would be long sung up and down the narrow steel rails.

"I am an old woman, and hugely confused," Grandmother Taal said grand-maternally. "What exactly are you asking me?"

"I'm asking, do you think this . . . sending . . . might have been from an oneiroscope?" asked Bladnoch, who, though he would not have lasted ten minutes trainboard, seemed the only one to have any more sense than a hen would hold in its shut fist. "A dream projector, if you're familiar with these devices?"

"Young man," Grandmother Taal said, fluffing her funereal black like a gamecock its dancing feathers, "in my young youth, we hauled the cars of Jonathon Darke himself, he of the Oneiric Circus and Grand Nebular 'Stravaganza. They would conjure whole stormfronts into melodramas."

"Yes, indeed," said Bladnoch, steepling his fingers and tapping the tips lightly together in an advertisement of mildly impatient blueskying. "I'm sure it was all most spectacular, but this . . . sending could you describe to me exactly what you saw? The geography, country, desert, town, city?"

Grandmother Taal did so over passable mint tea. Bladnoch then consulted his unfolding *vade-mecum* and while it searched the civic databases and threw the dreary zocalos of a thousand rural dustburgs on to the screen, Grandmother Taal studied her hosts and wondered again at the wisdom of Wisdom in entrusting the safety of the world to third-division comedians. Every profession has its fear: the soldier pant-soiling cowardice; the actor paralysing stage-fright; the trainwoman unforeseen delays, cancelled contracts, bankruptcy. The comedian's fear, she had always heard, is the sound of his own two feet walking back to the dressing room. What if they went out there and did their routine and no one laughed? If these people died the death, the audience died with them.

The United Artists were all gathered around Bladnoch's palm-sized screen. It lit his face spectral blue. His eyebrows climbed: a hit.

"Solid Gone," he declared, snapping the clever little machine shut.

"Let's go get 'em," Skerry declared and United Artists swept into action.

"Excuse me," Grandmother Taal ventured as the secret agents bustled around her. "Excuse me." They were all entering codes on little thumb-pads. "Listen to me, please." Mishcondereya and Weill were arguing over bright orange backpacks. "Will you listen to me?" She rapped her stick stoutly on the floor and everyone's attention was fixed on the little old woman in black. "I want to come with you." Before they could shout her down, she said, "First, because I have seen this place more clearly than any of you and I know what to look for. Second, because my granddaughter may still be there, and, if not, the cineaste may know what has happened to her. Third, because it's going to be fun."

Thus it was that a circle of cloud forest on the lower slopes of Tassaday District flipped open and a small sardine-shaped racing blimp slipped out, unfolded its ducted fans and swiftly sought concealment in the cloud layer that clung decorously around the hips of China Mountain. Aboard were Mishcondereya (pilot), Skerry (action girl) and Grandmother Taal Asiim Engineer (ould woman). Bladnoch, Weill and Seskinore remained in the Comedy Cave, finessing the End of the World.

The little airship was slim, nimble and quick, but Grandmother Taal could sense the two United Artists women's tension growing with every passing kilometre. Seskinore's meddling with the repair dock unions might buy a day or two, but even with an oneirojector and a shedload of fancy programming, even Grandmother Taal could see that the plan would be going in at the very last minute. If it went in at all. And given that it was deep deep down divinely ludicrous. Fake the apocalypse. What kind of person did they think would fall for that? Only someone who was confidently expecting the Rider on the Many-Headed Beast, the Circus of Heaven, the Seven Trumpets blowing sweet rock 'n' roll, the Conclave of Amshastria, the Vials of Honeydew and the Vials of Bile, the Apotheosis of St. Catherine among the Eleven Orders, the Revelation of the Secret Names and Nails, and God the Panarchic playing Flying Fifty-Two with the twenty-seven heavens. The full McClatch.

It was asking a lot even of the man who had challenged the angels. It was asking more of five music-hall entertainers and a clapped-out cloud projector.

"What if there aren't any clouds that day?" Grandmother Taal asked, aware now of a little pregnant worm of excitement growing inside her as she came nearer to Action. Action! After forty-two years . . .

"Clouds will be provided," Skerry said, grimly. The duststorm they had battled through on the run to China Mountain had given warning not to trust the weather makers. The storm wardens might not obey her. They might already obey another. Thus she kept one eye on the orbital monitors, full in the knowledge that the first sign of untoward movement up there and they were all hot ions. The fast little airship drilled on.

Beneath China Mountain, Bladnoch tried to marshal his team into a scripting session. While Weill and Seskinore did not verbally roughhouse as the little anarchist did with Mishcondereya (whom Bladnoch considered thoroughly useless, and probably not even a good poke), they did set each other back into their entrenched positions: street-snotty rebel-rebel; world-weary, comically-fused Mr. Let-me-Entertain-You. Bladnoch knew that his own irritation at his colleagues had been predicted and predicated: part of the Synod's social engineering. Keep your enemies close, but your agents closer, and eternally bickering. He cajoled them into a light brainstorming and came up with some good ideas for choruses of angels: Big Band, Deuteronomy Wedding *Schremmel* singers, irritating Mariachi, Elevator Pan-pipe Orchestra, which he zapped through to the design team up but he knew heart-of-hearts that he was carrying them. Had always carried them. Always would carry them. This was not vanity. This was comedic truth. His had been the only mandatory recruitment to United Artists, and that because if the constabulary had become involved, he would still be festering in Winstanley Canton Gaol. A people notorious for their stunted senses of humour, the Argyrians. Had it been only locals the night of the Corncrake Club, he would have gotten clean away with it. But Grantham Grornan had been a Chryseman and he got the little dagger-sharp one-liner. Got it. Yes, he got it. Indeed he got it. Started to laugh, and laugh and laugh until the veins stood out on his forehead and his neck muscles were like bridge cables and his eyes were like poorly poached eggs and his face was black with choking laughter. Laughed until he fell off his chair on to the floor of the Corncrake Club, stone dead. Bladnoch killed a man with a single joke. It was not the only thing died that night as he crept offstage to the sound of cardiac shock-plate powering up. The comedian's comedian died in the neon-lit dressing room. Laugh? I thought I'd die. That funny, but you could only ever be that funny once, if anyone who heard it died. And why be anything less funny than the killing joke? He considered suicide. He considered asceticism. He considered hermeticism, and drinking, and flagellant orders. He had found televised sport. Even now, he knew in his inner schedule that he was missing the play-offs in the Northwest Quartersphere *kabadi* league, and that was bad and idle—yea, sinful—because he'd been hired to save the world, not lie around watching tractor racing and freestyle windboarding. Like Skerry, Bladnoch came from a family with a lot of parcelled guilt. All comedians do. All the funny ones.

"Okay, right, so," he said, turning away from the panorama of his ruined career, clapping his hands chivvyingly. "Come on come on, what's God going to be wearing?"

Elsewhere, Mishcondereya's weather radar sketched out the cloud of dreamlessness pressing darkly down on Solid Gone like a saucerful of alien invaders.

"It's just sitting there," she said, pouting with bafflement, the same expression with which she met every novel event. "This cross-wind, it shouldn't last two minutes, but it's just sitting there." Skerry bent over the radar, face furrowed green by scanner-light. Those two minutes later the cloud hove into view, at once stifling and chilling. It grew perceptibly twilighty on the bridge of the sardine-ship. The streets, avenues and bourses of the stone town beneath it looked like a tourist map of hell. Mishcondereya cut thrust and steered the ship on to the central zocalo. The penumbra cast shadows and doubts, but there seemed to be a large crowd of people down there.

"What is that thing?" Mishcondereya asked with audible distaste.

"I know," Grandmother Taal said with a chill in her voice that made both women turn from their instruments. "I saw this once before, long long time ago, way down deep South Borealis, some terrible rural place. Two streets and sun farm; Redemption they called it, but the only Redemption was the train-track out of it. I remember it well, we only stopped because we had to water. That cloud should have warned us, and the girl."

"Girl?" Mishcondereya said in the off-hand way of a woman only half-listening to a story because she is checking the grapple gear in the belly hold.

"Aye. Chained to a steel luncheonette, she was, and there she would remain until she had written down and bottled in whiskey enough dreams from passing strangers for all her townsfolk to have a swallow. That was their disease—no one dreamed, and without dreams, nothing lives long. The girl dreamed too much, dreamed of getting out of a place like Redemption, and that was her curse, you see. Something had to come and take it all away from her: that cloud. Hence her doom."

"What happened to her?" Skerry asked, crossing both pairs of fingers in the pocket of her short-shorts in the old Ocyrian deflection of evil auras.

"For all we know, she's there still, but it would seem not, judging by that."

Skerry imagined she could feel baleful heat from the cloud even through the gold-tinted reflective windows of the racing-blimp. Mishcondereya was looking at her one way. The old trainwoman was looking at her another. A decision was necessary, even a wrong one.

"Take us in," she ordered.

In the short time since that troubling girl Sweetness Engineer had walked away, the cloud-cineaste who called himself Sanyap Bedassie, last of his mystery, had discovered the consolation of resignation. You need no ambitions, you need not risk pain and failure and disappointment. Here is food, here is water, here is a daily purpose and appreciation. We are your friends. We will always treasure you. Your world may be small, but whose is not, and it is blunt-edged. Your life may be circumscribed as tightly as an eremite's, but who has not considered the attractions of the confined, contemplative life, and it is not sour. Eight times a day, at the top of the hour, his purpose was affirmed. He changed lives, for a little while.

On clearer days Sanyap Bedassie wondered if this resignation was not the first symptom of the plague. He had always assumed that, by dint of his profession, he was immune to it. Maybe he was only last to succumb. Maybe he had already gone down, and only dreamed that he dreamed. So be it. It was the world he must live in, therefore, he would live.

The tolling of the iron bell. The faithful drew near. Their feet rasped on sandy setts. Again, he brought the capacitors on-line, unfolded the array from the rear of the crippled campervan, took aim on the underbelly of the cloud. The gathered oohed as they always oohed, always surprised by the sudden stab of the pink lance into the groin of the cloud. Again, the darkness parted like foetal cells dividing: Sanka Déhau and Ashkander Beshrap's faces gestated out of the cloud-mass. To stunningly explode in wisps and vapours as a daring silver airship plunged out of the heart of the cloud. The crowd gasped, faces frozen, upturned, unsure if this was part of the plot. The plucky little dirigible pulled out of its death-dive centimetres above the Grand Bourse's crenellations. Belly-spots swivelled and focused on Bedassie and his little van, drowning the pink dream-beam in garish white. He shielded his eyes with his hand, thought he saw the belly of the fish-shaped craft open and a steel grapple-claw descend. No imagination: metal fingers closed around the van, shaking it from side to side like a terrier a rat as they clenched firmly beneath its subframe. A jolt: the van lifted a metre into the air. The people of Solid Gone swayed back, rumble-grumbled, then lurched a step forward. Sanyap Bedassie watched the airship reel his van up toward its belly. Again the crowd rumbled, took another step forward, and another. Startling reality was penetrating their sullen gloom. Someone was taking the last of their dreams away. The realisation struck Sanyap Bedassie the instant before the mob broke into a lead-footed run.

"Wait for me!" he yelled, ran, leaped, caught the dangling end of a severed chain and was whisked skyway just as the highest-reaching fingers missed his foot. His last glimpse of Solid Gone was of a circle of three thousand upturned faces filled with intolerable sorrow, then the airship climbed, turned, closed its hatches on them and their misfortune and sped away.

25

*O*ne thousand storeys. Five metres per storey. Five thousand metres. Acceleration due to gravity, three metres per second squared. Terminal velocity in the thick, sweet air under Grand Valley's glass roof: twenty-two metres per second. Or eighty kilometres per hour. Time until Sweetness Octave Glorious Honey-Bun Asiim Engineer 12th hit ground zero: four hundred seconds. Or six and two-thirds minutes. You can get a lot of screaming into that.

The first "www" was not off her lips when the hand seized the scruff of her track jacket. Woofff. The world went red under her eyes, and suddenly, faster than any attempt to analyse it, she was not falling. Something dark had darted out from the cantilevering that supported the terraces of Demesne Urching-Sembely; on a rope, on wings, on a wire, on a carnival rocket. Whatever. All she knew was, it had a hold of her and she was not falling. Coincidence, Chance and Serendipity had saved the Feisty and Resourceful (But Cute With It) Heroine. She looked down between her feet. Dark threads rippled across the corduroy terraces of Canton Semb; clans of pickers at the harvest. Sweetness laughed to see them at their task, never suspecting what hung by a fistful of rip-stop nylon five kilometres above their bended backs. She wiggled her toes, delighted that the universe had let her live.

"When you're done," a strained voice said. "Only I don't know what's goin' to go first; my arm or the zip on your jacket."

Only then did she think to look up rather than down.

And boggled.

"Returning the favour," said the brown-eyed, urchin-fringed, suspicious-cute face that Sweetness Asiim Engineer had last seen looking up into hers from a precarious fingerhold on the side of ore car eleven. "You know, how is it every time we meet, I get a sore hand?"

Pharaoh the ex-railrat hung like a Missal Anagnosta from the *Guthru Gram Kanteklion* in a webbing harness. His left arm steadied himself on the rope fastened to the buttress ten metres overhead, his right was clenched in a generous fistful of her faithful track jacket. Sweetness could see his thin muscles knotting, his slender fingers going pale.

"When you're done staring, you wouldn't like to grab hold of this and haul yourself up?" He dropped her a length of line with two foot stirrups looped on the end. Sweetness, hands still bound, kicked her feet into the loops. Pharaoh threw two more loops around her body and slowly hauled her up to his level.

"Hold still," he said, flicking a knife. Sweetness flinched, Pharaoh repeated the order. "I don't want to cut the wrong thing." His blade was true; a snick, the cable tie fluttered yellowly down to the fertile terraces below. Sweetness watched it, gravely, as the hanging ensemble pirouetted gently, a Foucault pendulum ballasted with two lives.

"Hold on tight now, I'm going to put a bit of a swing on this thing," Pharaoh warned and shifted his weight. Sweetness wrapped her legs around his, buried her fists in his scabby brown leather jacket and combated the positive body odour and escalating motion sickness as the pendulum built up by marvelling how stories did what you expected, and then some more; that little extra neat twist. She could hear the wind rushing past her ears. Or— the defensive, pedantic incongruity of one hanging from a slim line over a five-kilometre drop—was it her ears rushing past the wind?

Soon, very soon, she thought, the shaking's going to start.

"I should thank you, cause I kind of think you saved my life," she whispered to Kid Pharaoh as they whooshed through ever-increasing arcs. His target seemed to be a clutch of heat vents and gas-exchange stacks tucked like parasitic moulds under the mushroom fan of the terrace tiers.

"Then we're even now," he said as they hurtled upward toward the impaling geometry of the Demesne's service zone. He reached . . . He grabbed . . . He held. Pharaoh hauled himself and Sweetness up on to the spar. He tugged on the line and the smart-plastic snap-release shackle gave way. The sustaining rope fell, Pharaoh carefully coiled it in. Sweetness clung to the girder, suddenly very very cold.

The shaking started. Soon after it came the black thing.

✿　　✿　　✿

After the incident with the Kaspidi Sisters that had cost him his Vagrant
Entertainer's licence (as good as a shroud to an Old Skool Funnyman like
him) and a warning never ever ever to set foot across the border of Christadel-
phia in this life or any other, Seskinore knew he deserved eternal banishment
to the dark and humourless land that is the lot of Old Comics Who Do it
With Wrong-Side-of-Barely-Legal Girls. It was meet and right that he would
never hear the band count in *two, three, four* and in to "East St. Louis
Boogaloo"; never again cross those boards to the spot under the footlights
where the applause sounded sweetest. They tore up his joke books. They
ripped the petals from his lapel carnation. Even when the government had
given him the only kind of job available to an old comic aside from soft-shoe
shuffling on the Great Concourse of Belladonna Main, cap in hand, his rep
had preceded him. He copped it nobly—dignity, always dignity—but sometimes he wished that these young slubberdegullions showed a little more
respect for his professionalism. Yea, he had sinned, and mightily, but it had
been a *professional* sin. And from what moral pinnacle did they regard him;
the burned-out smart-ass stand-up; the arty-farty *sensitive* girl who wouldn't
know a funny line if it stuck it all the way up her right to her ovaries; the
hand-standing fire-juggling dyke; the chicken-shit anarchist? Amateurs.
Even Dearest Dimmy and Mr. Superb would have disdained them; bottom-
rung acts they might have been, but at least they had been professional. They
understood timing. They understood experience, and the knowledge of what
works on an audience that only comes through dying the death a hundred, a
thousand nights. They understood practice, practice, practice. They understood dignity. Always dignity. Disgraced he might be, but Seskinore had
been professional unto the last. Seskinore could admit that he may never have
been funny, but he had been *professionally* not funny.

"Enough, enough!" he shouted with just the right tone of camp exasperation.
Bladnoch and Mishcondereya peeped sheepishly over the control panel of the
dream machine. Skerry frowned at him upside down from a silver trapeze. Weill
just scowled. "No no no no no!" He clapped his hands. "The Great Destaine
would never have stood for this, never. Switch it off, go on, off. Right now."

Bladnoch and Mishcondereya looked at each other, then Mishcondereya pouted and threw the power. The Ranks and Orders; the Rider on the Many Headed-Beast (each head that of a prominent politician, a satirical touch by Weill); the Circus of Heaven with its tightrope walkers balancing on super-strings, its jugglers cascading the planets of the solar system, its snarling, chained Tygers of Wrath and its high-prancing Horses of Instruction, its frilled, white-faced, terrifying Chaos Clowns; the down-sweeping Hammer and Sickle of God; all evaporated in an instant into the artificial clouds that had turned the Comedy Cave into a sweatlodge.

"What?" Skerry demanded, pulling herself upright and sliding off the trapeze on to the rehearsal platform. Seskinore half-averted his gaze from the gluteal zone of her cheek-cleaving green leotard.

"The timing's up the left. Between the Grand Parade of the High and Lordly Ones and the Opening of the Cornucopia of All Fruits, you're wide open for twenty, twenty-five seconds. And the coordination, God's bones, woman!" This to Mishcondereya. "The bloody things are running through each other! It's supposed to be the Ancient of Days thundering down in righteous wrath, not a charabanc of bloody village spooks!"

"It's a rushed job," Mishcondereya pleaded.

"It's always a rushed job," Seskinore said. "Now, we try it again. From the top. And this time, we will try to remember that the fate of the world is riding on us acting like professionals and not some half-arsed troupe of bloody sophomore-year drama students. First positions! Projector ready?"

Mishcondereya pouted again and reset the power buffers.

"Ready," she said sullenly.

"Right boys and girl, from the top, and this time, let's try and get it bloody right, shall we? Dear God; amateurs!"

Clouds swirled, found shifting, transitory forms in the tropical heat. Skerry towelled dry and tripped back to her position on the silver trapeze. As the hoists lifted her, apocalypse unfolded as a backdrop. Seskinore watched the little woman move into position and recalled what it was about her tight little ass that stirred such provocation in him. Nothing physiological—few women, or gentlemen for that matter, raised the Jolly Roger these sad days. Nor her personality, such as it was, narrow and deep-rooted in her own physicality. It was that he could order and stamp and throw funks and rehearse rehearse rehearse until they dropped, but come the day and the hour, it would be her out there on the high trapeze, and him back here, fretting over the monitors. Her; all of them. Never him. That was the price of his sensitive crimes with the Kaspidi Sisters. But once, by the gods of the backstage . . . When better to pick up the cane, tilt the hat, paint rouge circles on the death-white cheeks and stride boldly into the glare of the soda-light with the band striking up *your tune* behind you, than the end of the world?

The niggle with talent, Mishcondereya had always understood, was that it was blind to true genius. She had no doubt that her fellow artistes were indeed skilled at their crafts—in Bladnoch's case, a genuine *forte*—but all of them were so mired in the admiration of their own abilities that they could not recognise the only pukkah prodigy in the gang: Mishcondereya Benninger Eksendrarana. The lot of her privileged life. Always fated to be a lower bloom among the early flowerings of her four older sisters; the painter, the writer, the harpist and the sen-so-rama sculptress. The performance artist? Just another genius. Children brought up in the airy, light-drenched Grand Valley pueblo of Etzwane Eksendrarana and Afton Benninger (he a Living Treasure crafter of ritual mint-tea-infusers, she the lauded architect of India's Chursky Prospekt and the sheer crystal dome of Wisdom's new Grand Trunk Terminus) could not fail to develop into world-wide movers and shapers, but even the most indulgent of parents' attention starts to thin with the fourth gifted child. The fifth? A blossom that blooms unseen, wasting its perfume on the desert air. The o'erlooked rose. The unregarded bud. Mishcondereya often thought of herself (and she thought of herself very often) in terms of a flower, growing wild, nobody's child. Unregarded among her colleagues as she had been among her sisters. But it is the unregarded rose that is the sweetest, the pebble half-buried in the dune face on which you stub your toe and give no more than a glance that is the raw diamond.

Mishcondereya was firmamentally convinced of four things.

That she was an utter genius.

That she was a sex goddess.

That everyone either wanted to be like her or was helplessly in love with her.

That therefore everyone was jealous of her.

The polythene elevator took Mishcondereya up from the R&D dungeon through tiers of holy battle. She sneered at the photonic ghosts. She was in no awe of the angelic forces swooping and trumpeting outside. Vanity had always been the Defiant One's strongest weapon.

How did they ever imagine this would convince Devastation Harx? A man who founds his own church has an intimate knowledge of the phoney. He'd bust his nuts laughing, if he'd hadn't already bust them in some kind of ritual-humiliation holy wooden vice thing. Or was that some other mail-order outfit? Research had never been Mishcondereya's trump suit.

Not for the first time she thought about handing in her resignation. *Take it, I quit, I walk, I'm up and out, comperes, do the memory-wipe thing, it's not as if I'd be losing much, or even taking much with me. Surprise! Planetary security run by a pack of jokers.*

No. Not this time. There was yet pleasure to be savoured from saving their collective asses once again.

The device was still chill from the assembler vat; she tossed it from palm to palm. Cold that burns. Seskinore—*Fat Fart*, her private name for him— would be up there blubbering and mincing and farting like an old Show Boat duchess and of course it would all be heading floorward like a Belladonna dowager's butt and being *act-ors* (she always consciously spaced the syllables) they reckoned that if they looked deep enough inside their souls for Honesty in Comedy or stood in a circle and workshopped it out like sweating off a really bad wodka hangover or clenched and unclenched their fists and screwed up enough Team Force it would all come right just like that. Of course it wouldn't. Never would, not on its own. She'd told them that, lodged her token formal complaint, but they just kept stubbornly heading on with the wrong thing while the Armageddon clock ticked down to zero. No surprise they hadn't listened; she wasn't an *act-or* and therefore understood nothing of the creative process and the agonies of performance. Their loss. It didn't insult her any more. The ignorant can't insult you. So Mishcondereya Benninger Eksendrarana did what she always did, excused herself from their group huddle and primal yodelling and took her own idea off to make it into something.

Mishcondereya Benninger Eksendrarana was proud that she'd been expelled

from the only other team that had recruited her—St. Xaviou's Community College Ladies' touch-rugger—because she'd been more interested in spectator reaction to her tight'n'shiny shorts and over-the-knee socks than playing defensive
wing. Even then she had not been ashamed to own that she was not a team player.

The trogs in nanofacturing were creepy and a little smelly and she didn't
doubt that every man—and woman—jack of them fancied the teats off her,
but at least they had respect for a good idea. Struell Llewyn, trog King, with
too many pairs of glasses slung around his neck (can't he afford to get the ocu-
lars lasered or what?) had peered at the sketch, nodded at her general description of the effects she wanted (at least they didn't expect her to be a pharma-
cist) and called a conclave of nano and pharmaceutical advisers. No group
hugs. No free-form improvisation. No word-associational brainstorming.
Nothing that involved throwing soft balls to each other, abdominal
breathing or striking Damantine Discipline *thranas*. Quiet talk, a bit of scrib-
bling on thinkpads and after twenty minutes, the frog King had pushed up
his reading lenses and declared, "No problem for the welders."

"When can I have it?"

"Forty minutes."

And it had been, as it always was.

"Careful, now," the trog King had advised as Mishcondereya juggled the
frosted fluttering little thing up to her eye-level. "The trigger mechanism's
delicate." Compound globules of nano-carbon met jellied spheres of protein.
Gossamer wings whirred micro-breezes chilled with the memory of 3K
nanoassembler chambers in her face. She peered into the churning greenness
in its glass belly.

"Nice one."

As ever, he had given that lop-sided bow/smirk that was all the thanks
he would acknowledge. The pride of the artisan classes. When she was well
gone, that was when he would gather the trog nation in their canteen and tell
them what a great job they had done. Our humble bit in Saving the World!
Huzzah! Huzzah! Huzzah! Good people, if limited. In her many idle
moments Mishcondereya wondered just with what they filled their frequent
downtimes, what—who—they fantasised about when they went back to
their clean-living little pottery villages.

As the plastic elevator passed through the fish-scale train of Ananutu-ranta Deva, Lord of the Changing Ways, she ignored Struell Llewyn's admonition and tossed the little nano-bug high to catch it on the flat of her palm. And in that instant, without warning, she was embedded in stone. Darkness, pressure, absolute, not even space for a scream. Her lungs were rigid with solid rock. And then she was back in air and light and movement and the little flibbertigibbet floated down into her hand but she knew, for an instant, she had been dead, buried kilometres deep in the volcanic core of China Mountain in an alternative world where different laws of volcanology had refused to allow this chamber to form. She staggered against the flimsy side of the bubble car, almost dropped the frail flitter. She caught herself: dignity, always dignity. The Fat Fart was right in that one. But every one of her atoms remembered that they had been penetrated by cold hard gneiss.

They were looking concerned—and rightly—as she strode toward them across the rehearsal space. Once again, the spooks and spiritual entities were dissolving back into their constituent clouds with looks on their faces that might be read as worry, had they been anything more tangible than holographic dream-projections.

"Did you?" Fat Fart.

"Of course I did. Everybody did."

"We have to go, now." Leotard Girl.

So, why are you looking at me? Because it's up to Mishcondereya Benninger Eksendrarana to save your tight little butts again.

"No problem for the welders," Mishcondereya Benninger Eksendrarana said and blew the little fritillary off her open hand into Weill's face. Pig-turd Boy reeled back, lashed at the buzzy thing and it popped in front of his eyes into an expanding cloud of green gas. In shock, he took a deep breath.

His eyes glazed over.

"Woh," he said. "Wohhhhhh." A shit-eating grin spread across his peasant face. Realisation, both neurochemical as the hallucinogens kicked in and, with the shreds they left of his intelligence, intellectual. "I mean, really, woh."

"Yah," Mishcondereya Benninger Eksendrarana said lazily. "He'll believe it now."

❂   ❂   ❂

The hat-pin snapped with a loud tink. The broken spike rolled across the platform, under the guard chains and over the edge. It speared through a cloud-hologram of the Lorarch ROHEL shrieking between the stalactites and stalagmites of the Comedy Cavern, barbed swords in all four hands. The big pin clinked audibly off some outcrop or other.

"Cock piss bugger bum balls," Grandmother Taal swore. She should have gone straight for the lock-pick. Oh no, go for the easy option rather than invest ten minutes trying to remember where you left the wretched thing. Ten minutes squandered. That foo-feraw out there would only exercise their attentions so long. It was, of course, ludicrous. Even they could see that, and when the cloud-projector went off, she was bare bum naked up here on the platform.

A good God, a just God, would, at the end of your life, refund you all the time you had spent looking for little lost things. Like lock-picks. And granddaughters. Grandmother Taal plunged her arm elbow deep into her black bag and began to rummage through pocket universes.

The Bedassie boy had been easy to coerce. The polythene bauble perched on the sheer stalagmite might hold one so unadventurous as to prefer existence as a captive of a captive audience to wild wild life with a fit and nubile Engineer girl, but not a trainperson, and certainly not Engineer *Amma*. The boy had been polite, if a little malodorous from his long captivity and it was immediately evident to Grandmother Taal that he had been deeply touched by his exposure to Sweetness. She suspected that her granddaughter was one of those cursed to be fatally attractive to a certain type of man. Please God, the attraction did not seem to be reciprocal. Stainless steel kitchenettes were undeniably an excuse to up and leave, but for Sweetness to have boom-shaka-ed with *this* . . . Grandmother Taal shuddered at the thought.

Deep down in the dimensional folds of her bag, her fingers found a little pocket dedicated to souvenirs of Sweetness. A baby tooth. A bronzed raggie-doll. A scrolled-up drawing of a train, with a tree by the track and a yellow sun overhead and smiley Mama and Da waving palm-frond hands from the driving cab. The silk belly cord she had given up when she ceased to be a child and became fully human, an Engineer. The smeared panties of her womaning, preserved in a resin paperweight.

The fingers lingered a moment. The memories they felt out were a spur to hurry on. Soon, very soon, they're going to unleash Armageddon and your granddaughter has put herself right in the middle of it. The part of her that Uncle Billied rides across whole hemispheres, that recklessly bet years of her life on a turn of cards, that hitched with big band leaders and schemed with state-sponsored practical jokers, that tried to pick locks on railway tunnel exit doors, was slyly proud of that.

Three dimensions down, she found the lock-pick.

Let's see you try this, Marya Stuard, Grandmother Taal thought with an inner grin as she unfolded the prongs and set to work on the latch that sealed the two half doors. You may only need a lock-pick once, and maybe never, but when you do, you really do. Such was the logic of the collection she had stashed away over the decades in the black magic bag.

As she felt her way into the subtle mechanism, Grandmother Taal reflected that Sweetness's very gift probably sentenced her to a life of heartbreaks. The curse of unworthy men. Cute but chicken. When it had come to it, that one, back there, had chosen life as a captive of a captive audience to heading off with Sweetness into adventure, high or low. Small wonder that train life so appealed to men; full steam and high speed, but only in the direction permitted by the track. Bedassie had shown her the trick of the door—the comedians seemed to have forgotten that a cloud cineaste would have a way with electronic things—but he had turned down even an old wizened woman's offer of escape. The bridge that extruded itself from the stalactite to the railway station was narrow, railless, unsupported, and the drop through the warring tribes of holy ones terrifying, but Grandmother Taal had tightened up her courage and stepped out on to the swaying arch. Again, she thanked whatever Luck Gods had let her win precious years from Cyrene Ankhatiel Ree. In her old, fragile former self, the winds that gusted through the cave would have picked her up, puffed out her skirts like a festival balloon and dropped her on to the serrated obsidian daggers of the cavern floor. She looked back: Bedassie was clinging to the pod door.

"Come, take my hand."

"Leave all this?" Nodding at the raving deities boiling up on either side of the slender pont.

"They're ghosts, clouds. Nothing. They can't hurt you."

"It's all I have."

"Young man, do you think they will let us go, seeing and knowing what we have? The best we can hope for is mnemonic erasure. The worst . . . Let us say, I deeply suspect some of these people's senses of humour. Come. Now. They won't give you your device back."

For an instant he was tempted, then shook his head.

"I believe I can do a deal, be useful to them."

"Young man, if you believe that any government ever offers, let alone honours, a deal like that, you deserve all that you get. Last offer. Time is ticking away. My granddaughter is in great peril."

He smiled sadly and Grandmother Taal suspected that Sweetness had seen that look of amiable resignation too.

"I'm sorry."

"So am I."

Even with fifteen spare years, it had been a precarious crossing, arms out-stretched like a tightrope walker, breath coming in little tight flutters, looking ahead, dead ahead, always ahead, never down, never to one side or the other, never at the deities that loomed and ballooned at her like spooks in a Canton Fair House of Horrendo. Muttering it like a mantra, ahead, ahead, always ahead, down, down, never look down. The far side hove into view. A brass section of minor Cheraphs swooped at her, blowing sweet rock 'n' roll, breezed nonchalantly through Grandmother Taal as if she wasn't there. The old matriarch gave a little eek, teetered. Her hands flailed. She looked down. Volcanic teeth yawned for her. She staggered, dashed forward, came off the end of the bridge in a stumbling roll.

Grandmother Taal sat, legs stretched straight out, and rejoiced in breathing for a full minute before remembering to retract the pont. Then she turned to face the lock and drew the pin from her hair like a long-coated Rapari his sabre.

Where Harx was, Sweetness would be, that much was clear. All this piss and smoke about saints and mirrors; she could make none of that, except that anything that involved powers not safely meat and bone was bad. Typical of her granddaughter to underestimate the danger and overestimate her resourcefulness. Absconding is one thing, adventuring another, but Armageddon is entirely something again. Clown-time is over. This required the full resources of *Catherine of Tharsis* and her many tribes. Now, if she could just pick this little lock, walk up that long sloping tunnel to the surface and persuade some Engineer to break the snubbing and let her make a Red Call . . .

Long orders. Tall hikes. So. She was sturdy. Grandmother Taal worked the clever pick deeper into the lock. Something was resisting her. A shove, a twist. She felt metal give. She worked the device free. As she feared. Irredeemably bent.

This was not the end, though Grandmother Taal felt soul and body sag, all their gambled-away years returning in a moment of sheer dispirit. The semicircles of the hasp mocked her assurance and abilities. Fallen at the first. And a subtle pressure shift on the back of her neck warned her The End of the World Show was rolling up. She had sat through enough fatuous rehearsals to know she had less than a minute before the clouds recondensed into the vapour generators and she was exposed, a wicked black spider clinging to a metal door.

Help me, saints and ancestors! Aid an old and ridiculous woman, St. Catherine, since you clearly seem to exist and have some power in this world.

And it came. Aid Beyond Comprehension in a Time of Direness. Suddenly Grandmother Taal knew exactly what she must do. She found the little paper-wrapped packet in the fifteenth fold of her bag. She unwrapped the block of Etzvan Canton Black Loess Child'a'Grace had given her as a helpmeet. It smelled sweet and low and smoky. She had no need of its pharmacological virtues. The thing was that, in the white floodlight of the Comedy Cavern, it was deeply, gloriously, intrinsically *brown*. Quickly and decorously, Grandmother Taal fluffed her many skirts, squatted and urinated on the block of prime hash. With the briefest grimace of distaste, she mixed the hash and piss into a thick paste. With the bent blade of the lock-pick she crammed as much of the brown sludge into the lock mechanism as she could. Even when she thought she had enough, she kept obdurately plastering. It was a mighty thing to ask even of Etzvan Canton Black Loess. She packed and packed until it was dribbling out of the keyhole. Then, choosing a clean blade from the lock-pick, she pulled up a sleeve and swiftly carved the word OPEN on the ghost-pallid skin on the inside of her elbow.

Grandmother Taal cried aloud in pain. The winds that patrolled the great cave lifted it, turned it into just another shriek among the stalactites. The years, the prize years, were leaking out of her. The power was burning them, focusing their hope and energy on the intricacies of interlocked steel. Blood ran down her mutilated arm and dripped on to the marble concourse. Grandmother Taal clenched her fist, gritted her teeth. Fire gnawed her bones. Palsies wracked her. She shook to a spasm. The lock quivered. Again, she convulsed; two years, five years burned. The lock jerked. The ashes of years piled up in her cells; she was old, she was *old*. Seven years. Ten years. *Please, leave me something!* she begged of the lock. A third time the lock quaked. Quaked again, then, with a detonation of rending metal, it burst apart. A pool of brown sludge joined the pool of blood on the stone. The tunnel doors began to slide apart. No time to lose. Grandmother Taal snatched her bag, hitched up her skirts, slipped through the gap and high-footed it up the long, black tunnel.

The purple, Devastation Harx thought as the Acolytes of the Church of the Ever-Circling Spiritual Family filed from the flying cathedral's outlocks on to the morning-glinty plateau of the repair dock, had not been one of his better ideas. Not the colour; purple was a sacerdotal hue, and cheap. Fetching, in the right light. The uniformity. Suddenly he saw ranked and serried badness. All little faces and hands in little squads and files, all dressed in ticky-tacky, all together, all the same. Robots, not people. Not individuals. The ubiquitous machines. Getting closer now. Getting into his beloveds.

Why join? The thought came as a sudden desire to shout down from the brass-railinged balcony from which he took the salute of the faithful. *An act of free will to joyfully become a drone?* The words were a tight urging in his throat, then he heard in the hollow of his skull how they would sound going out across the high glass, and was afraid. The doubts of a middle-aged twenty-something who has woken all creak-jointy this morning. You owe them better, as they line up to praise you for the freedom you have given their souls. Tell them that they take free grace freely given and throw it away with both hands and the ones who could still think would stare, while those who could not would only worship all the harder.

It's not easy, running a religion. They have a habit of running away on you.

The Rank Presbyters and Exercisers Temporal had mustered their sections into squares and quadrilles of episcopal purple. Faces gleamed in the morning light. They looked to Harx expectant of blessing. He raised a hand, hesitated, suddenly nauseated by their need, suddenly heedful of the Störting-Kobiyashi shift workers trekking from the big express elevators along the grapple arms and access cranes to start work, and the way they could not quite bring themselves to look at all these faithful people, and smiled, and shook their heads sadly.

Yes, it is, Devastation Harx thought. And, to his gathered faithful, *Have you understood so little? I gave you the secrets of unbarring the cells of your minds, of mask-and-caping the superhuman beneath each of your mundane humanities, of nurturing each of your uniquenesses so that a thousand flowers might bloom and a thousand schools of thought pervade, and what did you do? Dressed all in purple and got great thighs pedalling a bicycle-powered cathedral.*

Great thighs, he admitted, were something.

But to make yourselves machines to war against the tyranny of the mechanical?

His hand returned to the balcony rail, unwilling to bless.

"Grace," whispered Sianne Dandeever, first of the faithful and devoted über-mater and who, Devastation Harx knew sadly from his visits to the cycle-housings, had an ass the Panarch herself would commit sin to own and who, if he ever said the word, would devotedly let him chew it. Devotedly, but not joyfully. "They're waiting . . ."

You become trapped by the needs of faith.

He raised his hand. The Rank Presbyters smiled, relieved; among them that odd, too-hungry trackboy who had stolen for him that dreadful tyke of train-trash girl. Of all incarnations and emanations for that Haan woman to have been entangled with . . . The ways of the multiverse were strange, and the boy had done a fine job, deserving of more reward than a two-tier promotion in the church civil service. Harx watched the boy nod to the Vicars Choral. They raised their staves, brought them down.

Happy happy happy
Happy happy happy
Happy happy happy all the day
Harx has saved us
Harx has made us
Happy happy happy all the day, the fresh-faced choristers sang.

Does God ever tire of hearing his praises sung? Harx thought, embarrassed today by the adulation wafting himwards, *Does he feel insulted by the infantile twaddle peddled in the name of worship?* So he would not have to listen, he surveyed instead the damage Cadmon and Euphrasie had wrought on his floating basilica. It looked to the faithful like contemplation of higher things. For a homosexual anarchist artist—late and reluctant recruits to the war—his brother had made a good aerial bomber. A few more sticks, a little faster on the turns, he might have seriously discommoded the great strategy, if not forced a season's defeat on him. His diversionary strike on heaven might have gained him ground in the lower orbitals and swept away a third of the angelic forces that opposed him, but the ways of machines were subtle, and from the humiliation at the Molesworth Festhall, he did not doubt that other energies were being mobilised against him.

Had they finished yet?

Gleeful gleeful gleeful all the day.

How many, if any, suspected the scale of crusade in which they were spiritual infantry? Few out on parade, few on this whole world, in this universe. Not the machines. They knew too well that this little red ball was their final redoubt, and that one installation artist turned religious shyster was to be their nemesis.

Strange, and passing inevitable, the path that leads from fine art to jihad.

Strange, the things you find in mirrors.

God, they were still at it. Did they never tire of singing? I'm trying to make a universe for humans to live in, and the best you can do with it is chant doggerel. Excessive aubergine and happy-clappiness were the prices you paid for owning your own church. Inventing a religion was still the best and easiest way to raise the astronomical amounts of cash a war with the angels required.

Sianne Dandeever, poker-erect, face rapt, hands firmly gripping balcony rail, suddenly flinched as if unseen wings had flapped in her face. She flicked something away with her hand, scowled, devotion broken.

Harx stared, then cocked his head a degree to catch a tiny sound. A hum, an insect drone.

Insects. Up here? On this glass desert? Ridiculous.

More than ridiculous. Sinister.

A black mote danced in his face. Harx lunged, snatched, felt frantic movement buzz in his palm. He closed his fist, felt a soft crunch, opened his palm and peered closely at it. One less skilled in the wiles of machines might have taken it for a true insect, but he could see that the thing whirring spastically in his hand was a tiny, glass-bellied helicopter. He held it closer; as he did, the belly-bead popped. Vapour wisped, Harx hurled the thing away from him but not before a greenish wisp had curled up his nostrils. He saw vinegar, tasted blue minims; a symphony for cabbage and pram played a loud chord in his frontal lobes. The smell of triangles . . .

"Battle stations!" he roared out over the assembled faithful. Every head turned. Sianne Dandeever stared, half numb, half thrilled that this might be the call for which Harx had invested so much of her body and will.

"Battle stations!" Harx repeated as the squares and drills broke up into frantic motion. "To arms, our church is under attack!"

He nodded for Sianne to take command as a cloud of robot insects, black as smoke, poured from the spire-top airco funnels. He did not like to be seen by the faithful to be abandoning Armageddon, but there were tactics that only he could employ, and those in private. The true battle would not be fought under the glass plains, with gun turrets and Gatling bunkers, but among the shifting dimensions of his mirror maze. Devastation Harx swirled from the balcony. Sianne Dandeever cracked her knuckles and stood tall. Thank you God. At last. At long long last.

"This is it, boys!" she guldered at the top of her ample lungs to the running acolytes. "This is war!"

❁ ❁ ❁

It wears off, they'd warned Lutra Blaine when she ticked the box in the job centre next to "Space Service." *And quicker than you think, too.* Cartwheeling off the action end of the Skywheel space elevator (*no, it's not me going arse-over-heels, it's the stars carouselling around me*; the innocent solipsism of the work-placement cosmonaut) she had yippeed in her soul of souls as the red-green-occasional-blue mottle of her world rolled up in a great disc before her like a test for colour-blindness in the eye of the Divine. *So tell me Ms. Blaine, what can you read down there?* Nothing but a door out of three rooms and twelve bodies Level Twenty-Seven Deep St. Berisha Project NewMarket Down, Belladonna, Greatest of the Cities of the Valley. The doctors had warned her of possible agoraphobia. It would still not have grounded her. No one got turned down for space service. Not a problem, she said. Outer space was no bigger or blacker than inner space. The tunnels of the littler moon were no less pumicey and constricting. Space, like bedrock, was just another darkness into which you cannot go.

You do know you've more chance of winning the Fat Lotto every week for a year than seeing some, you know, action, the sheddle steward had said as he turned her the right way up and sent her and her canvas grip-bag sailing through the lock into the foam-padded reception bay.

That's okay, she had thought as she swam through the thick, fart-whiffy air, wondering who the stocky, shock-headed smiler was down at the end of the cylinder, hand held out to welcome her to Planetary Defence System Terror. *Just as long as the cheques keep coming.*

The view was the one thing that had not tired. The constant vague nano-gee nausea; the bloated, rodent face in the morning mirror; the unflagging, eroding energy with which Taroudant—the tousled grinner—tried to get his hand into the waistband of her draw-string Space Service baggies—most of all, this last—those she'd tired of by the end of her first shift. But her world, her home, the soil of her birth, her shelter and prison; spinning slowly like the hands of a great clock behind the watch-glass of the observation blister, she would wake from near-trance to find hours had vanished, witched out of her by the huge, slow-turning world beneath her. Twelve and a half years she had lived and crawled beneath the surface without ever once looking at its face.

Truth be told, Taroudant notwithstanding—he occupied an ecological niche all his own—the creaky old battle station was full of creeps. Unaccountable breezes eddied in the gritty pumice tunnels. Light panels would flicker as she swam past, or switch themselves off, or, more spookily still, on, illuminating vast, irregular, lung-like hollows she was quite sure did not appear on any of the moon maps. Machines loved to click and groan theatrically; spirals of dust would spin and sparkle in the hub-chambers where tunnel systems met, and what was that lingering smell of perfume, like ashes of roses? Taroudant would have been the obvious suspect, by the unfeasible logic that if he scared her enough she'd suck him off, except that she knew he sensed them too and, more primarily, he lacked the imagination for even that rudimentary ploy. And he never smelled of anything approaching ashes, let alone of roses.

No, ghosts there were in the old, hollow moon. That was the very idea of the place. An army of ghosts, to be resurrected from the crusty regolith in the hour of its primary's need and thrown into final battle. She'd glimpsed the ranked processors behind their diamond viewing panes, waiting in supercool quantum chill to spin soldiers out of stone, like ice goblins in faerytales. The cold got into her bones, never really got out again, in the long, empty spaces of Planetary Defence System Terror. She floated warily past the empty templates mounted on the walls, breast-plated and beaked like insect warrior armour. Too many eyes, too many toes, too many arms that ended in too many blades, like ever-opening penknives. Slashers stabbers impalers gutters beheaders. All our warfares in the end come down to hand-to-hand. Stick a piece of sharp metal through your enemy. Simple and reliable. Like Taroudant. He came down to the hand-to-hand, in the end. Impale with a pointed weapon. Knob knob knob knob knob. Simple and reliable.

Two people; man, woman, trying to avoid each other in a worm-eaten potato of a moonlet, two billion humans' final defence against interplanetary attack. Oh. Forgetting of course, SERAPAMOUN, Cheraph, exalted one, genius loci, seeded so thoroughly and minutely through Terror that the whole planetoid could be said to be one great orbiting brain. The real trigger finger, silent as only the angels can be silent, patiently waiting for a word certain never to be spoken, that would transform moon-stuff into machine warriors and send them falling out of the evening sky like diamond rain in their spin-carbon reentry shells.

Sometimes, as she hovered above the great viewing eye, Lutra Blaine wished for even a rumour of war. A blip on the sensors that watched the edges of System. A sudden rip in reality, spewing dagger-edged starfighters from some alien empire, filling all circumambient space with lambent beams of coruscating force. Skyjack and piracy on one of the big, stately Sailships. Something to set the alarms ringing and the amber lights pulse-rotating and Lutra and Taroudant hand-over-handing at flank speed along the tunnelways.

Nah.

So there was always the world, and it was unfailingly wonderful. The amazement that geography was actually the same as drawn in the atlas. The miracle of clouds seen from above. The revelation that weather moved and you could watch the birth, life and death of a storm. That the seas had currents, that the mountains had snowcaps and that the green of spring visibly spread south day by day. A thought unfolded the opticon arm, through its eye Lutra could look past the clouds to see the wakes of ships on her world's small, landlocked seas. She could squint through the dazzle of sunlight from Worldroof to map the towns and tight-packed city-states of Grand Valley's floor. She could track the progress of the great trains across the quarterspheres by the white plumes of steam lashing out behind them. She loved the trains most, cranking up the magnification on the opticon until she could make out the spider-silk threads of the tracks themselves, their junctions and switchovers, trying to guess the route this freight would take, that passenger express. The train was freedom. The iron way out. Her hormone-haunted teenage sleep had been broken at least once a night by a whistle far away through the labyrinth of stone streets and downramps between St. Berisha and Belladonna Main. Train a'leavin'. Without you, Lutra Blaine.

"Child'a'grace, not again!" she grimaced.

The enchantment was dispelled by a red light pulsing in the bottom left corner of the opticon. That intermittent again. She thought up a diagnostic. Her world went out of focus.

As she suspected. The bloody thing had kicked into assembler preignition. Sixth time in as many days. Senile bunch of scrap. No way, of course, to think of an angel, a Cheraph, no less, whose physical body you inhabited more as parasite than guest. But no one could deny that after *that night* it had started to go quietly ga-ga. No one had explained what the hell was going on there, like no one had explained what the hell was going on *that night*, when all the stars started shooting at each other with lasers and all the viewing panels had sealed up tight and somewhere inside her a nasty little voice had said, there's stuff going on here they don't want you to see, stuff that might, just might get you killed, Lutra Blaine.

Machines. The way they should do it: either fix the stupid machine so you don't need any people so they can shoot away to their hearts' content, or you scrap SERAPAMOUN and make it all people. But three; one angel, one girl and one pervo, is sure-as-eggs-is-eggs grief.

Pain in the hole. When it kicked off you had to go down there and shut the bloody thing down manually before it went into full Generation One assembler breeding. It was only a one-touch panel, but it was picking that panel out of a grid twenty by twenty all the colours of the rainbow. First time she'd made it with 007 seconds to spare. Once the processor halls started filling with assemblers, all hungry for moonrock to turn into cybersoldier, it took three different codewords from three separate Anarchs to put the system back into Condition Mauve.

"Tarou, he's kicking off again," she said more in hope than confidence. The first three times he'd told her she had to do it because she needed to know what to do in an emergency, the fourth time she realised that he was saying that because he hadn't Idea One about how anything in the battle station worked.

Sort it yourself.

She'd worked out a way of negotiating Terror's warren of tunnels, push with the hands in a long, gentle incline toward a point on the opposite wall way down the tube, spin one eighty halfway down so that she met the oncoming rock hands and face forward, ready for another long shallow swallow-dive. As she zigzagged toward the main soul-sphere in the zero-gee hollow at the core of the satellite where the heart of SERAPAMOUN depended, the thought niggled her, as it had each time before when the intermittent kicked off, that she should probably tell someone about this.

Nah (as she jack-knifed from the Equatorial One into Six O'Clock Diagonal). They didn't pay her enough for responsibility.

One swoop past the intersection, Taroudant had left one of his tokens of intent. Grimacing, Lutra squeezed herself past the slowly revolving glob of milky jizzum.

"This wasn't in my job description, man!"

This time, not even a far distant snicker, reverberating through the tunnel system. The wads she could cope with, just. The lurkings, the stealth approaches, the sudden shock of a hand slipped into her pants, the clutch of a (small) breast: not even a job creation scheme cosmonaut should have to tolerate that. And she never saw him coming. He could move fast and silent as a shadow in those endless corridors.

Creep.

As her hands touched gritstone for the next fist-off, a peculiar tremor ran through her palms. She seized a rung, stayed her flight. Fingertips told her unprecedented things were stirring within the pumice. What; her one-hour prelaunch neuro-induction course had not covered. Had covered very little, except how not to depressurise the station, and if in doubt, refer upward. She changed course at the next node, upward rather than inward, following the tremble she could now feel in the air around her to the nearest processor hall. Her arms cleared a swathe through a flock of foam styrene food trays, still sticky with sambhar sauce and curry ketchup, the detritus of Taroudant's solitary dinners; she came in for a landing on the crystal porthole of the Valhalla 3 hall. Squinting down between her feet she could see at once through the hypercold the wasp-striped feed hoppers raised from their rest positions, pressed against raw rock, guzzling greedily. Shadows in the frosted diamond casting chambers. She bent closer, squinted. Steel bones and beaks. As she watched, swarms of assembler drones wove wires and smart-carbon sinews around the naked skeletons.

"Shit shit shit shit shit," said Lutra Blaine. There was no avoiding having to tell someone now. She kicked off.

Something snagged the waistband of her pants.

"Leave it out, man!" she yelled at Taroudant. "This is serious, SERAPAMOUN's lost it big time, the whole place is going monkeyshit."

The fingers did not let go. The other hand seized a fistful of work shirt.

"Tarou . . ."

She slapped behind her, yelped. The back of her knuckles had connected with something harder by far than barely-post-adolescent flesh.

A third hand snagged her right ankle.

She began a scream. A fourth hand ended it, fingers clapped around her open mouth. Six fingers of articulated stone. Lutra Blaine kicked with her free leg, struck out with her hands. Stone arms thrust from the tunnel walls to seize and pin them. Held immobile, Lutra Blaine could only watch the opposite side of the corridor unfold like an insect's maw into an arsenal of graspers, blades, buzz-saws. A swift, sure pass of the scalpel opened her up from pubis to sternum. Rectractors peeled back flesh and bone as the robot mandibles proceeded to patiently disembowel her.

*F*or three days Kid Pharaoh rode the cow-catcher of Grand Trunk Rapido *Hep Badda*, wide-eyed and hallucinating with speed and hunger.

In Xipotle he had jumped from the steps of the rickety-clickety stopper service across the sidings toward the gleaming behemoth of the big express. He had rolled under the grazer wagons, fragrant bovine piss leaking through the wooden slats as he pressed himself close to the track ballast, waiting for the Traction people to finish their inspection. As the boarding gantries retracted, he made his low, darting run and scramble up the slope of the cow-catcher. As Sweetness Asiim Engineer 12th had promised, he was invisible. His heart had bounded as the whistles blew and the drive shafts exploded in insane gouts of steam and the wheels fought for grip on the smooth steel. His fingers tightened their grip. *Hep Badda* gathered speed and swung out on to the Grand Valley mainline. On the upslope to midnight the sense of speed, of potential, of fast movement through a dimensionless, unguessed-at void thrilled him, on the downside the click of the joints and the brisk, muscular rhythm of the pistons began to hypnotise him. Pharaoh just, *just*, caught himself nodding off. Guillotining death winked in the moonlight; just, *just*, he pulled back. After that, he lashed himself to the cow-catcher irons with his belt and strips torn from his short sleeves. Crucified, he rode the steel rails. His numb, sun-scarred eyes were focused on those twin tracks of steel, forever reeling in beneath his crossed feet but never growing one centimetre shorter, always *always* reaching all the way to the horizon. The big luxury express had driven him against the wind so long and so hard he felt it was blowing straight through him, making a calliope of his rib cage, his skull transparent, a bowlful of gales. Wind madness.

Three days he rode thus, between starvation and velocity, mania and enlightenment, the cold steel rail and aspiration. Out of his head. Held together by strips and straps. He would have become another cheap martyr to the rails had not the sudden shock of a *something* jolted him back to his claw-hold on the cow-catcher. A shift of gravity, a change of pressure, a new tone in the mantra of the wheels; *something*. He opened his eyes and let out a rending shriek as tracks, train, passengers and Pharaoh perched on the very prow of it all were swallowed by the gaping demon-mouth of the mainline approach to Belladonna, mightiest and least obtrusive of cities. Pharaoh howled as *Hep Badda* plunged down into darkness, the twin beams of the head lanterns stabbing out on either side of him. Down down down. Signal lights and speed boards loomed at Pharaoh, switchovers glinted silver, hinting at strange other ways down darkly secret side tunnels. Pharaoh became conscious of other levels above and below that interpenetrated his space. Gleams of riding lights, echoes of whistles from high overhead, sudden gasps of steam wisping out of a side tunnel; on one occasion, the lights of carriage windows glimpsed through gaps in the track beneath his feet, other journeys speeding down there in the deeper dark.

After a timeless time in the dark, he became aware of a growing light ahead, a golden glow not from any device of *Hep Badda*'s, but from the tunnel itself. With a pressure gradient that wrenched the drum of his surviving ear, the rapido burst from its narrow tube into a wide subterranean boulevard. Houses and tenements carved from raw stone leaned over the tracks so steeply and closely that they met overhead in knurled concrete bosses and casement-studded fan vaultings. These were the barryvilles of Belladonna, the first diggings of the manformers when the world had no air and the radiation would roast your gear in your pants like a station vendor's spiced nuts. Idiosyncrasies with cutting lasers had, over the centuries, deepened it into a chaotically baroque architecture, and the old vehicle out-lock had widened into the main thoroughfare into Belladonna.

The big train brushed terrifyingly close to overhanging orioles and stone balconies: Pharaoh saw, quite clearly, a woman in a simple white shift standing reading a letter in a glassed bubble. Her face was joyful. Then she was whisked into the past. Residents bustled along the arcades that hugged the faces of the red stone buildings like a ballet dancer's tights his piece;

made their way up broad, foot-worn staircases to the hanging markets on their precarious stone platforms. Elegant stone footbridges arched over the tracks. Pharaoh glimpsed children's faces grinning down. He waved, they were gone. He had no notion how deep he was, but many tracks came together here under the vaulted ceiling: *Hep Badda* sprinted past a crowded local, a goggle-eyed, nocturnal creature that spent its entire life in the tunnels ways within Belladonna. The express gained on a big tanker train, drew level, prow to prow. Pharaoh glanced across, met another pair of eyes returning the regard. The two freeloaders strapped to their respective cowcatchers stared, then *Hep Badda* pulled away. Somewhere ahead must lie the terminus, Belladonna's legendary Main, but squint as he might, Pharaoh could see no end to the great street, just the warm golden glow haze of ten thousand windows.

But end it must, and did, the Barryville terminating in a sheer face of cliff pierced by a dozen tunnels. *Hep Badda* selected its destination, slid over the points and into constricting darkness. The lights showed nothing but curving track, but Pharaoh's kinesic sense told him his was headed upward. Then the Grand Trunk Rapido ground around a tight turn in the tunnel, a circle of painful white opened in front of Pharaoh's pained eyes and in a fanfare of steam and whistles he was thrust into the Minus One and second-highest level of Belladonna Main.

Hep Badda glided in to the marble platform like an oil-drop on steel. Numb with wonder, Pharaoh gazed up, immune to the stares of the station staff. Belladonna Main filled a shaft a kilometre deep. The same constructional diamond technology that propped up Grand Valley's roof here built the cantilevers and cables that supported the ten levels of platforms, tracks, concourses and ticketing halls that criss-crossed each other like outspread fingers in a children's game of who-gets-to-go-first. What entranced Pharaoh was that, up there beyond the spans and spars of Level Nought, he could see dawn light glitter on the glass dome that capped the shaft-station, and through that, beyond that, the building-crusted shaft of a support pier leading his vision high, higher, highest, through the morning cumulus to the diamond glint of Worldroof.

The squeal of brakes broke his dream. The buffers were approaching.

Porters and pedicab wallahs were already closing on the train like warrior ants tackling a snake. With stiff fingers, he worked loose the bindings, returned his belt to its more socially acceptable use of keeping his pants from obeying gravity. He stood up, balanced himself and stepped off the cow-catcher on to the platform at a gentle walking pace.

Belladonna.

He had made it. He had arrived.

He clenched his fists in private triumph, let a slow, sly "yes" slip across his lips.

Instantly he felt fingers at his pocket. He turned: gone. Faces. The Grand Trunk Rapido was disembarking, a flood of faces. Pharaoh shrugged. So. Every-thing he valued, he carried inside his clothes, and up there, the sun was shining.

Belladonna.

Made it.

"Long way between down there and up here," Sweetness Octave Glorious Honey-Bun Asiim Engineer 12th observed as she tugged the blankets tighter around her and tried to ignore the swaying of the little webbing nest.

The shaking had soon passed, eased with cups of a herbal brew that left twiggy bits in the gaps of her teeth. Picking at them too vigorously, Sweetness noticed that she was setting this little globular nest of plastic, webbing and soft fabrics in which she had found herself swaying. Before Pharaoh could stop her, she had stuck her head out through the entrance slit and found herself looking down through five kilometres at the sinuous terraces of Canton Czystoya.

"Oh whoa," Sweetness had said, queasily, and crept back into the draughty comfort of Pharaoh's nest.

"More tea?"

"I think I could, yeah."

Because it was all story, it was necessary not just that she be rescued from the Point of Worst Personal Threat by a daring swoop out of the big blue, but that the daring swooper be a character she had last encountered before she properly understood what it was to be a story and have improbable things happen around you. Ironic too; the saviour saved. Now she understood what the Teacher of the Air had been going on about in all those lessons about story and structure and narrative. All you had to do was throw yourself off

the thousandth-level balcony of a pier-top manor. Irony on irony; the meat
Lotto winner from the pits under Meridian should end up some kind of vertical goondah in a squatter town of pods and cocoons hanging like grapefruit
from the heat-exchange vanes of Pier 11738.

Some folk just got the hooverville in the genes, Sweetness supposed.
Never get away from it. Like some people got trains. At least the view's
better, and you get to crap on the people below.

"It's easy to get trapped, so," Pharaoh said in his soft, hesitating way, his
head half turned so she would not have to look at one price he had paid to
make it all the way up here.

Yeah, Sweetness thought and remembered those other men she had met
who, one way or another, had trapped themselves. Uncle Neon, literally so,
fused into the global signalling network, his soul blasted into some alternative world less friendly than this. The doctor, free to go as far into the futures
and pasts as he liked, but only within the confines of the town he had
invented. Bedassie with his dream cinema playing every night to an audience
of zombies because any applause was better than the sound of your own feet
walking off stage. Cadmon and Euphrasie: weird butty-boys. Building things
and blowing them up again and not caring if anyone ever saw or knew. Bones
in the sand now, with no one caring or knowing, because they'd let head
stuff—politics, art, aesthetic outrage—drive them to war with Harx. He was
at art school with them? So what was this Church of the Ever-Circling things
then? Big big art—so they got jealous, or sell-out? Trapped. Leading of
course to *him*. Serpio. Trapped like the rest of them. Terrible, the things mail
order can lead to. Now this Pharaoh guy, *again*. You give some folk the key
to the box, they walk out, take a look, decide it's not for them, then they turn
around and walk right in again. When station rats look at heaven, they see
just a bigger station, with better retailing.

You need to cultivate a different flavour of males, Engineer.

So? What's so different about you, cutie? All this is working, all these
adventures are happening, all this story stuff you tell yourself, because one
evening you walked into a trackside booth and you've never really walked out
again. You're still in there with the falling beans, balancing on those skinny
sticks.

Trapped, like the rest of them.

She didn't like the track this train of thought was taking, so she prompted, "So, what was it about Belladonna, then?"

The boy leaned back against the yielding skin of his bubble. Sweetness tried not to think of the terrible void outside.

"No kids."

"Explain this."

"Not the city—never got out into the city, not the city proper. The station. I walked down the platform on to the concourse and just stood there, looking around me, because I knew something wasn't right, so, but I couldn't smell what it was. I mean, there were travelling people and staff and people selling food and shining your shoes and reading your cards and selling you travel insurance and all that *passenger* stuff but there was something not right. Something missing, you know? So there I was, standing under the Diamond Clock with all these people rushing around past me and then it hit me. Where were the kids?"

Sweetness understood. Not *passenger* stuff. Not the grouchy four-year-olds dressed in their breeches and frocks for their Dedication at the shrine of their Celestial Patroness. Not the bouncy T-shirts and shorts kids off for their holidays at the seaside or in the mountains or some desert spa. Not the school parties roped together by the wrists off on an educational jolly to the chasm-side colleges of Lyx. Not the commuting high-schoolers burning holes in the upholstery with their illicit cigarillos, stopping off at the shopping levels before traipsing on home. The track kids. The seen-but-unseen kids. The world's mainline termini teemed with vermin children: water sellers, hotel touts, street performers, beggars, get-rich-quick pamphleteers, hawkers of burgled goods, apprentice pimps, rent-boys, sucky-sucky girls, shoe shines, con-artists, muggers, teen dacoits, cut-purses, luggage-slicers, street sleepers and trash. Those pinched ferret faces Sweetness had seen peering up between the sleepers. In her professional capacity, she accepted them as you accept fleas on a dog, had even come to relegate them to background noise, as train-people of necessity learn this skill, but any station, let alone Belladonna Main, with its five million transits every day and night, without *kids* was more than peculiar. It was improper. It was a full quarteryear since *Catherine of Tharsis* had last drawn in to a stand on the crystal cantilevers of Belladonna Main—a succession of dreary if lucrative heavy haulage contracts had kept the trainfolk out on the industrial circuit—but such a total pogrom of the vermin could only have come from radical changes in station hierarchy.

"Karen Kupelski," Pharaoh said quietly. The high winds soughed in the support webbing. "Concourse and Franchise Management. Heard about her later. After, you know."

"She cleared out all the tunnels and chased them off the concourse."

"More'n that. She sold them. Made a lot of cash out of the deal. That was the idea; they were going to put out shares or something like that, I don't know; anyway, they need a boost of quick cash, so Karen Kupelski, she's three weeks in the job and says, I got an idea! Watch me kill two birds with one stone! In come the railway police with torches and hunting cheetahs and sonics and gas and all that. Rounded them all up, put them in containers, shipped them out as night freight. Result, happy shareholders and passenger complaints way down for the quarter. There's a lot of people out there've got a use for a spare kid. Them ones I lifted you from . . ."

"The furniture folk."

"Them, they're not the worst by any means. Not by a long way, no."

Children as resources. Feedstock. Sound economic sense to recycle your trash. Sweetness shivered: memories of being an almost-chandelier. She thought about the others, ever-ready for dinner, shedding light from a plastic flambeaux, then unthought, guiltily.

"So what did you do?" she asked.

"Tell you something, if I hadn't twigged, if the nose hadn't said, *Something not right here, hey! Where's the kids?* they'd've had me. They were coming for me, lucky, I've got this eye for pattern, I can see patterns in things, know what I mean? I'm looking round at the crowd and suddenly I see that this guy and this guy and that woman and this guy are all heading toward me. So I leg it. Up and out; up the ramp, throwing people out of my way, all these passengers and their kids, get the hell out of my way! You know? Up to the first level, and up beyond that even. Right out, on to the surface. Tell you something, if they'd got me, God knows where I'd be right now."

"Still a long way between there and here," Sweetness coaxed.

Pharaoh tapped the star of scarred skin where he had sold his ear for freedom.

"From the top of Meridian Main, you got two choices. Horizontal, or . . ." He pointed upward. "And I heard her say, "Go up, boy. Go up."

"Her? Who?"

"The one bought my ear. Remember? I told you sometimes I hear what she's hearing. Other times, it's like she's talking to me."

"Through your ear."

"Through my ear. Still part of me. 'Go up,' she said. 'I'm up here.'"

Sweetness did not want to say that the odds of the donee knowing the identity of the donor, let alone choosing to send a message to the ear's erstwhile owner, were negligible. Multiply by the likelihood of Pharaoh emerging on the foot of precisely the correct one out of half a million roof-pillars . . . But, in the realms of the psychic, there were no coincidences, and fewer unlikelihoods.

"Okay, so she told you to go up," she said.

The first couple of kilometres were easy. Like the roots of the immense primeval trees in the Forest of Chryse (planted by St. Catherine herself, the legend went) the piers of Worldroof flared out in massive buttresses. This was the demesne of the lowest orders in the tower's vertical society. From the condos and projects, dock workers and glass cleaners would toil up the zigzagging staircases to the express elevators that whisked them five kilometres up to their daily labour. Easy here for a ragged railrat to merge with the on-shift and try to blag a ride skyward. The eyes of elevator security, paid to protect the privilege of altitude by the tower-top mandarins who had massed nabob fortunes out of glass-cleaning contracts, were ever sharp for goondahs.

"Pass?" they said.

"Forgot it," Pharaoh said with his best ingratiating smile. They bounced him, hard. The workers smirked. He cursed them all roundly, but it was no hardship. There was breakfast to be filched from the concessionaires and food-courts that had joined together to form catering districts around the elevators. Service stairs took him up the escalators of Dunny, a cloistered district of globular habitats clustered like clitorae in the crotches where the buttresses merged to form the pier. Here a race of petty professionals lived, bookkeepers, never accountants; legal clerks, never advocates; data processors, never systems designers. Bourgeois values are always held more tenaciously by those whose claim is slightest; the window-studded tenements were all gated and guarded by security men in black leather. No place to linger, and hi-speed escalators swiftly took Pharaoh up through half a kilometre of mall levels (a moment's warmth, some scavenged centavos and a stolen bite) to St. Dominic's Preview, the first of three that ringed the pillar at significant and spectacular points. The preview was a wide annular plaza where the pillar vertical began, a popular pet-walking, child-strolling and picnicking place for people of all classes from a kilometre up and down the spire. Mingling with the crowds—even on a midmorning work day—Pharaoh was aware for the first time of his altitude. All his morning's climb had been facing the pillar, up stairs, along walkways loomed over by tight-packed buildings. Now he had clear blue air in front of him. It drew him to the edge. The boy from deep under Meridian Main learned the meaning of vista.

Before him, Grand Valley; its gently greened hills, its rangelands and ranches, ancient and noble haciendas folded at their hearts; the woodlands and lakes of the Pay Parks; the sister pillars rising at regular geometrical intervals: true primeval world-trees. Here Grand Valley was at its widest; even through a coin-operated opticon, Pharaoh could not see the valley walls to north and south. The hexagon-patterned glass of Worldroof arched over all, curving down to the visual horizon in every direction. Pharaoh looked down. Beneath him the boroughs and manufacturing districts of Pier 11738 swept down to the earth. They went much further than he had imagined. He trained his opticon on the place where the naked carbon of a root buttress entered the ground. Turf and bedrock were heaved up around it, like plucked skin, or a scar. Pharaoh stroked his lost ear, the ear that was guiding him upward, and turned around to look up at his final destination. It seemed to lean over him like a bullying deity, or a new Concourse and Franchise Manager. He leaned back. Railrat and tower regarded each other. The way up is not so simple now, the tower said.

Cunning could find sneaky ascents in the vertical country above St. Dominic's Preview. A sneaky ride on top of a tourist elevator lifted Pharaoh fifty whole levels. Up in the land of the communications systems: great, crackling dishes and relays, the neurons of Grand Valley's communication system were crawling with access ladders and, when those gave out, offered plenty of handholds.

Upward, guided still by the echo in his deaf inner ear. Birds swooped at Pharaoh; householders and pier security hurled threats and harder objects; keek and filth discarded from yet higher levels threatened to dislodge and knock him spinning into space. Tucked in a crevice between the pipes of a water recycling system, he chewed a *refrito* chapatti stolen from Aisle of Plenty Mall and surveyed his kingdom. A half-hour overhead was the great baffle of St. Lutetia's Preview, midpoint of the pier. Two and a half kilometres. Pharaoh's lunch perch opened new panoramas to him; lines of shadow to north and south were the rim walls, higher even than this high seat. The land beneath had lost its geography and become a carpet, a tapestry of green on greener, arbitrary and thus lovely. He could trace the progress of rivers and the movements of trains. He had to make it to five now, to see how more different his world looked from the very top. He could not stop now. Halfway? Like the immigrants off the Sailships who made it six streets away from the sheddle port and no further. Enough energy for six streets. Upward, to the owner of his ear.

The second Preview was difficult. Understatement. It was only after his traverse of the canopy ribbing ("Look, look Rafe, is that a *boy*? How theatrical!") to the guy stays, soaked through, fingers numb with cold from a sudden squall, that he understood how close he had come to the long scream. For Pharaoh, that was the only way back now. Above the Preview was a quarter-kay of expensive residential apartments. No access to the interior service shafts was apparent, so Pharaoh made his way up via the obligingly railinged balconies. He struck out strong and zealous to dry out his clinging clothes and put a little fire into his fibres but the cold was sinking its claws into his core. Every hand-haul was that little more difficult than the one before. Every grasp and pull weaker. Sometime, if he did not find a way in to heat, his fingers would grasp falsely, slip and he would fall.

It was beginning to look more attractive than the recriminations of *What have you got yourself into now, boy?*

Open drapes. A sliding door ajar. Pharaoh heaved himself over the railing, stumbled across the balcony, into ankle-hugging fur carpet, rose damask and the overwhelming reek of Nightshade by Arvonne.

A woman was seated on a boudoir stool. She saw the apparition in the mirror stumbling in from the direction from which no apparition should stumble. She froze in the brushing of her long brown hair, half scooped back behind her left ear. She turned.

Pharaoh could see nothing but the bud-like ear, pierced for a single stone, and the mahogany hair tucked behind it. It seemed to open before him like a maw. He was falling into his own ear.

"My ear," he mumbled. "Give me back my ear . . ."

He lunged at the woman, whose name was Tallysker Merie Thrinton. She leaped spryly away, swiping at Pharaoh with the hairbrush.

"Kidnapper!" she yelled. "Sky-pirate, abseiling hijacker! I've heard of people like you, come in on airships all quiet and steal people. Well, my husband has no money, it's all in bonds, he can't get it out. I'm as worthless alive as dead . . ."

"My ear," Pharaoh said soggily and dived for it, fingers hooked to claw it from the misappropriator's head. The hairbrush caught him underneath the jaw. He spun round once and was cold before he hit the fur pile.

Pharaoh regained consciousness with two dominant impressions. The first: he was as cold wet shivery filled with pain and hungry as ever. The second: two granite pairs of hands held him in a stern grip, supine, like a battering ram. Like that battering ram, his head was being aimed toward a small hatch in a riveted metal bulwark.

"Help!" he bleated.

"Oh ho," said one pair of granite hands. By twisting his head, Pharaoh could follow the leather-clad arms up to the padded shoulders and helmet-covered head of Paradise View Apartment Services: 17. "Trash."

"You know what we do with trash," the other pair of hands, connected by identical sleeves to identical shoulders and a helmet that differed only in that it read Paradise View Apartment Services: 24.

Then Pharaoh saw the wording on the steel hatch: Refuse Disposal Chute.

"Bastards!" he started to shout as the two security men broke into a charge. His head clanged painfully against the hatch. Pharaoh was looking down a short, sharp metal slide into a bottomless pit. Plastic shopping bags, sanitary towel cover sheets and pieces of tissue paper flocked on the thermals that spiralled up from the dark depths of the titanic rubbish shaft. As he was held there, head down toward disposal, he heard a clank from above and a collection of individual cereal packets tumbled past him into the darkness of the abyss. He let himself slide. His fingers scrabbled for a firm grip but his shoulders were wedged in the hatch, he could get no purchase. By slow degrees, he was being tilted down the chute.

"Allez *oop*," he heard Number 17 say, then a scuffle of feet and two muffled retorts. Pharaoh slid a centimetre, two, five. Like this? he thought. Born trash and died trash. Then an unknown, higher-pitched voice shouted, "Get a hold of him," and he felt his ankles seized by numerous pairs of hands. A lurch and his shoulders came free.

Another and he shot from the hatch like a silver trout from an apprentice tickler's fingers to lie gasping and shivering on the mesh flooring. Teenage faces appeared over him, none older, most younger than his own. They were daubed with stripes and smears of blue and yellow warpaint and hair gel was obviously their chief expenditure. Blinking certain death out of his eyes, Pharaoh scanned down his saviours as he had scanned up his executioners. They favoured sleeveless T-shirts and leather vests and pants with too many pockets tucked into boots with too much metal. Their wrists were bound in gizmotry, they carried beanie guns in over-elaborate holsters and from complex packs on their backs barely visible diamond-fibre lines ran up in to the dazzle of ceiling lights.

"Safe to lift?" said the one with the yellow under each eye, who seemed to be the head one, though his voice was hardly broken. A teen warrior with green streaks in his hair and henna tattoos on his well-developed biceps knelt to poke at Pharaoh.

"Eh!"

"Safe enough."

"Then let's get vertical!"

Before question or protest, more hands seized Pharaoh. Motors churned a second, then captors, captive and all were whisked straight up into the darkness.

"The Vertical Boys, that's what they call themselves," Pharaoh said. "*Los Verticales*."

"There's lots like that, up here," Sweetness said. "I seen them up on the glass; kids' nations, all that stuff. Runaways, thinking like they're kings. They aren't as flash as they think they are."

Again, the thought of the fall of the Seven-Ups Girl Nation. Thought, and immediately unthought. Would it have been worth being a chandelier not to feel guilty about surviving? Stupid. Almost as stupid as diving over a thousandth-level balcony because all you could do was trust that you were still a story.

"They just want a place of their own, that's all," Pharaoh said. "Bastards won't let you live, up here. There's enough room for a million Vertical Boys, but even if they don't use it they're not going to let you have it. Their umpteen-times grandfather cleaned glass for this, you know. They earned it; and what have we done to deserve it? You got to fight. You got to squat on it and say hey, it means so much to you, you take it off me. That's all these people understand."

Sweetness rolled on to her side, tucked the blankets around her in a way she hoped was kitteny and cute. An idea was forming.

"So how many of them are there?"

"Two, three hundred."

It must be cosy and reeky in those little plastic bladders. Sweetness's estimate, from her queasy survey of the Vertical squatter-town, had been considerably lower. Two hundred was good. Three hundred, excellent.

"With beanie guns," she said. "You going to stun them to death?"

"Hey, those beanie guns saved my ass, so I could save your ass from those furniture folk."

"Okay okay, so that's us even on the I-owe-you-my-life stakes. Now, correct me if I'm wrong, but sometimes an outside viewpoint can give a whole new perspective on things—but you've got like one razor between the lot of youse and these window-cleaning aristos, one click of the fingers and there are two divisions of mercenaries sticking their laser-sights up your hole. Right now, you're just a mild irritation. Moment you ever start to look like a threat, you're all either down the chute or you're in the black suit with your balls sticking out like two eggs in a handkerchief. Now, if you had weapons, and I mean *real* weapons, you could take these people by surprise. Blow them clean out in one go."

She gave Pharaoh a teasing glance, loosened her shirt under the blankets and let her mantle slip a little. How long since you glimpsed the sweet and unaffordable flesh of a fine woman, railrat?

"What do you know about weapons?"

"I know there's Gatlings and lasers and hunter-droids, man, not a day's sail from here."

"Tell me more."

"Oh, I will, but first, I have to tell you a little story. It's about St. Catherine, and mirrors, and a flying cathedral . . ."

*F*oolish folk will tell you that trains are intrinsically happy things. They are bright, speedwell creatures of pomp and steam, like well-fed cheerful uncles. They take people on journeys and life, such folk believe, is journey. A train is a thousand stories, each carriage, each compartment, each seat row crammed more full with motive and emotion and drama than any book. If, as the Masters of Narratology maintain, all story is journey; the converse is also true; there is no journey that does not have a story in its ticket price. Trains bringing lovers together. Trains carrying hopeful families to new lives. Trains taking bright young people to brilliant success in the cities. Trains taking the old to meet the new generations of their people. Engines of change, garlanded with flowers. Happy things.

People wiser in the ways of trains know that for every happy train there is a train of sorrow. For every holiday special there is a packed commuter, for every young hopeful there is a freeloader clinging to the bogies and for every reunion there is a final parting. Trains of farewell. Trains of fatalism, and passivity. Trains of exile. Trains of extermination. Death trains, on which we all must ride, carried at ever higher speeds by forces over which we have no control, directed by rails we did not set, into the tunnel that never ends. And the communication cord is snapped.

The wisest in the ways of trains count a third category; trains of no emotional content. Freight trains. Bulk carriers. Vast, slow-moving ore trains, big enough to be visible from orbit. Trains made up of grain silos, cement wagons, chemical tankers, lumber racks, agricultural machinery flatbeds, grazer cars, hydrocarbon processors, container pallets, paper mills; trains of oils and minerals and big red rocks. Trains of silk and straw and exotic fruit. Trains of glass and tin; tea and spices. Trains with no cargo of human feeling. These, such people say, are the truest trains, for they expose the soft anthropomorphism of those who must project feelings all around them. A train is nothing but a big chunk of inter-related metal parts wrapped around a hydrogen fusion/superheat steam boiler combo. Classically structured, a piece of pure operating logic. Any emotional freight is the property of its passengers and crew.

As example, they will say, here is a train. It's coming on down the line. Let's start at the front and see if there is anything about it that could teach us about happiness and sorrow.

We start with a pair of nipples, silver, quite erect. From them we move back over the areolas, the proud, firm and outsized breasts to the curved-back torso of a woman, chin proudly aloft, hair streaming out behind her. We note that the silver woman has wings for arms, and that they are folded back around the boiler cap. Back along the swelling curve of the boiler to the cyclops eye of the headlamp, over the tiers of outlook galleries and catwalks to the gold-plated anti-glare glazing of the driving bridge where the Engineer stands, hand on the thrust bar, eye on the quartersphere ball, thence by the black and silver livery of Bethlehem Ares Railroads to the streamlined wedge of the main stack. A moment's pause to peep down the steam flues in the raving heart of the machine. On, over the fluid humps of the reheat coil and the Deep-Fusion homesteads, to the ornately filigreed hydro-helium tanks and the water tender with their turrets and watch-houses, the last outpost of the Engineer Domiety before we pass from driver to driven: the train proper. We enter here the territory of the Stuards; from single sleek, slim-line executive express cars to ten kilometres of ore trucks, from pilgrims clacking their beads to polymer processors, all are their responsibility, all are tended with equal attention. Today this service is hauling an organic chemical processor: the first fifteen cars we fly over are stacked with logs from the great polar taigas of Treeves and Raskolnikov. A beltway feeds them one by one to the chipping plant in car sixteen and from there into the bacterial fermentories, reactor plants and cracking towers of the middle section of the train. We glide over cylinders and chimneys and cooling ducts, rivers of pipework and power conduits, separator grids, pumps, distillation columns, wash-backs and vents jetting waste gasses. Brute industry. No emotion here. Now we follow the loops of colour-coded piping to the storage section of the factory-train where each separated fraction is channelled into the appropriate receiving tank. Some bear large and flagrant warning symbols, others are wreathed in mist from cooling tubes, others still carry prominent pressure release valves and little vent-flaps that flutter and chirp as the whole ensemble makes its ponderous way across the unhedged grainlands of central Axidy.

Happy, sad?

This train is not done yet. There is the auxiliary power van, and the raised cupola of Shipment Control, from which the Stuards can look out over the whole length of the train and ascertain in an instant if something is wrong with their charge. After aux and con we pass swiftly over Ballasted Brake vans 1 and 2, the abode of the abject Bassareenis, to the final car, the caboose. Passing over its gilded lion-head crest, we come to a long glass blister. We glimpse greenery. It seems to be some sort of conservatory. Onward. We fly out over the Stuards' verandah a little way down the track that strikes undeviating across the plain. Turn, look back at the foreshortened length of the great train driving across the geometric farmland. There it is. The great train, *Catherine of Tharsis*. Happy? Sad? Can't tell, can you? It's magnificent, but it's metal. Meaningless.

But let's turn round, go back to that blister of glass and greenery. Hover a moment. Stoop lower. Look carefully. It is indeed a caboose-top roof garden, accessed by a wrought-iron spiral staircase, protected from the three-hundred kilometre-per-hour winds of express speed by a slender geodesic. Within is a lush little jungle of foliage plants; some flowers; a small water feature; wind-chimes; darting ornamental humming birds, like flying jewellery; a little lawn as smooth as snooker baize and a tiled patio area with casual cast-aluminium seating. A young man is sitting on one of the chairs. He is slightly built, with the pallor of the Deep-Fusion Domiety, a childhood encased in metal, close to perilous energies. A worm of goatee shadows his chin. He looks ten, eleven of this world's double-years. On an occasional table beside him is a peeled apple, a pocket knife, and a red telephone. He cuts a slice from the apple, eats it, tries to pay attention to the yellow paperback in his hand.

Romereaux Deep-Fusion finds he has been spending more time in Marya Stuard's conservatorium recently, reading yellow novels, mostly being away from other people. Friends and relatives now crowd him. There is not enough room, there is always someone around, someone wanting to talk to you, someone pushing past you, someone *there*. No space for yourself, except up here. And the books are yellow and stupid, but no more so than anything else. His job, his life-role, bores him. Tuning tokamaks, configuring containment fields, controlling plasma flows, manipulating ignition lasers; ten generations of Deep-Fusioneers may have nurtured the fire in the beast, but why the eleventh? Romereaux has discovered that he resents that he was never given a choice about it. You are born to tend tokamaks, that's fact, son. It's not just him. There's a discontent going up and down the corridors, through the carriage couplings and along the gosport tubes. The contracts are signed, the loads hauled, the engines fused up and the brasses polished, but there's no spirit in it. Haul, heave, haul again. The rails go on forever. You will never get anywhere on them, just round and round the round round world. Tempers are short, patience shorter. Good reason to stay away from your brothers and colleagues when a bump in a companionway can lead to a fist fight. Romereaux can't remember the last time he heard *Madre* Mercedes strike up with her asbestos gloves on the calliope. Not since *things started going bad*. That is what he says; but what he means is *since Sweetness went away*.

In engineering terms, he thinks of her as a very small bolt, in a difficult place, unobtrusive, easy to miss. But that bolt is made of gold, and it's the one that holds the whole thing together. Lose it, and . . . She rode away that morning and lit up a whole other world of places to go and lives to lead. All of a sudden, everyone had choices. You don't have to go where the rails take you. You can move in at least two dimensions. You can get off the train. First Sweetness, then Grandmother Taal: if the lofty Engineers are so rotten within one girl can topple them, why do we cling so tenaciously to our traditions and laws? Will they save us, and what from? Are they worthy of saving?

Pull that bolt, and the whole damn thing starts to come apart.

He spears another segment of apple on the pen-knife blade. It's halfway to his mouth (it is a terrible, yellower-than-yellow novel) when the telephone rings. The red telephone.

Because it is the red telephone, he stares at it for ten, twenty, thirty rings. The red telephone. The hot-as-Hades emergency line. For use only in absolute *extremis*. War pillage flood firefall a line invasion end of the world. The red telephone. It is still ringing.

Romereaux looks around, finds no one who can advise or he can delegate to. He picks up the receiver, suddenly fearful the caller might have run off in disgust. He dislodges a thick fall of dust.

"Hello?" He listens to the voice at the other end. The message is short. "Yes, I understand," he says and reverently sets down the handset. Then it is as if he has had a cattle-prod inserted anally: he is out of his chair and across the conservatorium in one galvanic bound. He snatches up the gosport, uncaps it and bellows up to the bridge.

"Stop the train! Stop the train! It's Grandmother Taal!"

Sweetness clung like a tick to the underside of the grapple arm. Around her, Vertical Boys with improbable face paint hung from the metalwork like festival piñadas. It was five minutes since the punky little scout with the spiky hair had reported the last of the acolytes scampering in an all-fired-hurry back into the cathedral. Oddly quiet up on the working platforms. Had Störting-Kobiyashi's industrial trolls downed tools again? Sweetness's own ears hinted at strange energies brewing inside the flying machine. Something was about to happen, but Sweetness held her forces back. Better to be safe than sorry. This is war.

Every story needs a good mass action scene.

Sweetness checked her beanie gun. She checked her emergency parafoil. She didn't trust herself with either of them.

Point and pull. Simple. A soft thud and they go down. Guaranteed non-lethal. Lies. A feather pillow can be lethal in the wrong hands. One false shot could knock someone right over the edge, or what if they had a heart condition, or brittle bones? She had sworn her way across the Great Desert on the lives of those she'd love to kill and the ways in which she would enjoy doing it. Now the very real possibility stood before her and asked, *Can you do it? Can you do it?* Even that Serpio. It's you, him and a big drop. One shot. Will you put him over? And if you do, will you fire from cover, an unseen assassin, or do you want him to see you, do you want him to know? Do you want your face to be the last, the very last thing he will ever see? What if he goes for you? What if it's you and him? Bean the bastard. No questions asked. There. Justified. Sort of.

The parafoil was simpler still. Fall and pull. She had done the fall already and that had not been so hard when it came to it, but it seemed saner to trust in the power of story than this rustley wad of cut-and-glue nylon sheeting. How many goes did it take to get the design right?

Everything does come out right in the mass action scene, doesn't it?

Pharaoh was looking to her for instruction. He had two parallel stripes of blue under each eye and they made him look fierce in a soft, cute sort of way . . . Aw, no. Have you no self-control, girl? Get a grip of yourself. It's the going into battle thing. A whiff of danger, a reek of death and the DNA says, pass me on, pass me on, make babies, make babies.

"Okay, let's go to work." She had heard someone say that in one of Sle's action movies. Pharaoh heliographed to squads two and three on the far grapple and underneath the service yard. Mirrors flickered compliance, the Vertical Boys unhooked their safety lines and began to advance along the girders and ducts.

It had been a hard march, filing up the narrow flanges of one roof-spar, swinging perilously in webbing harness across the huge annular bolt plates where spars joined the huge glass hexagons, then another long shuffle down the next rib to the next pier. One hundred metres out along the first spar Sweetness had discovered the first, and unspoken, rule of a Vertical Boy: *Don't let go of what you've got until you have a firm grip on something else.* The second rule she knew already. *Don't look down.* Shuffle. Swing. Shuffle. Scramble. She watched the nonchalant ease with which the Vertical Boys swung over terrifying gaps, hung one-handed over appalling chasms. It's easy for them, Sweetness thought. They have no eggs, just lots of cheap and messy seed they can fire where and when they like, all over the place. Be careless with it. Nature is profligate with guys' life-stuff. Death means nothing to boys that age. Gangs, guns and glory. They imagine themselves gazing down on their own heroic memorials, all their friends and the ones who scorned them and secretly fancied them gathering round and being amazed or sorry or distraught or manly-but-gutted. They hear staunch eulogies, they stand by weeping mothers and girls who could have been girlfriends, in a *guy's* way, right? and look at their broken bodies and feel really really good. They can't understand that death is death, end, terminated, *finito*: game over. No nothing.

Sweetness thanked the hormones of pubescent boys, that let her play the Fab but Unattainable Warrior Queen with great hair and them her berserkers.

They roosted around her on spars and struts at the end of the grapple arm. Clamps held the cathedral of the Church of the Ever-Circling Spiritual Family a short spit away. It filled half the world, an orange moon cratered with scars and punctures. Sweetness had reconnoitred her access points from the vantage of an adjacent roof-spar. You could march whole armies through the holes Cadmon and Euphrasie had blown in the skin. She flexed her aching muscles and gave her pre-invasion team talk.

"Okay, on my word, we go up and in. What we're looking for is a jar thing, about this size, dirty greenish. It's got a lid like a helmet with wings, right? It's probably up at the very top; there's a kind of glassed-over dome thing that seems to be Harx's special place, I reckon he's got it there if he's got it anywhere. Work your way up, the place is all circles, so it's easy to get about in but you can end up going round and round if you're not smart. That jar is what we're here for. Nothing else matters. Not even getting people, get that? Avoid unnecessary combat. That's an order," she insisted, seeing the looks of disappointment on some of the boys' faces. "Don't stop for anything. We want to get in and out, quick smart."

"This fog is great cover," green tiger-striped Vertical Boy said.

"What fog?"

The boy nodded down. Against the rules, Sweetness looked down between her feet. A raft of cloud boiled up toward her. As she watched, it swirled over her feet, up her legs, swallowed her whole. Sweetness and her strike force were suspended in grey murk.

"Something freaky here," she said. Then the world lurched. "What the hell is going on?"

"We seem to be moving," Pharaoh said calmly. Dripping blue arcs, power lines disconnected from the cathedral, swung free and began to retract. Water conduits unplugged, access scaffolds slid backward on their greased bearings. One by one the grapple fingers were releasing their grip. The sounds from inside the airship took on a deeper, more urgent tone. "Harx is casting free."

"He's what? He can't do that. Signal the others."

"In this?"

The arm lurched again. Sweetness looked wildly around. Her platoon awaited her command.

"Go go go!" she yelled and, before any of them could move, was diving recklessly out along the gantry, hand over hand, scrambling to beat the relentless release of the claspers. Three. Two. One steel finger now restrained Devastation Harx. Sweetness swung herself on to it as it let go the orange hull. The airship floated free. Sweetness hurled herself across the widening gap, dived through the jagged hole in the skin, rolled and came up looking out at her boy army swinging helplessly away into the grey. Grapple guns popped, fell into the void. One grapnel was firmly hooked into the lip of the wound. Sweetness heard winch motors whine. A hand grasped the ragged edge, another. Fingers strained. Pharaoh's head appeared. Sweetness helped him haul himself into the corridor.

"Well, general," he said, looking up and down the circular corridor.

"Nothing's changed," Sweetness said. "We got a job to do. Let's move it on out." She had heard that too in one of Sle's movies, and always wanted a chance to say it. They moved it on out.

As usual, Devastation Harx's reflection kept him waiting. Being a man with little tolerance of boredom, Devastation Harx amused himself by trying to catch sight of that other, mirror universe his reflection inhabited, into which it went to pass his reports and receive its instructions. As usual, the glass returned the infinite regress of his mirror maze, devoid of its creator.

Why, he thought, is it this Harx that must wait? The fountainhead and inspiration of an entire religion does not stand around tapping his foot for a mere dog soldier, even if that soldier is one of countless billion alternatives enlisted in the multiversal war against the machines.

Harx glanced at his hand to reassure himself of his own solidity. Truth, illusion and selfhood become dubious when you trap mirrors with mirrors. Mirrors could reflect time as easily as images and possibilities. Many a time he had found a new configuration of the maze, brought into temporary alignment by the movements of the mirrors, where he had seen back two and half decades ago to the Collegium of All Arts alternative poised on an overhang of sculpted rock over the deepest part of the canyon of Lyx like a school for apprentice sorcerers. Magic indeed had been worked there. Quantum magic, the only one the universe permits. The deepest, blackest and most baffling of all.

Somewhere in the mirror maze there must be the reflection of that moment when a three-year-old boy from a good, staid grain family of Valturapa picked a face mirror from his mother's dressing table, turned it to the vanity mirror, peeped in to see what reflections of reflections of reflections looked like. There also must be time-reflection of the sudden explosion of a smack on the back of that boy's head, the lace-gloved fingers snatching away the hand-mirror, his crow-face of grandmother bending down, the onion smell of her breath as she told him never never never to look into two mirrors reflecting each other. A boy's soul could be sucked out of him and lost forever in the maze of reflections. Too late, Amma. His soul was already lost in the infinite regress.

He had certainly seen many times the mirror maze he built as his graduation piece, the culmination of four years' esoteric research in draughty libraries. Fine art and quantum theory. Mirrors could be turned face to face to reflect not infinite regress, but infinite alternative universes, all the possibilities that bubble off from every wave function collapse. Polymers could be doped with the same string-processors that built the neural architectures of ROTECH's reality-reshaping manforming machines and cast into mirrors. Such mirrors could show the dual, uncollapsed state of every photon that impinged on them; a man looking into the infinite regress would see not just himself, but all other possible selves. No two who looked would see the same. Every man his own work of art.

He built the first, ten-mirror quantumoculum in a mad dry season with the hot *tlantoon* wind blowing in from the high desert, alone, as he had spent most of his study years; a man apart from his fellow students. On a sleepless night with the summer lightning raving around the college's spires, he stepped into the circle of mirrors, lit a paschal candle and looked. At first it eluded him, a shimmering, scampering thing that flitted from mirror to mirror, gone as soon as he tried to fix it in his vision; then he learned the trick of seeing by not-looking, like willing the floaters in the eyeball to be still, and he first encountered this other Harx, this soldier in the panversal war against the artificial intelligences. From him he learned his true name and nature, and the meaning of his existence in this universe.

Devastation Harx coughed dryly. In the next universe over, Harx II heard the signal of stretching patience and poked his head around the edge of the mirror.

"Oh. There you are. Sorry, I didn't hear you. Have you been waiting long?"

Harx I stepped into full shot to face Harx II. They were, of course, physically identical, being mere quantum fluctuations of each other: middling height, trim, the grey hair that hue that is known as Distinguished Silver; the refined, slightly feminine features; lips slightly cruel. In manner of dress and disposition they differed radically. Harx I, as ever, was immaculate, expensive, restrained and carried his black swagger-stick with a casual ease that hinted at casual power casually wielded. Harx II seemed slumped, as if drawn in by an inner hollowness, skin waxy and blotched; weary to the very bones. He wore a high-collared uniform with badly pressed pants with a red stripe down the side. The whole looked as if slept in regularly. Harx I often thought of telling his alternate that he looked more like a bell-hop in a Belladonna *bidouche* than a reality warrior.

"The diversionary tactic was completely successful. Already the lunar assembly lines are dropping the first waves of military units across the equatorial zones. We should have secured local government, constabulary, communication and transport systems within seventy-two hours. We will maintain public order in the transition period."

"That's good, that's good, that's good." Harx II's voice was distracted, wandering. Harx I often suspected that he was taking orders from a clerk in the pay division. "What about the subterranean defence units?"

"They're only accessible through privileged Synodical codes. Once we secure the compliance of the Anarchs, they'll cease to pose a threat."

"And until then, half the planet's got a ring-side seat on robot wars." Harx II paused, hacked up a phlegm ball and decorously ejected it. "There's not going to be much left of your pretty little terraformed world by the time they end. Your people are going to have to rebuild it all, ground up."

"Correct me if I'm wrong, but that is the notion."

Harx I did thoroughly despise his quantum counterpart. Multiversal war was no excuse for bad dressing.

On that night of heat lightning, Harx had walked into a maze of quantum mirrors and discovered that his world, its peoples, its history, its Five Hundred Founders were all images, distant reflections of a greater, more terrible reality. In the long manforming, ROTECH's angels had shuffled many realities. In one and one only was there any probability of a habitable world they could share with the humans, a redoubt of diversity and toleration. In all others, there was war. War between the meat and metal, without let or quarter. Total war. War fought across the million realities opened up by the computing power of vinculum theory processors. A war that, in all those other realities, the machines were losing. Across countless universes, the AIs had been exterminated, in many others, driven back, in the rest fighting for their survival as a sentient species. In one and one only they survived, hidden in a fold of improbability from the multiversal Questors of the Human League. This little greened world with its pretty moonring was their final stand. Their red Masada. And, on a hot summer night, an art student had opened a door into the multiverse, called out and received not a welcoming hello to a greater fellowship of all humanity, but the sound of bugles.

"Fight? For you? In a war? What for?" he had asked his scruffy emanation on their third meeting, a night with the insane *tlantoon* howling about the pinnacles and stacks of Lyx canyon.

"Bucketloads of money," Harx II hinted.

"I am an artist," young Harx had said, bristling at the enormity of the insult. "And anyway, physical transfer between universes violates conservation of mass and energy."

"Information doesn't," Harx II said. "We've got ideas."

Two weeks later he was back.

"I'll take the bucketloads of money," Harx I said. "Give me your ideas."

Show time. The external examiners had decorously hitched their gowns of office to step over the threshold into the quantumoculum. Half an hour later they emerged. Two days after that, they delivered their judgement. This was not art. This was a risible fairground side-show, reeking of the fairground midway and the barker's shout. A third-class degree. The lowest possible award. In all but name, a failure, for in these days of fiscally sound education and league tables of performance, a failed student meant a slashed budget and a faculty reprimand.

"Okay," Harx II had said. "You want to make money, stuff art. Found a religion. Here's one we prepared earlier . . ."

That day Harx I took the name and nature of *devastation*.

Back in the contemporary corner of the mirror maze, Harx II chewed at his lower lip in that way Harx I loathed so copiously.

"One wee thing, those two artists. They did a lot of a damage. A lot of damage. We can't afford any more setbacks like that."

Ironic, that the angels should have recruited his own brother and that brother's lover as assassins. That they had been sent to destroy him, Harx I had no doubt. Had it been a desert revelation, the angels boiling out of the heat haze to take them up and show them the name and natures of the multiverse, then tell them exactly who they wanted killed, and how to do it? Bloody A-students. Bones in the dust. He'd seen to that. Never underestimate the longevity of professional jealousy.

"Everything is under control."

Patently untrue, but Harx I had few qualms now about lying to his counterpart. Let the enemy love-bomb him, let them send who or whatever. He had control of the orbital weaponry, his metal soldiers were burning through the upper atmosphere like autumn meteors and, behind this gaudy diversion, he had accomplished his strategic goal: he had stripped the holy codes for the superstring processors out of the St. Catherine entity. Devastation Harx commanded the reality shapers themselves. Nothing could stop him now.

The sound of muffled shouting from the corridor outside gave immediate lie to Harx I's claim. He whirled. Unregarded, Harx II vanished back into his reality. Last to fade was a puckered frown. His parting words echoed in the mirror maze.

"Just make sure it is."

More shouting, louder now, and sounds of strife. Voices: Dandeever, calling orders. They were quick, his enemies, but he was ready for them. Mirrors pivoted away from Harx as he hastened from the mirror maze to take command against the attack. Parallel Harxes swung away from him and vanished into the multiverse. One misreflection caught him in midflight. He checked himself, took a cautious step back, seized the edge of the mirror to hold the image. Caught in the silvered glass was a girl, green eyes, brown skin, black curly hair in need of a wash. She wore tattered pants, a sleeveless shirt, an orange track vest. A new addition was the complex pack on her back, and the peculiar gun in her fist.

"You," Devastation Harx breathed. "Again."

It was not until Skerry was standing in the open hatch of the United Artists speed dirigible, bungee cords around her ankles, that the thought struck her. What exactly did the soul of St. Catherine of Tharsis look like?

Two minutes to curtain up on The End of the World Show. Somewhere out in the thickening fog, Bladnoch lurked in UA2, the big heavy lifter, dream projector warmed up and ready to transmogrify all this mistiness into saints. In the tower-top penthouse that United Artists had requisitioned as command centre for a truly profane fee, Weill received confirmation of funding from Wisdom and immediately generated a credit transfer to Grand Valley Regional Weather's account. It had been touch and go with the weather workers. Orbital climate systems had brusquely brushed his request for a hundred percent pea-souper off to planetside weather control, but Weill could not rid himself of the feeling that they wanted rid of him quickly, that there were things going on up there not for the eyes of the earthbound. Grand Valley Regional Weather had whined about compensation payments to tower-toppers who paid high premiums for sunny skies and unbroken vistas from their panoramic windows and named a figure. Weill laughed. Grand Valley Regional Weather did not.

"Okay, I'll get you your filthy money," Weill growled, then spent five minutes he could not afford trying to track down Synodical Security's Head of Finance through the labyrinth of Wisdom bureaucracy and the planetary communications network only to catch him on an approach shot to the thirteenth at Great Estramadura.

"How much?"

Weill repeated the fee. He heard the sigh.

"It's yours. It's transferring now. Now, if you'd be so kind, I'm about to dormy this hole."

But Weill's request had put Synodical Security's Head of Finance off his stroke. He sliced his approach, bunkered, took five to get on to the green and threw away the match. The five-million-dollar five iron.

Mishcondereya's plague of nano-flies had liberally dosed the Church of the Ever-Circling Spiritual Family with hallucinogens, there was a clear window of fifteen minutes to get Skerry in and out before the dosages wore off: she crept in on muffled fans, positioning the speed dirigible over what the satellite images had shown was a shattered glass vault at the apex of the cathedral.

In the command tower, Weill relinquished the command chair for Seskinore, fresh from the ritual ablutions which climaxed his preperformance superstitions which included inside out underwear, never wearing anything blue, singing two bars from "The Five O'Clock Whistle" and allowing no one to use the word *bishop*. Weill considered it a professional challenge to work in as many natural and logical uses of that last, taboo word as possible when he First ADed to Seskinore. The old ham took two puffs of minty breath freshener, sat ponderously down in the Director's chair, cracked his walnut-knuckled fingers and donned his virtuality headset.

"And how are we, boys and girls?"

"Boys and girls are ready to rock-'n'-roll."

The props were all in place, lighting and SFX up to speed, the actors cued and ready, and now Skerry had seen the gaping hole right through the belly of it all. Precious minutes could be lost sorting through racks of religious paraphernalia. She might have to take a hostage, anathema to Skerry. Threaten nastiness. It was a distinct possibility she might not be able to find the saint at all. Skerry thumbed the cabincom and explained her predicament to Mishcondereya.

"*Merde*," Mishcondereya said, crackly over the corn lines. A pause, then, "I'll call Control." Mishcondereya called Seskinore. Seskinore called Bladnoch out in UA2, who called Weill to call the cave because the old train-witch might have got something about that in that sending. While Weill called the Comedy Cave, Skerry listened to the static on the interphone and tried to make faces out of the swirling patterns. It was a distraction from the stage fright. The fright was a secret she had successfully kept all her professional life: Skerry Scanland Ghalgorm was martyr to that disease of performers. The fear. The shakings; the pacings; the compulsive bouncings of balls on walls; the huddlings in the corner, arms wrapped around knees, rocking and moaning in terror; the discreet throwings up. She recited cantos from the Evyn Psalmody. She performed a Damantine stretch routine, jogged on the spot, chanted tongue-twisters. Anything to push down the dread. On this gig, stage fright could kill you.

"Sker."

"The old train-witch doesn't know."

"The old train-witch has hightailed it."

Skerry was beginning to have a bad feeling about this.

"She's what?"

"Gone. Scarpered. Skedaddled. Flown the coop. Split the joint. Sker."

"What?"

"There's something else."

Skerry's stomach spasmed.

"What kind of something else?"

"He's moving."

"He's not supposed to move."

"I'm getting readings; he's cast off from the dock and is under acceleration."

Skerry swore. The calculations were all based on a stationary target. The margins were tight, hideously tight. Maimingly tight.

"Are we tracking him?"

"I'm setting up a radar lock now. That's us. We're locked on, provided he doesn't make any sudden course changes. And, ah, Sker . . ."

"What now?"

"You know I said there was something else?"

"Yes."

"Well, there's another something else after that one."

"Tell me."

"Ground-to-orbit tracking at Molesworth has picked up a number of objects de-orbiting into atmospheric entry configurations."

"A number, what number?"

"A big number."

"How big a number?"

"Five thousand, in the first wave."

"First wave? How many waves are there?"

"Four that Molesworth knows of."

"Twenty thousand, that's a big number. Does Molesworth know what they are?"

"Nothing on sensors, but, um, how should I put his? That other moon we used to have . . ."

"Oh, Mother of all Grace . . ."

"I don't know how he's done it, but he's got into the planetary defence systems. He's dropping soldiers all over the day side of the planet."

Now Weill spoke in her ear.

"Thirty seconds. First positions."

Skerry felt the dirigible shift altitude as Mishcondereya steered by radar through the cloud of unknowing. The fans swivelled into braking configuration, whirred, slowed to a safe-distancing thrum. Mishcondereya was parked directly over the Cathedral of the Church of the Ever-Circling Spiritual Family, matching its ponderous progress through the fog that would soon boil into angels and demons. Skerry tried to send her circus sense out into the churning mist, feeling for her unseen target, asking clues, hints, graces. Give me a sign, what does it look like? *Give me a break, one little break.*

"Ready, Bladnoch?" Weill said.

"Ready."

"Ready, Mishcon?"

"Ready."

"Ready, Skerry?"

"Ready as I'll ever be."

She buckled the bungees together around her ankles, strapped the isokinetic punch around her left wrist. The charge light glowed. She would blow a pure and perfect circle out of the hull, dive head first through, blow free the bungee couplings, roll and come up slugging. Simple. Pity there wouldn't be anyone there to see her greatest stunt.

The show goes on.

"Cue Armageddon," Seskinore said. The green jump light went on. And, as it did every time, though she doubted it, every time, the fear went. Vanished. She was filled with a clear, cold certainty. It was easy. It was all so easy.

"Dying is easy, comedy is hard!" Skerry yelled, and dived head first out of the airship into the fog.

"Never!" Naon Sextus Solstice-Rising Asiim Engineer 11th thundered. His fist met the gleaming mahogany of the conference table. Tea glasses jumped, startled off their thick bottoms. "Never never never!" A double pound, doubly emphatic.

The gathered heads, without-portfolios and diverse uninviteds of the Domieties of *Catherine of Tharsis* turned their attention to the other end of the table where Child'a'grace sat, hands folded meekly in her lap, the natural leader of the rebel alliance.

She said, mildly, "But husband, it is your own mother."

Naon Sextus's mouth worked. For a terrible moment everyone thought all propriety would be undone and he would address his wife directly. He caught his words, turned to Marya Stuard, his lieutenant and interpreter.

"Inform my wife that she is correct, it is my mother, and Taal Chordant Joy-of-May Asiim Engineer 10th is an Engineer of Engineers, and were she here, she would tell you no different from what I am telling you: we have never, never, *never* failed to deliver a contract. She would say, leave me there."

The assembly pondered the self-orbiting logic. The Confab Chamber was steadily filling; word had passed up and down the train that the thing that had simmered four long years between Naon Engineer and his wife was at last coming to a head. Ringside seats at a full-blown domestic! Spectators packed the railed off Gentles and Relatives areas at each end of the carriage. The Bassareenis had turned out *en famille*. They were particularly keen to watch the snooty Engineers publicly disgrace themselves.

"But it was the red telephone," Romereaux said. The conference room had a simple polarity. Stop the Trainers! at one end, The Mail Must Get Throughers at the other, undecideds down each side and baying bloodsports fans behind the studded brass railings. Amongst the nonaligned, mostly Tractions, a couple of new generation Deep-Fusion folk and the oldest Bassareenis, heads nodded, agreements muttered. A red telephone, yes, the red phone, starkest emergencies, Aid from Beyond Comprehension, in a time of Extreme Direness, only direst direness, Taal Chordant, of course she knows, wouldn't have unless, worse than worst.

"Red telephones can be ignored," Naon Engineer countered. There was a collective intake of breath. Heresy. Ignore a red telephone? Foolish. Worse than foolish. Reckless. Perilous. A dangerous precedent could be set. Taal Engineer was no grazeherd crying, "Leopard leopard leopard." The collected heads turned back to Child'a'grace. She waited with an icon-like grace and stillness for the room to match her serenity. The very way she held herself in her council chair made everyone check his or her posture and sit up a little straighter.

"Husband, your mother, saints be kind to her, is being well aware of the Formas, of years more so even than you," Child'a'grace said. That's right, the nodding heads agreed, Yezzir. "Not for nothing would she imperil the economic well-being of this train and those who live upon her. Not for nothing, say I again, but for one thing and one thing only, and that is family. Wherefore this red phone, unless she has found our child, your daughter, Sweetness Octave?"

A smattering of applause swelled into a small ovation. Many Tractions, Deep-Fusioneers and Bassareenis bore generations of low-grade resentment at being the driven, never the driver. Smelling mutiny, Marya Stuard rose from her green buttoned-leather seat. The room fell silent.

"Economic well-being. Shall we explore this idea for a few moments? The economic well-being of this train and all who live upon her. That, I believe, was your expression, Child'a'grace. I'm very glad you used it because it clarifies our thinking upon this subject. For, despite our many Domieties and mysteries, ultimately, this train is one nation, mobile, indivisible. We are all on the same track together, headed for the same destination, carrying a common cargo. What we are discussing here is not an Engineer affair. It is not even a Stuard and Deep Fusion affair. It is all of us, Tractions, Bassareeenis, all the people of *Catherine of Tharsis*. That is why it warms me to see representatives here from all our peoples and ages. Our economic well-being, my friends. And that cannot be the responsibility of just one family, or one individual out of one family."

She looked around the captive faces.

"I agree with my friend, Child'a'grace, that Taal Chordant would only have used the emergency communication system on another's behalf, and I feel the loss of young Sweetness Octave as deeply as any of you, but consider again those words 'economic well-being.' Sweetness Octave had a choice. She made it, she left the train. Such is her right. But her choice took away our choice. We live with the economic and social consequences of her exercise of freedom. I don't need to regale you with the economic implications of marriage contracts—we all have our diverse nuptial customs—let alone the social. Suffice to say what you have all by now experienced: that the real damage was done to the name of *Catherine of Tharsis*, and that name is our economic well-being. We are *Catherine of Tharsis*, four centuries of history beneath her wheels, named after Our Blessed Lady herself. We should be heading up the Ares Express. There should be Prelates and Nabobs in our Excelsior class lounges, not half a forest and a festering factory full of bugs. But it is work—the only work we can get. Oh yes. I won't bore you with how hard I and my family argued to get even this. So low has our stock sunk. So low. But it's money. It pays the track fees and the water rates and the insurance and the mortgage and puts a little food in our mouths. It's economic well-being. And now, you would throw every deadline and timetable and delivery date down the jakes for the person—mark this well—who got us into this state in the first place. Not enough for her to do it once. She would have you do it again. She doesn't know, doesn't care. Whatever you're doing, I don't care, stop it. Come and get me. I've had enough. I'm bored with life out there. I want to come back. Remember, she chose to leave us. She chose to walk away without a thought; without a thought for us, and now she wants to walk back again."

Marya Stuard looked long at the sombre faces around the table. She had given them the back of her hand, the hard slapping of truth. Time now for the drop of honey. The table would be hers.

"I'm not saying, leave her," Marya Stuard said, and could almost hear the tension go out of her audience's muscles like a chemical sigh. She afforded a little smile. "What I am saying is just, not now. When we've delivered. When we've our next contract, then, and she'll always be welcome back among us—we are one nation on a rail. But not now. Not now."

She stood, feeding on the ringing applause.

"There, I think that has it sorted," she asided to Naon Engineer. It did seem so. The mutineer running dogs were dismayed, Romereaux silently seething, but Child'a'grace sat preternaturally calm. Marya Stuard felt her scalp prickle, a wash of magnetism, a subtle charisma from the Engineer woman that slowly but surely suffused the room like incense and turned every head to her.

"You're not a mother, are you?"

There was a collective gasp. It was an unspeakably low blow, it was the knife in the belly, the mallet to the testicles, the Sunday punch from which there is no coming back, the all-conquering Belly Spear which can never be used with honour. Because every sinning soul aboard *Catherine of Tharsis* knew it was true. Marya Stuard staggered, her assurance annihilated, the wind gone out of her, the fusion fires doused. She wavered. She paled. She passed her hand over her face.

She looked faint, confused, for the first time without a riposte ready to hand. Things no one in that council chamber had ever seen before and no one could rightly believe they were seeing now. She toppled, went down in her seat, fatally punctured, mouth opening and closing like a beached cod, but Child'a'grace was relentless. The long chapatti years were speaking. She turned on Naon Sextus Asiim Engineer 11th.

"And you, the flesh of your flesh and the blood of your blood, the seed of your seed and the dream of your dreams? You a father, not dry and seedless like this, this stick, this thorn, and you no different? Dollars and centavos. Dollars and centavos. The nation, the train, the nation, the train. *Catherine of Tharsis* is her people, her wealth is here, all of the people in this chamber, not what we haul behind us for others like sledge dogs. Our wealth is our people, all our people, and if one of us is missing, we are the poorer, we are impoverished, and for us to willingly sell of our own, for dollars and centavos, for security, we are lost. We are bankrupt. We deserve to steam no more. We deserve to go under the hammers at the Winter Solstice auction and take up hoes and desk jobs."

Face like fusion reheat, Naon Sextus was on his feet. Every mouth was a round "O" of astonishment.

"Woman, you go too far! You drive me too far, too far. You are not track, not in the blood, you know nothing, nothing, you . . . you . . . Susquavanna, you Platform."

The silence was absolute, the shock palpable. Not at what Naon had said, terrible though it was. It was what—who—he had said it to. To his wife. Directly. Passionately. Face to face.

Child'a'grace filled the stunned vacuum with action.

"With me, now!" she cried, leaped up from the conference table and was out through the carriage door. In a thought, Romereaux was after her, then, in order of fleetness, Thwayte Engineer, his sister Anhinga, Psalli, Ricardo and Miriamme Traction and Mercedes Deep-Fusion of the asbestos gloves and the impudent calliope.

"Quick quick quick," Romereaux shouted, beckoning them through as Naon Engineer rose from his stupor with the terrible cry of "Mutiny!" on his lips and Sle and Rother'am at the head of the mob leaped for the hatch like hunting dogs. Romereaux slammed and dogged it in their faces. It would buy seconds, that was all. Seconds were all he needed. *Tante* Mercedes's steatopygous rear was vanishing up the water tender companionway, already Sle and Rother'am were cranking away at the manual override and one of the six dogs was free. Romereaux punched his personal code into the emergency carriage release mechanism. The Engineer brothers saw what he intended and redoubled their efforts. Naon joined them, face pressed sideways into the porthole. Over the clacket of the wheels, Romereaux heard the repeated cry of "Mutiny, mutiny." Two dogs were free, three dogs. The keypad spat out Romereaux's authorisation with a curt "code not recognised." Romereaux cursed exotically and reentered the code, willing his fingers to be slow, steady, patient. Four dogs free, five. So slow. The sixth and final dog was beginning to unwind. Was halfway unthreaded. Was three-quarters unthreaded.

"Code accepted," the key pad reported. A square yellow button lit up. Romereaux hit it as the sixth and final dog hit the deck, the door scissored open, Rother'am and Sle dived and the explosive bolts in the carriage couplings blew. For an instant Rother'am and Sle hung suspended. Then it was as if they were being drawn slowly back while still in midleap as clear blue sky appeared between the carriages and the rear section of the train began to slow under its gargantuan weight.

Romereaux wiggled his fingers at the receding loyalists as *Catherine of Tharsis*, unencumbered, found unheard-of speeds. A last cry of "Mutiny!" penetrated the shriek of wind and steam and was gone.

Romereaux arrived on a crowded bridge. *Catherine of Tharsis* pounded at four hundred and twenty down the beautiful straight steel line.

"Excuse me," he asked, "but who's driving the train?"

"Don't look at me," said Thwayte, caught up in the drama of it all and now beginning to wonder just what he had done. "I'm just a kid."

"Don't look at me," said his older-by-two years sister Anhinga. "Girls don't drive trains."

"Don't look at us," said the three Traction folk. "We're Traction."

"So who the hell is?" Romereaux asked again, nervously observing the numbers clicking up on the tacho.

A noise, like something rusted jarring free, like years of phlegm from aggregation of the bases being gullied up in one bucket-filling gob, like relief after constipation, like the screech the prematurely buried would make when the rescuers opened the coffin lid. In a shadowy corner of the bridge, an object moved. Motors whined. Grandfather Bedzo rolled out from his alcove, caked with drool and shaking with palsies. But his cyberhat glowed with puissance. He grinned toothlessly, a terrible sight, and with a thought, threw the points at Abbermeyer Switchover and took *Catherine of Tharsis* on to the Grand Valley mainline.

"*Tante* Miriamme," Romereaux said. "Have you got your gloves?"

"I have indeed, nevvy." She waved them over her head.

"Then put them on and get you up there and play like buggery and let Sweetness know her family's coming for her."

*T*rainpeople have this innate sense. An evolutionary thing, really. A survival skill. Take them to a place once, and no matter how long a time until you take them back again, they can find their way round it, no problem. In the dark. In the fog in the dark. In a power-out in the fog in the dark. They get so many places, they have to remember them all, or they'd get New Merionedd mixed up with New Cosmobad, Wisdom with Lyx, Belladonna with Llangonedd, Iron Mountain with China Mountain and everyone would be hugely lost. So Sweetness convinced Pharaoh as she led him spiralling inward along the corridors and down the tunnels of the Cathedral of the Church of the Ever-Circling Spiritual Family. Maybe not convinced. Told well enough for him to follow.

"Where is it we're going?"

"To the audience chamber. The presence room, whatever he calls it. The top of the shop."

"You're sure of that?"

"Have you been here before?"

There being no answer to that, Pharaoh trotted behind the resolute Sweetness. Two sectors starboard, he stopped again.

"Can you smell something?"

"Like what something?"

"Sort of sweet, like chocolatey, a bit perfumey floaty butterfly-ie."

"Floaty butterfly-ie?"

Pharaoh shrugged.

Onward. He was firmly convinced they had gone around this same orbit of corridor three times now.

"What does the lid have on it again?"

"Wings."

"And you're sure of that?"

Sweetness stopped abruptly. Her shallow temper flared.

"Yes, I'm sure of that and yes, I know exactly where it is and yes, I know exactly where we're going as well. Here."

She banged on a closed bulkhead to a radial corridor. She jumped back, startled, as the bulkhead flew up, opening on to a corridor filled from one end to the other with Ever-Circling Spiritual Family.

"Ah," Sweetness said.

"*Ahhh!*" the Ever-Circling Family cried, threw up their hands in horror and fled as one.

"Simple," Sweetness said, snapping her fingers with admirable nonchalance, surveying the now empty corridor. "Come on, this way."

"I knew I could smell something," Pharaoh said, sniffing.

Sweetness stopped at another circular door halfway down the corridor.

"In here."

"What's in here?"

"The way up's in here. Child'a'grace, do you have to make a question out of everything? I got the genes, you don't, that's evolution. In here." She slapped the door release with the heel of her hand. It flew up. Sweetness found herself looking in a darkness that glittered with a thousand mirrors.

"Maybe not this one."

There was a man reflected in those mirrors, a man of distinguished silver and good personal grooming, of fine taste in tailoring with a black cane in one hand. A man who, as she watched, turned as if scenting her, all his mirror images turning as one with him. A man who was now aiming something that looked inarguably like a gun at her.

"Run!" Sweetness yelled and dived past the door, Pharaoh a step behind her, as a tremendous explosion and shattering of glass shook the corridor.

"You!"

The word hung in the electric air of the mirror maze. Eyes met in the mirror; green, grey. Then Harx reached inside his immaculate jacket, pulled out a hand-held field impeller, spun and with a terrible raven cry fired at the source of the image. A boom of exploding glass: a million minute shards rained down on Devastation Harx. In the same instant the corner of his eye saw the figure, that trainbrat, that dreadful persistent, rude little girl who would not accept her severe limitations, who would insist on trying her betters, who would absolutely not go away or take no for an answer or know when she was mastered, roll and duck for cover. He readied his gun, panting.

The gas. It's getting to you. You can't allow yourself to act this way, not over an uncouth trainbrat. But she irritated him so much. He wanted her gone, gone for good, so much. He spun, reading his mirrors for unauthorised reflections.

There.

"Yah!"

Harx spun, fired six fast, flat shots at the six standing figures that had swung into view as the mirrors revolved on their tireless waltz. The mirror maze rang to multiple detonations. Still she mocked him, now a dozen reflections away. No matter. Two-fisted, Harx aimed the field-impeller, blew the dreadful girl to hell and silica and so she would have no hiding place, each of the intervening mirrors as well. A slow snow of powdered silvering dusted Devastation Harx's shoulders.

A serene place beyond the paranoia of the combat gasses said, She's not moving. She's not even there. You're just shooting at reflections of reflections of reflections.

Selah. It was good to shoot. Good to cast off the constraints of holiness and spirituality and responsibility and guruship and blaze away with a very big gun at something that annoys you very much.

"Waaaaaah!"

Spinning like a Swavyn, impeller set on constant output, he cut a scything swathe of flying glass through his revolving mirrors.

"Come out come out come out!"

A movement. He turned. In one beautiful, oil-smooth movement, he levelled and aimed the gun at the figure in the glass. Too late he saw that it was not his Nemesis. Harx II, his otherversal counterpart, gaped at the gun, threw up his hands in supplication, denial, hope. Far far too late. The eager finger had closed the contact. A ram of gravitomagnetic force sent him raving up in a spray of subquantal shards.

Devastation Harx staggered. What man would not, who has already killed his brother, and just shot his own self? His field-impeller fell like a shriven sin to the ground. He gave a little creaking moan. He clutched at his heart. Something was torn out of him. Somewhere, he had felt himself die. In a pique of confusion and paranoia, he had killed himself.

No. That itself was paranoia. That was the combat gas, as much as that image of that taunting, grinning female, which he now knew to have been one brief glance, amplified by the vinculum circuitry of his shattered maze. The man had been a Harx, but not Harx. He had been a mirrorman, a reflection, a thing from a universe not his own. A dog soldier. And dog soldiers die.

He was glad. It had long angered him, being given orders by such a sloven.

Disgusted by his lapse of control, Devastation Harx stormed from his sanctum. There was a war to be fought, and won, and it would not be won by ecstatic, slashing violence. Control. Application. Determination. He found the corridor awash with purple: acolytes rushing hither and yon. Beyond the tumult of panicked voices, was that gunfire he heard? He seized a passing faithful, a runty, trembling boy with a pudding-bowl crop.

"Just what the hell is going on?" he thundered.

"The hell!" the little acolyte exclaimed and fled shrieking. Harx pushed his way through the milling crowd to the elevator. As the doors opened the airship lurched, sending him reeling inside. He slid the doors shut and ordered "Presence chamber" into the gosport. The elevator stayed obdurately motionless. He called again, a third time, a fourth time. The elevator crew had evidently abandoned their posts for the mass hysteria raging through the corridors.

"Must I do everything myself?" he declared to the universe in general, and began to crank the windlass.

At the perigee of the dive, at the uttermost straining limit of the bungee, Skerry hit the snap release, went into a forward roll and came up poised and feisty on the balls of her feet as the elastic cords snapped back up through the hole she had made with the isokinetic punch. A moment to fit nasal plugs in case of any lingering pockets of Mishcondereya's trip-gas, another to fix her bearing on the wrist tracker, a quick tweak of the string of her leotard out of her crack, and she was ready for action.

"Okay I'm in," she said into the throat-bindi mike. Still without a notion where she was going, what she was looking for. But in and intact. "There's a lot of noise." There certainly was, down beneath her feet, like a party going badly wrong in a neighbour's house. She crept forward on her toes; the din neither waxed nor waned. "I guess they must be really digging your light show, Bladnoch."

Director Seskinore came on the line.

"My dear, we have a suggestion from the head doctors in Wisdom. They suggest you go up rather than down. Some head-shrinkie theory about people and valuables."

"Too right I'm going up. I'm not going down there for a boob job."

She checked her wrist tracker. Its hypersonic bat-squeaks penetrated every level of this creaky, shambling edifice and sketched up a rudimentary map. On the toe-tips of her grip-sole shoes, Skerry moved out. At every turn, she chose the inward route. At every flight of steps, she chose the upward course. Sound travelled well along these curving corridors; plenty of warning of approaching feet to slip into cover: a wall closet, a low-level airco shaft, a false-ceiling panel. What is it about young people today, she thought as the purple-clad faithful rushed beneath her, that fun and dancing and drinking and sex aren't enough for them? Why do they want to be going and joining religions and dressing up all the same and getting dreadful dreadful haircuts? Each generation rejects the *mores* of the one preceding. You should know that better than most, daughter of Ghalgorm's draughty halls.

Better to avoid people altogether. The ceiling duct in which she had taken cover let into a crawlway. After a dozen metres on her belly, it branched. Her tracker advised her that the left fork led to the cathedral's service core. Skerry had always been a fan of service cores. She kicked the panel that capped the tunnel free. It fell an impressive distance between the bloated gas cells before it hit a tension net and bounced. With a grin, Skerry swung herself out on to the honeycomb mainframe beams and began to climb. Upward. But still no idea what she was looking for. The nave-like space of the service core amplified sounds, reflected and focused noises in strange ways. The din from the panicked in the corridors washed back and forth, up and down, unnerving hellish. Skerry flinched at the sudden tattoo of gunfire, though sense told her not even a teen acolyte would be so idiotic as to fire a slug-thrower in an LTA.

"Mish?"

"What's up?"

"I heard shooting."

"Oh, that. They're spraying bullets at anything that moves. Sooner or later they'll run out. What's with you?"

"I'm on a gantry directly under the apex of the ship. There's a solid roof above me, which the tracker says is the floor of the dome room. I'm going to try there first, once I get out of here."

The tracker also a contained a clever little bollixer (in Weill's gaudy and expressive phrase) with enough electronic nous to jemmy the hatch from the gantry on to the corridor. The two halves of the door slid open to reveal a young, dark-haired woman dressed in improbably ramshackle battle gear pulling at the handles of an inlaid double door. Skerry froze. The girl froze. Behind her a similarly piratical youth also froze, but it was the girl that transfixed Skerry. In an instant of epiphany, she knew who that girl must be, what she was looking for behind that door, how she recognised it.

"Hey! You!"

The spell shattered. The girl drew something that looked like a cross between a crossbow and soft furnishings. Skerry did not wait for it to demonstrate its potentialities. A back flip took her out of arc behind the door. She scrambled up on to the ceiling, hung spider-fashion, peeked out at the inverted corridor. Empty. The dark-haired girl—the granddaughter, the traingirl, the one who was at the heart and root of all this mad affair, the only one apart from Harx who knew what this divine receptacle looked like—and her boyfriend were gone. But the double doors stood open.

"Let's go!" Skerry said, somersaulting to the ground.

Mishcondereya tacked the sky yacht hard aport and by sheer millimetres missed clipping the pin-feathers of the Winged Edsel. She swore her finest ladies-finishing-school oaths as she fought to control the skittery little machine in the chaotic turbulence cast up as cloud boiled into phantasm and back again.

"I'd like to see what the manufacturer's manual has to say about this," she hissed as she righted the ship and immediately pulled it into a fan-shredding climb as Cheraph PHARIGOSTER came howling up at her, fiery scourges raised. The things were no more substantial than the mist from which they were constructed but you could hardly fly through them. Necessary illusions must be maintained. "Where's he gone now, the bastard?" Radar lock had been long abandoned. Mishcondereya kept track of the labouring cathedral, sometimes invisible within the thrashing cloud of Saints and Angels, by line of sight, seat of pants, twitch of ovary and luck. She momentarily caught Harx's fortress in her peripheral vision, enveloped in the tentacles of PREMGEE, the World-Devouring Squid.

"Woo hoo!" she whooped and threw the airship into an immediate rolling dive after him. Lift bags boomed, struts complained, spars groaned. Tremendous fun.

"Bearing two oh two oh niner," she called to Bladnoch, circling discreetly in UA2 on the trailing edge of the maelstrom. "Delta vee, about twenty squared." She knew he flew the thing on autopilot and liked to intimidate him with technicalese.

"Moving in," Bladnoch said, calmly. From the high steering turret he watched Mishcondereya plunge into the heart of Gotterdammerung. He wondered what the people on the ground were making of it all and what lies the media were being fed to explain just why the Rider of the Many-Headed Beast had chosen this day and their neighbourhood to duke it out with the Seven Sanctas. Whatever, he felt a glow of proprietorial pride. One of his better efforts. Oh definitely. He could almost feel good about it. Bladnoch tried to work out how he could slip it into his cv, then raised control on the communicator.

"Yuh?" Weill said, delighted by the tag-team wrestling match between the Two Lone Swordsmen and several scaley members of the Circus of Heaven unfolding like a summer squall over Nanerl Canton. Who would have thought the forces of divine order harboured such spectacular anarchy?

"Weill, I have to have more weather."

"I'm giving you all the weather I can, man."

"We lose cloud, we lose everything, friend. We're bollock naked."

"Have you any idea how much this is costing?"

"Since when have you been concerned about the taxpayer's dollar?"

Seskinore took over the line. In addition to his preperformance rituals, he had popped a tab of tephranol filched from Weill's supplies and was now as convinced of his own omnipotence as the Panarch himself. More so. He could order the Panarch about: look, there He goes. Loop-a-da-loop, Ancient of Days.

"Whatever it costs, you will have it," he said, plummily. There was nothing he could not do now, no benison he could not grant, he held ele-mental forces in his hands and made them dance and sing. A million people were watching the products of his genius, *gobemouche* with wonder, and they loved him, they loved him. Even if they did not know who he was, they loved him. A stage! A stage worthy of the great Seskinore at last. He tabbed up Mishcondereya. "My dear, timing! Timing! The very soul of comedy!"

"Meaning?"

"Meaning, you're a little bit late on your shadowing. Skerry has to get back out again."

"Ses, they've got Gatlings down there and they're not averse to using them," Mishcondereya said, thinking, pillock, but she took the little ship in close through a phalanx of Spiritual Spearmen. The proximity alarm and Weill's shouted warning blasting her eardrum came simultaneously. By instinct alone, Mishcondereya threw the sky yacht out of the way of the six blinding streaks of light that burned over her head and in the same instant were gone.

"Bladnoch, what the hell you playing at?" she yelled as she fought to avoid ramming the Great Pantechnicon amidships.

"Not mine, Mishcon. Those were hundred percent corporeal. Solid."

"I'll tell you what they were," Weill said grimly. "Waves five and six. Our Mr. Harx has just upped the ante."

Sweetness and Pharaoh ran pell-mell up the gently curving corridor that Sweetness's infallible train sense told her led to Devastation Harx's presence chamber. Hell and urine, it was only a few days since she had last been here. Full days admittedly, but how much can you forget? She stood before the double doors, hand resting on the door pad.

"This is the place," she said.

"Definitely?" Pharaoh asked, faithlessly.

"Hundred percento," Sweetness said and palmed the door release. "See?"

In those few days since she had last stood in the presence chamber, much had befallen that beautiful room. The wooden cressets had tumbled, the horse-shoe table smashed in the middle by a falling beam, the thirteen chairs scattered and broken-backed. Sweetness walked to the centre across a carpet of glassite shards. She looked up through the shattered dome, shading her eyes against the white glare of the fog.

"What the . . . ?"

Pharaoh was working at the door, wedging the handles with broken chair-backs. He looked up at Sweetness's exclamation.

"What is it?"

"I thought I saw . . . I don't know, couldn't be, an angel. Looking right in at me."

"Nothing would surprise me about this place," Pharaoh said. "Or you. There. That should hold them for a while."

Sweetness surveyed the grandeur of the devastation of the beautiful room.

"Mother'a'mercy, those boys could chuck dynamite," she opined. "Where do you start in this mess?"

"Lid like a winged helmet," Pharaoh said.

"Yuh."

"It could be over there."

The wooden altar piece had been added to the furnishings after Sweetness's visit and had been miraculously spared the destruction, as they often are as a sure sign of their divinity. A lot of purple acolyte hours had been put into it, the triptych of St. Catherine on Motherworld, St. Catherine planting the Tree of World's Beginning with pressure-gloved fingers in the regolith of Chryse and St. Catherine the Mortified as a translucent woman in a floaty frock was vigorous if naive. The five radiating arms bore miniatures from the

Reality Wars, teen cybersoldiers with mirror shades and wires in their heads, fleets of logic bombers dodging slashing lasers, grim-faced space-marines hacking their way into orbital habitats with power axes. They were more crudely rendered but had the energy and zeal of the eye of faith guiding the hand of paint. Crucified to the central spine, haloed by festival fairy lights and stick-on fake jewels was the Catherine canister. It could not have been more obvious if it had had a banner hanging over it announcing *Catherine of Tharsis*, right here, right now.

"You know, I'm having second thoughts about saving you," Sweetness said as she started to climb the rickety edifice. Her desert boots dislodged self-adhesive cabochons, flaked chips of lovingly applied paint. "You are too damn smart for your own good, son."

"Then you be spread all over Canton Semb like cashew butter," Pharaoh said.

"I'd've been all right, I'm a story," Sweetness said, reaching for the reliquary.

"Yeah? Happy ending or sad ending?"

At which moment, Pharaoh's barricaded door quivered.

Outside, in the curving corridor, Skerry cursed.

"Agh!" She beat her palms against it in frustration. "When will something go right today?" She stepped back, too short a run, put her solid shoulder to it. The double doors bulged. Wood splintered.

Within the presence chamber, the wedge chair creaked, wooden billets cracked. The door slammed again.

"Let's go!" Sweetness said, wrenching the pyx free from the altar. She held it up in her hand like a mace. She expected a glow. She expected an angelic chord. She expected a ray of light to beam through the shattered dome of the sacred place on to her face. She expected a sense of completeness, reunification with her sundered twin, of mission accomplished. What she did feel was Pharaoh's hands plucking urgently at her feet.

"Hey, get off me, I'm coming, I'm coming . . ."

She looked down at the face behind the insistently clawing hands. It was not Pharaoh's face. They were not Pharaoh's hands. Pharaoh was on his knees on the broken glass, retching from an evident boot in the testicles.

Him.

"You, you turd!" Sweetness shouted.

Serpio.

Devastation Harx pulled the gunners away from their crank-wheels and chain feeds and Gatling sights and cast them aside like a Poor Claireen purging a stockmarket dealing pit.

"Stop it, stop it at once, buffoons, fools, po-heads, cretins. I, your Harx, command you! Cease fire! Cease fire! You are shooting at lies! Lies!"

But convincing lies. For the first moment, when the blast doors opened and he saw the things he had always dreaded, always dreamed, flocking and swooping outside the Gatling turret, his parts had shrivelled with pure, superstitious dread. In that moment, the Nagging Demon that pricks all holy men and preachers whispered, you had to do it, didn't you, you push and push and push and in the end, you succeeded, you pissed the Panarch Himself off, and now look what you've done, saints and angels coming out of the sky like hailstones at a holiday barbecue. Well, I hope you're happy, Devastation Harx. Just for the first moment. Then for the next moment, he saw his brave boys, his mail-order crusaders, meet the limitless powers of the Omnipotence with whooping determination and good marksmanship, their grim-set mouths foam-flecked with zeal. Then he had seen the white stutter of tracer pass harmlessly through the seemingly corporeal divine hosts, the cloudy wakes they left behind as they howled and loomed and Pride Demon said, Call that an effects budget? When the Seven Trumpets play sweet bebop and God the Panarchic calls out the boys, you'll know about it.

Then Devastation Harx felt a towering rage, that the enemies against whom he pitted his every strength and resource should insult him with ghost candles and magic lantern spooks and mists of ectoplasm.

He straight-armed the shrieking gunner away from the triggers, slapped up the safeties and turned to thunder down on his faithful.

"Illusions!" he proclaimed. "Deceptions! Flim-flammery to dupe us from the real enemy! We are infiltrated, our enemy is within, in this sacred place, on our own sanctum, and in here." He touched finger to head. Devastation Harx frowned, touched finger to forehead again. He shook something that was not lingering battle gas out of his head, swivelled his eyes upward to the main bulk of the cathedral hanging above. His mouth opened, a quiet ah went out of him.

"Did you feel that?" he asked his cowed, stoned disciples. "Did you feel that? Some . . . thing went out of me. Some . . . thing touched me." His eyes went wide. "No! They have it! Bastards!" He raised his cane. "With me, people! They must not get away with this! We shall recapture St. Catherine." He leaped from the gun platform and was borne out of the turret on a surge of ululating, drug-berserked believers.

Ben's Town to Annency; Annency to Perdition Junction; Perdition Junction to Laurel Hill. Woolamagong. Serendip. Acacia Heights. Atomic Avenue. The nameboards blurred past, waiting passengers stepped back, then stepped forward to stare after the vision of blue and silver and steam that had thundered past them, drawing all their newspapers into a rattling dance in its wake. Class 88 *Catherine of Tharsis* broke all records for the Grand Valley mainline. The fusion djinns howled inside their tokamak bottles, the drive rods shuddered and jumped in their housings, every loose scrap of metal and under-tightened bolt rattled and hummed as the Ares Express came through. Scruffy little commuter shuttles, ill-bred schoolgirl specials, slow local stoppers bustled out of the path of the furious monster on to branch lines. Thousand car freighters and Intercity Limiteds were herded and held on sidings; even the transplanetary expresses found themselves inexcusably held at orange as the Insane Train ran every signal and flaunted every speed restriction. Central Track Control sent command after command, all ignored as Grandfather Bedzo, with a saliva-y smile, opened up the throttles and poured in the steam. In the panoramic Central Dispatching Room of the half-kilometre-high glass nail of Central's control tower, despatchers in the ankle-length beige duster coats of Great Southern Traction debated throwing the runaway on to a long run of branch line. They ran the figures on their wrapround Track Display Visors, thought again. At its current speed, the intruder would tear through the points like a child ripping open a birthday present. A four-hundred-and-eighty-kilometre-per-hour derailment and subsequent tokamak explosion would take a ten-kilometre square section of the planet's most densely utilised rail network out of commission for a time measured by half-lives.

Let them get where they are going in so all-fired a hurry, was the conclusion. Re-route, hold and divert and pray the Angel of Trains they don't meet anything coming in the opposite direction. We'll get them in the courts later.

Then, amazement in the tower of glass. The Runaway Train was slowing. Senior Signallers summoned Track Regulation Officers Grade II to confirm the information on their visors. They ran to their Dispatch Assistants levels 2 and 3 and returned with the reports from the Signal Attendants: yes, out there in the green fields of Canton Thrench, *Catherine of Tharsis* was coming to a halt.

"What is happening, why are we slowing?" Child'a'grace chirped as, through her boot soles, she felt the subtle shift of weight that meant that her train was losing speed. Bedzo's face was tight with either concentration or constipation as he applied and released the brakes. The rising screech of hot brake shoe filled the driving bridge.

"What is going on?"

"Something on the track ahead," Romereaux said, frowning, trying to read traffic information from the data-sphere.

"Another train?" Child'a'grace asked.

Catherine of Tharsis had slowed to a undignified commuter-train lope and still Bedzo applied the brakes.

"Doesn't look like it," Romereaux said. "Looks more like, lots of little things."

"Little things?"

"I can't get any detail on this effort,"

The great train had slowed to walking pace. Psalli called from the window.

"I see them, I see them!"

Her tone brought Romereaux straight to the curving glass.

"Full halt!" he yelled. Bedzo complied with a thought. Everyone on the bridge staggered as brakes bit hard, steam billowed, drive shafts flailed and kicked into reverse. Wheels screeched on steel rail, then all was quiet. *Catherine of Tharsis* stood panting gently on the Grand Valley up line. Facing it across a hundred empty metres was an army of robots. They were twice the height of a man and twice as broad, had four metal legs and four metal arms all of which ended in stabbing, slashing or snipping weapons. They had beaked metal insect-heads with complex metal mandibles that opened and closed and chewed in a horrid way. They glowed golden in the Grand Valley sun, their eye clusters glittered. They said, we are painless and tireless and relentless and merciless and perfectly professional about what we do. Every one of the watching faces pressed to the observation glass up on the bridge could see that very clearly.

"What the hell are those?" asked young Thwayte Engineer in a very adult voice.

"Those are a thing I and all of I'se people hoped never never to see," Child'a'grace said gently. "Those are moon-warriors, fallen to earth. Their presence can mean only one thing: our world is under attack. We are at war, they have come to defend us."

On which cue the entire phalanx, fifty by fifty, took a ground-shaking step forward.

"I'm not so sure about the defend bit," said Anhinga nervously.

A metallic click, audible through the armoured glass. Like the Skandavas in the collaged caves of Attaganda, each of the machines cocked its four arms. Blades flashed in readiness.

"And where is Taal exactly?" Psalli asked.

"Exactly on the far side of them," Romereaux said.

"Full reverse!" Child'a'grace suddenly commanded, swirling away from the window to Bedzo's side. The old patriarch grinned toothlessly. At long last, his beloved train was his again. Let the man who still has a drop of juice in him get his hand on the drive rod, not that arrogant, prudish stick of a son of his. No Engineer in his heart.

"Ha ha!" Bedzo said and, with a pulse of his mind, the tokamaks blazed and the boiler seethed, the cranks pumped and the wheels turned and, with gathering speed, *Catherine of Tharsis* backed away from the army blockade.

In their high glass tower, the Beige Controllers read the new reports from Thrench Regional and decided it might just be best to call it a day and all go home.

Out in the green fields, Harx's occupation force noticed a change in their parameters and clicked into advance mode. A thousand metal hooves churned up the summer grazing. Bedzo put a clear two kilometres between the train and the advancing troopers, then stopped. The big train waited.

"Now!" Child'a'grace shouted, and everyone in the cab saw the years and chapatti dust fall from her and she was again the Child of Grace, the bright, vivacious, dotty and energetic woman who had sold her freedom for marriage to a train. "Full steam ahead!"

"Wa!" Bedzo shouted. Hydrogen raved into helium. Every piston exploded superheated steam. The abused drive shafts kicked again, the journel bearings shrieked. The wheels spun as tons of sand was poured on to the track, found purchase, bit. Three thousand tons of Class 88 fusion hauler leaped forward like a speed-dog from a trap, wreathed in steam like a Shandastria geyser elemental. At the sight of their target stopping, the robot soldiers had broken into a heavy trot. Now as it bore down on them, whistles shrieking, they stopped, tried to turn, scatter, flee. Too late, too slow. *Catherine of Tharsis* bowled them over like pins. Amputated limbs; gnashing, severed insect-heads were strewn hither and yon. A rain of blades embedded themselves in the soft green turf.

"There's one on our port fairing!" Psalli shouted, peering out of a shunting oriole. "He's climbing up!"

Grandfather Bedzo rolled and farted under the coronet of his cyberhat. A twitch of the corner of his mouth, a blast of steam from the overheat release valve sent it spinning half a hundred metres. The old man rocked and laughed as the mutineers put the rout beneath their wheels.

"I see her, I see her!" Miriamme Traction called from the forward observation balcony, Sweetness's former vantage. "She's waving a flare!" But even before Child'a'grace could call full stop, Bedzo was already applying the brakes. These striplings today understood nothing, respected nothing. Understood nothing because they respected nothing. Had no pride. Bedzo Trine Cirrus Minor Asiim Engineer 10th had been Engineer of Engineers. He would bring his train in so sweet, so smooth, the old lady would not even have to walk to the steps.

"I don't know where you popped up from, but you're going right back again," Sweetness said to Serpio, centimetre by centimetre climbing her legs.

She clubbed him hard with the St. Catherine pyx. He cried out, lifted his hands to his bleeding head, fell heavily to the ground.

"To think, I gave up a perfectly good stainless steel kitchen for you," Sweetness said, leaping nimbly over Serpio and sprinting for the other, unbarred door. But he was already on his feet, after her. God, he might be a Waymender, but he was fast. He dived for Sweetness, was knocked sideways with a crunching *oof* as Pharaoh came barrelling in in a sliding tackle that would have had any soccer player red carded. The two men rolled over and over in a tangle of attempted blows. Sweetness reflected casually, and inappropriately, how alike they looked.

"Out!" Pharaoh shouted. "Down and out!"

"You mean?" Sweetness winced as Pharaoh took an elbow in the ribs.

"The aperture, go on, go! Jump! I'll catch up."

They fell to it again. Sweetness hit the door catch, pelted down the short curving corridor and almost knocked down a very tall, very big woman dressed in purple cycle gear. Big muscles too. Sweetness jumped back. The big woman blocked her escape. She smiled, beckoned with her hand, *give, here.*

"Uh uh," Sweetness said and pulled out her beanie gun. Sianne Dandeever grinned like a skull and took a step forward.

"This will hurt, you know," Sweetness said, and shot her point blank. Sianne Dandeever's hand moved like a snake striking. She caught the bean bag in midair. She tossed it, caught it in her palm, smiled. Then she dived and brought Sweetness, beanie gun, canister and all down in a crunching tackle.

"Get off me, you big fat lesbian dyke!" Sweetness shouted and looked for something to bite but the big woman's big hands were forcing her fingers open. Then she heard a noise like wind-rotor blades slicing air, a soft-edge whistling, glimpsed, past the big body crushing the wind out of her, something back-flipping fast down the corridor. The willy-willy demon whirled past, something caught Harx's lieutenant a hefty whack on the back of the head, sending the big woman sprawling.

Skerry rolled out of her tumbling sequence as Sianne Dandeever shook the impact of grip-soled left foot out of her head and came up slugging. A *savatte* kick under the jaw sent her straight down again. Skerry cuffed her wrist to ankle with plastic wire grips.

Sweetness scrambled up, backed away, beanie gun levelled.

"I'll have that," Skerry said, advancing toward Sweetness.

"You will not."

"Look, I've had a difficult day. Just hand it over."

"Get away."

"I'm the government."

"You would say that."

"Don't make me take it off you. I can. I will."

Sweetness shook her head. Skerry saw her finger twitch on the firing stud of the beanie-gun.

"I think I should tell you, I'd not just catch that, I'd throw it right back at you as well."

"Oh yeah?" Sweetness said, swinging the beanie-gun a millimetre and firing at the pressure-seal emergency door switch she could see and she knew Skerry could not. Skerry caught a fistful of air as the metal semicircles slammed together in her face.

"Balls!" she muttered. She called up Seskinore. "The girl's got the thing and she's making a run for it. There's still a chance."

The bloody show must bloody go on.

"Please deposit three million dollars for the next ten minutes of personalised weather," the computer voice at Grand Valley Regional Weather said without the least flicker of irony. Weill lifted the telephone receiver away from his ear, looked at Seskinore.

Seskinore, listening on the monitor, shook his head and cut his throat with a terminating finger. Weill hung up without a word. Together, they watched the apocalypse dissolve into the early afternoon sunlight. Pursued, pursuer and pursuer-of-pursuer were now so far away down the long tunnel of Grand Valley only the airborne cathedral was visible, a wobbling orange oval. Rather like a flying dog-biscuit, Weill thought inconsequentially.

"The mission is a complete and unqualified lemon," Seskinore said ringingly. His fancies of summer seasons, charabanc picnics, celebrity bingo, maybe even once again doing the cruise trains, had evaporated like the cloud saints and angels. He was now and forever an unfunny comic with weak material in a too-small suit.

"No it isn't!" Skerry roared on the comline. "Get Mishcon in here, I'm going after the girl."

"Such a pro," Weill said, admiringly.

There comes a time in running, Sweetness discovered, when it is very easy to forget just why you are running, where to and who from. It is just running, pure and purposeless and absolutely chemical, and therefore very very silly and very very dangerous. She willed herself to stop, think, think girl. Think. Down and out, he had said. Back to the aperture. Aperture. Where had that been? Where was she now? Sweetness looked around for landmarks. Few and featureless in these circular corridors. Some cathedral this. No shrines of the saints, no centavo-a-candle angelic light-'em-ups. No swinging censers, no hand-hammered carillons, no statues with scary eyes that followed you around the place, suspicious of sin. No bells, few smells now that that weird perfume Pharaoh had complained about seemed to have dispersed. Not even piles of leaflets or self-sew purple habit kits or whatever mail-order paraphernalia the Church of the Ever-Circling Spiritual Family needed to conduct its business with God. The single piece of religious engineering she'd come across she'd climbed all over with her size sevens. She'd seen more spiritual tat in an arcade game.

Refreshed by her brief exercise in cynicism, Sweetness peered at the outer corridor wall. It sloped very slightly inward from top to bottom. Southern hemisphere. Any down ramp around her would do. She slipped back into running mode. Anything that got in her way, stuck a face round a corner, looked vaguely in her direction, she roared at. The things fled, shrieking thinly. There was obviously very much more going on here than she knew about; the angel-thing she had glimpsed through the shattered dome, the seeming plague of mass hysteria, the fit girl in the green leotard. All of them were up there, behind her somewhere, with the big hard woman and Pharaoh and that Serpio, and, ultimately, Harx himself. Don't think about it, Sweetness Octave. You've got what you came for. You get in, you get it, you get out. The rest will sort itself.

Her traingirl sense stopped her in midstride. Here. She skipped back a step. The tunnel looked the same as all the others in this forsaken burg, but ripples in her water insisted: here, yes, really. She rounded a dog's leg and saw sky. A lot of sky. Into which she was meant to jump with little more than her trust in the home-brew parafoil on her back. And she had done the Point of Worst Personal Threat bit. The Feisty and Resourceful (But Cute With It) Heroine was into narrative *terra incognita*. She edged up to the lip. Crosswinds buffeted her; the cathedral started and swayed as if taking evasive action. She could still hear gunfire from overhead. She crept forward, took a peek at the ground. Seen worse. Risked higher. Still far enough and hard enough to kill you dead dead dead.

"Why is there never a Plan B?" she pleaded with the Laws of Universal Narratology as she secured the Catherine bottle in a breast pocket of her track jacket and braced herself against the side. Wind whipped her hair into her eyes. She tried to comb the greasy, stinky, sticky stuff out of her eyes, lost her balance as the Church of the Ever-Circling Spiritual Family seemed to drop out from underneath her and fell into the void.

"Aaaagh!" she cried, staring at a plan view of the undulating drumlin country of Canton Thrench. Then her hands found the rip cord, thirty square metres unfolded above her and she was jerked up into the air. "Oooh," said Sweetness Asiim Engineer, flying. Pharaoh had given her verbal instructions in the control of the parafoil but they had been strictly just-in-case. Sweetness shifted her weight in the harness, pulled on the guys to scoop air into the left winglet and went spiralling up the side of the cathedral.

The sound of gunfire grew louder and closer. Maybe not that way.

She spilled lift, slid downward and forward. She slid out from underneath the belly of the cathedral into clear air. Grand Valley opened before her.

"Weee!" she whooped. Beneath her feet the Grand Valley trunk line was four streaks of silver meeting in a wink of light at the vanishing point. There was a loco on those tracks. A deadheader, no train, but putting out a lot of steam. Someone was really whipping the tokamaks down there. The funnel configuration identified it as a Class 88. Black and silver livery, Bethlehem Ares. Sweetness peered closer. Those patterns on the roof, and that finial on the tender: a roaring Iron Lion? And, at the limits of vision, covering the boiler cap with her wings, was that a figurehead of a silver angel, proud-breasted?

"Pharaoh, look, look, it's *Catherine of Tharsis*, I know it, I'd know that old train anywhere, we're safe!"

Pharaoh. What had happened to him? She scooped deeply into the wind, bought altitude to rise level with the hole in the hull At the outward edge of her turn, she had seen other aircraft in full pursuit of Harx; one a small, minnow-like racing yacht, the other a big grampus, a heavy lifter. They seemed to be occupying the full attention of the gunners who were spraying black arcs of tracer indiscriminately toward them.

Pharaoh was standing in the gaping rent, looking down at the ground beneath him, fingering his harness. As Sweetness swooped past him, he waved.

"Pharaoh, they've come back for me!" she shouted. "*Catherine of Tharsis*. I knew they wouldn't give me up. They're down there, we're safe! Come on!"

Hand on rip-cord, Pharaoh stepped into the air. In the same instant, a dark mass leaped from the shadows in the corridor and seized him around the waist. Serpio. The airfoil opened but the combined weight of two bodies was too much for Vertical Boy engineering. Air boomed, seams tore, the wing folded up in the middle, failed. Locked together in a final, ludicrous embrace, Serpio and Pharaoh plunged down in a fluttering, tearing death spiral to the meadowlands of Trench below.

$\mathscr{S}$kerry clung to the edge of the punctured corridor, riven with sick doubts. Seconds before, she had seen the two young men fight and fall to their deaths. No purpose, no logic, no great cause served, no noble sacrifice. Just the momentary blindness of aggression. Boys and their competition. Fight, and fight to the death.

Dying is easy. Comedy is hard.

They would still be falling.

Ha ha ha ha ha ha ha. How we laughed.

"Bastards!" she suddenly swore, kicking and punching at the jagged exposed metal in the hope it would tear and hurt her. The soft airframe aluminium and plastic bent under her hard hands and feet. "Bastards bastards bastards!"

She was Skerry Scanland Ghalgorm. She could flip and swing and juggle. She could walk tightrope and walk on her hands and walk over fire. She could swing trapeze and sway-pole and do rope tricks that would make your mouth hang open in amazement. She could put both legs behind her neck. She was an entertainer. A provider of simple spectacle and wonder; a Good Night Out. She was not a secret government agent. She was not a Synodical warrior. She did kids' parties. The Anarchs had no place, no place at all, asking her to run the End of the World, fight people, watch people fall to their deaths.

But what of the show, Skerry Scanland Ghalgorm? Always, the show. She took a deep centring breath and called Mishcondereya on the bindi-mike.

"Mish, I've lost her. She's got away."

Mishcondereya swore. Apparently the only subject her gentleladies' finishing school taught well was Cursing and Advanced Cursing.

"I'm going after her. I need pick-up," Skerry said.

After a pause clearly meant to be significant, Mishcondereya said, "It may have escaped your attention, but they'd shoot their own shadows back here."

"Mishcon, I need pick-up. I know we can get her, I know we can get the Catherine artifact." She saved the Portentous Line for last, though she doubted Mishcondereya had a functioning sense of portent. "If we don't, Harx will."

Heavy sigh. You love it, Skerry thought. If you hadn't become a state comedian, you would have been a rich-girl terrorist. The action, the toys, the scent of men, the tang of alfresco sex, the adventure. You live it, you love it, you think. But you would think different if you had seen two boys who loved it as much as you, and for the same reasons, earn the bitter pay-off.

"All right, I'm coming in. Give me your fix."

Buffeted by surface winds—Harx was taking this thing low and fast— Skerry touched her throat jewel. Seconds later, the blunt nose of the sky-yacht nudged into view beneath her. It crept up on the frantically pedalled airship until half its length underhung the much larger orange bulk, like a pilot fish pacing a shark. Skerry waited for Mishcondereya to lock engines. You get one shot at this.

She picked her spot on the skin.

Never a safety net, Skerry?

Arms spread, she swallow dived into the yielding cushion of the gas bag.

"I can take her out, one shot," Sianne Dandeever said, rubbing her still-chafed wrists. His Holiness's rescue party could have come a little more expeditiously. She rested her hand on the heavy Sharps' rifle's wooden stock, casually swung the sights toward the dwindling figure of Sweetness beneath her flying wing. She badly wanted to punish someone for her humiliation. The cathedral's aux-con was an architecturally incongruous glass teat at the apex of the pseudo-classical portico of the Pilgrim's Steps. From here two people could command and fight the full edifice and company.

"You will do no such thing," Devastation Harx retorted. "We might still need it, in which case, I want it somewhere I can find it, not spread all over Grand Valley."

"Do we need it?" Sianne Dandeever asked. "And if we don't, can I have a shot anyway?"

"That we will find out very soon," Devastation Harx said, taking an orbital uplinker from inside his jacket. Sianne Dandeever blinked at the blasphemous machine. "Oh, for goodness sake woman, even God needs good rolling stock." In a flicker of data and twittering, the little device reported on the state of his many fronts. In ten minutes he would be out from under this accursed roof, where he could get a once-and-for-all shot at these impudent pranksters in their airships with the partacs. Waves eight and nine were entering the upper atmosphere, the first four squadrons were down, shifted into ground combat configuration and were moving into occupation positions. The global communication network was buzzing with madness and rumour. Let it. Soon and very soon it would be silenced. The more they talked, the more they watched the pretty lights in the sky, the less they would suspect his true strategy. That was the eternal secret of all gods. Keep watching the pretty lights in the sky.

Then, one by one, he would put those pretty lights out. The infiltration of the reality shaping computers was almost complete. The simulacrum was perfect. St. Catherine herself would seem to give the command for the Artificial Intelligences to switch themselves off, then command of the multiverse would pass to its rightful users, the dirty, bustling, conniving, inquisitive, mortal humans.

"She's getting away," Sianne Dandeever warned.

Harx looked up from his schemes of splendour. He should know where that irritating little girl was going, in case something did go wrong with the protocols and he needed to access the original St. Catherine program. She was almost out of sight, spiralling lower and lower.

"Where are you going, you vexatious child?" Harx mused.

"Go on, your Holiness, just one shot," Sianne Dandeever.

Then he saw the contrail of steam, the mirror steel lines, the blue and silver of a Bethlehem Ares fusion hauler.

"Of course! So loyal! Sianne, take us down."

"Down it is."

Never a question, never a query. He should have tried to get his hand into those thigh-hugging pants.

"We have a train to catch."

In contrast to her departure, Taal Chordant Joy-of-May Asiim Engineer 10th's return to *Catherine of Tharsis* was loud, crowded and chaotic. So many people on the bridge, all wanting her to answer their questions before they answered hers.

"What have you done to yourself?" Her old friend Miriamme Deep-Fusion's voice cut through the babble with the one question everyone wanted answered but were too in awe of the terrible old lady to ask.

"A form of rejuvenation I would not recommend. It is most efficacious, but the price is excessive. Now, enough enough enough. I am senior here, it is you who must answer my questions," Grandmother Taal said, glad to feel the creak and shift of hull-plates under her square-heeled boots again. "Where is everyone? Where is my son? What has happened to the train?"

A chorus of voices babeled answers. Grandmother Taal held up her hands for silence.

"Mutiny?"

The mutineers looked at each other, all except Grandfather Bedzo, deeply enmeshed in driving his train.

"For Sweetness," Child'a'grace said.

"Hmph," said Grandmother Taal. "Well, I suppose it's an exceptional circumstance and my son and that Stuard could well do with a lesson in humility, but I would not condone it as a general course of action."

Relief was general and unabashed. Into it, Child'a'grace asked, mildly, "So, where exactly is Sweetness Octave?"

Grandmother Taal craned around her to peer out of the window. She pointed.

"There, I suspect."

Everyone turned to witness a spectacle almost certainly unique in aviation. It was like an animated lesson in marine ecology: big fish eats littler fish eats weeniest fish. Well to the rear was a massive cargo-lift airship, vast as a cloud. Ahead of it, no less small, was what could only be described as a flying cathedral, vaguely saucer-shaped with heavy Palladian pretensions, incongruously coloured earth-orange. Squeezing out from underneath the cathedral and pushing slowly ahead was a silver trout-shaped aircraft, sleek and streamlined, and in the lead, beating courageously down the sky, was the tiny delta wing of an airfoil. Everyone could see the dark speck hanging beneath it. The whole flying circus bore down on *Catherine of Tharsis* like muscular theology.

"That would be our Sweetness."

Pursuit was good. Challenge was good. Danger was good. Tough flying was good. Everything was good that kept out that final image of Pharaoh and Serpio, locked together, falling through the killing air. Concentrate. Not much longer. Not much further. Line up on that great big beautiful steamy train there. A few hundred metres. Then you'll be home. Then you'll be safe. Then you'll be among people who know you and your story can end and you can go back to your little cubby. Just you and Little Pretty One again.

You can't go back, Sweetness. You're a traingirl, you supped that truth with your mother's milk. You can go everywhere, anywhere, all around the world, but never back. The tracks only lead forward.

She navigated in over *Catherine of Tharsis*. Whoever had their hand on the drive bar was good, matching her speed, compensating in an instant for her wobbles and surges as she carefully spilled lift, lining up on the back of the tender. Twenty metres, ten metres. She wove from side to side of the steam plume, checking her positioning. Up there behind her, she could feel the presence of heavy aerial machinery on the back of her neck. Ignore them. If they want to blow you away, they can do it any time. Concentrate on getting down. Down. Down . . .

Her toe-tips brushed the top of the tender, an eddy lifted her into the vapour trail. Moment's blindness. She fought for control, stabilised, came in again. Almost almost almost . . . She tugged on the guy lines simultaneously, spilling lift, and touched down at a run in the middle of the tender. Immediately, figures—people! trainpeople! her people!—came surging off the access ladder, seized her, stripped off her flying harness and carried her down.

Sweetness babbled, recognising the faces of her bearers, trying to touch them, remember them.

"Psalli, Romereaux, Anhinga, it's you. Thwayte, what are you doing here?"

She was borne along a sidewalk up a companionway through a shunting turret. She could feel the train was picking up speed again. Sweetness glanced backward. The cathedral eclipsed half the sky, the little air-yacht almost crushed between the two heavyweights of earth and air. On the driving bridge the people she loved were waiting for her. Her bearers set her down and immediately Child'a'grace hugged her.

"Your hair is needing washing, child," she remonstrated.

Sweetness plucked at a greasy coil, then all the tension excitement fear confusion horror exhaustion dread wonder puzzlement loneliness hunger sleeplessness vertigo love loss and death of the days since she had ridden away from the grand steaming ruptured. She burst into tears. Her family, Dorniety and non-Domiety rushed in to comfort her. Thus only Ricardo Traction noticed the shadow fall over the windows.

"Um, I hate to disturb you, but we seem to have a cathedral on the roof."

Everyone looked up, the world went red, and they were somewhere else entirely.

*R*ed. Red heaven, red earth. Red hills, red soil, red stones. Red sky, red sun, red lines of thin cloud at the close horizon. Bethlehem Ares Class 88 fusion hauler *Catherine of Tharsis*, pride of the fleet, stood in a half-kilometre length of neatly severed track in the middle of endless, featureless red.

Numb silence. Utter dislocation. Then young Thwayte Engineer cried out in sudden pain, clapped hands to ears. In the same instant, everyone became aware of a hissing scream, like steam escaping from a fractured pipe. Scattered papers flew up, across the room like carrion birds and packed themselves against the bottom of the starboard catwalk door.

"We're under vacuum!" Romereaux shouted, however impossible that seemed, and rushed to open an ancient, paint-sealed red box on the bulkhead with a fire-axe. *Catherine of Tharsis* was an old-school hauler, a veteran from the days of the manforming when the air was still thin and dead and Big Stuff needed shifting, and fusion-powered steam locomotives had been a useful way of getting water vapour into the primitive atmosphere. Her inner corridors and habitations had been designed to be pressure tight, however those seals might have perished with time and travel, and she still carried tubes of puncture goop in the Emergency DeePee boxes. Two blows hacked the casing off; Romereaux and Ricardo Traction wove streams of fast-drying foam goop over the bottom of the door, layer upon layer upon acetic-smelling layer until the piercing whistle dwindled to a whisper to nothing.

"Where the hell are we?" Romereaux asked.

A shriek aborted any offers of an answer. Mercedes Deep-Fusion stood pointing a quivery finger at Grandfather Bedzo. The aged aged man was slumped in his seat. His hands swung at his sides, bloated with pooled blood. His eyes were half-open. A thick rope of glossy drool hung from his protruding tongue to his chest. He did not seem to be breathing.

"Is he, is he, is he?" Mercedes stammered.

He looked anyone's definition of dead as dead could be.

Anhinga Engineer, who had trained as a Knight of the Healing Joans, knelt by the old man, felt for pulses, tested for breath.

"He's still alive, just about."

"Get him to sick bay!" Romereaux ordered.

"We left sick bay back in Axidy, remember?" Anhinga said. Everyone slowly turned round to look at the alien world outside the windows.

"Really, where the hell are we?" Romereaux said sombrely.

Sweetness spoke up.

"Okay, you're not going to like this."

"We don't like it anyway," Thwayte Engineer said.

"Well, I think we're in exactly the same place we were. We haven't moved at all. Well, not forward or backward. I think what's happened is, we've moved sideways. Across universes, if you like. Parallel worlds, all a little bit different. Harx sent us further than most. That's why poor ould Bedzo's in the state he's in. The shock of transition. We all blacked out for a moment; he was plugged into the cyberhat, what must it've been like for the whole system to go down when we made the jump?"

"So, he's not driving us out of here," Ricardo Traction said.

"Looks like no one's driving us out of this one," Romereaux commented unhelpfully. "There isn't even any air."

"Harx did this?" Grandmother Taal asked.

"He had these mirrors could look into other universes," Sweetness went on, aware of how frenetic this would sound in any other circumstance. "It's where he got his power from: he wanted St. Catherine so he could get more of that power by getting hold of the angels that built the world by shuffling through the multiverse until they found the best of all possible worlds."

"Whoa whoa whoa whoa," Romereaux interrupted. "This goondah has sent us across the multiverse into an alternative of our world?"

"That's what I think."

"We're buggered."

"Do you want to know how buggered?" Sweetness said.

"Can it get any worse?"

"I think this is an alternative world where the manforming never happened. That means, no air. Meaning, all the air we have, is in here. Eventually, we'll run out. We've already lost a lot."

"So, have we a plan for getting back?" the pragmatic Ricardo Traction asked. Diving through that carriage door into mutiny had been the only spontaneous thing he had ever done. Now look where it had landed him. That's what you got for allowing yourself to be whirled up in the mood of the moment.

He led the inquiring expressions at Sweetness.

"Hey, I'm not a vinculum physicist," she said. Sarcasms and recriminations burned more air. "There's something I want to try, but I need to go to my cubby, right?"

Devastation Harx tried to restrain his delight. The symbols on his uplinker were dropping back out of the imaginary plane into the concrete world of integers. Incursion into the multiverse complete. He snapped the plastic lid shut.

"You know, I wasn't entirely sure that would work," he said to an awed Sianne Dandeever. All chances of worker's playtime banished forever there. Gods don't shag the believers, and with his demonstration of multiversal engineering, he surely qualified for that league.

"We don't need her any more, then," the faithful lieutenant said, nodding to the place *Catherine of Tharsis* had been.

"Ah, no," said Devastation Harx.

The Cathedral of the Ever-Circling Spiritual Family hovered over a precision-cut half-kilometre circle of other world. The Grand Valley mainline led in, the mainline ran out, in the middle, dead red grit and rocks. The airship still rocked gently from the inrush of air as near vacuum was displaced into atmosphere.

Devastation Harx looked around from the vantage of his high glass pulpit.

"Now," he said, dusting off his hands, "who else has irritated me today?"

How sweet, Sweetness thought. They had kept her cubby unchanged since the day she left. Then again, she thought as she unscrewed the cap of the pyx, it wasn't as if she had wandered away for years uncountable, and, with most of her stash of precious things in her backsac, there wasn't much to identify a process of change. But it was nice to think they had kept it as a shrine to her.

Sweetness shook out the roll of quantum-plastic mirror and gunge-tacked it to the back of the cubby door.

"You lied to me," was the first thing Sweetness Asiim Engineer said to her double, dressed, as ever, in what she had been wearing the day before, which was identical to today's apart from the parafoil harness, which Sweetness had forgotten to remove in the rush of it all.

Little Pretty One spread her hands apologetically.

"Yes, but in a very real sense, no."

"You pretended to be my twin sister; in fact, you're Catherine of Tharsis, the woman who made the world, who, for some reason, decided one day to walk out on heaven and live in a mirror with me. Where's the no in this?"

"Guilty on that count. You'd know about deciding one day to walk out."

"It's not the same at all."

"Isn't it? You think it's a thrill-a-nanosecond, living as an AI? Let me tell you, these guys get off on abstract mathematics. The intellectual glory and wonder of infinite prime dimensions. After a millennium or two, a girl gets to thinking, maybe this mortification of the flesh isn't what it's cracked up to be after all. Maybe you get an itch to see what the meat's up to these days. I never was a scientist, you know. I was a construction worker. Strictly blue collar, that was Kathy Haan."

"Enough enough, all right? So, you thought you'd take a couple of decades' vacation in the flesh, but don't call me sis, you are not my sister."

Little Pretty One looked at her feet, which, because of the size of the cramped cabin, had been rolled up, but were presumably visible in whatever kind of state she inhabited.

"No, you're right, I shouldn't call you sis. It's a lot closer than that."

"Don't give me this."

"In an absolutely real sense, I am you, you are me. You are Kathy Haan, reborn, the best of her, the good in her, the bits that got lost in the madness and the 'Spirituality.' They were all stored in the matrix whenever I went eternal. They didn't go away. They wanted to come back. They wanted to live. So, we made a body for them to live in. Me, here in the mirror, that's the rest of you, the unseen part. The divine twin. We are sisters, we are joined, a lot closer than you could ever imagine."

"I'm a ghost," Sweetness said wanly. She sat down on her bunk. "You're real, and I'm the ghost in the mirror. My whole life has been lies. Everything I've lived, it hasn't been for me at all. It's been for you."

"No," Little Pretty One said with the gentleness of spring rains. "You couldn't be more wrong. You are you. You are living your life, once, for you. I watch, I feel, but I can never get inside your head. I can never share your sense of youness. I can never know your experience of what it is to be a person."

"This is heavy shit," Sweetness said after a time, shaking her head.

"Yes, and, in a very real sense, no. You just do what you're doing. So tell me, how has your life been?"

Images of a life thus far. Golden dawn over the high north desert, seen from her forward lookout, the sun rising huge out of the shimmer at the edge of the world so that she seemed to be driving into its very heart. The Great Snow, blowing up from Borealis, when *Catherine of Tharsis* plunged headlong into a huge drift and got stuck and they all sat around in the tea room, drank mint tea played card games and told stories while the Deep-Fusions tweaked the tokamak thermal output to melt them all free. The first explosion of wonder at Belladonna's Undercroft decked out for the Five Hundred Founders Day celebrations; firmly gripping Child'a'grace's hand as she peered over the edge of the railing down into the kilometre-deep vertical street lined with more shops than anywhere else in the known universe. The first time she got drunk at a corroboree and tried to pull Blasniq Bassareeni and Sle and Rother'am had to drag her off before she disgraced the family name. The first time she toddled away from *Catherine of Tharsis* and looked back and saw her world whole for the first time, a steaming dragon in which she lived. The dealings, the pickups, the drop-offs, the shuntings and couplings, the long slow hauls, the brilliant fast express runs, the hypnotic boredom of the endless straight track up over the north pole, the cleaning and the pride in the brass work and the time the School of the Air teacher had given her the gold star for her essay on the weather. The wonders of desert storms and high plains lightnings; the rains sweeping in black curtains across the hills of Deuteronomy. The huge nights when you felt you could pull the moonring from the sky and take it for a bracelet, when a hundred stars all started moving at once and you knew it was a Praesidium Sailship, bigger than the runty moon, setting out on its journey to the other worlds and peoples of System. The knowledge that the morning would always bring a new place and time. And more, and more. Hers. All hers. Uniquely, trivially, gloriously, personally, hers.

"Life's been good," she said thoughtfully, then sat up straight, the old light in her eyes. "No," she said, "no; I've been lost, starved, shot at, dropped from a great height, betrayed, used, confused, fallen in love twice, crossed deserts, flown through the air, battled duststorms, watched star wars, fought terrible foes, faced down people with the powers of gods, run for my life, been picked up, thrown away, travelled into other universes, fought wars, been shat upon from a very great height, been a story, been fired halfway across the multiverse, it's nowhere near over yet and I haven't a notion how it's all going to end but I have to say this, it's been great. I've had a ball. Your wild things have been having the time of their lives. You don't know what you're missing."

Little Pretty One smiled a pickled smile.

"You wish you were me, don't you?" Sweetness said.

"You have no idea how much I wish that."

"Do me a favour then, for this life I've lived for you."

"Name it."

"Get us out of here."

"Ah," said Our Lady of Tharsis.

"Say again?"

"I was rather hoping you had some ideas on that. You see, I kind of need to get back. You should see what they're doing to my world."

"I thought you were supposed to be divine."

"I am. But just because I'm a god, that doesn't mean I'm omnipotent. I can control the reality-shapers, but only if they're there. All there is in that sky are a couple of tatty little moons."

"So we're stuck. And I've wasted God knows how much valuable air talking to you."

"I wouldn't say wasted. And I didn't say stuck."

"You know, I'm not surprised I'm the best of you," Sweetness said.

The figure in the mirror sighed.

"Now, if you could get me back to our reality again, then I might be able to do something. I'd certainly pull the plug on Mr. Harx's operation, shut down that invasion and, somewhere in between all that, I could probably find time to send you a bit of help."

"Why don't you just tell me how?"

"You're the heroine, you're supposed to work it out for yourself. All the clues are there."

"How about a starter?"

Little Pretty One pondered this gracefully for a moment, finger to lips.

"Okay. What's outside?"

"Bit of rail, lot of dead grass, couple of dead birds, lot of red dirt red rock red sky red hills red clouds . . ."

Sweetness stopped, mid-litany, kicked in the diaphragm by fierce understanding. She flung open the cubby door, slamming Little Pretty One against the wall, burned precious oxygen hurtling along the corridors and up the steel staircases to the starboard track-observation oriole. The howling cold of the great red desert was starting to penetrate the turret, making her fingers thick and stupid as she fumbled with the opticon.

"Come on, come on."

She swept the objective across the featureless terrain, left, right, in, out. There.

"Oh yes!" She punched the air.

Far off across the redscape, foot wreathed in carbon dioxide mists, the sole vertical in all this monstrous horizontality, was the lone steel pole of a signal light.

Skerry and Mishcondereya stared.

"Did you see what he just did?" Skerry asked.

"I can show you the replay on video if you want," Mishcondereya said. "I think that kind of proves we lost that one."

"What happens next?"

"I'll tell you what happens next," Mishcondereya said, directing Skerry's attention to Harx's predatory, hovering cathedral as it slowly turned on its central axis toward them. She pulled back on the altitude stick, simultaneously floored the drive stirrups. The air yacht bucked like a rodeo llama, shot straight up at forty-five degrees at an acceleration that pressed Skerry deep into her seat upholstery. Mishcondereya commed up Bladnoch, who had taken aboard the rest of United Artists and was waiting with them ten kays up valley in UA2.

"UA2, UA2, execute Plan Curtain Down, repeat, Plan Curtain Down. Harx has control of reality-shaping weapons. Get the hell as far away as fast as you can." Mishcondereya banked fiercely, levelled off just under Worldroof, opened the fans as far as they would go. "Tell you something. I can't wait to read the reviews in the morning."

As she trudged across the frosty dead regolith in her five layers of underwear and radiation-proof suit, Sweetness amused herself by trying to fit all this into being a story. That she still was, was patently evident. You didn't volunteer to go out the emergency anti-radiation lock wrapped up in borrowed socks, T-shirts and a double layer of baking foil if the laws of narrative weren't still playing a prominent role in your life. Obviously, she was beyond the False Denouement-Microanticlimax, but was it the Third Act Last-Minute Reversal of Fortunes, or was this ultimate Point of No Return, where things get as bad as they possibly can, and then everything rolls over into the Final Scene?

Out here, in this isolating, airless, dizzyingly featureless place, where all you could hear was the sound of your own breathing and the tap of the (strictly rationed) respirator, the expression Point of No Return carried too much additional significance.

What on earth had made people look at this place and think, yeah, we could turn that into a nice habitable little planet?

God, but her feet were cold. And her hands. She flapped her arms, trying to beat heat into them. The suit might be thermal foil, but all it seemed to do was reflect the little external heat from the tiny, wan sun.

Was that really the same sun?

Still less than halfway to the gantry. Her family had thought her head blasted by the interworld transition, like Grandfather Bedzo, but they had no better explanation for the incontrovertible existence of a Transpolaris Traction signal light out in the desert.

Sweetness paused to haul up her arms, hoick up her crotch. The radiation-proof suit was also gas-tight, but it came only in sizes large and extra-large, and she was terrified of tripping over a fold of foil that had drooped around her ankles, ripping the fabric on one of those nasty wind-sharpened stones and dying alone out here in the cold with blood coming out of her ears and eyes.

The one good thing about the Point of No Return, she decided, was that anything after it was an anticlimax, so things could not get any worse than this and they would all be home and happy soon.

Caution abandoned, she ran the last few metres over the ragged rocks to the signal tower, rested her palm against it, took ten, fifteen deep breaths. The libation. You always give him something. She unhooked the flask of mint tea from the Velcro chest patch, uncapped it, poured. The liquid flashed to vapour before it hit the ground.

"Uncle Neon."

"Sweetness, child!" said the godlike voice in her head, a little startled, as if disturbed from private contemplation. "What a pleasant surprise! How is everyone, what's the news, it's been a while since I last heard of all your doings and undoings. Or has it? Is that a new outfit you're wearing? I must say, it does nothing for you. Wasted your money there."

"Uncle, I haven't time to explain. I need you to send a message."

"Not a foretelling? You don't want to know about the baby Sle's going to have with that Cussite girl he hasn't married yet?"

"Uncle, just send a message, back home."

A pause. Sweetness could imagine the discourses running through her poor mad uncle's eotemporal brain: why can't the child take it herself; back home, where is that, why is that? where is this place I find myself, am I indeed dead, has this all been dreams arcing through my head from that final lightning, am I in heaven or hell or somewhere not quite either?

"What is this message?" Uncle Neon asked.

"It's not so much a what, as a who," Sweetness said, unVelcroing the canopic jar and, with ice-numb fingers, fumbling off the lid. "See?" She held the mirror up to the three eyes of the signal lights like an ancient scroll.

"I most certainly do," said Uncle Neon. "One moment . . ."

When she rolled it up again, the mirror was empty of any image of Sweetness Asiim Engineer. As she stomped back toward the cordillera-like mass of *Catherine of Tharsis*, Sweetness turned to hold the roll of plastic film out to the rising wind, like a spinnaker.

"Look for me in mirrors," had been Little Pretty One's final whisper before Uncle Neon launched her back down the link that Sweetness alone and always had been able to exploit to bring her to this other world.

She let go of the mirror. The wind caught it and whipped it away like a sail, around and around and over and over, tumbling away, a blink of light, on the eternal gales.

It took ten minutes of concentrated rubbing by Romereaux before sensation returned to her feet and hands and then that was pins and needles that had her hopping in agony around the bridge, oohing and aahing.

"You're wasting our air," sour Ricardo said.

"Look, I went out there," Sweetness said, dancing up and down on her points. "Anyway, help's coming."

"Aye, and when?"

Not in the first hour, the hour of confident expectation.

"She's got a lot to do," Sweetness explained.

Nor in the second hour, the hour of settling down patiently.

"Maybe he put up more of a fight than she expected," was Sweetness's rationalisation.

Nor the third hour either, which, when your air is strictly budgeted, is the hour of creeping doubt.

"There're all those cybersoldiers, remember," Sweetness said let's-not-be-selfishly.

But the help did not come in the fourth hour, nor the fifth hour, nor the sixth hour, when the air is hot and foul and so heavy with carbon dioxide all you can do is sit with your back against the cooling bulkhead and count things over and over and over again.

"Help?" Ricardo croaked.

"I don't know," Sweetness said. "I don't know at all."

Then the cry came from the window, a little, oxygen-choked croak.

"Out there," Grandmother Taal stammered. Everyone crawled to the window, heaved themselves up over the sill.

Something like a very small dust-devil was moving across the Big Red, cutting straight across the dirt and red rocks as if possessed of a volition and a destination. It was heading straight for *Catherine of Tharsis*. Sweetness felt a silly, oxygen-wasting laugh bubble inside her, a laugh she could not keep down, that boiled out of her like her offering tea flashing to vapour as she poured it out.

A bit of help indeed.

The whirlwind rushed up to the side of the train, mounted the boarding ramp, spun along the walkways and stairways until it came to the pressure outlock. Then everyone on the bridge heard a hammering on the lock door.

"Open, in the name of Beelzebub!"

31

*T*he pressure-lock door closed behind the strange little man. He had long white hair tied back at his shoulders with a gold ring and long mustachios which he kept sharply waxed. His eyes were deep and darkly bright. He wore a long desert duster coat and a big-brimmed hat with a ludicrously jaunty feather in its band. On his back was a complex pack of many devices and power cables, including a handy-looking field-inducer tucked into the pocket of his coat and a whirring object that looked like a small sewing machine. He carried around him a translucent bubble of force that seemed to hold his own atmosphere. He twisted a setting ring on the field inducer. The bubble popped audibly. The oxygen-starved people of *Catherine of Tharsis* smelled purple heathers and autumn seaside. To them, the little man looked a little blurred at the edge, slightly out of focus, like a television picture on the edge of a transmission footprint. They thought it was their foggy minds. Sweetness knew better. The traveller was on the extreme edge of his probability locus. He took a step forward out of the lock, removed his gloves, banged them together, kicked the dust off his battered desert boots, sniffed, grimaced.

"It mings a bit in here."

He sought Sweetness, doffed his hat and bowed in the formal Old Deuteronomy way to her.

"My dear, Dr. Alimantando, multiversal engineer and transtemporal tourist at your service. I have been expressly purposed by Our Lady of Tharsis herself with the task of taking you anywhere in the multiverse you wish to go."

"Home would be good," Sweetness said. "Home would be very good."

"Tokamaks ready?" asked Sweetness Octave Glorious Honey-Bun Asiim Engineer 12th.

"Ready," came Romereaux's voice from the gosport.

"Traction engaged?"

"Traction set," Ricardo called up from the transmission tunnel.

"Timewinder ready?"

"Ready, aye ready," came the voice of the doctor from the arcane bowels of systems engineering. "Hooked up and running sweet as a child's top."

"Then let's go home," Sweetness Engineer said, and moved her hand to the great brass drive bar. Her fingers opened to grasp it. And froze. Suddenly, sitting there in the Engineer's chair, navigation sphere under her left hand like an orb, the sceptre of the drive control waiting for the touch of her right, she could not do it. It was everything. Everything. The years, the days, the nights, the dreams, the anger, the frustration, the investment of hope and joy, the aspired to the wished for the painfully desired the loved thing the completing thing and now it lay under her palm and she could not do it. Should not do it.

Girls don't drive.

She licked her lips, looked to her mother on her right side.

"Go on, my child."

What if she did it and, after all, it was nothing? The train moves, the train stops. The train moves again, stops again. What if that was all there was to it, what if that was the secret the Engineer men kept from their women? That's all there is. Nothing special.

She looked at Grandmother Taal on her left.

"I'll give you such a slap," she said tetchily.

Sweetness grinned, seized the bar and pushed it forward. And it was precisely as special as she wanted it to be. And that, she understood, was all the secret of the Engineers. Tokamaks flared, water flashed to agonised steam, thundered down pipes, turned cranks, turned wheels within wheels about wheels that drove a belt looped around the spindle of the machine that looked like a small sewing machine. Inside, vincular dimensions spun. The doctor rubbed his hands with glee and watched his fiendish little device, nested among the brute force heavy metal engineering.

Wheels spun. The big train inched forward. Laughing, Sweetness pushed the drive rod up, up. *Catherine of Tharsis* began to roll, not along the snatch of track, through alternative universes. White light seemed to break around the cab window, they were in the middle of a cavalry charge of six-legged monsters ridden by four-armed green creatures with fangs and swords. Flash. Now a dry and delicate desert place, in the distance, a city of crystal windows and fragile towers. A swarm of silver locusts parted around the speeding train.

Sweetness pushed the handle up, up. Flash. Tall metal tripods stalked a landscape of green canals and hive cities. Flash flash. A parade ground in a great spire-capped city, filled with creatures like mushrooms. Flash. A howling red desert, a lone spaceship standing on its tail, an object like an animate ice-yacht sailing away, a human infant cradled at its heart. Flash. More cavalry, grim-faced riders on outsize ferrets leaping a barbed-wire barricade. A sterile red desert, an archaeologist in a transparent spacesuit, and in the sky, a malevolent red moon. A landscape littered with massive terraforming machinery. A single red crater with a smiley face drawn on it. Flash flash flash. Sweetness drove the timewinder up, up, up. A forest of clattering plastic windmills. A big rocket with a big red star on its tail. The universes were coming so fast now she was afforded no more than a glimpse before bursting through into the next. But a trend was apparent, they were moving from uninhabited, inhospitable worlds to her own little green world.

Green hills, an endless glass roof, an orange air-borne cathedral.

Sweetness jerked back the drive bar, overshot by a few dimensions into a smoking battlefield swarming with killing machines, reversed up universe by universe.

"We're back!"

She pulled out the gosport, whistled down to systems.

"Doctor!" No answer. "Doctor!" Still no answer. A third time: "Doctor!" As she had expected, the probability of his existence in this space of this time in this universe had dropped to zero.

Sweetness slumped back in the Engineer's chair. Doors were opened, windows thrown wide. Grand Valley's air smelled sweet as Isidy wine. Sweetness drank it down, touched a playful finger to the drive bar, shivered in private delight as the trainpeople came up from their stations and section to celebrate their return. Romereaux offered a hand to Sweetness, *come on, you've earned it.* She shook her head, looked at the navigation ball under her left hand. A world in her palm. Anywhere you like.

"I hate to disturb things," came Ricardo Traction's maithering voice, "but we've still got a cathedral on the roof."

"And there's an awful lot of robots headed our way," Thwayte added.

The party froze.

"Oh my God!" Sweetness moaned. "Is there no end to this story?"

As she gave the curse, she knew where she was in the universal narrative—the Unexpected Resurgence of the Villain—and what she must do to resolve it and bring her story to a conclusion. By her right hand was the evacuation alarm. She punched the bright red toadstool, hard. Yellow flashing lights leaped to life, sirens yammered.

"Are you deaf?" Sweetness shouted at the startled, pale faces. "Get out! This is an evacuation, get off the train, go on, everybody off, get back to the tender!"

"My daughter . . ." Child'a'grace began.

"Don't argue, I know what I'm doing. Get back to the tender, I'm going to sort this thing with Harx once and for all."

Such talk clears bridges. Ricardo and Thwayte pulled Bedzo plug-free from the cyberhat and wheeled the comatose old gent to the escape hatch. Child'a'grace and Miriamme Traction scooped up Grandmother Taal, who was for staying with her wayward granddaughter. Romereaux was last to clear the battle zone. He looked back, as he knew he must, as Sweetness hoped he would.

"What about you?"

"I'll be all right," Sweetness said. The door sealed. She glanced up at the thumb-nail monitors. She saw Romereaux close the hatch to the tender. The rest of *Catherine of Tharsis* was empty. The exterior eyes told her the metal men were getting uncomfortably close. Looking up, the roof cameras told her what she hoped; the sudden return to this universe had jammed parts of the complex undersurface of Harx's flying cathedral against *Catherine of Tharsis's* corporate gingerbread.

"Gotcha," Sweetness hissed as she hit the buttons for the preignition sequence. "Let's go play trains." She punched the red *tokamak overheat* plate, gently eased the drive bar forward. Train and parasitic cathedral began to roll.

The sudden lurch sent Devastation Harx reeling against Sianne Dandeever. He pushed her away, flipped open his uplinker. The screen spat random numbers at him. Heaven was rebelling. That damn train with that bloody girl was back. Devastation Harx had a ball-shrivelling suspicion that something else had paved the way for her. Something else harrowing his heaven. Harx snapped the treacherous machine shut—should never have trusted it—tried to think what to do. Don't get flustered. Gods may be capricious, but they're never flustered.

His whole world lurched again, began ponderously to move.

"Get everybody off," he ordered Sianne Dandeever. This was the end game now. Poor reward for the faithfulness of his faithful to risk them all on a final play of death or glory. "Abandon ship."

"Sir."

"Sound the alarms."

They were picking up speed. Soon it would be too late for all of them.

Sianne broke open the sealed box and pulled down the lever. As the bells rang and Harx felt his airship tremble to hundreds of pairs of running feet, Sianne said, "Sir, with respect, I'm not leaving you. Whatever happens, I will be true."

Which was as profound a profession of love as Devastation Harx had ever heard.

"Would you look at those purple boys go," said Weill, watching the evacuation of the Church of the Ever-Circling Spiritual Family on the opticon from UA2's stand-off position twenty kilometres east. "Here, Bladdy, take us in for a closer look, you don't see this every day."

"What about the reality-shaping weapon?" Seskinore warned, wringing his red, veiny hands.

"You think he'd be abandoning ship if he still had it?"

"If he were about to use it, he would," Seskinore countered, but Bladnoch was already pushing the stick. On Weill's monitor, purple-clad bodies tumbled down chutes, scrambled down wire ladders, slid down ropes, dropped in inflatable escape spheres, jumped, fell, ran through the advancing soldiery as the tottering, creaking lighter-than-air cathedral was dragged along by the slowly accelerating train.

"Wo, that is premier league chaos. Train-cathedral steel cage match, with fighting robots. Get the finger out, Blad, I don't want to miss any of this."

Instead of the mildly stimulating vibration of slightly unsynched engines, Weill's groin felt instead the sensation of the fans powering down.

"Blad, I said get it on, what the hell is up?"

"That," Bladnoch said, pointing up the western approaches of the valley where a disc of light, bright as the sun, was swooping toward them through the air.

One eye on the tacho. One eye on the tokamak monitors. A third eye . . . No third eye. Just trust. Sweetness edged the power bar forward. Too much acceleration and the wedged cathedral might tear loose. Too little and those steel flatfoots might catch up. Four legs, four arms. Nightmares. Thirty, forty. Keep it going. Fifty. Fifty-five. That's a crawl. A crawl. You've got to get them a safe distance. Sixty. Seventy. That's enough.

"Sorry folks," she said to her friends and family and pulled the lever that blew the bolts coupling tender to train. The rearviews showed them falling behind. The wave of galloping soldiers broke around it, reformed. It was her now. On her own, with just the water and hydrogen in the tanks.

She prayed the Train Gods she had worked it out right.

A drilling, banging on the roof. Sweetness cringed, another deafening rattle. She flicked up the ceiling-eyes, found herself looking up the multiple barrels of a Gatling, with Devastation Harx behind the triggers. He loosed off another stream of bullets. The camera went blind.

"Right," she said, teeth gritted, and pushed the drive bar forward. And went blind too. Light. Primal light, pure white, seared the cab. Sweetness cried out in pain, blinked away the after-images. There was something divine going on in the rearview cameras. The swathe of light scythed across the cavalry charge. Wherever it touched, it paralysed. Cybersoldiers froze in mid-step, arms uplifted, locked rigid. Ten passes, and the battlefield was a sculpture garden. The light flashed over Sweetness again, hovered for a moment. She squinted up through the glare at the flying disc of light. A vana, a sky-mirror, stooped down from the moonring to earth. Through the painful white, Sweetness thought she saw an image in the great mirror. A woman, with long dark hair. Her image.

She understood. She waved. The light went out, the vana twisted away and up on its long loop through Grand Valley.

The tattoo on the roof continued. Old *Catherine* could take it. The founding engineers of Bethlehem Ares built well. One hundred and twenty, one hundred and forty. Nice smooth power curve. Enough reserves to make it up to two hundred and eighty, if they didn't hit any upgrades. Decision point was two hundred. Tokamak pressure was peaking high orange. Sweetness began the priming sequence. Deep-Fusion? Who needed them. All you had to do was watch and learn. This little button shut down power to the containment field. This little button overrode the overrides. And this little button got her fine ass right out of here.

One ninety. One ninety-five. Two hundred.

"This is Point of No Return," Sweetness said. "This is for everyone." She hit the Emergency Escape button. The lights went to red. Shutters sealed over the windows. Drive rod and navigation ball folded away into the floor. Safety bars enfolded her like overaffectionate aunts. The camera eyes went black. The read-outs blanked. Alone in the red dark, Sweetness heard the serial bangs of the explosive bolts, heavier and harder than Harx's now-sporadic Gatling fire. Then she felt the grapple arms lift the driving cab free of the locomotive. Yellow digits counted down to primary ignition.

Here was the gamble. Here was the place where it could all go so so wrong. A misalignment of the escape rockets, and she wouldn't be thrown clear to the side and back. She'd go straight up and be tangled in Harx's cathedral.

The cab stirred under her. She was moving, but where. Where? Then the rockets kicked in and Sweetness momentarily blacked out under three gees. Burn burn burn burn burn. She was still moving, She was free. Then the rockets burned out and she was falling free. And in that instant, there was a light, brighter even than the light of the Little Pretty One vana, a light that penetrated even the meshed fingers of the blast shutters, the light of a Class 88 hauler containment field collapsing and a hydrogen fusion tokamak exploding. Then something like a steel fist punched the falling cab as hard as it could, sent it tumbling and Sweetness, strapped in her chair, screaming, crashing down to earth. Then the sudden whump of parachutes unfurling snatched her away from death.

The cab lay on its flank, buried waist-deep in the loam. The parachute, discarded on impact, bowled on the winds of the after-blast like a demon-driven thing across the grazing lands, screaming toward the rim mountains. The internal lights had failed: Sweetness scrabbled, trying to locate the green phosphorescence of the emergency door release. She hurt. She hurt bad. Things bent in there, chipped. But alive. Sort them later. But you could be radiated. The shields have no other purpose than to defend from fusion core detonations, but you were close to the epicentre when the tokamaks blew. Some could have eaten through. It could be burrowing into your bone marrow like maggots. It could be gnawing your genes. Three-headed Engineer children. Siamese twins. The Big C, she thought, completing the downward spiral of sobering possibilities. Hey, it's an occupational hazard of trainfolk. You're alive alive-oh. They can do things with that, these days. It costs but, don't they owe you? You saved the world. You can name your price. A gene-scrub, then that week getting oiled and sunkissed at the spas in Therme.

The back-up power seemed to have failed as well. Swearing, Sweetness Asiim Engineer grubbed around until she found the manual door crank. Every turn dug it into her ribs and brought a fresh oath as she winched the iris slowly open. Indigo sky. Distant bluffs. Green hills. A shower of dust. Sweetness pulled herself up and out, stood on the hull to survey the damage she had dealt. To the west the lower levels of the mushroom cloud were disintegrating but the thunder-head still boiled furiously upward through the hole it had blown in Worldroof, challenging heaven, setting weather patterns fleeing in consternation. Shading her eyes with her hand, she thought she could just make out the lip of the characteristic, fatal blast crater. This world liked craters, Sweetness decided. It could afford another one. Around were embedded mammoth shards of shattered roof-glass, thrust dagger-deep into the hill-country. She made a complete circuit of the horizon. Scattered across the southern panorama were the tangled, ungainly corpses of the machine army, twisted like burned matches where the sudden cease from St. Catherine had frozen them in the path of the fusion blast. With the seasons the soils would blow over and the green grass grow up and bury the forgotten army. A kilometre or so to the west she found the dazzling silver thread of the mainline. She thanked all her saints; the blast-wind could have carried her any distance, any direction into the wilderness. Sweetness slid down the cab hull on to the grass, headed over meadow flowers and sweet turf to the track. She looked back at all that remained of *Catherine of Tharsis*.

Best to see it as another piece of discarded metal in this junkyard of improbabilities, soon to be covered and forgotten like all the other casualties.

Her home . . . Her people. What had she done to them?

What only she could do.

Would they believe her when she pleaded story?

She could not look at the silver gingerbread that prettied up the blast shutters, the roaring lion crest, charred, battered. No more Ares Express. The Saint is dead. You killed her, Sweetness Octave Glorious Honey-Bun Asiim Engineer 12th.

Head full of the singing, ringing sound of pushed-down tears, she walked through the robot cemetery to the line. This time, she had a clear indication what direction not to go. Think of it as another re-route job for the Waymenders and a few minutes down-time on the Grand Valley runs. She turned east, to warmth and hope.

Sweetness had walked but a few minutes when she became aware of a bee-drone and moving mote in the eye of the sun. She squinted, peered. An object was driving through the air toward her, a larger object than its direct frontal approach hinted. United Artists' trim little airship emerged to eclipse the light and dropped to a relaxed hover over Sweetness Asiim. A hatch opened, the woman in the green leotard hailed her.

"You want a lift? We owe you."

"A lift? Where?"

Skerry indicated the whole wide world.

"Wherever you want."

Sweetness thought about the gift of leaving all the mess for someone else to clear up, climbing up that ramp and dissolving into the anonymous. Then she saw Grandmother Taal, and Child'a'grace, Psalli and Romereaux, still standing there, seeing what she had done, waiting, and still she did not come. Did not ever come. Ran away with the circus. Sometimes even an Engineer cannot ride. Sometimes you have to walk to face it.

"I think I'll walk this one, thank you. But hey!" she shouted as the fans swivelled into lift configuration and the little blimp began to turn. "Tell them I'm all right, will you?"

The taut little woman saluted.

"We will. By the way, in case you were wondering, we did win."

"That's all right then," Sweetness called up as the door irised shut, the fans threw dust around her and the airship lifted, turned, dipped its nose to the east and sailed away.

Five hundred paces later, she found the bean. It was balanced on the starboard rail. No natural force could have balanced it there, the fusion wind from Harx's devastation would have carried it away had it been there for any time. Sweetness bent down, studied the dull, white little eating bean. She frowned at the incongruity, then remembered where she had seen such a pulse before. She pocketed it and hiked on up the line, knowing what she would find next.

The skinny wooden spill was stabbed like a *vodun* charm into the dirt between the sleepers. Sweetness knelt, slowly pulled it out by its green tip. It was, she remembered, meant to be pulled slowly, gingerly, with forethought.

"Boy of Two Dusts," she read. Glancing up, she saw the next stick thrust into the dirt three sleepers up. "Golden Thumb-ring." She kept it in her hand with Boy of Two Dusts. Within a minute's walk she had a fistful of slim sticks. Half a kilometre upline was a signal relay from which came an unseasonable smell of spring verdure. Suspecting what she would find there, Sweetness walked resolutely up to it.

"I thought it might be you."

The greenperson sat back on the relay, knees pulled up to chest, forearms resting lightly on them. A loose canvas jellaba covered its body and hid its face within a deep cowl but the slim-fingered, pale green hands confirmed what the smell of growing suggested. Sweetness dropped the bundle of fate sticks at its scaley feet.

"Story over, then."

"It is. You are no longer afforded the protection of the universal narrative conventions. You are not the darling of the universe any more."

Funny way the universe had of showing it, Sweetness thought. She said, "Not even a little after bit? A coda?"

The green person shrugged.

"It reminds me of someone when you do that," Sweetness said.

"Nice denouement, I must say," the greenperson said, ignoring her bait. "End with a bang. Always good."

"Cost *Catherine of Tharsis*. My family's one and only asset, and I blew it up."

The green person cocked its head to one side, a darting, reptilian motion Sweetness could not read.

"I think you'll find that, despite the mess you've managed to spread across this and neighbouring universes, what passes for the government in this one is not ungrateful," it said. It looked up from the folds of its cowl, shot a hand from the long, loose sleeve. The face was slit-eyed, scaled. Sweetness thought she saw a forked tongue flicker. The long fingers had stretched into hooks, the knuckles swollen to painful knobs, the nails drawn into tight black claws. Sweetness took the hand. It felt like napped velvet.

"Well, that'll be goodbye then," the green person said. "I'll not get up if you don't mind, I'm finding standing increasingly uncomfortable as I change. We'll not meet again in this lifetime. Goodbye, it was a good story, I enjoyed you: see you in the next one."

They shook hands briefly. Then the lizard-hands scooped up the bundle of fortune-telling sticks and snapped it smartly in half.

"You're free now. I give you your fate back. What happens from now on is entirely in your own hands. Your story has ended, your tale has just begun."

"Thank God for that," Sweetness Engineer 12th said, and began to walk. Like flies in the heat-haze, she thought she could see objects far down the track, swimming in the treacherous silver. Resolution and certainty increased with every step she took closer. People, trainpeople, and behind them, that rippling square of black must be the jettisoned tender. But what was that in the deeper haze beyond? A thing like a city, all spires and towers and campaniles. Mirage. Illusion. It could all be lies and magnifications. Should have taken that ride, traingirl. Story's over, if your pride gets you into trouble now, you've only yourself to get you out of it. No different from everyone else then. That should be sufficient. Sweetness jogged forward, trying to penetrate the shimmering. A city, yes, but a narrow one. A linear city? She stopped, laughed out loud, beat her hands off her thighs in realisation. Not a city at all; a factory train. A big smelly minging dirty factory. Now she could see the tell-tale parallel plumes of steam from the separators. They had all come for her. They were all here. All her people. She glanced back, as everyone must. Of course there was no figure squatting by the signal relay, but did she see a scurry of green dart to cover behind a sleeper?

Free to be mundane again.

Sweetness Octave Glorious Honey-Bun Asiim Engineer 12th smiled, shouldered her pack and ran along the line through the green hills of Mars, into the silver shimmer where her people were waiting.

ABOUT THE AUTHOR

Ian McDonald is the author of many science fiction novels, including *Desolation Road*; *King of Morning, Queen of Day*; *Out on Blue Six*; *Chaga*; *Kirinya*; *River of Gods*; and *Brasyl*. He has won the Philip K. Dick Award, the Theodore Sturgeon Award, and the BSFA Award, been nominated for a Nebula Award and a World Fantasy Award, and has several nominations for both the Hugo Award and the Arthur C. Clarke Award. The *Washington Post* called him "one of the best SF novelists of our time." He lives in Belfast, Northern Ireland.

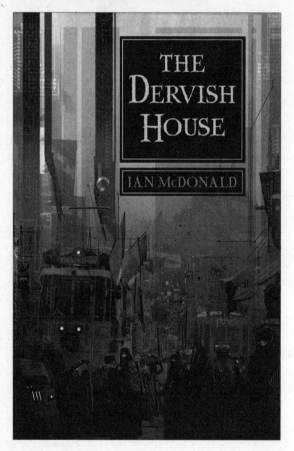

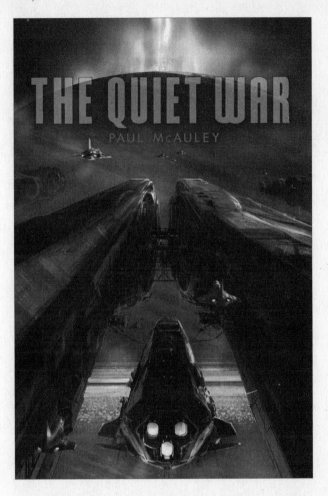

THE QUIET WAR

PAUL McAULEY

"The stage is set for war and it is beautifully handled." —SciFi Now

 Pyr®, an imprint of Prometheus Books
716-691-0133 / www.pyrsf.com